The Golden Dawn Journal:
Hermetic Wisdom for the New Age

Discover an enriching and empowering source of spiritual guidance based upon the rituals and teachings of the Golden Dawn. The gods of the ancient world reveal themselves through the idealized concepts of Venusian love, Martial strength, Jovian laughter, Osirian rebirth, Maatian justice, Athenian wisdom, and more. They help us to see and understand our potential, our strength, magic, and inherent spiritual beauty.

The Hermetic Order of the Golden Dawn is the best known and most influential magical organization to have emerged from the 19th century magical revival. Its members, both past and present, are responsible for writing, or at the very least, influencing many of the best books on the subject of magic and spiritual growth.

The Golden Dawn taught tolerance and respect for all religions, for they all possess their own, unique value to humanity. *The Magical Pantheons: A Golden Dawn Journal* continues this tradition by providing a fascinating and informative look at the major deities of the Western Esoteric Tradition who continue to inspire us through their myths, mysteries, and magic.

About the Editors

Both Chic and Tabatha Cicero are Senior Adepts of the *Hermetic Order of the Golden Dawn*. They are the authors of several books published by Llewellyn and are active in the larger magical community. Sharing an enthusiasm for the esoteric arts and a love of cats, the Ciceros live in Florida where they work and practice magic.

To Write to the Editors

If you wish to contact the editors or would like more information about this book, please write to the editors in care of Llewellyn Worldwide and we will forward your request. Both the editors and publisher appreciate hearing from you and learning of your enjoyment of this book and how it has helped you. Llewellyn Worldwide cannot guarantee that every letter written to the editors can be answered, but all will be forwarded. Please write to:

Chic Cicero and Sandra Tabatha Cicero
C/o Llewellyn Worldwide
P.O. Box 64383, Dept. K861-3
St. Paul, MN 55164-0383, U.S.A.

Please enclose a self-addressed, stamped envelope for reply, or $1.00 to cover costs.
If outside U.S.A., enclose international postal reply coupon.

THE
MAGICAL
PANTHEONS

The Golden Dawn Journal
Book IV

Edited by
Chic Cicero
Sandra Tabatha Cicero

1998
Llewellyn Publications
St. Paul, Minnesota 55164-0383

FIRST EDITION
First Printing, 1998

Cover design: Anne Marie Garrison
Cover illustrations of gods and goddesses: Eric Holtz
Interior design: Sandra Tabatha Cicero
Cross and Triangle artwork © Sandra Tabatha Cicero

Chapter art courtesy of Dover Publications.

Material quoted from *The Bahir*, Aryeh Kaplan (translator), is used with permission from Samuel Weiser, Inc., York Beach, Maine.

Library of Congress Catologing-in-Publication Data
The Golden Dawn journal / edited by Chic Cicero, Sandra Tabatha
    Cicero
        p. cm--(Llewellyn's Golden Dawn series)
    Includes bibliographical references.
    Contents: ---bk. 4 The Magical Pantheons
    ISBN: 1-56718-861-3 (v. 4) $14.95
  1. Hermetic order of the Golden Dawn. 2. Cabala. 3. Magic.
  4. Symbolism. I. Cicero, Chic, 1936- . II. Cicero, Sandra Tabatha,
  1959- . III. Series.
  BF1623.R7G57   1994   94-39664
                                                                   CIP

Publisher's Note
Llewellyn Worldwide does not participate in, endorse, or have any authority or responsibility concerning private business transactions between our authors and the public.

All mail addressed to the editors of this book is forwarded, but the publisher cannot, unless specifically instructed by the editors, give out an address or phone number.

Llewellyn Publications
A Division of Llewellyn Worldwide, Ltd.
P.O. Box 64383, Dept. K861-3
St. Paul, MN 55164-0383

Also by the Editors

The Golden Dawn Magical System
  including:
  The New Golden Dawn Ritual Tarot (deck)
  The New Golden Dawn Ritual Tarot (tarot)
Secrets of a Golden Dawn Temple
Self-Initiation into the Golden Dawn Tradition
The Golden Dawn Journal Series
  including:
  Book I: Divination
  Book II: Qabalah: Theory and Magic
  Book III: The Art of Hermes
Experiencing the Kabbalah

Forthcoming

The Middle Pillar (Third Edition, edited and annotated)

For Maria Babwahsingh, Jim Kaelin,
Bob Gilbert, Allan Armstrong,
and Francis.

Contents

Illustrations

Romans worshipping the God Neptune.

Introduction: Gods and Humans

Chic Cicero and Sandra Tabatha Cicero

And the Gods were seen in their Ideas of the Stars, with all their Signs, and the Stars were numbered with the Gods in them.[1]

Many people in this world go about their lives assuming that there is only one way of looking at spirituality—in the religion that they were taught as children. It never occurs to them that the spiritual beliefs of others, if different, could possibly have validity. For some reason, perfectly rational and intelligent people, who otherwise uphold the idea that "there are two sides to every issue," will obstinately stop short of saying that the same is true for spiritual beliefs. One can almost see the wall of religious intolerance come down behind their eyes, to firmly close their once-open minds against ideas and beliefs they are unfamiliar with.

The fact that humanity has developed a dazzling variety of deities and a plethora of ways to worship them, should point to the marvelous ingenuity of the Divine, which seeks to express itself throughout all world cultures. No single culture or tradition has exclusive rights to divine knowledge, for as it is stated to the candidate in the Neophyte ritual of the Golden Dawn, "Remember that you hold all Religions in reverence, for there is none but contains a Ray from the Ineffable Light that you are seeking."

Diversity of ethnic and spiritual practices makes the world a far richer place. One glance at nature should be enough to convince anyone that the Divine loves variety. How interesting would the earth be if there were only one type of animal, one species of flower, and one kind of tree? How intriguing would the world be if all human beings on the planet held the same opinions, voted for the same politicians, went to the same type of school, wore the same style of clothing, ate the same kind of food, and had the same kind of occupation? Frightfully boring!

Most humans, when given a choice, will opt for diversity of personal expression. Why should we expect our most personal and sacred beliefs to be any different? Do we neuter the religions of others so that we can force their "square" beliefs into our nice "round" circle

1

of dogma? Coercing others into falling in line with one's own spiritual doctrine is a *human,* not a divine, obsession. It is a product of the *lower ego,* telling us that our opinions are right (good), and the opinions of others are wrong (evil). This misguided dualism has no place in the divine universe, where natural polarity is considered part of a greater unity. (The dualism of the black and white pillars of the Qabalistic Tree of Life is a perfect example of opposing forces that complement and enliven each other.) The divine creator(s) of this mysterious and splendidly colorful rock upon which we spin around the solar system is certainly not interested in our petty, childish squabbles over whose interpretation of scripture is correct or whose holy books are true.

If only all of humanity could take an objective and open-minded look at the world mythologies, they would come to the conclusion that there are basic religious themes that are venerated by us all:

> *We have the same Gods with us now as always. They have not changed essentially, though we have altered our formalized concepts of them....*[2]

The orthodox religions have always striven to label and separate the various forms of spirituality. For the sake of description, we shall do likewise, although we do not believe these divisions are so rigid as some would claim. A *pantheon* is a collection of all the gods of a particular people or nation. *Monotheists* believe in only one god. *Polytheists* believe in the worship of more than one god. And *pantheists* believe that the deity and the created universe are *one*—they cannot be divided or separated. Pantheists believe in the worship of *all* gods as universal expressions of the totality of the universe.

Monotheism Versus Polytheism and Pantheism

Since the beginning of human history, mankind has maintained the belief in a supreme being or divine force that created the world. Although this basic tenet has been expressed in diverse ways, the universal truth at its core unites us all.

Some see this divine and eternal force as singular—an indivisible monad. Others see it as a diverse tapestry composed of a profusion of deities. What is interesting, however, is that both monotheists and pantheists share the same basic beliefs, even if they describe those beliefs in different terms.

Most polytheists and pantheists believe in a primal creator being that existed before all other deities (the Babylonian *Apsu*, the Egyptian *Nu*, the Greek *Chaos*, etc.). From these ancient beings, other gods and goddesses were generated. However, these creator gods were not often seen in ancient times as the most potent, or even the most important, of the deities. Eventually, a dominant god and a dominant goddess were born. Other (lesser) deities ruled over particular areas of deific influence (such as the god of war, the goddess of love, the god of medicine, etc.).

Monotheists believe in a single creator god who is all powerful. However, this divinity created lesser deities known as angels and archangels. These beings had certain duties; they governed a specific area of divine influence—not unlike the lesser gods and goddesses of other pantheons (the angel of childbirth, the angel of death, the angel of annunciation, etc.).

Polytheists and pantheists seem to agree that all the gods are but one god and all the goddesses are but one goddess. In other words, the various goddesses and gods that comprise the pantheons are nothing more than the multi-faceted expressions of the archetypal creator beings—the Great Mother Goddess and the Great Father God. But even this idea of a "universal duad" is a bit of an illusion, since ultimately, non-monotheists believe that "all is one." Thus it might safely be said that polytheists and pantheists hold a basic belief in a universal unity that is forever *unfolding* into various personalized gods and goddesses that are readily accessible to human worshipers. The archetypal images of Mother and Father are together considered a sacred unity—a union or marriage between two divine halves that by themselves are incomplete. The pantheistic tenet of a "god of gods" is not an affirmation of the Judeo-Christian doctrine, but rather a recognition of the indescribable force that created everything in the manifest universe.

In spite of their differences, monotheists, polytheists, and pantheists are probably more alike in their spiritual beliefs than is generally believed by the public at large.

Do the Gods Exist?

Some people believe that the gods and goddesses are real and very powerful beings who dwell in another dimension and have existed since the beginning of the known universe. Others hold the opinion that the gods are thought-forms—anthropomorphic images created in the mind of humanity—and that these thought-forms have been empowered and brought to life by centuries of continuous prayer and veneration. This later view holds that the divine realities behind the gods and goddesses are enormous reservoirs of energy that are fed by the strong, passionate devotion and focused thoughts of human worshipers. These ancient reservoirs are still in existence, and although centuries of neglect have depleted them, they can yet be re-energized through the ceremonials and invocations of modern-day priests and priestesses. These deific energies may be asleep, but they never cease to be.

In *The Ladder of Lights*, William Gray says:

> *A wit once wrote; "God created Man is His own image—and Man was so pleased with the results that he returned the compliment." Our anthropomorphic Gods and Goddesses are both human projections to a higher level and Divine projections to a lower one, the result of such an impact on meeting each other being what we may term a "God." These "Gods" are very real constructions formed mutually by Humanity and Divinity as points of common conscious contact, and they are certainly to be treated with the respect they deserve.*[3]

The gods are archetypal images that have a life of their own. These *divine ideals* have had enormous influence over every aspect of human life. All deities have a validity in their specific function. Each deity symbolizes *one facet* of the eternal creative force of the universe. Through the personalization of every single part of the Divine, humanity is better equipped to connect with and comprehend the whole, which is so abstract in its sum total that human understanding of it is impossible. Humans will always require some reference point in order to grasp abstract thoughts. By giving human form to these divine images, the abstract becomes something that can be related to the human experience and deeply felt within the soul.

This brings us to the importance of emotional force in spiritual expression. Worship of the gods involves a great amount of *emotive energy*. Human beings have an intrinsic need for religious articulation. Gray states that:

> *A God is to be experienced, felt, moved by with, and in, so that we are affected by the nature of the God concerned. Two factors move man, thinking and feeling. Ideals move our*

minds, but only the Gods move our souls. We must be in a state of empathy with them so that effects take place throughout our sentient souls and we undergo an actual experience of that particular God. Such a relationship is a personal one in the most intimate sense and unless it can be established and maintained between God and human, they will be lost to each other.[4]

Having a belief in the Divine, be it "god" or the "gods," is vitally important to the physical and psychological well-being of our species. Many people in this day and age have lost interest in any type of religion or spirituality. When life runs at an even keel, this lack of a spiritual foundation goes unrecognized. However, when hardships arise, it's another story. That's the time when people reach out for answers and begin to reflect upon the meaning of existence. Acknowledgment of our eternal source is fundamental to human evolution and growth. Whenever a group of people renounces a belief in that eternal source, the result is usually the disintegration of the social fabric. According to psychologist Carl Jung:

It is the role of religious symbols to give a meaning to the life of man. The Pueblo Indians believe that they are the sons of Father Sun, and this belief endows their life with a perspective (and a goal) that goes far beyond their limited existence. It gives them ample space for the unfolding of personality and permits them a full life as complete persons. Their plight is infinitely more satisfactory than that of a man in our own civilization who knows that he is (and will remain) nothing more than an underdog with no inner meaning to his life.[5]

What are the gods—real beings, or thought-forms that are vitalized by our belief in them? The answer, like the existence of the gods themselves, will always be difficult if not impossible to prove using the physical tools of modern science and the biased logic of the rational mind. But ultimately, the debate over the existence of the gods, is unimportant. They quite simply *are*. The universe itself certainly acts as if the gods do exist.

Ritual Worship of the Divine

Very early in our history, symbols became important tools of spiritual expression. Humans have always used physical objects as emblems of the eternal and inscrutable source of the universe. It is no accident that mystics always describe their inner experiences with visual images, as well as the sensations of smell, sound, and touch. By using symbols, we can relate and compare the concepts encountered in mystical experiences with the occurrences of daily life.

Even the ancients knew, however, that symbols only *represented* the reality—they were not the reality itself. Most statues of gods and goddesses were designed to be visual aids for divine concepts—not as objects of worship in and of themselves.

Magicians, priests, and priestesses are able to access the various power reservoirs represented by the gods and utilize them in ritual/devotional workings. Through extensive training in the development of a focused mind, will power, and the imaginative faculties of the psyche, and by the active use of sacred symbols as points of concentration, magicians are able to tap into these vessels of god-energy and use them to mold the *astral light*—that plastic interpenetrating substance that theurgists use to create change in both the physical and non-physical realms. Since the image of a deity is a *personalized* representation of a specific portion of the eternal source, working with these deities gives the magician easier access to the divine creator. The god or goddess employed acts as a direct channel of intercourse between human beings and the eternal source—a divine channel that the magician can identify with and have strong feelings for. These empathic communications are transmitted along an inner conduit (via the invoked deity) to the divine source, which is able to communicate spiritual knowledge back to the theurgist.

During an *invocation*, the magician calls forth a deity, essentially reaching into one specific reservoir of god-energy. He allows this god-energy to use his body as a temporary vehicle for communicating with the physical world. It is a powerful way of connecting with the energies of a particular god or goddess. In her description of Egyptian theurgic practices, Florence Farr wrote:

> ...the most potent magical formula was the identification of the Ritualist with the God whose power he was invoking. So increasing himself to an immeasurable greatness he lept beyond all bodies, and transcending time became eternity. He

became higher than all height, lower than all depth. He knew
himself part of the great chain of Creation....[6]

In truth, all pantheons are magical. Although the orthodox religions of the world would have us believe that their forms of worship do not involve magical practices, it takes no effort of the imagination for the objective individual to compare the prayers of the Christian, the Jew, and the Muslim to the invocations of the Neo-pagan, the Druid, and the Hermetic magician. The trappings of ceremony and devotion are virtually the same; only the deities change.

Here we will briefly explore the primary gods of the western world—those ancient deities who are especially important to today's Neo-pagans and Hermetic magicians. This is not to say that the magical traditions of the east are unimportant to western readers. Eastern spiritual beliefs and magical practices will be the focus of another issue of *The Golden Dawn Journal*.

Some effort will be made to compare the gods of one civilization to those of another. Although "all the gods are but one god," it should be remembered that each deity has its own unique characteristics and nuances, however subtle they may be. These differences are created by the multifarious cultural and environmental influences.

The following section is intended to provide only a rudimentary knowledge of the major deities of the Western Magical Tradition, as well as a small sampling of the vast historical factors that shaped each particular pantheon. This material should be supplemented with a few good books on the various pantheons, some of which are listed in the bibliography at the end of this introduction.

THE MAGICAL PANTHEONS

Mesopotamia

The one factor that seems to be most responsible for propelling Stone Age peoples all over the world into the coming Age of Civilization was the challenge of controlling and irrigating river valleys. This was made possible only through the centralized authority and coordinated effort that the first city-states provided. The land "between the rivers" of the Tigris and Euphrates, just north of the Persian Gulf, is credited with being the birthplace of civilization. It was here that humanity built the first cities, began creating tools out of bronze, and developed the first system of writing (cuneiform). Here the rivers would play a major role in shaping the social and religious outlook of all the various ancient cultures who would make the "Fertile Crescent" their home.

The Sumerians (4000–2350 B.C.E.) built the first civilization in Mesopotamia. Their culture eventually outlasted them and became the basis of all later Babylonian civilization. Their way of life, style of writing, architecture, and attitude toward the gods were preserved in the Tigris -Euphrates river valley throughout ancient times by the civilizations that followed them—the Akkadian, Babylonian, and the Assyrian.

The Fertile Crescent was a land of extremes—scorching heat, choking dust storms, violent winds, and disastrous floods. No matter what they did, the Sumerians could never completely control the flooding of the rivers. Low water levels often resulted in drought and famine. During the rainy season, the turbulent rivers would sweep aside levees and drown whole villages. In addition to these natural threats, the Mesopotamian valley was constantly exposed to the man-made dangers of raids and invasions from neighboring tribes of the desert and the hills.

As the first people to carve civilization out of a hostile environment, the ancient Mesopotamians saw life in general as a struggle against unfriendly forces. They thought nature to be brutal and unpredictable. This outlook was reflected in their understanding of the gods, many of whom were warlike and powerful.

The Sumerians were an agricultural people, and thus they worshipped the great natural forces of the universe that governed the fertility of the earth. The relationship between gods and humans was compared to that between parents and children. There were cosmic gods, city gods, and gods of nature. Oftentimes the functions of these different classes of divinities overlapped. To the Sumerians, certain gods were naturally put in charge of both cosmic forces and their earthly counterparts—the cities of Mesopotamia—whose existence was maintained by the surrounding farmland. Humanity was seen as a vessel of the divine will—it was the duty of humankind to carry out the divine will on earth, implementing a divine order that would secure the fertility of the land. The gods were honored with great temples that were the cultural and economic centers of the city-states. A city itself was considered the property of its primary deity, and the temple was the god's earthly abode. In fact, it was in service to the gods that the Sumerians conceived many of their most important contributions to civilization, including writing, which developed from the need to keep track of temple assets. Every human endeavor, whether for peace, war, agriculture, or commerce, was performed for the benefit of the gods; the gods were depended upon for everything.

Sacred rites were performed in the temples by priests and priestesses, but there were also several great festivals in which the common people took part. The biggest of these festivals was the *hieros gammos* or "sacred marriage," which celebrated the union of the deities Inanna and Dumuzi.

Below the realm of the gods was the realm of spirits, both good and evil. Magical arts and incantations were developed as ways of appeasing friendly spirits and driving off malicious ones. The average Sumerian often employed the services of astrologers and *magi* (hereditary priest-magicians) for divination, healing, blessing of amulets and talismans, purification, cursing, warding off evil, etc. Private homes usually contained shrines to the owner's personal god or goddess, where prayers and sacrifices were made to attract the deity's favor. Dreams were considered divine messages, and dream interpretation dates back to 2450 B.C.E. Thus the practice of magic played a very important role in the interaction between gods and human beings in Mesopotamia.

The following deities were known as "the seven who decreed the fates." These were the primary gods and goddesses that were worshipped in Mesopotamia, but there were also a host of others.

Sumerian Gods

The Cosmic Triad

An (equivalent to the Babylonian **Anu**), the god of heaven, was probably the main god of the pantheon until 2500 B.C.E., after which his importance eventually declined. His name meant "sky" and he resided in the uppermost region, which was called the "sky of An." The main principle of creation, An was the supreme and distant king of the gods. Most of the other deities of the Sumerian pantheon honored An as their father or chief. His consort was Ninhursag, the Great Mother goddess. An symbolized power, protection, justice, and judgment, and was often represented by a tiara on a throne. His royal emblems were the scepter, the diadem, the horned cap, and the staff of command. His army, which was used to destroy the wicked, were the stars that he had created (called the "soldiers of An"). Never leaving the heavenly regions, he occasionally traversed a portion of the sky reserved only for him called "Anu's way," located in the uppermost part of the heavens. More benevolent toward sovereigns than to commoners, An presided over the fate of the universe.

Enlil (equivalent to the Babylonian **Ellil**), the son of An and Ki, was lord of wind and storm. His name meant "air god," and he was said to have separated heaven and earth with a pick-ax. After 2500 B.C.E., Enlil became the main god of the pantheon and "king of all the lands."[7] The other gods were not even allowed to look upon his splendor. Enlil symbolized the forces of nature, especially the destructive ones (hurricanes, storms, and floods), and was considered to be the master of humanity's fate. The air god was also a creator god who brought forth the dawn, vegetation, and the fruits of harvest. He was credited with inventing the plough, and he ruled over disasters, prosperity, and destiny. Like An, he had a reserved promenade in the heavens called "Enlil's Way," but his usual abode was the Great Mountain of the East.

Enki (equivalent to the Babylonian **Ea**), was "lord of earth," king of the underworld, and ruler of the waters. His primary domain was the *Apsu*, the fresh water abyss that was thought to surround the earth and provide water to all the springs and rivers. He was the main divinity of all fluid and watery substances. The waters of the earth were a source of great abundance, fertility, and treasure, as well as knowledge. Therefore Enki became known as a god of wisdom and friend of humanity—creating man from clay and counseling human beings when other deities sought to harm them. He taught humanity the crafts of constructing, farming, writing, and magic. Some of Enki's titles are "lord of wisdom" and "lord of incantation." Enki guarded the sacred *me* (pronounced "may"), which were the divine decrees, wisdom, and invocations that spread civilization and the arts. The *me* were distributed in an orderly fashion to humanity by Enki. Enki is also said to have blessed the beautiful land of Dilmun (Eden) with water and palm trees. The god is often portrayed as a goat with a fish's tail, or sometimes as a man with waves of water springing from his shoulders or from a vase, which he holds.

The Earth Mother

Ninhursag (equivalent to the Babylonian **Aruru**), was the goddess of the earth whose original name was thought to be *Ki*. Her more common epitaphs are *Ninhursag* "queen of the mountains," *Ninmah* "exalted lady," and *Nintu* "the lady who gives birth." As the wife of An, Ninhursag is the mother of the gods and the great creative principle. Many Sumerian kings liked to refer to her as *their* mother as well. She assisted Enki in the creation of humankind from clay, and created eight new trees in the land of Dilmun. The goddess is often represented wearing a leafy crown and holding a branch symbolizing fertility and regeneration.

The Celestial Triad

Nannar (equivalent to the Babylonian **Sin**), the moon god, was the chief among the astral triad, which also included Utu and Inanna, who were his children by his wife, Ningal. The lunar god was known as "he whose deep heart no god can penetrate" because of his mysterious transformations during the moon's various phases. The full moon was his crown, and thus he was known as the "lord of the diadem" and the "shining boat of heaven." Nannar was said to rest in the underworld every month, where he decreed the fate of the deceased. The lunar god was the enemy of those who did evil, and he was also the god of the measurement of time. He ruled over destiny, secrets, and predictions. A very wise god, Nannar is sometimes pictured as an old man with a beard the color of lapis lazuli and riding a winged bull. The crescent moon was his boat, which navigated the night sky.

Utu (equivalent to the Babylonian **Shamash**), was the god of the sun and lord of judgment, truth, and justice (since the sun was thought to see all things). The god was said to rise out of the eastern mountains of heaven in a chariot with the solar rays radiating from his shoulders. He represented the sunlight, which illuminated the life of man and caused plants to flourish. Each night he entered the underworld through a gated mountain. Utu governed laws, oracles, courage, victory, vitality, judgment, and retribution. He was also a warrior and a protector of the righteous. He is often portrayed with a ring and scepter in his right hand, and has been shown with a pruning-saw.

Inanna, (equivalent to the Babylonian **Ishtar**), the goddess of the star of Venus, was the most important goddess in the Sumerian pantheon. To all that she ruled, she had a positive and a negative side—kind one moment, cruel the next. A complex goddess of many roles, Inanna, whose name meant "lady of heaven," had three distinct functions: 1) goddess of Venus, the morning and evening star, 2) goddess of love, and 3) goddess of war. In one tradition she was said to be the daughter of An, and was depicted as the goddess of love. She had many lovers and was not considered a mother goddess. She had the power to arouse desire and the ability to procreate in all creatures. She was "courtesan to the gods," and sacred prostitution formed an important part of her cult. Although she often displayed her kindness, she was also regularly cruel to her many lovers, and her affections were sometimes fatal. Her love for the harvest god Dumuzi eventually caused his death. In one story, Inanna decided to visit the underworld to witness the funeral rites of Gugalanna, the Bull of Heaven, only to become her sister Ereshkigal's prisoner. Eventually she was freed with a powerful magic spell by the god Enki.

In the tradition where Inanna is seen as the daughter of Nannar, she was perceived as the goddess of war, who is fond of battle. She was said to stand beside favored monarchs as they fought.

Inanna was also a goddess of wisdom. It was she who tricked Enki and stole the holy *me* for her followers. The goddess ruled sexual love, fertility, revenge, warfare, resurrection, and initiation. She is usually represented as a winged warrior goddess who wears a triple-horned crown and flowing robes. Sometimes she is portrayed armed to the teeth, and at other times surrounded by stars. Her symbols are the lion, the rosette, and the eight-pointed star.

Some Lesser Deities

Dumuzi (equivalent to the Babylonian **Tammuz**), was a god of trees and vegetation. His name means "son of life" or "only son." As a mortal, he was the shepherd king of Uruk, but after his marriage to Inanna, he assumed divine powers over the fecundity of animals and plants. After Inanna's rescue from the underworld, it was decreed that someone would take her place there. Dumuzi was caught and slain by galla demons and taken to the underworld, where he was to stay six months of the year. His annual return from the underworld marked the fertile return of spring.

Ereshkigal, whose name means "queen of the great below," was the dark goddess of the underworld—a place of the dead, which was guarded by seven gates. She was the sister of Inanna and the wife of either Gugalanna, the monstrous Bull of Heaven, or of the god Nergal. She is also the mother of the goddess Nungal and the gods Namtar and Ninazu. When her sister Inanna attempted to gain entry into the underworld, Ereshigal turned her into a corpse and held her prisoner.

Nammu was the goddess of the Apsu or watery abyss. She was the mother of many of the ancient gods, including An, Ninhursag, and Enki.

Ningal was the wife of the moon god, Nanna, and the mother of the sun god, Utu. In later Babylonian times, she was worshipped under the name of Nikkal.

Ninlil, whose name meant "lady of air," was the wife of Enlil. A merciful and benevolent mother goddess, she often aided the cause of mortals. Initially raped by Enlil, who was banished to the netherworld for this offense, Ninlil followed the air god and subsequently bore him a son, the god Nanna, along with three other children.

Cross-cultural Developments in Mesopotamia

The cultures of Mesopotamia emerged through the interaction, friction, and amalgamation of different groups of people with various beliefs, gods, languages, and social structures. In early times Mesopotamia encompassed two regions—Sumer to the south, and Akkad to the north. The Akkadians were among the earliest Semites. Around 2370 B.C.E., the Akkadian ruler, Sargon, conquered both regions, uniting Mesopotamia for the first time. The Akkadian Empire maintained its rule over the area for several generations. Their grip on power was lost to invaders from the northeast around 2200 B.C.E. Several new Semitic tribes entered the area about two hundred years later. During this time, the Amorites from Syria rose to power and widened their rule under king Hammurabi to create the Old Babylonian Empire. Eventually, a group of Indo-Europeans from Iran, known as the Kassites, brought an end to Hammurabi's dynasty in 1530 B.C.E. Then came the rise of the Assyrian Empire, which lasted from 745 to 538 B.C.E. Like the Akkadian and Old Babylonian cultures before it, the Assyrian civilization was based on the Sumerian model. Its pantheon of gods was very similar to those of ancient Sumer, although much more militaristic and severe—like the Assyrians themselves, who ruled by terror. When the Assyrian Empire's leadership faltered, the people it had once ruled destroyed it completely. The final phase of Mesopotamian greatness was ushered in around 612 B.C.E. by the Semitic Chaldeans, who established a New Babylonian Empire full of magnificent cities and temples, including the Hanging Gardens of Babylon, one of the Seven Wonders of the World. This final Babylonian revival ended when the Empire was conquered by the Persians in 538 B.C.E. The Persians broke with the Sumerian/Babylonian pantheon of gods and set up an entirely different group of deities under the fiercely dualistic religion (good versus evil) of Zoroastrianism.

The following is a list of some of the more important gods of the later Babylonian Empires. These deities were added to the growing pantheon of Mesopotamia.

Assyro-Babylonian Gods

Adad or **Hadad** (equivalent to the Sumerian **Iskur**) usurped Enlil's position as lord of thunder and storm. The son of An or Enlil, Adad was partially responsible for floods as well as storms and hail, but this deity also had a beneficial side as a god of fertile rains and streams. Adad is usually depicted with a thunderbolt in each hand and standing upon a bull or a lion-dragon. At times he is shown with a thunderbolt in one hand and an ax in the other. Storm clouds were often referred to as "Adad's bull-calves." Adad was also known as the "lord of foresight" who could read the future.

Marduk, the son of Ea (Enki), was the patron god of Babylon who absorbed the attributes of most of the other Babylonian deities; taking over their various functions, characteristics, and even their names (the "fifty names of Marduk" were for the most part the names of gods he had usurped). The name of Marduk was said to mean "bull-calf of the sun." He became the central deity of the Babylonian pantheon and king of the gods. It was Marduk who organized the universe, fixed the course of the stars, and gave the gods their heavenly abodes. Known as the "lord of life," he created man from the blood of a slain god. He was a gifted healer and a great magician.

In the Babylonian story of creation, Tiamat, the great chaos dragon of the primordial ocean, waged war upon the elder gods. Marduk, champion of the gods, engaged Tiamat in battle. In single combat, Marduk forced an evil wind down the dragon's throat, shot her with arrows, crushed her head, and split her body into two pieces. With one half of her body he created the heavens, and with the other half he created the earth. Tiamat's saliva become the clouds and her two eyes became the rivers of the Tigris and the Euphrates. After this feat, all the gods honored Marduk as their king.

Marduk is pictured as a mature, proud man. He is said to have four ears and four eyes. His symbol is the *marru* or triangle-headed hoe, possibly alluding to his early origin as a god of agriculture. When he speaks, fire emits from his mouth. His token animal is the snake-dragon. Marduk is often shown armed with a scimitar and battling a dragon (Tiamat).

Nergal (or **Erra**) was "the lord who prowls by night." In his persona of Erra, he was a warlike god who ruled over forest fires, plagues, and fevers. Once he became the husband of Ereshkigal, Nergal became lord of the underworld, co-ruling with his dark wife. Nergal is depicted wearing a long robe that is open in the front—one leg is bare and extended, with the foot on a raised support or crushing an enemy. His symbols are the scimitar and the double lion-headed club.

Ninurta was originally a Sumerian god who became widely worshipped by the later Assyrian kings because of his warlike nature. The son of Enlil, Ninurta was a celestial god who was identified with the constellation of Orion. Once a god of the fields and canals who brought fertility, Ninurta became known as a hunter-warrior and champion of the celestial gods. He was called the "strong one who destroys the wicked and the enemy." His weapons are the bow and poisoned arrows, along with the mace, *Sharur*—a club flanked by two S-shaped snakes.

Asshur, the national god of the Assyrians, became the main deity when the Assyrian Empire took control of the region. Like Marduk before him, Asshur absorbed the attributes and characteristics of all the earlier gods. Thus he became the self-created king and father of all the gods, who created mankind and ordained the fate of humans. Above all, Asshur was a warrior god who fought alongside his people in battle, encouraging them on to victory. The symbols of Asshur include the horned cap and the goat. He is sometimes represented mounted on a bull.

Canaan

Around 1700 B.C.E., a group of Indo-Europeans known as the Hittites established an Empire in Asia Minor and extended their reign over Syria and Palestine. Their closely guarded secret of iron smelting gave them superior weapons technology against their neighbors, but after 1200 B.C.E., this technology was spread across the archaic world. The next people who came to power in Syria and Palestine were the Semitic Canaanites. The culture of the Canaanites was derived from both the Egyptians and the Mesopotamians, since they were a kind of "buffer state" between those two great kingdoms. Due to the region's continual mingling of cultural elements and almost constant state of warfare or invasion, it is almost impossible to pinpoint a single Canaanite culture or pantheon. Sitting in the middle of the crossroads between many foreign empires meant that the Canaanites were never able to unify under a single native ruler, but instead maintained a number of independent city-states (such as Ugarit and Gubla), each with differing lists of local gods. Many local gods were simply called *Baal* or "lord." The pantheon of Canaan was not only composed of several local deities, but also of some Egyptian and Mesopotamians gods as well. Even Yahweh, the tribal god of Israel, found acceptance among some of the syncretic religions of Canaan.

One of the Canaanites' greatest contributions was the development of the first true alphabet, which used twenty-nine symbols to represent the consonants. This simplification spread the art of writing from the highly secretive scribal class down to the average person. As a result, literacy was greatly expanded.

From 1300 to 1000 B.C.E., the city-states of Canaan came under fierce attack from the Israelites and the Philistines. They lost much of their land, but managed to hold on to a narrow strip along the coast known as Phoenicia, which included the cities of Sidon and Tyre. These later Canaanites were called Phoenicians, and they developed a talent for commerce and sea-trade. The alphabet of the Phoenicians was later adapted into what would become the Greek alphabet.

To the Canaanities, religious practice was no longer exclusive to the temples. There were several natural places of worship, including open air sanctuaries, which were often located near water, trees, or hills (the biblical "high places"). The gods of the Canaanites reflected the relative austerity of life in the region. They sought to appease the gods of natural forces—deities of atmospheric phenomenon, agriculture, and fertility.

Canaanite Gods

El was the supreme god of the Ugaritic pantheon. He was known to his followers as "Bull El" and the "father of the gods." Pictured as a wise and kindly old man with gray hair and beard, El was called "the father of the years," "the favorable," and "the merciful." El's abode was the source of the cosmic rivers. As a young god, El courted two women by the sea, who later became his wives and gave birth to the "gracious gods" *Shahar* ("dawn") and *Shalim* ("peace" or "twilight"). El remained an aloof deity, a creator god who supervised cosmic order from afar.

Athirat (or **Asherah**) was the "lady of the sea" and mother of the seventy "gracious gods." The wife of El, she was presumably one of the two women he courted by the sea. In some stories, she is the consort of Baal. As Asherah (which has been translated as "grove," "straight," or "pillar"), the goddess was worshipped in the form of a tree or a straight wooden staff. She is the goddess of planting and childbirth.

Baal (or **Hadad**) was the son of El. His name means "lord" or "master." He was often called the "calf" or the "young bullock" as a reminder of his lineage to Bull El. A god of fertility, vegetation, rain, and storm, Baal was also "lord of earth" and "mightiest of warriors." Although Baal was subordinate to El in authority, he was much more active and much less remote—he generated widespread worship among his devoted followers. Baal was considered the provider of food to humanity, but to do so, the god had to leave his abode and fall to earth in the form of rain. During the heat of the summer, Baal was said to stay in the underworld as a willing sacrifice—a prisoner of Mot, the god of death. In a famous creation story reminiscent of Marduk killing Tiamat, Baal had a feud with Yamm (Naher or Lotan), the dragon god of the seas and rivers. Eventually Baal broke Yamm's back and was declared king of the gods. Baal carries a lightning bolt in his hands and his voice is thunder. His ship is a cloud. In some Canaanite traditions Baal has supremacy over El.

Anat was the daughter of El and the sister of Baal. A virgin (meaning independent) and "progenitor of the people," Anat was one of the nursemaids to the "gracious gods." She was renowned as a fertility goddess as well as a fierce hunter and warrior. Even the gods feared her. In some stories, Anat is the one who killed the dragon Yamm/Naher and slaughtered all the enemies of Baal. After Baal's death, Anat found his body and buried it on Mt. Zaphon where it was presumed that Baal would continue his resplendent reign. Anat went to the god Mot (death) who she cut and scattered like grain (a clear reference to an agricultural fertility myth). She is sometimes pictured with bow and arrows. Her animal is the lion.

Athtart (or **Astarte**) was the wife of Baal and the "queen of heaven" who was associated with the planet Venus. Known as a huntress and warrior, she was primarily worshipped as a goddess of love, sex, and fertility. Her worship included sacred prostitution and astrology. Athtart was said to have descended to earth as a flaming star (meteorite), which was kept in her temple at Byblos. The goddess is sometimes portrayed wearing the horns of a bull. Her symbol is the eight-pointed star.

Elements of Mesopotamian and Canaanite Mythology in the Old Testament

History is replete with examples of beliefs and ideas that have spread from one culture to the next. Usually, certain characteristics of an earlier civilization are absorbed by a later one. In spite of the fact that the Israelites later despised Babylonian religious beliefs, several key portions of the earlier Mesopotamian religion (and its gods) found their way into the mythos and writings of the Hebrews. Most of these elements can be found in the book of Genesis. The creation story of Genesis mirrors that of the earlier Sumerian version, where the world is created out of a watery abyss (Apsu), and the heavens and the earth are divided from each other by a solid vault containing the atmosphere. In fact, many biblical accounts of the stormy, war-like Hebrew god Yahweh are remarkably similar to those of earlier creator-storm gods, particularly Marduk and Baal.

The biblical story of Eden is based on the Sumerian legend of the paradisiacal land of Dilmun, and the creation of man out of clay first appeared in the story of Enki and Ninhursag. Eve, created from Adam's rib, was originally the goddess Ninti ("lady of the rib"), who healed the rib of Enki after he was cursed by Ninhursag for eating the sacred plants of Dilmun. And the serpent in the tree initially appeared in the Babylonian epic of Gilgamesh, the oldest book in the world.

One of the best known Sumerian legends that was later adapted by the Hebrews is that of the great flood. In the Mesopotomian version, the gods decide to send a flood to destroy humanity. The god Enki (Ea) took pity on the pious king Ziusura (or Ut-napishtim) and instructed him to build a great boat to save his family, a few craftsman, several animals, and precious metals. All else is obliterated. At one point, Ziusura released a dove from his boat to see if land was near. Eventually the waters receded. For saving humans and animals, Ziusura received eternal life.

There was also a Sumerian myth that formed the basis of the Biblical story of Cain and Abel. In this story, the god Enlil resolved to establish agriculture on earth. To this end, he produced the brothers Emesh and Enten, and gave them each a particular assignment. Emesh became jealous of Enten's role as "divine farmer," and challenged his brother. Enlil favored Enten's position because of the good work he had done.[8]

The sea-dragon known in the Old Testament as Leviathan, who was killed by Yahweh, is none other than Yamm/Lotan, the dragon of the sea, who was vanquished by Baal in a Canaanite myth. This is itself based on an earlier Babylonian story where Marduk slays the dragon Tiamat of the primordial waters.[9] And even this myth can be traced back to the Sumerian legend of the evil serpent Kur, who was killed by Enki.

The Canaanite creator god El was never vilified in the Bible as was his son Baal. In fact the name of El, the single most common Assyro-Babylonian name for "god," is a commonly used name of the supreme deity in the book of Genesis. And it is no coincidence that El, "the merciful," lent his divine name to the Qabalistic Sephirah of Chesed, the sphere of mercy. In addition to this, many Hebrew names such as Israel, Michael, and Gabriel use the suffix "el" to indicate that they are "of god."

Athirat or Asherah, the wife of El, was worshipped by the Hebrews for six centuries—even in the first and second temples at Jerusalem. Her statue had been brought to the temple by king Solomon. Her tree-symbol was eventually replaced by the image of the menorah.

There are a number of places in the Bible where the existence of other gods is acknowledged. The word "Elohim," or the plural of El, (literally "gods") is found throughout the Old Testament. In the Book of Psalms, Yahweh, like El before him, is seen as the king of the gods— the leader of a divine court or family:

> *God stands in the assembly of the gods. He judges in the midst of the gods. How long will ye judge unjustly and lift up the face of the wicked? Selah. Judge the poor and fatherless; do justice to the afflicted and needy. Deliver the poor and needy. Deliver them from the hand of the wicked. They neither know nor will understand; they walk in darkness; all the foundations of the earth are shaken. I have said you are gods, and all of you are sons of the Most High, but you shall die as men, and you shall fall like one of the princes.[10] (Psalm 82:1–7)*

The assimilation of pagan beliefs into the Hebrew monotheistic religion is proof of the scale to which spiritual doctrines can be absorbed regardless of geography, time, and cultural bias.

Egypt

> *They [the Egyptians] are religious to excess, far beyond any other race of men.[11]*

The Nile River, the life-blood of ancient *Khem*,[12] snakes northward across the North African desert toward the Mediterranean. In ancient times the Nile Valley was composed of two states that gradually coalesced into the two kingdoms of Upper and Lower Egypt. Upper Egypt, the narrow valley so named because it was closer to the river's source, was the southern state. Cities of Upper Egypt included Thebes, Abydos, and Edfu. Lower Egypt (which included the cities of Memphis and Heliopolis), was the northern state, which encompassed the wide flat Nile Delta. Around 3100 B.C.E., the "kingdom of the two lands" was unified by a conqueror named Menes, who became the first pharaoh. The monarchy governed from Memphis, and over the ensuing five hundred years of dynastic rule, Egyptian culture formed into a pattern that would govern the life of its people for the next two thousand years.

The classical age of ancient Egypt was known as the period of the Old Kingdom from 2600 to 2150 B.C.E. This was a time of great stability and confidence, which saw the building of the pyramids. The power of the pharaohs was eclipsed by the priests and the local rulers during the First Intermediate Period from 2150 to 2040 B.C.E., until the monarchy regained most of its authority in the Middle Kingdom (2040–1659 B.C.E.), ruling this time from the city of Thebes. The invasion of the Hyksos, a people who had superior military technology in the form of horse-drawn chariots, ushered in the Second Intermediate Period (1650–1567 B.C.E.). They held the ancient Egyptian government for almost a century until they were ousted. This was the time of the New Kingdom, from 1567–1069 B.C.E. It was also a time of imperialism, when the Egyptians, having learned the military techniques of the Hyksos, now began to set out and conquer Syria and Palestine. Internal conflicts and a series of invading conquerors, including the Assyrians, Persians, and finally the Greeks under Alexander in 332 B.C.E., finally put an end to Egyptian rule.

Although Egyptian and Mesopotamian civilizations were both born out of the taming of rivers, their culture and style were vastly different. This was partially due to differences in environment. The flooding of the Nile was much less severe than that of the Tigris and Euphrates. The weather of Egypt was generally kinder as well. In ancient times, the population of the area was relatively small, thus food and other natural resources were enough to sustain it. Also, the land of the Nile was surrounded by deserts, which protected Egypt from the constant invasions that plagued Mesopotamia.

Generally having enough resources to go around, moderate weather, and few invasions (especially in the early period), meant that life in ancient Egypt had a certain pleasant regularity about it. As a result, the Egyptians were inclined to be optimistic, self-assured, and secure. They assumed that they were singularly blessed by the gods. Egyptian art, architecture, and literature tended to portray a sense of tranquillity, confidence, and felicity. The essence of Egyptian mentality was one of benevolent tolerance.

It was during the Early Dynastic Period (3200–2600 B.C.E.) that hieroglyphic writing became a true literary vehicle. The Egyptians made achievements in irrigation, physiology, and medicine that were exceeded only much later by the Greeks. Their knowledge of astronomy was used to create a solar calendar of 365 days, which was far more precise than the Mesopotamians' lunar calendar.

Unlike the pessimistic Mesopotamians, who tended to regard the afterlife as a rather dreary existence, the Egyptians saw life after death as a positive attestation of eternal life. Although the religious beliefs of nearly all ancient civilizations contained the theme of death and resurrection based on the observance of the seasons and agriculture, the Egyptians brought it to a new level of spiritual development with the Osiris-Isis myth. Osiris, a god who was killed and resurrected, became a symbol and an ideal of salvation and eternal life in the afterworld based upon the personal merits of the individual. Life after death was considered a more perfect existence, a continuation of life as it was *before* death—only better. The art of mummification developed because the Egyptians believed that although the spirit left the body after death, it was free to return. This necessitated the preservation of the body through embalming.

Egyptian religion was a kaleidoscope of gods, legends, and beliefs that, although seemingly contradictory to the modern mind, was a perfectly natural arrangement to the ancients. Mythological concepts varied from region to region, even in regards to the same deities. When newer beliefs came into contact with older ones, they were blended together, even when the result was paradoxical. To the tolerant Egyptians, it was simply an appealing organic process of unification in which there were several different ways of expressing the same basic beliefs.

The universality of certain cosmic gods was recognized by the ancients, so that no matter what their differences were, certain deities were identified with one another. One way the Egyptians united various cosmic beliefs and national gods was to join the name of two deities together. The result of this religious syncretism was the creation of composite deities such as Re-Atum, Amon-Re, or Ptah-Nu. These amalgamated gods were said to inhabit one another—they had personal characteristics, but not singular identity. Thus the composite deity of Ptah-Nu would be the energy of Nu expressing itself through the persona of Ptah.

Many Egyptian gods were portrayed as having the bodies of humans and the heads of animals. This probably stems from an extremely ancient belief that certain animals had specific powers and thus were held to be sacred. A god was thought to take the shape of a particular animal, which was regarded as its *ba* or soul. Nevertheless, the gods of the Egyptians, like those of other pantheons, had human personalities.

The Egyptians had a great multitude of gods. In the ancient texts the gods were sometimes organized into an Ennead or "company of gods," which usually began with (but was not restricted to) a group of nine deities.

Egyptian Gods

The Primordial Waters

Nun (or **Nu**), whose name indicated "water," was the god of the great primordial ocean, which contained the germs of all things before the Creation. Often called "the father of the gods," he was conceived of more as an intellectual concept or abstraction—having neither temples nor worshippers. Nun is represented as a figure standing waist-high in water, holding his arms up to support his offspring—the gods.

The Great Ennead of Heliopolis

Tum (or **Atum**) was a primary creator god. He was considered the head of the Heliopolis Ennead. His name comes from a root word that means "to be complete." Early on, his followers identified him with Re, the sun god. Said to have existed as a still, formless spirit inside Nun before the Creation, Tum carried within him the sum of all existence. Legend has it that one day the god issued forth the gods and all living things. Thus he was considered the ancestor of humankind and the lord of peace and rest. Later, Tum was seen as the setting sun and was merged with the sun god as *Re-Atum*. The god is often represented wearing the *pschent* or double crown of the Pharaohs.

Re (or **Ra**) was the major sun god, "the great god and lord of heaven," whose name meant "creator." He was also known as the "supreme power" and was recognized all over Egypt as the eternal creator and ruler of the world. The source of heat and life, Re was worshipped in the shape of a giant obelisk, which symbolized a petrified sun ray. Through his persona as *Re-Atum*, he fathered Shu and Tefnut. Each morning Re was said to enter his royal solar boat in the east and ascend the sky to inspect his kingdom—the earth. During this daylight journey, Re was youthful and vigorous, but at night he was thought to "die" in the western sunset and journey through the underworld in his sacred barque. The twelve hours of the night were a perilous time for Re—he had to avoid the attack of his eternal nemesis, the great serpent Apep. But the forces of Re always triumphed over Apep and the sun god was reborn each morning at dawn.

　　Re was the favorite god of Pharaohs, who referred to themselves as the "sons of Re." He ruled over prosperity, destiny, truth, and righteousness. The god is represented in many forms—sometimes as a man with a ram's head, but more often with a hawk's head surmounted by the solar disk.

Shu was the god of air. His name means "to raise" or "he who holds up." Shu is the atmosphere that blankets the earth. Equivalent to the Greek Atlas, Shu was the one who supported the sky. The creation of Shu made possible a space between the heavens and the earth, into which the sun could shine. Because the sunlight immediately followed the creation of Shu, he is sometimes identified with light. Acting upon orders from Re, Shu slipped between Geb and Nut, separating earth from sky. He is always represented in human form, usually wearing an ostrich feather on his head.

Tefnut was a goddess who was more of a theological concept than a person. Her name is probably derived from a root word meaning "to moisten." She was the sister and wife of Shu, who she helped to support the sky. Tefnut was the goddess of the dew, mist, and rain. Each morning Shu and Tefnut received the newborn sun as it broke free from the mountains of the East. She is depicted as a lioness or a woman with the head of a lion.

Geb (or **Seb**) was the god of earth and the father of Osiris, Isis, Nephthys, and Set. The earth itself formed the body of Geb. He is usually depicted as a man who wears upon his head the white crown or crown of the north, to which is added the *Atef* crown. The color of his skin is either black or green, the color of the fertile mud of the Nile and of plants. Geb is also symbolized by a goose of the particular species called *seb*. He was the god of the earth's surface, which gives rise to vegetation, and he was important to the mythology of the underworld as well—having authority over the tombs of the dead. Geb figures prominently in the first act of creation, when the earth god and the sky goddess, Nut, were locked in a lover's embrace. Geb's father Shu, the air god, interceded and lifted the starry body of Nut off that of the earth god, thus forming the earth, the starry heaven, and the air between the two. Geb governed crops and fertility.

Nut (or **Nuet**) was the sky-goddess and personification of the starry heavens. She was separated from her lover Geb (the earth) by the air god, Shu. She is often represented as a blue-skinned woman with an elongated body, who touches the earth with fingers and toes, while her star-spangled body is supported by Shu. She therefore forms the arc of the heavens. Nut sometimes appears as a cow whose four legs are each held aloft by an appointed god. When in her human form, she often wears a round vase upon her head, the symbol of her name. Her maternal starry likeness was painted on the inner lid of sarcophagi to watch over the deceased. The children of Nut and Geb included Osiris, Set, Isis, and Nephthys.

Osiris (or **Asar**), the son of Geb and Nut, was originally an Egyptian god who died with the harvest only to be reborn in the spring. His name might have meant "strength of the eye." Osiris later became the god of the dead and of resurrection. In early legend he was also a water god who represented the fertility brought by the Nile. In certain texts he is simply referred to as "God," something that was not done with other deities. And no other Egyptian god was equal to the exalted position of Osiris, or thought to possess his specific characteristics.

Legend has it that Osiris instituted the cult of the gods, built the first towns and temples, and laid down the laws governing religious worship. He was given the title "un-nefer" (*onnophris* in Greek), which some claim means "the good one." As the story goes, Set, the evil one, plotted to kill his brother, Osiris. Set entombed his brother's body in a chest and flung it into the waters. The chest later ended up on a shore where a tree trunk grew around it. The tree was later cut down and used as a column in a king's house. The chest containing the body of Osiris was eventually recovered by his wife, Isis, but Set found it and dismembered the body into fourteen pieces, which he then scattered. Isis patiently searched for the remnants and reconstituted the body, all except for the phallus. Isis, aided by Thoth, Anubis, and Horus, was able to restore the dead god back to life.

Osiris represented a being who was both a man and a god; someone who by virtue of his suffering and death, humans could identify with—more so than the other gods. But he also offered the hope of resurrection after death; the idea that humans, too, could triumph over death and attain everlasting life. Thus Osiris became the god of the underworld, with the power to bestow eternal life upon the dead, who after passing the ordeal of the judgment (the "Weighing of the Soul") were allowed to live in the underworld. Osiris became known as *Osiris Khenti Amenti* or "lord of the west-erners," because the dead were thought to go into the west, the direction of the setting sun.

Eventually Osiris was thought to be even more powerful than Re, the sun god—taking on the powers of a cosmic being and the cre-ator of all. He governed initiation, eternal life, judgment, water, agri-culture, religion, discipline, order, and law. Osiris is represented standing or sitting on a throne and dressed in mummy wrappings. He wears the *Atef* crown, which is a high white miter or cone flanked by two ostrich feathers. His hands, which are folded across his breast, hold a crook and a scourge.

Isis (or **Eset**) was the most important of all Egyptian goddesses. She eventually absorbed the functions and attributes of all the other god-desses combined. Isis was the sister and wife of Osiris, to whom she bore the child Horus. Mother goddess extraordinaire, Isis was also the most powerful magician in the universe, even rivaling the great Thoth. Her many deeds included learning Re's secret name of power, protecting the infant Horus from the evil Set, and resurrecting Osiris from the dead. Isis taught the arts of healing, cloth-weaving, marital devotion, and the magical arts. She ruled over marriage, fertility, med-icine, weaving, magic, maternity, divination, and protection. The god-dess is usually depicted as a woman who wears a throne (the symbol of her name) upon her head. Sometimes she appears with wings or wearing the solar disk and lunar crescent.

Set (or **Seth**) was the destructive brother of Osiris who represented the violent storms of the desert. In very early times, Set was the lord of Upper (southern) Egypt who was overthrown by Horus, lord of Lower (northern) Egypt. His name is said to mean "he who is below." Set quickly became known as a force of darkness that, in the guise of the Apep serpent, sought to prevent the solar god Re from appearing in the eastern sky. Eventually Set came to be known as the incarnation of evil, destruction, and all that is unclean. Whereas all good came from Osiris, all perversity came from Set. Out of jealousy, Set killed Osiris and cut up his body into fourteen pieces, which he then scat-tered. Horus, the son of Osiris, fought many ferocious battles with the evil one, and in due time he avenged his father's death and Set was banished to the desert for all eternity.

All noxious creatures, desert beasts, and certain water animals were considered symbols of Set. One of Set's opponents was the hippopotamus goddess Reret, who kept the powers of the evil god fettered with chains.

Set is depicted as a strange animal with a curved snout, box-like ears, and a forked tail, or simply as a man with the head of this unusual beast. He is sometimes said to have red hair, a trait that the Egyptians disliked.

Nephthys (or **Nebt-Het**) was the sister of Isis, Osiris, and Set. She was also the wife of Set and the mother of Anubis. Her name means "lady of the house," and she originally represented the desert's edge, an area that is alternately fruitful and barren. Although Nephthys was regarded as the female counterpart of Set, she always remained the devoted sister of Isis. After Set murdered Osiris, Nephthys abandoned her husband, joined the defenders of Osiris, and helped Isis embalm his body.

Nephthys was a goddess of death, but she was also associated with the renewal of life, which follows death. She was a symbol of passive darkness, who always upheld and seconded the light of her sister Isis. So inseparable were the sisters (who were opposites in every way), that they were often called the "twins." The dark goddess is pictured as a woman wearing the symbols of her name—a kind of basket marked with the sign for "house."

The Memphis Triad

Ptah was the primary god of the city of Memphis and one of the oldest Egyptian deities. He existed before all else in the watery abyss of Nun. Through thought and speech he brought all living things into existence. His name means "sculptor," "engraver," or "maker," and he is associated with metal-smithing, casting, and sculpting. He was the great architect of the universe—the designer of heaven and earth. Some legends say that Ptah fashioned the universe under Thoth's command. Ptah is usually portrayed as a bearded, balding man who wears a tight headband and is clothed in a close-fitting garment or mummy wrappings. From an opening in his garment his two hands project to grasp a phoenix scepter, an ankh, and a *djed* wand.

Sekhet (or **Sekhmet**), whose name means "the powerful," was Ptah's wife. Goddess of war, Sekhet personified the burning, fiery, and destructive heat of the sun in late summer. Sekhet and the cat goddess Bast worked together to destroy the enemies of the sun god Re. Her lust for battle was so extreme that Re had to restrain her from killing off the human race. The goddess is represented as a woman with the head of a lioness crowned by a solar disk encircled by an uraeus.

Imhotep was the son of Ptah and Sekhet who replaced the god Nefertum as the third member of the great triad of Memphis. The god, whose name means "he who cometh in peace," was said to have brought the art of healing to humanity. In later times, this god of medicine absorbed many of the scholarly attributes of Thoth. He became scribe of the gods. Imhotep is represented as a bald, seated man with a roll of papyrus on his knees.

The Theban Triad

Amon (**Amen** or **Amun**) was the patron god of the city of Thebes, whose name means "hidden," implying that this self-created deity was mysterious and ineffable to his followers. Until the period of the Middle Kingdom, Amon was just another local god; but after the Thebans conquered all of Egypt, Amon became a major primordial power. He was a god of generation and reproduction. His worship rivaled those of Re and Osiris, and huge temples were dedicated to him. At times he is represented as a ram, but more often as a bearded man wearing a headdress of two tall plumes. God of the most potent Pharoahs, Amon became known as the "king of the gods," and eventually his identity merged with the older cult of Re, the sun god. The Theban deity assumed all of Re's powers and came to be known as *Amon-Re*, enthroned on the solar boat.

Mut was the wife of Amon, whose name means "mother." Mut was a sky goddess who is usually depicted as a woman wearing a vulture headdress and the *pschent* crown. She was the mother of Khonsu.

Khonsu (or **Khensu**) was the god of the moon, whose name means "the navigator" or "the traveler" or "he who crosses the sky in a boat." Khonsu was a messenger of the great gods and was later identified with Djehuti, another moon god. In this form he was worshipped as Khonsu-Djehuti, the Twice Great. As the new moon, Khonsu was likened to a mighty bull, and as the full moon he was said to correspond to a gelded bull. As the crescent moon, Khonsu shined his heavenly light so that all female creatures would become fertile and conceive. He was thus the source of generation and reproduction. In one story, Khonsu was beaten by Thoth in a game of senet and consequently lost some of his light each month in the lunar cycles. The god is sometimes portrayed with a hawk's head, but he is usually represented swathed in mummy cloth like Osiris and holding the scepters of crook, scourge, phoenix, and *djed*. His head is shaven except for the heavy tress of a royal child on one side. He also wears a skullcap mounted by a disk in a crescent moon. Later he became known as an exorcist and a healer.

Other Important Deities

Khepera (or **Khepri**) was the god of the rising sun symbolized by a scarab beetle, which like the sun, was thought to emerge from its own substance. Early on, he was incorporated with the other solar gods Re and Tum. To the Egyptians, the scarab pushing its ball of eggs buried in dung symbolized the sun god pushing the solar disk across the sky. The root of this god's name comes from the Egyptian word for "scarab beetle," as well as a verb that means to "create" or "transform." Khepera was the god of the transformations that manifest and regenerate life. He governed rebirth, compassion, and new beginnings. Khepera was sometimes portrayed as a man with a beetle for a head, or just as the beetle itself.

Anhur, whose name meant "sky-bearer," was a god associated with the creative power of the sun. Later he became identified with Shu and was invoked under the name of Anhur-Shu, a warrior aspect of Re. Anhur became very popular in the New Kingdom, and was often invoked for protection against enemies under the titles of "the savior" and "the good warrior." He is represented as a warrior who carries a lance and wears a long robe and a headdress ornamented with four long feathers.

Horus (or **Hor**) was the son of Isis and Osiris, whose name means "he who is above." The word "hor" sounded like the Egyptian word for "sky," and Horus probably represented the "face" of the heaven. The sky itself was seen as a divine hawk that had the luminaries of the sun and moon for eyes. Horus was a solar god who was represented as a hawk or as a man with a hawk's head. The hawk was probably the first animal worshipped in Egypt—it was considered a symbol of an omnipotent and eternal being. There were many variations of Horus, several of which need to be mentioned here:

Harakhte or "Horus of the horizon," represented the sun on its daily path between the east and west horizons. Early on, Harakhte was confused with Re and gradually expropriated Re's characteristics. Re in turn assimilated all of Horus' characteristics and was

worshipped under the name Re-Harakhte. The god is usually portrayed as a man with a hawk's head who wears the solar disk.

Harparkrat or "Horus the child." In this form, Horus is represented as an infant, the archetypal divine child. His human head is
shaved except for a single lock of hair. He is often depicted sitting on
the lap of Isis, who suckles him.

Hor Wer or "Horus the elder" was the god of the sky. Son of Re
and brother of Set, the perpetual battle between light and darkness
was symbolized by the battles between the two brothers. At one point,
Set tore out Horus' eye, and in turn was castrated by the hawk-headed
god. Eventually the gods ruled in favor of Horus over Set.

Heru Behutet was named after a district of Edfu. One of the
most important forms of Horus, Heru Behutet personified the most
powerful heat of the sun at midday. He is depicted as a winged disk,
a hawk-headed man carrying a spear or club, or as a lion. His battles
with the evil Set earned him the title of "smiter of the rebel." The god
symbolizes the power that dispels evil and darkness and fills the
world with brilliant light.

Hathor (or **Het-Hert**) was a sky goddess who became associated with
the morning and evening star because the sun god resided within her
breast, enclosed every night within the body of Hathor, to be born
anew each morning. Her name means "house above" or "house of
Horus." She was revered as the goddess of love, joy, and merriment,
and the mistress of dance and music. She also governed women, flowers, beauty, marriage, alcohol, prosperity, the arts, and family. Her
temple was the home of intoxication and a place of enjoyment. Hathor
was sometimes represented as the great celestial cow, whose milk
nourished the young Horus. More often she is depicted as a cow-
headed woman, or a woman with cow's ears, sometimes crowned
with horns and the solar disk. The sistrum, a musical instrument used
to drive away evil spirits, is Hathor's special implement. Sistrums
were usually engraved with her image.

Anubis (or **Anpu**) was the son of Nephthys, and his father was either
Set or Osiris. He presided over funerals and embalming, having
invented the art when he preserved the body of Osiris so that the great
god would live again. Pictured as a man with the head of a jackal,
Anubis became known as a god of the dead from very early times
because jackals were always seen prowling around tombs. Anubis
was considered the companion, guide, and protector of the dead. He
acts on behalf of the deceased in the Hall of Judgment.

Upuaut was another jackal-headed or wolf-headed deity who is sometimes identified with Anubis. His name means "opener of the ways." In early times he was shown as a warrior god who guided his armies into enemy territory. Eventually, he came to be seen as a god of the dead, along with Osiris and Anubis. It has been suggested that Anubis was the opener of the roads of the north and the summer solstice, while Upuaut was the opener of the roads of the south and the winter solstice.

Thoth (or **Djehoti**) "lord of books and learning," was the patron god of wisdom and inventions, science and literature. His name is derived from the Egyptian word for "ibis," a bird that is sacred to this deity. He was the spokesman of the gods, as well as the record-keeper and moon god. Self-begotten and self-created, it was he who invented all the arts and sciences: geometry, arithmetic, astronomy, astrology, surveying, medicine, music, drawing, writing, and all knowledge in general. He is also the god of magic and the world's first magician and priest. The disciples of Thoth claimed to have access to the god's magical books. When deciphered, these formulas could command all the forces of nature and subdue the gods themselves. This infinite power is the reason his followers referred to him as "Thoth, three times very, very Great," (which became the basis for the Greek version *Hermes Trismegistus*). Thoth is the one who divided time into months, years, seasons, and aeons. He is the divine calculator, adviser, arbiter, chief historian, and keeper of the divine archives. Herald of the gods, he also served as their clerk and scribe. In the Hall of Judgment, he acts on behalf of the gods. Thoth is pictured as a human figure with the head of an ibis, wearing the kilt, collar, and headdress (sometimes with the disc and crescent) of the Old Kingdom. In his hands he holds the tablet and writing stylus of a scribe.

Maat (or **Meet**) was the goddess of truth, justice, law, order, and "straightness." She was indicative of all that was true, genuine, and moral. Regarded as the female counterpart of Thoth, Maat indicated the consistency of Re's daily trek through the sky. Her moral power of truth was tremendous, and she came to be regarded as the destiny that awaits each individual based upon a lifetime of good or evil deeds. In the Hall of Judgment, where the deceased's soul was judged by the gods, Maat waited to hear the confessions of the dead. The deceased's heart was weighed against the feather of Maat, and if he had lived a pure life he was judged to have "done maat." The goddess is portrayed as a woman who wears a single straight ostrich feather on her head.

Egypt's Contribution to Western Magic

According to Clement of Alexandria, "Egypt was the mother of magicians." The Egyptians, like the Mesopotamians, believed that the first magicians were the gods themselves—the glorious creators of the universe and of humankind. Magic was said to come from the gods. Therefore, some of their greatest gods were connected with the magical arts. Thoth was first among magicians, but the great lady Isis was nearly as powerful.

In ancient Khem, there was no real distinction between religion and magic. In fact, any attempt to separate the two would have been thought of as ludicrous. To the Egyptian way of thinking, the word "religion" would have been meaningless—there was no religion without *heka*[13] or "magical power." Heka was used by the creator god to form the world out of chaos. Heka was used by the gods to produce humanity, and it was also seen as a gift given by the gods to humanity to deflect the blows of fate. Since heka was the energy continually used by the gods in the process of creation, the Egyptians reasoned that it could also be used by human beings in their endeavors. The people of Khem had an overwhelming faith in the powers of magic. Thus Egyptian priest/magicians performed ritual acts of magic for the benefit of whole communities and individuals alike. Magic was employed in all questions of life and death, health and illness, love and war.

A central theme in Egyptian magic was the belief that words, names, and images had creative power. The name (or *ren*) of a being was considered an essential part of his or her soul. In the story of Isis and Re, the great goddess obtains power over the sun god by finding out his secret name.[14] In the same manner, Egyptian priests hoped to appease, influence, and sometimes threaten the gods or spirits using a host of names and epitaphs associated with the deity. This practice could later be seen in the "barbarous names" of evocation found in fragments of later Hellenistic magical papyri. Medieval magical grimoires were no less influenced by this method, as attested to by the great number of divine Hebrew, Egyptian, and Greek names found therein. Modern magicians can look to Egypt for the origins of the practice described in the Golden Dawn's Neophyte Ritual: "For By Names and Images are All Powers Awakened and Re-awakened."

In magical ceremonies, priests and priestesses often took on the personas of different deities. They identified themselves with various gods and acted out certain divine myths. By ritual performance of a particular myth, such as that of Isis raising Osiris from the dead, the priest/magicians hoped to magically accomplish something similar—like the raising of a deceased person to eternal life. This technique of deity emulation would later become a major part of Hermetic magic known as the "assumption of godforms."

The Egyptian practice of commanding lesser gods and spirits into carrying out the will of the magician through the repetition of certain names and formulae developed into techniques used in evocation and talisman consecration. The widespread use of amulets and talismans was perhaps the best-known aspect of Egyptian magic. Objects of this sort were employed for the living as well as the dead. But these objects were not considered powerful in themselves; they had to be ritually consecrated. Purification rites were essential in these ceremonies. Perfumes and incenses were commonly used as well.

Apotropaic wands made of ivory or precious stone were engraved with various figures and used as weapons for banishing hostile spirits and for creating a circle of protection.

The priest/magicians worked sympathetic magic and practiced an early form of what we know today as the "Law of Correspondences." They sought to understand the primary essence of all beings and objects, as well as the points of connection between them. These shared points of similarity included color, sound, appearance, and a host of other correspondences. Once this type of connection was made between two things, the magician manipulated one in order to affect the other.

The Egyptians were skilled metal-workers, and the legendary Hermes Trismegistus was reputed to have been the first practicing alchemist. In fact, the name *"alchemy,"* containing the ancient name of "Khem," is said to mean "the Egyptian matter," referring to the Egyptian origins of the art. The name of "khem" literally referred to the fertile black soil of the region, but it had additional connotations in the symbolism of alchemy to the black ore that was said to be the active principle in the transmutation of metals. Alchemy came to be known as the "black art" for this reason.

The Egyptians were prolific writers. A collection of various religious passages, hymns, and rituals can be found in *The Book of the Dead* (or more correctly, *The Book of Coming Forth by Day*). This might well be considered the first real magical grimoire. Egypt had a powerful effect on the surrounding cultures of Canaan and Israel. It seems likely that at least a portion of the religious literature of the Hebrews, such as the Psalms, was influenced by Egyptian writings. And many beautiful invocations directed at the great gods of Egypt were the forerunners of the most sublime Judeo-Christian prayers:

> *Praise to thee, O Re, lord of Truth. Thou whose chapel is hidden, lord of gods. Khephre in his bark, who gave command and the gods came into being.*
>
> *Atum, who created mankind, who distinguished their nature and made their life; who made the colours different, one from the other.*
>
> *He who heareth the prayer of the prisoner; kindly of heart when one calleth to him.*
>
> *He who rescueth the fearful from the oppressor, who judgeth between the miserable and the strong.*
>
> *Lord of Perception, in whose mouth is Authority. For love of him cometh the Nile, the sweet, the greatly beloved, and when he hath come men live.*
>
> *He causeth all eyes to open...his beneficence createth the light. The gods rejoice in his beauty, and their hearts live when they behold him.*[15]

Greece

Long before the Golden Age of classical Greece (or *Hellas*) came into being, two earlier Greek civilizations flourished in the Aegean: the Minoans of ancient Crete (2000–1400 B.C.E.) and the Mycenaens in southern Greece (1580–1120 B.C.E.). Little is known of these sea-faring cultures, but portions of their mythologies were later absorbed into Hellenic[16] legends. Invaders from northern Greece put an end to the Mycenaean culture and began the so-called "Greek Dark Age" lasting for several centuries from 1120 to 800 B.C.E., during which time the people of Greece lost the art of writing.[17] The darkness began to lighten in the eighth century with the emergence of the Homeric epics. The works of the poet Homer have been studied for their brilliance ever since.

The Hellenic culture, which emerged after the Dark Age was based on the model of the individual city-state known as the *polis*.[18] These small independent states (such as Sparta and Athens) had their own customs, deities, and political systems that encouraged participation in community affairs. The years from 750 to 550 B.C.E.

were a period of expansion as a number of Greek poleis began a process of colonization across the Mediterranean. Greek city-states and Hellenic ideas flourished in Sicily (Syracuse), southern Europe (Neopolis in Italy, and Massilia in France),[19] west Asia (Byzantium),[20] and north Africa.

Revolutionary ideas about democracy and personal freedom were developed in the polis of Athens in the fifth century B.C.E. All native male Athenians were given citizenship and the right to a voice in the city Assembly, which decided all matters of public policy. A smaller group known as the Council of Five Hundred was chosen by lot to run the day-to-day affairs of the polis. It was a government of the people, for the people, and by the people.

During the sixth century, Ionia in Asia Minor was the cultural center of the Greek world. Contact with Near Eastern peoples gave the Ion-ians their own distinctive outlook. It was here that lyric poetry, Greek philosophy, and Hellenic science came into being. The open-minded philosophers turned their attention to the study of logic, humanity, and the rational investigation of the nature of the universe. The ideas of the two greatest philosophers, Plato and Aristotle, would later have an enormous impact on all of western philosophy and spiritual thought.

Compared to the cultures of the Near East, the world of the Greek polis-system was versatile and intense. Greek art, especially sculpture, reflected a style of freedom and naturalism not seen before.

Internal pressures and inter-city warfare put an end to the Golden Age around 404 B.C.E. The poleis declined until Philip of Macedonia conquered all of Greece in 338 B.C.E. Soon after, his son Alexander the Great went on to conquer much of the then-known world and began the Hellenistic Age—the final stage of the ancient Greek civilization.

The Hellenic gods had various origins—some were local, some were remnants of the earlier Minoan and Mycenaean cultures, and a few were imported from areas of Greek colonization, such as Asia Minor. By the time of the poet Homer, most of the myths had coalesced in a hierarchy of deities that were common to all of Greece. Probably influenced by the creation stories from the Near East, the poet Hesiod provided the *Theogony,* which was the story of the origin of the universe and the birth of the gods, most notably the Titans (the first gods) and the Olympians (their divine successors).

One of the main functions of mythology is to make the divine more accessible to humans. Thus the Greek gods were entirely human in form and in behavior. They displayed all the human traits of anger, love, jealousy, favoritism, etc. But they also possessed superhuman characteristics such as immortality and the power to transform. Universal belief in the Olympic pantheon was a unifying factor in the otherwise stubborn regionalism of Greek society. Yet each city also had its own native deities whose worship garnered feelings of family devotion, city prosperity, and local patriotism.

Rivaling the Olympic gods in popularity were the ancient agricultural fertility cults of death and rebirth, such as those of Demeter and Dionysus. These deities remained the focus of annual festivals and initiatory rites, which were considered sacred religious observances.

The essence of the Greek mentality was a dynamic interplay between two methods of thinking: logic and myth, reason and legend—objective truth (which can be proven to all) versus subjective truth (that which can be understood but not verified by tangible facts). It is mind-boggling to some people that the most logical and rational of the ancient civilizations was also the one with the most fantastic and colorful myths. However, the rational side of the Greeks was perfectly balanced by their intuitive, imaginative side. In the Hellenic world, there was no dogmatic religious authority that imposed provisions of faith upon the populace. The priesthood held little power here. The temples contributed much to the Hellenic pantheon, but they were not the sole repositories of Greek religious thought. Each individual was free to believe or question the veracity of the Greek legends.[21] Their mythos was pliable and fluid, often manifesting great variation in the same story from one region to another. Poets, writers, philosophers, and artists often adapted legends of the gods as they pleased, sometimes speaking of them as symbols and metaphors in order to describe a certain human condition, argue a point, or emphasize a particular moral principle. When the Greeks freed their emotive religious beliefs from the bonds of their rational logical side, their mythology became one of the most productive areas for human contemplation and creativity, as witnessed by the appearance of the pantheon in virtually all areas of art and poetry for several centuries after the Golden Age came and went.

Greek Gods

The Titans

According to the *Theogony*, there existed only chaos in the beginning. This was pure space in which nothing could be described. The "elder gods" who evolved out of this chaos were known as the Titans. They were considered the first divine race. Some of them were quite nebulous and ill-defined, with no distinct personality. The Greeks honored these primordial cosmic forces as the ancestors of humanity and the creators of magic and the arts. They were also the ancestors of another divine race that eventually overthrew them—the Olympians.

The Titans included: **Gaea,** the deep-breasted earth, first appearing out of chaos. Her son **Uranus,** the sky, became her husband. Together the ruling couple produced many children, twelve of the Titans among them: **Oceanus** (the ocean), **Coeus** (intelligence), **Hyperion** (light), **Crius, Iapetus, Cronus** (time), **Theia, Rhea, Mnemosyne** (remembrance), **Phoebe** (the moon), **Tethys** (wife of Oceanus), and **Themis** (justice).

Uranus, horrified by all his children, locked them away in the depths of the earth. But Cronus, aided by his mother, castrated Uranus in his sleep and became ruler of the Titans. His wife was Rhea. To ensure that he would not share the fate of Uranus, Cronus devoured his children once they were born. When Rhea gave birth to Zeus, the first of the Olympians, she saved him by tricking Cronus into swallowing a rock instead of her son. When Zeus reached adulthood, he freed his swallowed siblings and led a revolt that defeated the Titans. Thus began the rule of the Olympians.

Other Titans were:

Prometheus (who foresees) was the Titan who created humankind and helped humans in other ways, including giving them fire.

Epimetheus (who reflects after the event) was a rather dim-witted Titan who accepted Pandora's gift to Zeus and was responsible for evil being loosened upon the world.

Atlas led the Titans against the Olympians and was punished by having to support the world on his back.

Metis was the Titaness of wisdom.

The Olympians

The new race of divine beings was the twelve gods whose abode was on Mount Olympus. These deities, who were all related, constituted a divine society with its own hierarchy and laws. The god Zeus reigned over this society with absolute authority. Beyond Zeus, however, there existed an ultimate power to which even the gods were subject—Moros or "destiny." Wise Zeus knew enough not to challenge the decisions of destiny.

Zeus was the god of the sky and of all atmospheric phenomena including winds, clouds, thunder, and rain. He is sometimes referred to as *Nephelgeretes*, or "cloud-gatherer." Zeus was said to reside in the uppermost regions of the air and on mountain tops. He overthrew his father Cronus and drew lots with his brothers Hades and Poseidon. Winning the draw made Zeus king of the gods. Later, he took on the characteristics of a supreme god who was omnipotent and all-knowing. A wise leader of gods and men, he ruled all in accordance with the law of fate. He punished liars and oath-breakers. To humans he dispensed both good and evil, but he was generally kind, protective, and compassionate. Zeus is usually depicted as a mature, robust man with a serious expression and deep-set eyes. Thick hair and a curled beard frame his face and a crown of oak leaves adorns his head. Sometimes nude, but more often wearing a long mantle that covers his chest and right arm, the god holds a scepter in his left hand and a thunderbolt in his right. He hurls the thunderbolt at those who displease him.

Poseidon was the god of the sea, a position he won after drawing lots with his brothers Zeus and Hades. His name is derived from a root word that means "to be master." It is likely that he was once a celestial god, as his symbol the trident (a form of the thunderbolt) would seem to indicate. Although he was the equal of his brother Zeus in dignity and birth, he was nonetheless subject to Zeus' power and authority. Next to Zeus he is second in power amongst the gods. In addition to being the lord of the sea, Poseidon was also the master of lakes and rivers. He could shake the earth at will, and would often split mountains with his trident and roll them into the sea to make islands. His personality was somewhat contentious—he often quarreled with other gods over cities. His palace was located in the depths of the Aegean Sea, and whenever the god left his palace, he would don golden armor, harness swift golden-maned horses to his chariot, and race across the watery plain with whip in hand. Sea monsters would pay homage to him and frolic in the waves as he passed by. The very sea itself would open up before him as he sped lightly across the waves. The appearance of Poseidon coincided with fierce storms at sea, a sign of the god's rage.

Hades became the god of the underworld and ruler over the dead (after drawing lots with his brothers Zeus and Poseidon). A possessive god, Hades continually tried to increase the number of subjects in his kingdom. The Greeks viewed him as a god of terror and the unknown. Black rams were his favorite sacrifice. Prayers to the god were performed by beating the ground with rods or one's hands.

Hades was also considered the god of buried treasure, precious metals, gemstones, crops, and all wealth that comes from the ground. Unlike the other Olympians, Hades did not make Mount Olympia his home. He rarely left his underworld kingdom. Whenever he left the underworld, he wore a helmet that made him invisible.

Hestia was the goddess of the hearth-fire of the household—fire that was beneficial to humankind. She was the sister of Zeus and a chaste goddess. Considered the oldest of the Olympians, Hestia was venerated in all of Greece, and the fire of the hestia or public hearth was used in sacrifices and was never allowed to go out. She was considered a protectress of home, family, and city. Hestia is pictured as a robed woman who maintains an attitude of immobility.

Hera was the queen of the gods and a patron of women, especially married women. She also has a connection with the three phases of the moon. Originally a sky goddess, Hera became the wife of Zeus, and the cults of the two sky-deities merged. Zeus initially tricked Hera into marriage. The relationship between the two divinities was always rocky due to Zeus' many infidelities and Hera's successive, jealous acts of vengeance. The noisy quarrels of Zeus and Hera were reflected in the storms and atmospheric disturbances.

Ares, the son of Zeus and Hera, was a murderous god of war. The Greeks viewed him more with a sense of terror than empathy. He was the god of brutal courage, rage, and bloodshed. In battle he was merciless and bloodthirsty. Ares was hot-headed and impetuous, often sneaking off to be with Aphrodite when her husband Hephaestus was away. The god is portrayed as a handsome bearded warrior with helmet, armor, and spear.

Athena was a virgin warrior goddess and the favorite daughter of Zeus. She had no mother, but sprang from Zeus' head fully-grown and dressed in armor. She was formidable in war, but benevolent in peace. She fought only when it was necessary to protect her people. Her functions were many—her skills in battle rivaled those of Ares, but she was also known as a goddess of the arts and of intelligence. Protectress of various industries, Athena was the patron of sculptors, architects, spinners, and weavers. Her renowned wisdom and valuable service to humanity earned her the titles of *Pronoia*, "the foreseeing," as well as counselor and goddess of the Assembly. She taught the skills of horsemanship, charioteering, pottery, cloth weaving, and embroidery. Athena was known for her healing arts and for her role as protectress of both individuals and entire cities. The goddess is usually depicted dressed in draping robes and wearing a helmet. In one hand she holds a spear and in the other a shield. She is the essence of wisdom and purity. Her symbol is the owl.

Apollo, the son of Zeus and Leto, and twin brother of Artemis, was one of the greatest gods of the Greek pantheon. A handsome deity, he was given special consideration, even among the gods. He was the god of music, healing, truth, and light. He was also a shepherd who protected flocks. His titles included *phoebus*, "the brilliant," *xanthus*, "the fair," and *chrysocomes*, "of the golden locks." As the god of solar light, Apollo made all fruit to ripen. He also protected crops. Every day he harnessed his chariot with four golden horses and drove the orb of the sun across the heavens. He was known as a god of divination and prophesy. Apollo had several sanctuaries (including one at Delphi) where oracles were dedicated to him. He was skillful with the hunting bow and with the lyre. All the gods were entranced when the fair sun god played music.

Aphrodite was the goddess of love in all its aspects. *Aphrodite Urania*, or the heavenly Aphrodite, was the goddess of pure, ideal love. *Aphrodite Genetrix* was the goddess of marriage. *Aphrodite Pandemos* was the goddess of lust and mistress of prostitutes.

In legend, Aphrodite was born out of the sea, from the foam of the severed genitalia of Uranus. All the gods were struck by her beauty and grace, for the goddess emitted an aura of seduction and charm. She owned a magic girdle that was endowed with the power of enslaving the hearts of mortals and immortals alike. Aphrodite often delighted in arousing the amorous passions of the gods and sending them chasing after mortals. Protectress of legitimate unions between men and women, the normally benign goddess could punish her enemies by driving them mad with passion. Her companions included the child-god Eros and the three Graces, whose presence gladdened the hearts of humanity. Although she was the wife of the deformed god Hephaestus, her lovers were many (the war god Ares among them). Aphrodite is usually portrayed as a voluptuous woman partially draped with a robe or nude. Her symbols include the dove and the swan.

Hermes was the son and the messenger of Zeus. It was his duty to bring the dictates of the gods to earth. Primarily a god of travelers, Hermes guided those who were journeying. As *Hermes Psychopompus*, he was charged with the duty of conducting the souls of the dead to the underworld. Because many journeys were undertaken for commercial reasons, Hermes became known as the god of commerce, articulation, and eloquence. He is often represented as a swift-footed, (sometimes bearded) athletic god, wearing a winged helmet and winged sandals. Hermes holds a winged staff with two serpents twined around it—the *caduceus*. The name of Hermes was invoked in later times to describe the esoteric tradition known as Hermetics.

Artemis was the daughter of Zeus and the twin sister of Apollo. She was originally known as a moon goddess and was associated with lunar light and the crescent moon. Later she became known as a goddess of the hunt and protectress of women in childbirth. Artemis is the goddess of untamed nature and the "lady of the beasts"—a virgin goddess who hunted deer with silver arrows. She was destructive to those who displeased her, but beneficial to her worshippers. Fundamental to the worship of this goddess were vivacious dances and the Sacred Bough, which was probably derived from worship of the ancient moon-tree, considered a source of knowledge and immortality. At times she is depicted as having many breasts, a reference to her powers of fertility. At other times she is flanked by lions, dancing with a stag, or holding a slain deer in each hand.

Hephaestus was the god of terrestrial fire. The son of Hera and Zeus, his name is derived from a Greek word meaning "heath" or "kindle." The element that this god represents was not the destructive fire, but the beneficial fire of the forge that permitted humans to smelt metal and advance civilization. Like the Egyptian Ptah, he was the divine blacksmith, the artisan who taught humans the mechanical arts and built the divine palaces of Olympus. His forge was a volcano, which he used to make armor and weapons for the gods. Hephaestus appears as a powerful, bearded smith who is lame in both legs. There are two different stories as to how he became lame. In one version, Hera flung him from Mount Olympus because he was an ugly child. In another tale, he argued with Zeus and was thrown off the mountain. Kind and gentle, he is the patron god of smiths and weavers. Hephaestus is depicted wearing a short, sleeveless chiton and holding a hammer and thongs, often working by flaming furnaces and pounding out metal on an enormous anvil. The metal-working companions of Hephaestus were a variety of subterranean fire genii, which included the Cyclopes and Dactyls.

Other Deities

Ascelpius, the son of Apollo, was a god of light, medicine, and healing. He was raised by the centaur Chiron who taught him the healing arts. Asclepius is sometimes represented as a serpent, but more often as a kindly middle-aged man with a staff around which one serpent was twined. (It was probably this staff that was intended to be a modern symbol of medicine, rather than the caduceus of Hermes.) The god brought dead mortals back to life with a vial of blood from the Gorgon, an act that angered Hades and instigated Zeus' killing of Asclepius with a thunderbolt. The cult of Asclepius was both a religion and a system of therapeutics. The priests of this god had a wide knowledge of the medical arts.

Demeter, the daughter of Cronus and Rhea, was the goddess of the fruitful earth. She represented the fertile, cultivated soil of fields as well as grain (especially corn, wheat, and barley), fruit trees, and the harvest. It was she who governed all agricultural activities and made the crops grow every year. Thus the first loaf of bread from the harvest was always sacrificed to her. Both she and her daughter Persephone were intimately linked with the seasons. Demeter is usually represented as a mature woman in a long robe, often wearing a veil that covers the back of her head. She is sometimes shown crowned with ears of corn or a ribbon, and she holds in her hand either a scepter, ears of corn, or a torch.

Persephone or **Kore,** the daughter of Demeter, was also a goddess of harvest and fertility. She was kidnapped by Hades and held prisoner in the underworld as the dark god's wife. At the loss of her daughter, Demeter cursed the world, withered plants, and made the earth barren and desolate. Alarmed, Zeus persuaded Hades to release the young Persephone, but first, Hades persuaded her to eat some pomegranate seeds, which made their union indissoluble. To settle the matter, Zeus decided that Persephone would live with her husband in the underworld for one-third of the year. During this time, Demeter grieves for her daughter and revokes her gifts from the earth in winter, when the world is cold and unproductive. When Persephone returns in the spring, the earth resumes its warmth along with its mantle of flowers and fertile crops. Persephone is often portrayed as a maiden crowned and enthroned. She sometimes carries an ear of corn or a pomegranate.

Dionysus, a late-comer and guest of honor among the Olympians, was the son of Zeus and Semele, a mortal woman. He is the only god in the pantheon to have a parent who was human. Dionysus was a complex god of wine, pleasure, and the forces of life. Credited with inventing the art of wine-making, Dionysus (like wine itself), can bring either ecstasy or rage. Unlike other deities, Dionysus could sometimes be perceived as dwelling *within* his followers. Called the "deliverer of men from their cares," Dionysus is depicted as a youth crowned with vine leaves and grapes and robed in the skin of a panther. In one hand he bears a cup of wine and in the other a thyrsus staff surmounted by a pine cone. The god is often accompanied in his travels by a band of satyrs, centaurs, maenids, nymphs, and sileni. The festivals of Dionysus were marked by frenzied activity, orgies, dancing, music, and pleasure. Eventually, these rites became the basis of Classical Greek drama and theatrical performance. Later, the god acquired the more mystical aspects of death and resurrection, when jealous Hera ordered him to be killed by the Titans. He was brought back to life by Rhea, and thus became a symbol of the forces of life. He was one of the few deities who could bring the dead back from the underworld.

Adonis was originally a Syrian vegetation god who was adopted into the Greek pantheon. His name was a Hellenized form of the Semitic word *adoni,* or "lord," which was chanted continually by his priestesses during the autumn festival of Adonis (called the *Adonia*). He was an extremely handsome god who won the affections of both Aphrodite and Persephone, who fought over him. To make peace, Zeus decided that the beautiful god would spend half the year on earth, and the other half in the underworld. Adonis was killed by a wild boar sent by jealous Ares. He was believed to return to life only to be killed and reborn with the harvest.

Eros, god of romantic love, was the son of Aphrodite. His arrows were magically treated to cause the person wounded by them to have either insatiable love or total disinterest toward the first person he or she saw. Eros is portrayed as a young, winged child. He is sometimes blindfolded to represent that "love is blind."

Helios was the god who personified the sun itself (whereas Apollo was considered the solar light). Drown in the ocean by the Titans, Helios was raised to the sky to become the luminary of the sun. Each morning the god emerged from the east in a golden chariot pulled by nine white, fire-breathing horses. The light of the god's golden armor and helmet shown down upon the earth illuminating both gods and humans. At dusk, Helios entered a boat in the west to rejoin his family until the next dawn. Like many solar deities, Helios saw everything from his lofty position in the sky—nothing escaped him.

Selene was the primary goddess of the moon and sister of Helios. Particularly associated with the full moon, she was also called *Mene*, and her bright crown illuminated the dark night. Every evening, after the journey of Helios across the sky, Selene began her own excursion after bathing in the ocean. Then the broad-winged goddess would dress in fine robes and fly across the sky in a chariot drawn by radiant steeds or oxen. In early depictions, she is shown as a cow with the ancient horns of consecration—the crescent moon. Selene is sometimes shown mounted on a horse, bull, or mule.

Hecate was a powerful moon goddess who presided over navigation, enchantments, and magic. She was known as the "mother of witches" and was particularly associated with the dark new moon. Her gifts were riches, victory, and wisdom—she was a powerful deity in the sky and on the earth. Later she became known as a goddess of the underworld who ruled over ghosts, demons, and cemeteries. Hecate was called the "invincible queen" who presided over purifications and expiations. Ritually prepared food was offered to the goddess as an act of appeasement, and her image was placed in front of homes to avert evil. Hecate is sometimes portrayed with three faces to represent the cycles of the moon. She is often accompanied by wild hounds.

Pan, son of Hermes, was the god of the woods, forests, shepherds, goatherds, and wild places. He is depicted as a man with the horns, haunches, legs, and hooves of a goat. Considered an excellent musician, he often carries the syrinx of panpipes. A merry and mischievous deity, Pan was fond of dancing and chasing forest nymphs, who usually rejected his advances because of his looks.

Greek Influence on Magic and Spirituality

With the conquests of Alexander the Great in 323 B.C.E., the Hellenistic Age began. The Greeks were now the rulers of the archaic world—Egypt, Syria, and Persia. Under their dominion, a magnificent cosmopolitan civilization emerged that was clearly Greek in flavor, but metamorphosed by the traditions of native cultures and the broad new surroundings, which the Greeks now controlled.

During this time, Greek religion was transformed as the ancient allegiance to the poleis gradually evaporated. This was a time of fierce individualism that manifested itself in a multitude of new spiritual ideas that emphasized the liberation and fulfillment of the individual above service to the city or community. As the Hellenistic realm grew to encompass the then-known world, the Greeks came to look upon all humankind as a legion of individuals, where one's ethnic origins, whether Greek, Hebrew, Egyptian, or Persian, mattered little. The Greeks themselves were heavily influenced by Near Eastern thought. A collective culture was developing—one with shared ideas and shared deities.

Some Greek deities, such as Iris and Hebe, were portrayed as graceful figures dressed in flowing robes with large wings protruding from their shoulders. Artistic renderings of these deities were probably the inspiration for later Christian representations of angels and archangels. Eros, the Greek child-god of love, was almost certainly the source for the popular image of the cute, rosy-cheeked "cherubs," who bear little resemblance to the Hebrew/Babylonian *Kerubim*—the fierce, many-winged, many-headed, guardians who were half-human and half-animal in appearance.

The worship of agricultural deities such as Demeter and Dionysus, which had always existed behind the great Olympian pantheon, came to the forefront as an interest in personal salvation and initiatory cults grew. Among these were the mystery religions of Eleusis, Samothrace, and Orpheus. Many of these groups stressed secrecy along with personal knowledge and mystical experience of the Divine. Members underwent potent ceremonies of initiation. In addition, several Near Eastern mystery cults were adopted by the Greeks, including the mysteries of Isis and Osiris from Egypt. Nearly all of these initiatory cults focused on the death and resurrection of a deity and the promise of the initiate's personal salvation. At the same time, there was a rebirth of interest in Babylonian astrology, divination, amulet magic, mysticism, and Egyptian theurgy.

And yet, in the Greek tradition of dynamic contrasts, many Greeks also turned to radical new ethical philosophies such as Skepticism, which questioned everything, including all knowledge of the gods, of humans, and of nature. Cynicism was a philosophy that rejected all human institutions, traditions, and possessions. But there were also some philosophical schools that managed to combine rational thought, ethics, and a hint of mysticism. Such were the teachings of the Stoics and Epicureans, who believed in reincarnation and an orderly universe. They compassionately taught that humans should seek out happiness or virtue in order to fortify themselves against the harsh conditions of life. Stoicism and Epicureanism both influenced human thinking and behavior for many centuries.

It was this cosmopolitan Hellenistic melting-pot of spiritual ideas that would set the stage for the numerous Greek cults of Christianity and Gnosticism. Hellenistic culture exercised an overwhelming influence on the Roman Empire, as well as the Persian and Byzantine cultures, and even Medieval Christian Europe. But the Hellenistic style of free-thinking and intellectual inquiry would not be seen again until the Renaissance.

Rome

The origins of Roman history are ambiguous; however, it seems likely that the city-state of Rome was formed around 750 B.C.E. when Etruscans from the north settled in the area and proceeded to mold early Roman civilization into a style that was heavy with Greek and Near Eastern elements, but was nevertheless amply distinctive in its own right.

The nobility of Rome overthrew their Etruscan king in 509 B.C.E. and set up a Republic with a government comprised of number of civic officials, advisory councils, and legislative bodies such as the Senate. The early Romans were committed to the state. Their outlook on life was serious, austere, and disciplined. By 265 B.C.E., much of Italy was under Roman control. During the Punic wars, from 264 to 146 B.C.E., Rome fought bitterly against Carthage, a city in northern Africa whose power rivaled Rome's. Eventually the Carthaginians were defeated. Contrary to the mystique of Roman military superiority, their military victories were accomplished more through pit-bull determination than skill. At the end of the second century B.C.E., Rome had conquered all the Hellenistic kingdoms of the Mediterranean world, and as a consequence Rome fell increasingly under the influence of Greek culture.

Eventually, the old Roman Republic was laid low by political corruption and internal conflict. When a military commander named Julius Caesar took authoritarian control in 48 B.C.E., the Roman Empire was born and conquest followed conquest. The five-hundred year reign of the Empire saw Roman dictators as brilliant as Augustus, and others as cruel as Nero and Caligula. Though individual Roman liberty lost ground during the Empire, for the most part, there was relative peace and stability. Among Roman citizens there was also a new sense of optimism. In the early second century C.E., the Roman Empire included a vast region of approximately three thousand miles from east to west. It included the areas of modern-day Italy, France, Spain, England, Egypt, Greece, Turkey, Syria, Iraq, and the northern coast of Africa. Under the umbrella of the Roman Empire, Graeco-Roman culture spread across the western world. One product of this combination of Roman political ingenuity and Greek contemplative thought, was Roman law, a body of social principles that has become the basis of western legal systems.

Roman Gods

From its earliest days, Rome was exceedingly receptive to spiritual influences from the outside. Some believe that the ancient Romans (753–43 B.C.E.) had no mythology of their own, but simply plagiarized and renamed the pantheon of the Greeks. However, there were differences between Greek deities and the Romans gods, even though the latter absorbed much of the character and mythos of the former. Thus the Roman Jupiter was not identical to the Greek Zeus, and Minerva was subtly different from Athena. The ancient origins of the Roman pantheon were generally Etruscan. Upon this framework, the Hellenic mythology was heavily layered.

Roman myths were generally less complex, less elaborate, and more coherent. Their gods were more abstract, utilitarian, and less personalized. Additionally, the purposes and functions of the Roman legends were different from their Greek counterparts. Whereas Greek mythology focused more on the deities themselves, Roman myths tended to emphasize how the gods affected history, social functions, and city life. The gods of Rome were mainly considered protectors of the state and of the family. But here, as in other parts of the world, agricultural deities always played an important role. When the politically savvy Romans conquered ancient lands, they built temples to the gods of the conquered peoples on Roman soil. Thus even foreign deities took on the responsibilities of protecting Rome and its culture. Throughout the Empire there were also numerous unofficial cults that existed under the tolerance of the state. There was no recognized monopoly on spiritual truth, and so a single person could be a member of several pagan cults. Thus the Roman pantheon was a mosaic of different elements, including Etruscan, Sabine, Alban, Syrian, Greek, Persian, and Egyptian.

The one truly Roman god was **Janus**, who originated as a solar deity. With time, Janus became known as the god of all doorways and gateways. He was also the deity of harbors, communication, navigation, beginnings, initiative, and of the creation of the world. According to Ovid, when the elements first separated out of chaos, the chaos took on the form of Janus. This "father of the gods" status was higher even than Jupiter. Janus is portrayed as an older bearded man with a double face that permits him to look within and outward. His symbols were the key (to open and close doors) and the stick (to drive intruders away from the threshold).

The correspondences between the most prevalent Greek and Roman gods are as follows:

Greek	*Roman*
Cronus	Saturn
Gaea	Tellus
Zeus	Jupiter
Hera	Juno
Posiedon	Neptune
Hades	Pluto
Hermes	Mercury
Ares	Mars
Aphrodite	Venus
Athena	Minerva
Artemis	Diana
Hestia	Vesta
Hephaestus	Vulcan
Apollo	Apollo
Selene	Luna
Eros	Cupid
Demeter	Ceres
Ascelpius	Aesculapius
Dionysus	Bacchus
Persephone	Proserpina

Later Trends in Graeco-Roman Spirituality

The same forces that encouraged individualism and restlessness in the Greek realm began to repeat themselves in the Roman world. The trend toward personal redemption, mystery religions, and salvation cults that started in the Hellenistic world continued on into the later centuries of imperial Rome. Another factor that added to this mystical inclination was the growing poverty and hopelessness among great numbers of the underprivileged.

Slowly the worship of the traditional deities of the state gave way to more exotic gods imported from conquered lands: Mithras, the Persian god of light; perennial favorites Isis and Osiris; and from Asia Minor came the Great Mother Goddess Cybele and her consort Attis (the "most high"), along with another deity named Sabazios.[22] In some areas Yahweh, the tribal god of the Hebrews, was worshipped alongside Horus and Jupiter. The shift in Roman religion began to turn from city god to savior deity.

Greek philosophy was also alive and well, and busy transforming the older Graeco-Roman gods into new transcendent symbols for Neoplatonic teachings. The school of Neoplatonism, based on the teachings of Plato as interpreted by Plotinus (205–270 C.E.), would become a predominant junction of philosophy, logic, mysticism, and magic. Neoplatonists believed in a transcendent god who was the source of all and whose main creation is the divine intellect. All things that emanated from god were considered degrees of light-energy. They believed that the human soul consisted of a higher and lower self, and that the latter was a reflection of the former. They also believed in reincarnation and stressed that the individual should seek out goodness and strive to reach god through contemplation of the Divine over the coarse of several lifetimes. Neoplatonic thought had a major impact on the development of western ceremonial magic.

During this time, interest in magic, astrology, and divination dominated the Graeco-Roman mind more than in any previous era. The ancient books ascribed to Hermes Trismegistus, known as the *Corpus Hermetica*, were written around this time (second and third centuries C.E.). In addition, numerous magical texts, collectively known later as the *Greek Magical Papyri*, were being written down in Egypt.

It was also around this time that the early followers of one of the salvation cults, known as Christianity, began to emerge in different forms—to the annoyance of some of the Roman rulers, who thought this new cult subversive to state interests and tried to eliminate it. Eventually, a single form of Christianity became the official religion of Rome, and all other faiths were outlawed. Monotheism had won out over polytheism in the western world. And that, some would say, was that.

But paganism lived on, sometimes in the most unexpected places. Many important intellectuals of the early Christian church, including St. Ambrose, St. Jerome, and St. Augustine, drew heavily upon pagan writers such as Plato, Homer, Cicero, and Virgil to enrich their Christian writings. Thus a form of "Christian Platonism" dominated Medieval thinking and remains an important part of Christian thinking as it exists today.

In many cases, paganism simply moved underground, especially in rural areas. The ancient pagan festivals were still celebrated as Christian holidays became attached to them. Gradually, many people forgot their polytheistic origins; but there were always some who remembered...

The Gods: Yesterday and Today

In our own time, the gods of old are enjoying a comeback. Many people in the New Age, tired of the spiritual numbness provided by several of the orthodox churches, as well as the hellfire-and-brimstone approach of various fundamentalist creeds, are turning to alternative belief systems. Some of these systems are fairly new and experimental; but others are based on the religions of the past; both eastern and western. These traditions are naturally being updated for the modern mentality, since today's neo-pagans face a far more complex world than did their ancient counterparts. These new belief systems also have a strong tendency toward religious tolerance, and many are themselves composed of an amalgamation of several diverse traditions. The deities of Egypt, Sumer, Greece, and other ancient lands have awakened from their long dormancy, aroused by a chorus of new voices who call upon their sacred names.

In previous pages we have examined how in antiquity, many ancient peoples saw no conflict in adopting deities from other lands. In Hellenistic times, just as now, there was a recognition that the diverse pantheons of peoples everywhere represented various portions of the same fundamental inner realities. In our argument for the universal truths that lie behind all spiritual faiths, we can do no better than to quote the Roman Senator/orator Quintus Aurelius Symmachus, a pagan who pleaded for religious tolerance in the early days of Christianity:

> *It is on behalf of the ancestral, the native gods that we plead for tolerance. It is all one and the same, whatever god any particular man adores. We all look up to the same stars; heaven is common to all; the same world surrounds every*

*one of us. Whatever rests above [these]—each in his own
wisdom seeks to know the truth. It is not by one single path
that we arrive at so great a mystery.*[23]

In our own time, religious freedom and tolerance have been re-established. Let's hope that we never lose it again.

This issue of *The Golden Dawn Journal* will examine several pantheons that are important to the Western Magical Tradition. Some of the articles presented here are devoted to an exploration of the Norse and Celtic pantheons. In "Ancient Ones of the Irish Faery-Faith," Kisma Stepanich examines the Celtic deities and festivals along with various practical formulae for visualization. Pat Zalewski demonstrates how to apply the Celtic and Norse pantheons to the Qabalistic Tree of Life in "The Incomplete Mythological Pantheons of the Golden Dawn." The origin and gematria of various god-names and angels of the Hebrew pantheon are explored in the chapters by Harvey Newstrom and James A. Eshelman.

In "Samothracian Fire," Steve Cranmer examines the oldest Greek mystery cult and its pantheon, which had a prominent place in the Practicus Ritual of the Golden Dawn. John Michael Greer describes the similarities between "Christ and Osiris," especially in regard to the appearance of these godforms in Golden Dawn ritual. M. Isidora Forrest compares the devotional and magical practices of pagans in ancient and modern times. And the question "Do the Gods Exist?" is the subject of an article by Donald Michael Kraig.

The magical pantheons of the world have served to enrich humanity, not only through inner communication with the greater divine self, but also through the heroic, graceful tales of the gods and goddesses revealed through their mythos. They have inspired us through literature, prayer, poetry, music, and dance. The gods reveal themselves to the human soul in the idealized concepts of Venusian love, Martial strength, Jovian laughter, Osirian rebirth, Maatian justice, Athenian wisdom, and more. And they continue to teach us about our ever-unfolding spiritual selves. These deities show us the many faces of the eternal source of the universe, as well as the multifaceted splendor of our own inner souls. The gods help us to see and understand our potential, our strength, our magic, and our inherent spiritual beauty.

What would be a world without the magic power of love of beauty and harmony? How would a world look if made after a pattern furnished by modern science? A world in which the universal power of truth were not recognized could be nothing else but a world of maniacs and filled with hallucinations.[24]

Endnotes

1. From the *Divine Pymander*.
2. William Gray, *The Ladder of Lights*, 83.
3. Ibid., 82.
4. Ibid., 84.
5. Jung, *Man and His Symbols*, 89.
6. Farr, *Egyptian Magic*, 12.
7. Still later in Babylonian cosmology, the god Marduk was revered as the primary creator and storm god, usurping all the powers of An and Enlil.
8. In the Biblical version, god preferred Abel over Cain because Abel could offer animal sacrifices.
9. See pages 476 through 478 in our book *Self-Initiation into the Golden Dawn Tradition* for more information on this.
10. The fall of the prince refers to the star of Venus.
11. Herodotus, *Histories*, 132.
12. The ancient name for the land of Egypt.
13. Heka was also the name of the god who personified magical power. A goddess known as Weret Hekau ("great of magic") was represented by a cobra. Wands in the shape of a cobra were often used by magicians. (As a note of interest, in the *Book of Exodus*, Moses and Aaron have a magical dual with the priests of the Pharaoh. Aaron's rod and the wands of the Egyptians are transformed into snakes. According to the Old Testament, Moses was "learned in all the wisdom of the Egyptians and mighty in words and deeds." To his Egyptian teachers, this would have indicated that he was "great of magic.")
14. Perhaps it was through fear of such practices that the ancient Hebrews insisted their tribal god's true name was unknown and unpronounceable.
15. Adolf Erman, *Ancient Egyptian Poetry and Prose*, 285.
16. Hellenic ("pure Greek") refers to that which belongs to the Classical Greek Age. Hellenistic ("Greek-like") refers to that which belongs to the age that commenced after the conquests of Alexander the Great.
17. The alphabets of Crete and Mycenaea were forgotten. Later, when the Greeks took up writing again, they used an alphabet adapted from the Phoenicians.
18. The plural form is *poleis*.
19. The modern cities of Naples and Marseilles.
20. Constantinople or the modern-day Istanbul.

21.   Some groups, however, such as the ultra-skeptical Sophists, continued to push Greek religious tolerance too far and were seen as detrimental to the social fabric and traditions of the poleis. At times they attracted the anger of traditionalists. The philosopher Socrates was condemned for his "subversive" ideas.

22.   Note the similarity to the Hebrew word *Sabaoth* or *Tzabaoth*.

23.   Frederick Grant, *Ancient Roman Religion*, 249.

24.   Franz Hartmann, *Magic White and Black*, 27.

Bibliography

Black, Jeremy and Anthony Green. *Gods, Demons and Symbols of Ancient Mesopotamia*. Austin: University of Texas Press, 1992.

Budge, E. A. Wallis. *Egyptian Magic*. New York: Dover Publications, Inc., 1971.

———. *Egyptian Religion*. Vols. 1 and 2. New York: Citadel Press, Carol Publishing Group, 1991, Volumes I & II.

———. *The Gods of the Egyptians*. New York: Dover Publications, 1969.

Divine Pymander, attributed to Hermes Mercurius Trismegistus. Des Plaines, Illinois: Yogi Publication Society, 1871.

Erman, Adolf. *Ancient Egyptian Poetry and Prose*. Mineola, NY: Dover Publications, Inc., 1995.

Farr, Florence. *Egyptian Magic*. Kila, MT: Kessinger Publishing Co.

Godwin, David. *Light in Extension*. St. Paul: Llewellyn Publications, Inc., 1992.

Grant, Frederick C. *Ancient Roman Religion*. Indianapolis: The Bobbs-Merrill Company, Inc., 1976.

Herodotus. *Histories*. Hertfordshire, UK: Wordsworth Classics, 1996.

Hollister, C. Warren. *Roots of the Western Tradition*, 4th ed. New York: Alfred A. Knopf, 1982.

Jung, Carl G. *Man and his Symbols*. Garden City, NY.: Doubleday & Company, 1983.

Larouse Encyclopedia of Mythology. New York: Prometheus Press, 1959.

Larouse World Mythology. New York: G.P. Putnam's Sons, 1965.

Moscati, Sabatio. *The Face of the Ancient Orient*. Garden City, NY: Anchor Books, 1962.

Perowne, Stuart. *Roman Mythology*. Middlesex: The Hamlyn Publishing Group, 1969.

Pinch, Geraldine. *Magic in Ancient Egypt*. Austin: University of Texas Press, 1994.

Scarre, Chris. *Smithsonian Timelines of the Ancient World*. New York: Smithsonian Institution, 1993.

Spence, Lewis. *Ancient Egyptian Myths and Legends*. Mineola, NY: Dover Publications, Inc., 1990.

———. *Myths of Babylonia & Assyria*. London: George G. Harrap & Company Ltd., 1928.

Thompson, C. J. S. *The Mysteries and Secret of Magic*. New York: Causeway Books, 1973.

Selene, Goddess of the Moon.

Pagans and Neo-Pagans
Five Elemental Reasons to Claim Our Pagan Polytheistic Heritage

M. Isidora Forrest

> *Hellenic spirituality differs from much Christian spirituality in that it is not based on a particular revelation and does not recognize any ex officio spiritual authority; in that it is free, unorganized, and without special spiritual institutions; and in that it retains close links with the archaic piety of the Divine in nature...it must be recognized as a real and deep spirituality which has continued to be powerful after the end of the old Mediterranean world and can still challenge many of our common assumptions about the nature of spirituality.*
>
> —A. H. Armstrong, in the introduction to *Classical Mediterranean Spirituality, Egyptian, Greek, Roman*

hile this passage was written about the Pagans of more than two thousand years ago in and around the Mediterranean basin, it could just as well have been written about today's Neo-Pagans.

For those familiar with modern Neo-Paganism, the description in this passage is striking. Many of them would readily agree that Paganism's modern expression is "not based on a particular revelation," recognizes no overall spiritual authority such as the Catholic Pope, is decidedly "free and unorganized," and honors nature as divine. There are also important additions most Neo-Pagans would make to this characterization, such as the Neo-Pagan worship or honoring of the divine feminine as Goddess(es). This was not even an issue in the polytheistic world of the ancient Pagans. The existence of the divine feminine went without saying, but this is not so in the modern, largely Protestant, United States.

Yet there are more Pagans in the United States today than there have been since before the Pilgrims landed. Aiden Kelly, in his book *Crafting the Art of Magic*, estimates that there are more Neo-Pagans and Wiccans in the United States than there are Unitarians and Buddhists.[1] A conservative 1993 estimate for the number of Wiccans *alone* is approximately 200,000 nationwide.[2] And just as there are more

Neo-Pagans in society generally, so there are more Neo-Pagans in magical orders such as the Golden Dawn and GD-derived groups operating today. While most members of the original Golden Dawn came from decidedly Christian religious backgrounds and were exposed to a kind of Neo-Paganism through the order, experience shows that most members of these magical orders in the United States today come from Neo-Paganism or Wicca rather than from Christianity. For this reason it is important for those interested in the Golden Dawn and GD-derived magical orders, such as the readers of this *Journal*, to also be familiar with the traditions of Paganism and with its new and varied expressions in Neo-Paganism.

My task in this article, however, is not to define either ancient Paganism or modern Neo-Paganism. Due to the very diverse nature of Pagan polytheism, it is probably impossible to produce a definition with which all Neo-Pagans—or all ancient Pagans, for that matter—would agree. There are, however, a number of corresponding themes that can be identified in both of these expressions of polytheism. Therefore, the task I have chosen is to identify and discuss some of these themes, which both ancient and modern Paganism share, albeit in different forms. Some of these aspects of Pagan spirituality seem to flow organically out of polytheism itself and are manifesting themselves as naturally in the new Pagan communities of today as they did in the old Pagan communities of long ago. For other themes, Neo-Pagans consciously reach back into the ancient world, finding there inspiration for, and resonance with, their religious lives today.

Yet the Pagan revival is not atavistic. It is a *new* Paganism. The new Pagans reinterpret the old myths and rituals. They update them, expand them, and make them once again relevant for women and men who are alive and conducting their spiritual lives *now*. The roots of Pagan myth and ritual are in an ancient religious tradition; the leaves unfurl in the present—and the plant needs both to flourish. In this article, I will connect some of these ancient roots with today's healthy growth of leaves by showing a few of the ways Neo-Pagan religious expressions are connected to the Pagan polytheistic traditions from which they spring. Information sources will include the writings of ancient Pagans and scholarly opinion on the subject, as well as personal interviews and written questionnaires from modern Neo-Pagans. The brevity of the article prohibits an exhaustive list of the correspondences—and the article in no way addresses the many important differences.

My hope in outlining some of the ways the ancient roots connect to today's flowering of Neo-Paganism is to help strengthen Neo-Paganism's growing acceptance as another of the many genuine paths of human religious expression, a path with a spiritually rich past and an equally spiritually rich future. I believe that what A. H. Armstrong said of Hellenic Paganism in our opening quote is also true of Neo-Paganism: "it must be recognized as a real and deep spirituality which has continued to be powerful after the end of the old Mediterranean world and can still challenge many of our common assumptions about the nature of spirituality."

Our Specific Focus

In order to be able to grasp this subject at all, we must first narrow the focus. "Ancient Paganism" and "modern Neo-Paganism" are both categories far too vast to be able to discuss without constantly having to qualify the statements. So let me make my qualifications now. The ancient Paganism we will be discussing is classical Greek, Hellenistic, and Græco-Roman Paganism, from around 500 B.C.E. to the prohibition of Pagan worship. There are two reasons I've chosen this era of about a thousand years. For one thing, there is a lot of material available. Ancient philosophers, historians, poets, and playwrights all have much to tell us about the Paganism of their time, as do scholars who have studied these periods. The second reason is more subjective. From my own reading of the material, particularly the later material, I have come to believe that modern Neo-Pagans would have quite a lot in common with their ancient sisters and brothers from this period. They would understand much of the reasoning and the feeling involved in their ancient rites and mysteries. They would be able to "talk shop" with these Pagans. And while they would not necessarily agree with everything the Pagans would have to say about their religious outlook and religious expressions, I believe today's Neo-Pagans would at least be able to understand what they meant, what they were doing, and why they were doing it. In this, their understanding exceeds that of many academic scholars of ancient Paganism who, not being practicing polytheists themselves, sometimes approach the polytheistic people of their study as if they had an underdeveloped (i.e., not monotheistic) spirituality.

The Neo-Paganism with which we will compare the ancient is self-identified Neo-Paganism as expressed in twentieth century North

America and to some extent in England. This is simply because this is the Neo-Paganism with which I am personally familiar. I have also chosen to exclude eastern traditions from the discussion, even though there are continuous "Pagan" polytheistic traditions existent in the east. Again, it is a matter of focus. This is not to say that eastern traditions did not influence western Paganism (and *vice versa*). They did and continue to do so today.

The Arms of the Pentagram

We will be concentrating, then, on Western Paganism, both ancient and modern. Further, I have organized these Pagan and Neo-Pagan themes around the ancient Greek conception of the elements—Earth, Air, Water, and Fire—which were considered to be the building blocks of natural creation.

A fifth element, added by the Pythagoreans, is called Aether. It was considered finer than the others and thought of as a kind of spiritual Fire. (Today, most magical groups consider the fifth element to be Spirit.) Aristotle further defined the four elements in terms of pairs of qualities: Fire was "hot and dry," Air was "hot and wet," Water was "cold and wet," Earth was "cold and dry." The Stoic school of philosophy simplified this idea further and defined Fire as hot, Air as cold, Water as wet, and Earth as dry. These elements and qualities also showed up in Greek medicine, and thus in medieval medicine, as the four "humours" that make up the human body and that can also be associated with the four seasons of the year and the four stages of human life: childhood, youth, maturity, and old age.[3]

These days, Neo-Pagans symbolically use these ancient building blocks to construct the very walls of their places of worship when they invoke the presence of the powers of the elements to be present around their ritual circles; a tradition that came into Neo-Paganism through Witchcraft/Wicca, which picked it up from ceremonial magic via John Dee's elemental Watchtowers. In the case of Neo-Paganism, however, the elements are usually considered to be more organic "forces of nature" than the connotations of the term "watchtower" imply. The elemental categories can also be used as a method of classification.[4]

Each of these elements is further attributed to an arm of the five-pointed star called the pentagram. Like the Christian cross, the pentagram can have many different meanings. Some Neo-Pagans wear it simply as a symbol of their religion. Others interpret it as a symbol of the Divine in nature, with the top point of the star attributed to Spirit and situated symbolically "in the midst" of the other four elements (the other four arms of the star). These five elements are considered to make up the body of nature, including humanity. The Greeks, too, may have seen this relationship between the natural human being and the divine in the pentagram. The basic proportions of Greek temples and statues from the sixth century B.C.E. onward are the same as those of the human being—and these were abstracted into the pentagram.[5]

This conception of the elements and the elemental pentagram, kept alive in medical history, astrology, philosophy, the esoteric tradition, art, and architecture is all part of our Pagan heritage—as much a part as federal buildings constructed to look like Roman temples or as Easter egg hunts and Christmas trees. It is significant, and precisely to the point, that Neo-Pagans (and other western esotericists—whether or not they consider themselves Neo-Pagans) have found this ancient Pagan conception to be valuable. For this reason, I have chosen to use each of "the arms of the pentagram" to bring some order to my observations about the correspondences between ancient Hellenic Paganism and modern United States Neo-Paganism.

Earth: This Sacred Ground We Walk Upon

> *All this place is holy, and there is nothing which is without a share of soul.*[6]

Thus commented the Neoplatonist Plotinus on the essential sacredness of the entire material universe. This has always been the Pagan view of the world, from prehistoric times to the present. In the Hellenic and Hellenistic world we're discussing, it is the world view of a largely agricultural society, dependent on the land—a connection the people never lost, even when worshipping at the magnificent temples in their cities.

It was a world view that understood that the divine could be manifested in all the natural world, in all of human experience, in the savage forests, in the tamed fields, in the sane and ordered rationality of the human mind, and in its disordered madness. Deities permeated everything in this often animistic world in which the divine was deeply immanent. And while it is true that late Hellenism produced a number of body and matter devaluing sects, certainly most Hellenes retained their ancient connection to the Earth and the chthonic deities. Iamblichus, another Neoplatonist, refuted the split between the deities and the world:

> As to the first principle, that the gods dwell only in heaven, it is not true. Everything is full of them.[7]

Many natural things were said to be sacred, *hieros*: mountains, rivers, the day, corn. "Hieros is as it were the shadow cast by divinity."[8] While the Olympians were not specifically nature gods in that their personalities are not thought to have developed from the worship of particular natural phenomena, there were natural phenomena that were worshipped as deities. Crucially important among these is Gaia or Ge, the Earth herself. The worship of the Earth as Great Earth Mother is often thought to be the prototype of all worship. This is not only the current opinion of many scholars, but it was the opinion of the Greeks themselves, who, from the time of Solon, acknowledged the worship of Gaia to have been the first worship. In addition, they believed that Gaia not only provided sustenance for her children, but placed obligations on them in turn.[9]

The sacredness of the Earth has often been discussed in relation to Pagan "fertility cults." Fertility of field, flock, and family were, of course, vital concerns; life itself, as well as material prosperity, depended upon it. Pagan or not, fertility has always been an abiding human concern. As urban as many of our lives may be now, as a society, we must still rely upon our fields and flocks in order to feed ourselves. In Greek piety, a single example will serve to illustrate this continuing concern—the rites at Eleusis. During the thousands of years that seekers continually came to Eleusis, part of the ceremonies was the ritual cry to the Sky God Zeus to "Rain!" while Gaia, the Earth, was called upon to "Conceive!" From this alone it is clear that the Eleusinian rites retained their potent agricultural flavor—even when the main concern of the *mystai* was no longer fertility *per se*, but with their initiation into the deep mysteries of the afterlife.

As the life-sustaining Earth was sacred, so were the waters that fed it. Every city worshipped its river or spring, sometimes even constructing a temple for the God of the river or the Nymph of the spring. The winds, too, were worshipped, bringing as they did the important weather changes that affected the harvests. The sun and the moon, Helios and Selene, were prominent deities. The moon particularly seems to have been consistently referred to as "the Goddess." Even as late as 430 C.E., after Christian control of the Empire had been established and Pagan worship became a clandestine affair, people still honored the Goddess in the moon. An incident from the life of the Neoplatonist Proclus illustrates this:

> It was the twilight hour. They [the philosophers of the Athenian Neoplatonic school] were still engaged in conversation when the sun set and the moon made its first appearance after its conjunction with the sun. They were trying to dismiss the young man [Proclus], after having greeted him, inasmuch as he was a stranger, so that, once alone, they would be free to worship the goddess. But when Proclus started to move away from them, he took off his shoes, and before their very eyes, he began greeting the goddess.[10]

This daring earned Proclus the admiration of the philosophers as well as entry into their school.

Particularly beautiful natural places were also known to be sacred. In Sophocles' play *Oedipus at Colonus*, Antigone leads her father, Oedipus, to a shrine explaining that:

> This place is clearly holy, with its strong growth of laurel, olive, and vine, and a crowd of nightingales fly and sing beautifully within it.[11]

A. H. Armstrong comments that the outdoor character of most Hellenic worship, with the exception of the mysteries, had a particular (and to my mind, beneficial) effect upon the worshippers. Because their worship was outdoors where participants could see the whole city or the whole countryside—indeed, their whole environment—it was impossible for people to conceive of themselves as a "special people," set apart from nature, from other people, or from anything else.[12] The later Stoic school of philosophy, too, admitted no differentiation between matter and spirit. This acceptance of all things as divine may have contributed to the underlying and healthy Greek conviction that somehow the world was good and beautiful—no matter how harsh it may also be.[13]

This connection to the Earth, the Heavens, their cycles, and the immanent divinity in all these things is a truth of Pagan existence. While most Neo-Pagans do not directly "worship" the river or the winds, they do honor the divinity that is immanent in these things of the manifested world. Who is to say that these attitudes are not in ultimate harmony? In the early 1970s, during a period in which Neo-Paganism began growing rapidly, Theodore Roszak, then a history professor at California State University, wrote in support of this kind of magical world view, which saw deities and holy places everywhere:

> Why, one wonders, should it be thought crude or rudimentary to find divinity brightly present in the world where others find only dead matter or an inferior order of being? And with what justification do we conclude that this thing we call animism is a false experience of the world?[14]

Roszak speaks for many Neo-Pagans when he connects the old Pagan ways, which he calls the Old Gnosis, with the modern re-establishment of this ancient consciousness, which is, for him, "an urgent project of the times."

> From that rich source [the old ways] there flow countless religious and philosophical traditions. The differences between these traditions—between Eskimo shamanism and medieval alchemy; between Celtic druidism and Buddhist Tantra—are many; but an essentially magical world view is common to all of them. I will from time to time be referring to this diverse family of religions and philosophies as the Old Gnosis—the old way of knowing, which delighted in finding the sacred in the profane—and I will be treating it with no little respect, since I regard it as the essential and supreme impulse of the religious life. This is not, of course, religion as most people in our society know it. It is a visionary style of knowledge, not a theological one; its proper language is myth and ritual; its foundation is rapture, not faith and doctrine; and its experience of nature is one of living communion.[15]

The experience of living communion with nature, which Neo-Pagans seek, points out one of the arguments that some have with Christianity; they perceive that one of its legacies is a harmful indifference toward nature. This is aptly expressed by writer Lynn White's observation that, in its relation to nature, "Christianity is the most anthropocentric religion the world has ever seen. ...(B)y destroying pagan animism, Christianity made it possible to exploit nature in a mood of indifference to the feelings of natural objects."[16]

A Neo-Pagan in West Virginia connects this indifference with current societal ills, writing that "Unfortunately, we have been cut off from our source, which explains the sickness at the core of our society." Another Neo-Pagan in Arizona directly relates the solution for that problem to Neo-Pagan ideas and writes that "Humans are a part of nature, but culture has obscured the essence of that relationship, which can be renewed and restored through acting on the ideas inherent in Neo-Paganism."

A "guiding concern for the Earth and our place among her creatures," as another Neo-Pagan puts it, has led many Neo-Pagans to be involved with the environmental movement. This was expressed by the Council of American Witches in their 1974 statement of principles, among which is this clause:

> We recognize that our intelligence gives us a unique responsibility toward our environment. We seek to live in harmony with Nature, in ecological balance offering fulfillment to life and consciousness within an evolutionary concept.

An insistence on living and behaving in ways that are in balance with nature leads Neo-Pagans to accept their own human nature, and the products of that nature, including technology, as natural as well—although most advise a conscious balance between these elements and products of our natures with the needs of the natural world. Many Neo-Pagans also connect to nature through alternative medicines and healing therapies, many of which have ancient antecedents and are designed to work with the healing powers of the body. Neo-Pagans are also frequently involved with human potential growth groups, which acknowledge the essential rightness of all psychological process while attempting to release the natural healing powers of the mind. "Such skillful trust in nature is the essence of the Pagan outlook."[17]

In Neo-Pagan ceremonies, the divine is seen by worshippers in nature. Ceremonies regularly take place outdoors, offering Neo-Pagans the same sense of connectedness the ancient Pagans enjoyed. Nature metaphor is frequently the basis of ritual celebration; worship often taking place according to the cycles of the moon and sun. By tuning in to these eternal cycles, Neo-Pagans seek to live in connection with nature and in communication with the divine. An Oregon Neo-Pagan comments that "just transcendence makes it all 'way out there' and 'beyond' and denies the direct experience of the divine." It is this direct experience of the divine which so many Neo-Pagans seek and ultimately find as they commune with the divine through nature—in a "brightly present" divine world such as the one experienced of old.

Air: Unity in Ritual, Not Belief

Paganism did not have its basis in a specific revealed truth. It had no scripture. It had no creed. And although Homer's poetry has been called "the Bible of the Greeks," this is untrue. Not only did the poets disagree with each other, but anyone was free to disagree with them. The work of the poets and the philosophers was always open to interpretation and criticism.[18] Further, there was no Pagan concept of heresy. The word *hairesis* to Pagans meant a school of thought—not a false doctrine.[19] A proliferation of cultic devotions to a variety of deities promoted a tolerance of other people's religions, which allowed Paganism to flourish for uncounted thousands of years.

An example of Pagan tolerance comes to us from the last days of Paganism during the destruction of one of the most famous and awesome Pagan temples, the Sarapeum in Alexandria. The historian Socrates (not the much earlier philosopher) gives this account:

> When the temple of Sarapis was torn down and laid bare, there were found in it, graven on stones, certain characters which they call hieroglyphs, having the form of crosses [the ankh, the Egyptian sign for "life"]. Both the Christians and Pagans, on seeing them, appropriated and applied them to their respective religions: for the Christians, who affirm that the cross is the sign of Christ's saving passion, claimed this character as peculiarly theirs; but the Pagans alleged that it might appertain to Christ and Sarapis in common; "for," said they, "it symbolizes one thing to Christians and another to Pagans."[20]

Paganism was finally overcome not by its own polytheistic tolerance of diversity, but by the intolerance of radical monotheism.

What Paganism insisted on was not that a person believe a certain way, but that she or he participate in the community acts of piety that were thought to be essential for the proper honoring of the deities and the perpetuation of divine favor. The tradition lay in the performance of the ritual, not in the belief about the meaning of the ritual. In fact, the meaning of the rites changed with the spirit of the times. Yet attempts at reinterpretation never tried to destroy the old ways, but to make them comprehensible to the sensibilities of a later time. While the philosophers eventually came to criticize the foibles of the deities as portrayed in the ancient myths, they always understood that the old ways were needed in order to provide connection to the divine for the greatest mass of the people.[21]

A kind of faith, unformulated by scripture or creed, and implicit in the ways of tradition, permeated Pagan society. It was simply accepted by all, and in this way it united them—perhaps like the choruses of ecstatic maidens on Delos who were said to know how:

> *...to imitate the dialects and chatterings of all men; each would say that she were speaking herself: in such a way is the beautiful song joined together for them.*[22]

The importance of experience rather than belief about the experience is emphasized in Aristotle's comment concerning the mysteries. He noted that those who undergo the mysteries do not have to learn, "but to experience and be changed by the experience."[23]

This does not mean there were no beliefs—merely that they were unlikely to be uniform. The diversity of philosophical schools is just one example which attests to strong differences in belief. Private families, individuals, and small communities throughout the Mediterranean world also developed their own ways of worship as well as their own unique beliefs about that worship and the deities involved.

This same variety of belief exists in Neo-Pagan communities today. This is true not only in the opinions of the various "philosophical schools," or "traditions," but among the various individuals within those traditions. Yet all can come together in the larger festival gatherings to participate in ritual together, to play and talk together, and to be a community together—regardless of their individual beliefs. A leader in an Oregon Neo-Pagan community expresses it as "a lack of emphasis on 'correct belief.' ...(W)hat matters is what we do, how we live...the rituals we do, and not whether we think the right thing about them. Our differences in belief are not something that we think should 'split the church' as it has in some Christian experience." Another young Neo-Pagan states explicitly: "what you have to understand is that for me belief is secondary. It is important, but secondary, to religion."

The ability to come together for a common purpose while toler-
ating a wide variety of beliefs may very well be one of the natural out-
growths of polytheism; at the very least, we can say that it is a clear
correspondence between ancient and modern Paganism. Perhaps the
only difference is that Neo-Pagans are even more tolerant than their
ancient sisters and brothers—there is no insistence at modern festivals
that everyone choose to participate in the rituals.

In this same way, Neo-Pagans tend also to have a respect for the
differences in individual experiences within a particular ritual. They
would agree with Aristotle that what is important is "to experience
and to be changed by the experience." Further, they would understand
that any ritual experience is a very personal one. An anthropologist
who has studied Neo-Pagans, Wiccans, and magicians concludes, in
regard to this particular aspect of ritual, that

> *Magicians accept the variation in ritual response as an
> inevitable feature of training, experience, and idiosyn-
> crasy.... Everyone has their own internal magical land-
> scape, everyone responds in different ways.... In using
> immediate experience to judge the rite at the time, the
> variety and fallibility of human experience is consciously
> recognized. So in rituals magicians are not themselves;
> they get sick or weepy or want to fly; they can feel a hal-
> cyon oneness with Isis and with their neighbor an unut-
> terable sadness. Yet all states are said to testify to the
> power of the rite.*[24]

Water: Free-Flowing and Unorganized

Since, in ancient Greek society, religion permeated the culture and
there was no separation of church and state, there were indeed highly
organized forms of Pagan worship and other religious experience.
Festivals were celebrated city-wide or community-wide and supported by the political "machine." The organization that would allow
for the initiation of the yearly multitudes of *mystai* into the mysteries
at Eleusis would have been vast and efficient.

What then can the author of our opening quotation mean when
he says that Hellenic spirituality "is free, unorganized, and without
special spiritual institutions?" I believe he means this: that there was
no overarching Panhellenic spiritual authority that dictated how
worship should be. There was nothing analogous to a Pope or the

hierarchical structure of most Christian churches. No city was required to send a delegation to, for example, Eleusis (although peer pressure encouraged it). It did not matter that the worship of Artemis at Ortheia was quite unlike the worship of Artemis at Ephesus. No Ortheian priests accused the Ephesians of heresy. Each city or community organized its own worship as it saw fit.

Furthermore, not all Pagan mysteries—and certainly not all worship—required a temple complex or an organization such as that at Eleusis. The influential Orphic mysteries, for example, were enacted in private dwellings. This is one thing that accounted for their quick spread during the middle of the sixth century B.C.E.[25]

Since it is obvious that there is no Pagan state today, it is in these smaller Greek religious structures that we find striking similarities to modern Neo-Pagan groups. In his excellent study of the Greek mystery cults, Walter Burkert describes the groups of private worshippers that were called in Greek *thiasos* or *koinon*, and in Latin *collegia* or *sodalitates*. These were essentially religious clubs or associations that provide us with an ancient forerunner of many Neo-Pagan circles or Wiccan covens—as well as the temples and lodges of other magical groups—operating today. The Golden Dawn's Second Order still refers to its assemblies as *collegia*, for example.

A thiasos provided for "the coming together of equals in a common interest."[26] It provided a private setting for religious activities as well as a body of comrades with which to attend larger city or community religious rites. Members remained independent in that they did not form a community separate from their own family and city. They contributed their time, interest, influence, and private resources to the thiasos. Sometimes the groups owned property in common, helped each other in lawsuits, and attended each others' funerals. The groups did have a legal status. While members held office in the group, there was no stable hierarchy and usually no charismatic leadership.[27] There was also a great deal of fluidity in these groups. They formed as they wished, dissolved as they wished, and allowed individuals to go their own way as they wished without sanction.

This is directly analogous to the loose organization of most Neo-Pagan groups in which members are free to stay or go as they please, yet which provide a warm fraternal camaraderie. According to Margot Adler's comprehensive study of Neo-Paganism in the United States:

> *Individuals may move freely between groups and form their own groups according to their needs, but all the*

*while they remain within a community that defines itself
as Pagan.*[28]

The Mithraic mysteries provide a model for the Wiccan practice of "hiving," that is, starting new covens from a central coven
that has grown too large. New Mithraic "caves" (so called since
meetings were usually held in an underground cave-like chamber)
would be established when the original cave grew to more than
twenty or so men.[29]

Even Greece's famous philosophical schools were actually just
small informal groups of friends meeting in private homes to discuss theological and philosophical issues. The school of Plotinus in
Rome met quietly in a private home. The Neoplatonists in Athens
were a small group in a university town and, because of their opposition to Christianity, were forced to keep a very low profile.[30] I am
personally acquainted with a Hermetic and Neo-Pagan discussion
group that has been meeting quietly in a private home like this for
over eight years.

Small groups such as these provided opportunity for religious
freedom for ancient Pagans and often allowed personal inspirations
to guide the development of cultic practice. Dionysos seems to have
been a God who particularly inspired his priestesses and priests to
innovation in his worship. For example, a priestess from Campania,
Italy was guided by Bacchus to alter his rites and succeeded in making significant reforms based on her personal inspiration from the
God.[31] In the play, *The Bacchae,* Dionysos impersonates his own
priest—a charismatic traveling throughout the countryside to insti-
tute the rites of Dionysos—and confirms to Pentheus that the God
inspired him with the knowledge of his rites. "Yes, face-to-face, he
gave these mysteries to me."[32]

Inspiration plays a significant role in Neo-Pagan rites as well.
While there are many, particularly Wiccan, groups with specific traditional rites and ways of worship, there are also many Neo-Pagans
who proudly identify themselves as eclectic and draw bits and
pieces from many traditions as well as their own inspirations. And
yes, the deities still reveal mysteries "face-to-face"; many are the
Neo-Pagan worshippers who receive ritual formulæ and other
direct information from the visions and the voices of their Goddesses
and Gods. "The same Gods who spoke to the ancient Egyptians or
Celts or to Native American Shamans still speak today," comments
one Wiccan.

The organizational freedom Neo-Pagans create in their groups and communities is a reflection of the freedom they seek in their religious expression and experience. Smaller, free-flowing groups provide the ideal environment for the experiential, experimental, and visionary style of religious communion Neo-Pagans seek. And while we cannot be sure to what extent ancient Pagans conceived of themselves as seeking free religious expression, we can be certain that many among them—for example, the initiates of the mystery religions—sought the same kind of deepening of their own religious feeling through the experience of deity (or deities) in new and more intensely personal ways. In this, they are true sisters and brothers to today's Neo-Pagans. We may agree with Walter Burkert in finding a great deal of value in these free and unorganized religious groups, both past and present:

> The general lack of organization, solidarity, and coherence in ancient mysteries, which may appear as a deficiency from a Jewish or Christian point of view, is outweighed by some positive aspects with which we may easily sympathize. The absence of religious demarcation and conscious group identity means the absence of any rigid frontiers against competing cults as well as the absence of any concept of heresy, not to mention excommunication. The pagan gods, even the gods of mysteries, are not jealous of one another; they form, as it were, an open society.[33]

Fire: Making Magic

If we wish to approach the world view of Pagans and Neo-Pagans, we must now address what Tom Driver, a student and advocate of ritual, jokingly refers to as "the M-word,"[34] magic—a reality that Pagans clearly accepted and that the vast majority of Neo-Pagans currently accept as an integral part of their religion. For many years, scholars have been trying to discover where to draw the line between religion and magic, between the so-called purity of the human religious impulse and the perceived contamination of magic. At what point does religion become magic? And conversely, at what point does magic become religion?

These were not questions that concerned the ancient Pagans. Nor do they particularly concern Neo-Pagans. The line between religion and magic for them is not only quite permeable, but for many, non-existent; one is a part of the other. Magic *"just is"* as one Neo-Pagan puts it. It is the way religion is done. It is a way of communication and communion with the divine. Magic may also be said to be:

> ...*the ceremonies, rites, and services that are the principal techniques of transformation employed by religion.*[35]

The roots of magic are prehistoric. Scholars of the subject find sufficient reason to believe that some fundamental magical beliefs and rituals go back to the religion of the Great Earth Goddess.[36] E. R. Dodds has used the term *shamanism* to apply to certain workings of Hellenic magicians and priests.[37] He notes that their magic was often for a religious purpose and frequently dealt with revelations of a religious character. The Egyptians, a people with a highly magical religion, named magic a God and considered him to be one of the primordial forces of the universe. It has been so often stated as to have become cliched that magician priests and priestesses were actually humankind's first scientists and psychologists in that they explored the natural world and the ways of the human soul.[38] Even Isaac Newton, the "father of modern science" and Carl Jung, one of this century's leading psychologists, both had strong interests in alchemy.

For Pagans and Neo-Pagans, magic is definitely not, as the Christian Augustine called it, "a criminal tampering with the unseen world." Rather for them, following Roszak, "magic, in its pristine form, is sacramental perception."[39] To understand more about magic, we turn to some of the ways magic has been defined; first, by Hellenic and Hellenistic magicians.

In the Greek magical texts, notably the magical papyri, a collection of texts written on papyrus rolls in Greek and Demotic that date from the second to the fifth centuries C.E., magic is called *magika heira,* or "holy magic," and the magician who is initiated into this art of holy magic is called "blessed initiate."[40] What is today called "high magic" or "ritual magic" was known as *theurgy,* literally, God-working or divine-working; and on the subject of theurgy, our Neoplatonists had much to say. Proclus defined it as:

> ...*a power higher than all human wisdom, embracing the blessings of divination, the purifying powers of initiation, and in a word all the operations of divine possession.*[41]

Iamblichus wrote that the theurgic union between the human magician and the deities, which activates the power of magic, is not a union caused by thought alone, but involves the soul, purification, and "the divine signs," the magical symbols that focus the attention of the magician and, by their affinity with the deities, call them to the theurgic union.

> ...(T)he divine causes are not primarily called into action by our thoughts, but they [our thoughts], along with all the best dispositions of our soul and our purity, must be there first, as auxiliary causes of a sort. What properly awakens the divine will are the divine signs themselves. Thus the actions of the gods are stirred up by themselves and do not receive from any of the subordinate beings any kind of initiative for their proper energy. I have discussed these things at length to make sure that you do not believe that the whole power of theurgic action comes from us....[42]

In the second century C.E., Apuleius of Madaura, the author of *Metamorphoses*, or *The Golden Ass*, in which his famous tale of initiation into the religion of Isis appears, found himself charged as a sorcerer. It seems he had married a woman much older and wealthier than himself and sorcery could be the only explanation for this unusual state of affairs. In his self-defense before the court, he gave this definition of magic:

> Aemilianus' [his accuser's] slander was focused on one point: that I am a sorcerer. So let me ask his most learned advocates: What is a sorcerer? I have read in many books that magus is the same thing in Persian as priest in our language. What crime is there in being a priest and in having accurate knowledge, a science, a technique of traditional ritual, sacred rites, and traditional law, if magic consists of what Plato interprets as the "cult of the gods" when he talks of the disciplines taught to the crown prince in Persia.... Listen to this, you who rashly slander magic! It is an art acceptable to the immortal gods, an art which includes the knowledge of how to worship them and pay them homage. It is a religious tradition dealing with things divine.[43]

Apuleius won his case.

The magician or theurgist, then, seeks "accurate knowledge, a science, a technique of traditional ritual, sacred rites, and traditional law." Through these things, the blessed initiate seeks to align her- or himself with the divine order so that "that which is below is as that which is above," according to the famous Hermetic axiom. The theory of correspondences or sympathies implied by this axiom says that there are deep affinities between the many things in the physical world as well as in the non-physical world—and that by these affinities, things *correspond* to one another. An overly-simplified example would be that a hot pepper corresponds to the hot-tempered War God Ares by virtue of its fieriness. By correspondences, one may choose appropriate offerings for specific deities or appropriate tools for a magical working. The doctrine of correspondences was held by many of the major Greek philosophical schools including the Pythagoreans, Platonists, Stoicists, and Neoplatonists.[44] In a talk before his students, Plotinus described how these sympathies worked.

> The effects of a prayer are real because one part of the uni-
> verse is in sympathy with another part, as one may observe
> in a properly tuned string on a lyre. When it has been
> struck in its lower part, the upper part vibrates as well.
> And it often happens that when one string has been struck,
> another one, if I may say so, feels this, because they are in
> unison and have been tuned to one another—one can see
> how far the sympathetic element extends. In the universe
> too, there is one universal harmony, even though it is made
> up of discordant notes. It is also made up of similar notes,
> and all are related, even discordant ones.[45]

Magic was a way of harmony. It could be used for deeply reli-gious purposes, such as communion with deities, and it could be used for practical purposes, such as success in business or healing. The surviving magical texts clearly attest to magic's use for all these laudable purposes, as well as for more coercive applications, includ-ing curses. Still, the ideas behind magic are noble. They express the essential affinities between the deities, human beings, and the nat-ural world—themes we have encountered before in Pagan and Neo-Pagan thought.

It is not surprising, then, to see these ancient magical themes echoed in Neo-Pagan considerations of magic. Many Neo-Pagans view magic as the method for practicing religion. "Magic is the prac-tical aspect of religion. It is what keeps it moving. It is the ability to see through a myth, dwell within it, and from that place work to transform it," comments a young Neo-Pagan. "Magic is one of the ways I express my beliefs," according to a Neo-Pagan in Mississippi. "Magic is the technology of religion. In Christianity they call it prayer," writes another in Minnesota. "Making magic is my way of worshipping the Goddess," a Wiccan in Indiana says. "I try to aid her, acting as a daughter trying to help her mother. ... I am trying to bring her presence closer to me and to make it more evident in the world."

To some, magic is both the technology and "what happens" when true connection with the divine is made. "I don't think you can define magic," says a Neo-Pagan in Oregon. "I feel you can be connected with it and participate in it—and recognize it. When you invoke magic, it is being in touch with the divine, a mystery. Perhaps another way I can put it is to be able to go into an open and childlike place and to see and experience the wonder." "Trying to define magic is like trying to define beauty," comments another Oregon Neo-Pagan. "You know it when you see it." Adds another, "Psychological, emotional, physical—it's everything—and when magic *really* works, all of those things are in sync and working together."

An obvious difference between Pagan and Neo-Pagan opinions about magic reflects modern access to and increased understanding of human psychology. For example, Neo-Pagans frequently mention the Jungian archetypes when discussing the nature of the Goddesses and Gods; and many Neo-Pagan definitions of magic focus on magic's effects on the *magician's* consciousness—even to the exclusion of any exterior effects it may have. Psychological effects on oneself, which in turn affect the world around one, is how many Neo-Pagans explain the working of magic. "Magic is the art of causing changes in the self at will," says a Neo-Pagan physician, while a Neo-Pagan psychologist comments, "One of the things I like about magic and acknowledge about magic is that while it is a *spiritual* technology, much of it is easily understood in psychological terms, sometimes biological terms. As a psychologist, I am well aware that many of the techniques we practice as magic have other names in psychological practice."

The ability to "make magic" for both Pagans and Neo-Pagans revolves around connection and harmony with the deities and the divine order and with the conjunction of human and natural-divine forces. For both, magic can be used for practical ends as well as for religious ones. The sympathies that the ancients believed existed between the human being, the things of the world, and the deities is expressed by modern Neo-Pagans as an understanding of a shared divine nature. As a part of the divine, we are naturally in sympathy and connection with the divine. And once this connection is deepened through the *technology* of magic, the greater magic of participation in the flow of nature, of communion with the divine, and of spiritual growth can occur.

Spirit: Diverse and Personal

Imagine yourself in ancient Athens, in the marketplace. The Athenians, who are known among the Greeks for their devotion to religion, have erected an altar to Mercy there, as well as one to Rumor and Effort. Near the marketplace is the gymnasium where there stands a series of stone herms, the sacred pillars of Hermes, and near the gymnasium is a sanctuary of Theseus. Close by is a temple of the Dioscuri, which is said to be quite ancient. As you descend past the town hall, (which houses statues of Peace and Hestia), you come to a sanctuary of the Græco-Egyptian Sarapis, which no one, not even the priests, may enter until they bury the sacred Apis bull. Near to here is a temple of Eileithyia, the Goddess of Childbirth. As you continue on, you come to the sanctuary of Olympian Zeus with its colossal statue of ivory and gold. Within the sanctuary are famous antiquities: a Zeus in bronze and an enclosure of Gaia. All this, and your tour of the religious places in Athens has just begun. You have not yet seen the temple of Pythian Apollo. Nor the temple of Aphrodite in the district called The Gardens, which is considered one of the most noteworthy sites in the city—nor, of course, the famous Parthenon itself.

   This short tour of one small part of ancient Athens was recorded in the second century C.E. by Pausanias, a Greek born in Lydia, in his *Description of Greece*. It illustrates the degree to which religion permeated the lives of the Athenians and shows the great variety of divine powers and beings who were honored—from marketplace Rumor (which, one suspects, was meant to be averting) to the primordial Goddess of Love. The diversity inherent in polytheism is one reason "ancient spirituality is bewilderingly free and various."[46] The deities were everywhere, always. They were honored and worshipped in public rites, in mysteries, and in personal acts of piety such as garlanding a stone herm or offering one's birthing garment to one of the Goddesses after the birth of a child.

   For the ancient Greeks, of course, the diversity of polytheism was the norm. Their worship was of "many divine powers in one divine universe."[47] The divine was clearly understood to have many names and personalities, and there were many different ways to interact with it. This meant, in effect, that there was a variety of different traditions under the greater umbrella of Paganism.

Something that marked all of them, however, was the very personal aspect of human relationships with the "many divine powers." There were numerous ways that people could relate to the deities, and the deities to them. One of these ways was the trading of favors, the exchange of offerings for divine aid. We find evidence of this amiable relationship in the votive offerings people made throughout their lives. A. J. Festugiere, a scholar who cataloged many of them, concludes:

> *A whole network of friendly relationships between the human being and his god embraced the Greek from his birth to extreme old age. This is clear from the gifts which the Greek offered to his gods. And evidence for such gifts is provided by the epigrams.*[48]

Not only did the deities do favors for their votaries, they often speak to them personally and individually as well. They might speak through priestesses or priests at one of the magnificent oracular shrines such as Delphi. They might also speak through other forms of divination or through meaningful coincidence. But the most personal communication of all was dreaming. People could seek divine dreams by sleeping in one of the temples where "incubation" was practiced, but unplanned dreams were also significant. Pausanias told a story about a dream of the playwright Aeschylus.

> *Aeschylus himself said that when a youth he slept while watching grapes in a field, and that Dionysos appeared and bade him write tragedy. When day came, in obedience to the vision, he made an attempt and hereafter found composing quite easy. Such were his words.*[49]

When the Christians finally converted the Parthenon to a church of the Mother of God, Proclus, who was particularly devoted to his city Goddess, dreamed that Athena came to him and said,

> *They have turned me out of my house, so I am coming to live in yours.*[50]

This personal aspect of religion was particularly evident among those who sought relationship with the deities through the mysteries. Initiates often expressed their devotion to the deities in terms of love.[51] Lucius, the hero of Apuleius' story of an initiate of the mysteries of Isis, expressed his love for the Goddess like this:

> *Thou in truth art the holy and eternal savior of the human race, ever beneficent in helping mortal men, and thou bringest the sweet love of a mother to the trials of the unfortunate.*[52]

These few examples give us some idea of just how personal Pagan relationship with the divine could be. We have also seen how the Hellenes found Goddesses and Gods immanently alive in the natural world. In the philosophical schools, Pagans thought in transcendent terms as well. Plato spoke of a transcendent "Form of the Good (*Agathon*)," which was "the ultimate object of learning" and "more excellent than being in its worshipfulness and power." In some of Plato's works, the Form of the Good seems not to respond to human contemplation of it, like Aristotle's unmoved mover; in others it has a more caring attitude, mostly leaving humans to their own activities until their folly threatens to destroy the world, in which case, the Form of the Good intervenes, heals, and takes control until the world is once more in order.[53]

The Hermetica, a collection of religious and philosophical, sometimes magical, treatises in Latin and Greek, probably written in the second and third centuries C.E. and ascribed to Hermes Trismegistos, also contain the idea of transcendent deity.

> *"In your mind* [in vision] *you have seen the archetypal form—the pre-principle that exists before a beginning without end." This is what Poimandres said to me.*[54]

In another of the treatises, Trismegistos explains "the incorporeal" as:

> *Mind as a whole wholly enclosing itself, free of all body, unerring, unaffected, untouched, at rest in itself, capable of containing all things and preserving all that exists, and its rays (as it were) are the good, the truth, the archetype of spirit, the archetype of soul.*[55]

Yet the incorporeal is distinguished from God, which, as in Plato, is the Good.

> *For the magnitude of the Good is as great as the substance of*
> *all beings, corporeal and incorporeal, sensible and insensible.*
> *This is the Good; this is God.*[56]

This theme of transcendent deity was simply another of the diverse strands of religious thought in Pagan minds and hearts during the Hellenistic period. Certainly it was more prevalent among the well-educated and well-born. Probably it was irrelevant to the Pagans in the countryside, to whom the destruction by monks of their temples was like:

> *...ruining the countryside itself at one and the same time.*
> *For to snatch from a region the temple which protects it is*
> *like tearing out its eye, killing it, annihilating it.*[57]

The diversity of polytheism and the search for a personal, experiential relationship with the divine are two more of the characteristics that unite Pagans with Neo-Pagans. The polytheism that allowed many deities to be worshipped at the same time, in the same place, and by the same person among the Greeks is still present today among Neo-Pagans. It is a polytheism that provides the opportunity for many realities. According to David Miller, author of *The New Polytheism*:

> *Polytheism is the name given to a specific religious situation*
> *...characterized by plurality.... Socially understood, poly-*
> *theism is eternally in unresolvable conflict with social*
> *monotheism, which in its worst form is fascism and in its*
> *less destructive forms is imperialism, capitalism, feudalism*
> *and monarchy.... Polytheism is not only a social reality; it*
> *is also a philosophical condition. It is that reality experi-*
> *enced by men and women when Truth with a capital T can-*
> *not be articulated reflectively according to a single*
> *grammar, a single logic, or a single symbol system.*[58]

Miller goes on to say that there is a difference between ancient and modern Pagans:

Yet, unlike their Pagan forerunners, for Neo-Pagans in the United States polytheism is a radical choice, not the socially-accepted one. Choosing polytheism emphatically states a belief that there is no one reality, no one truth, no one path. Instead, there are many, and as they lead to the divine Center, all have something in them that is valid and valuable. Polytheism allows that many points of view are not only possible, but reasonable—a view which promotes understanding. "Win-win scenarios are often made possible by polytheistic thinking."[59]

Within the polytheism of Neo-Paganism, one may also find duotheism and henotheism expressed. Many Neo-Pagans subscribe to a version of duotheism in which all Goddesses are understood to be one divine feminine principal and all Gods are understood to be one divine masculine principal. These two form the archetypal and activating polarity of the universe, which is unified by their love for each other. The Goddess and the God may be called upon by many different names and may also be understood as different aspects of the Great God and the Great Goddess. Other Neo-Pagans worship only the divine feminine as Goddess, but usually without denying the reality of other deities (henotheism).

However Neo-Pagans may conceive of the deities, they seem united in a desire for a deep sense of connectedness with them. "It is important to me to develop a radical sense of communion with the Gods—this seems to me the core of worship," says a young Neo-Pagan. "The meaning of the relationship between humanity and the Gods is to recognize that there is a relationship," says another. "Humanity turns to the Gods and Goddesses for a better and more balanced understanding of ourselves and the universe," comments a West Virginia Neo-Pagan. This "radical sense of communion" may take place for Neo-Pagans during ritual and in private meditation. It may also be experienced through one of the traditional forms of divine communication: dream, vision, and oracle. Some Neo-Pagans still make votary offerings in-exchange-for as well.[60]

Neo-Paganism also echoes Paganism's range of thought about the immanence and transcendence of the Divine. While many Neo-Pagans prefer to concentrate solely on the divine immanence in the expression and experience of their spirituality, many others recognize both its immanence and transcendence. As an Oregon Neo-Pagan puts it, "I don't think that anyone can adequately put into words the exact nature of the divine. But it is *as if* 'in the beginning,' before beginnings, was, is, and ever shall be, the divine. And that it became more than a great oneness, it became Goddess and God, and from them—the very 'stuff' of the Divine—were born all things, so that everything—that dried up seed on the bush, the rust on my porch—is the divine."

In whichever of the many and varied ways Neo-Pagans may conceive of the divine, the deity (deities) always remain close to them. Communion with the Goddesses and Gods is an intensely personal experience in which they continually participate.

Coming Full Circle

Readers familiar with Paganism, ancient or modern, will know this article hardly exhausts the subject. There are many areas upon which I have not even touched. Certainly, there are as many dissimilarities between ancient and modern Paganism as there are similarities. And while we cannot know the ancient Greeks directly, we *can* know Neo-Pagans—and they are a diverse group. In conducting the interviews for this article, I heard from Neo-Pagans across the United States, in Canada, and in England. There were repeated themes in their personal and thoughtful answers to my questions, to be sure. Yet for every answer given, there was just as surely another answer that completely contradicted it. In truth, there is no Neo-Pagan creed—just as there was no Pagan creed. Furthermore, few want one. Neo-Pagans wish to be free to explore their spirituality through their own experience and to come together as they choose to create community as they choose.

Neither is Neo-Paganism an insignificant religious fad. It may well be that the Neo-Paganism of the 1960s and 1970s was a forerunner, and perhaps even a goad, to the currents we see transforming mainstream American religion today—the re-emergence of God the Mother and the increased desire among many mainstream religious people for direct experience of their God, a desire that is requiring many churches to drastically change the way they worship—or to perish. The reemergence of God feminine, of Goddess, is *vitally* important to Neo-Paganism, yet the subject has been, and continues to be, so well-discussed in other venues that I felt comfortable not specifically discussing it in this article. Suffice it to say that connection with Goddess is, I believe, *the* most important religious reform of our times, and it is a correspondence between Paganism and Neo-Paganism.

If the Pagan deities no longer live in their ancient temples, there can be no doubt that, like Athena with Proclus, they are alive in the hearts of their worshippers. Perhaps they never really had a need for their fine houses. For they were always alive in the home shrines of the ancients, just as they are now alive in the home altars Neo-Pagans create in their honor. They were present in the mysteries and in the thiasos, just as they are present in the large festivals and the intimate groups in which Neo-Pagans commune. They cooperated and rejoiced in the magical workings of a theurgist, just as they make magic with Neo-Pagans now. Of old they guided in dream and oracle, just as they still do. And always, always, they were alive and numinous in the natural world, just as they are immanently, brilliantly present now in the mountains and fields, in the face of a lover, in a blade of grass.

There is much that is good, beautiful, and valuable in both Paganism and Neo-Paganism. I fully expect the Neo-Pagan religious revival to continue to flourish and grow. I hope that it can do so in freedom, in tolerance, in connection to its roots, and with a continual, bountiful growth of new leaves.

About the Author

Morgan Isidora Forrest is a Neo-Pagan who has been a practitioner of the Golden Dawn system of magic for more than twelve years. She is an accomplished ritualist and has authored many dozens of Hermetic and Neo-Pagan rituals, some of which have become a "tradition" of their own in Portland, Oregon, where she and her personal and magical partner, Adam Forrest, live, work, and invoke. She is co-founder of The Hermetic Society in America, Alexandrian Lodge, and often presents lectures to that group. In addition to her Hermetic and Golden Dawn work, Isidora is active in the local Neo-Pagan and magical community. She is a dedicated priestess of Isis and teaches in this capacity. She has served as a Pythia of Apollo, and is also, on occasion, divinely mad for Dionysos-Sarapis. Isidora has written articles for the *Golden Dawn Journal, Books I, II, and III,* and contributed materials to Chic and Tabatha Cicero's *Secrets of a Golden Dawn Temple.* In non-magical life, she is a freelance writer and an artist.

Endnotes

1. Aiden A. Kelly, *Crafting the Art of Magic, Book I, A History of Modern Witchcraft, 1939–1964* (St. Paul: Llewellyn Publications, 1991), ix.

2. Joel Beversluis, ed., *A Sourcebook for the Community of Religions* (Chicago: The Council for a Parliament of the World's Religions, 1993), 102.

3. Jim Tester, *A History of Western Astrology* (New York: Ballentine Books, 1987), 61.

4. For those unfamiliar with the elemental associations, a brief introduction: An airy nature might be bright, light-hearted, intellectual, or even a little aloof. Air is associated with the east and the dawn. A fiery nature is passionate, willful, inspiring, and energetic. Fire is associated with the south and with noon. A watery nature can be described as nurturing, emotional, and compassionate, but can also be unfocused. Water is associated with the west and sunset. An earthy nature is practical, wise, calm, steady, and even stubborn. Earth is associated with the north and night. The fifth element, Spirit, is considered to infuse all the rest, creating a unified web that weaves together all things and imbues them with the mystery of divine life. Spirit is associated with the center and the entire cycle of day and night.

5. Walter Wili, "The Orphic Mysteries and the Greek Spirit," in *The Mysteries, Papers from the Eranos Yearbooks*, edited by Joseph Campbell (Princeton University Press, 1955), 65. Wili cites the work of writer Lucie Wolfer-Sulzer working with mathematician Jay Hambidge showing that the proportions of temple, statue, and pentagram relate to human proportions.

6. Plotinus, "On Matter and Evil," cited in A.H. Armstrong, ed., *Classical Mediterranean Spirituality, Egyptian, Greek, Roman* (New York: Crossroad, 1986), 70.

7. Iamblichus, "On the Mysteries of Egypt."

8. Walter Burkert, *Greek Religion* (Cambridge: Harvard University Press, 1985), 269.

9. Ibid., 175.

10. Marinus, "Life of Proclus," cited in Armstrong, op. cit., 263.

11. Sophocles, *Oedipus at Colonus*, ibid., 70.

12. Ibid.

13. Armstrong, op. cit., 79.

14. Theodore Roszak, *Where the Wasteland Ends, Politics and Transcendence in Postindustrial Society*, (New York: Anchor Books, 1973), 108.

15. Ibid., 109.

16. Quoted in Roszak, 119.

17. Prudence Jones and Caitlin Matthews, *Voices from the Circle, the Heritage of Western Paganism* (London: the Aquarian Press, 1990), 31.

18. Armstrong, op. cit., 70.

19. Robin Lane Fox, *Pagans and Christians* (New York: Alfred A. Knopf, Inc., 1987), 31.

20. Frank R. Trombley, *Hellenic Religion and Christianization* c. 370–529 (Leiden: E.J. Brill, 1993), 142.

21. Armstrong, op. cit., vxi.

22. Burkert, *Greek Religion*, 110. Please note that the original translation of this passage used the masculine pronouns to refer to the generic maiden of the chorus (each would say that he were speaking himself...). I have changed the pronoun to reflect the gender of the maidens— and to allow the passage to make more sense.

23. Aristotle, "On Philosophy," cited in Armstrong, op. cit., 71.

24. T. M. Luhrmann, *Persuasions of the Witch's Craft, Ritual Magic in Contemporary England* (Cambridge: Harvard University Press, 1989), 136. This is an anthropological study of magic-users (Neo-Pagans, witches, magicians) in England, much of which applies to NeoPagans in the United States. If you have not read it, do. It is fascinating.

25. Wili, op. cit., 70.

26. Walter Burkert, *Ancient Mystery Cults* (Cambridge and London: Harvard University Press, 1987), 30.

27. Ibid., 32. Charismatic leadership was often found, however, in the philosophical schools.

28. Margot Adler, *Drawing Down the Moon, Witches, Druids, Goddess-Worshippers and Other Pagans in America Today* (Boston: Beacon Press, 1979), 33.

29. Burkert, *Ancient Mystery Cults*, 42.

30. Armstrong, op. cit., xiv.

31. Burkert, *Ancient Mystery Cults*, 33.

32. Euripides, *The Bacchae.*

33. Burkert, *Ancient Mystery Cults*, 48.

34. Tom F. Driver, *The Magic of Ritual, Our Need for Liberating Rites that Transform Our Lives & Our Communities* (San Francisco: HarperSanFrancisco, 1991), 167.

35. Van Gennep, *The Rites of Passage,* 13, cited in Driver, ibid., 168.

36. Georg Luck, *Arcana Mundi, Magic and the Occult in the Greek and Roman Worlds* (Baltimore and London: The Johns Hopkins University Press, 1985), 5.

37. E. R. Dodds, *The Greeks and the Irrational* (Berkley, Los Angeles, London: University of California Press, 1951).

38. Luck, op. cit., 8.

39. Roszak, op. cit., 107.

40. Hans Deiter Betz, "Magic and Mystery in the Greek Magical Papyri," in Christopher Faraone and Dirk Obbink, ed., *Magika Hiera, Ancient Greek Magic & Religion* (New York: Oxford University Press, 1991), 248.

41. Proclus, cited in Luck, op. cit., 20.

42. Iamblichus, "On the Mysteries of Egypt," cited in Luck, ibid., 128.

43. Apuleius, "Apology," cited in Luck, ibid., 111.

44. Luck, ibid., 4.

45. Plotinus, "Enneads," cited in Luck, op. cit., 119.

46. Armstrong, op. cit., 73.

47. Ibid., xvi.

48. A.J. Festugiere, "Anth Hon: La formule 'en echange de quoi' dans la priere grecque hellenistique," in *Revue des sciences philosophiques et theologiques*, cited in Armstrong, 202.

49. Pausanias, *Description of Greece, Books I and II* (Cambridge: Harvard University Press, Loeb Classical Library, 1918), 103.

50. Marinus, "Life of Proclus."

51. Joscelyn Godwin, *Mystery Religions in the Ancient World* (San Francisco: Harper and Row, 1981), 27.

52. Apuleius of Madauros, *The Golden Ass* in J. Gwyn Griffiths, *The Isis Book: Metamorphoses, Book XI* (Leiden: E. J.Brill, 1975), 101.

53. J. B. Skemp, *Socrates and Plato* in Armstrong, op. cit., 102–119.

54. Brian Copenhaver, *Hermetica, the Greek Corpus Hermeticum and the Latin Asclepius in a new English translation with notes and introduction* (Cambridge: Cambridge University Press, 1992), 2.

55. Ibid., 11.

56. Ibid.

57. Libanius, "Pro Templis," cited in Armstrong, op. cit., 200.

58. David Miller, *The New Polytheism* (New York: Harper & Row, 1974), 4., cited in Adler, op. cit., 29.

59. Valerie Voight, "Being a Pagan in a 9 to 5 World," in Chas S. Clifton, *Witchcraft Today, Book I* (St. Paul: Llewellyn Publications, 1992), 176.

60. A recent example is the offering of incense and prayers to Elemental Spirits made by a group of Oregon Neo-Pagans in exchange for good weather at a large Festival Gathering. While forecasts called for a deluge all weekend, apparently the Elemental Spirits responded; for while it did rain during the weekend, the rain stopped long enough for the important outdoor rituals to take place, and the last day was unexpectedly bright and sunny.

The Gods of ancient Greece.

Samothracian Fire:

Restoring an Ancient Greek Initiatory System

Steven Cranmer

Outside the popular worship of the Olympian gods, the Greek mystery cults held a special sway over the ancient world for almost a millennium. With secret and dramatic rituals celebrating birth, sex, death, and the afterlife, the mysteries were the prototype for many modern-day forms of ceremonial initiation. While the most well-known of the mysteries were those of Demeter and Kore at Eleusis and of Dionysos at Athens and Miletus, other lesser-known local cults dotted the sacred places of the Greek world. Of these, one of the longest lasting and most secret was centered around the northern Aegean island of Samothrace.

The Samothracian mysteries seem to have been a two-stage system of initiation. The degrees of *myesis* (connoting "secrecy" or "hiddenness") and *epopteia* (connoting "sight" or "awakening") corresponded roughly to similar degrees at Eleusis. Samothrace had its own deities, the mysteriously named *Theoi Megaloi* ("the Great Gods"), whose names and attributes were a secret revealed to initiates. The Great Gods had worshipers from as far north as Olbia on the Black Sea to as far south as Koptos on the Nile. Mainland Greeks encountering the Samothracian gods for the first time often confused them with other nearby deities such as the *Kabeiroi* (or Kabiri) of Lemnos, a fact leading to much confusion about their identity. Initiation into the mysteries of the Great Gods was thought to confer safety from danger, security in the afterlife, and (as many votive inscriptions can attest) protection from storms at sea. The famous statue of winged Nike found on Samothrace, and now in the Louvre, was erected in the second century B.C.E. to commemorate a victory won at sea.

With the air of mystery surrounding the identities of the Samothracian deities and the miraculous claims of initiates, it is no surprise that some aspects of these mysteries were included in the body of Golden Dawn ritual magic. The Samothracian "Kabiri" appear in the 3=8 grade of Practicus, anachronously reading from the Chaldean Oracles, and with nothing more to identify them as Samothracian than

their names. The inclusion of these divinities in this grade ceremony
has been criticized (by Aleister Crowley, for one) on the basis of over-
syncretic confusion and historical inaccuracy. It is possible, however,
to redeem the presence of the Great Gods in the G✳D✳ mythos in the
light of both modern archaeological knowledge and a little old-fash-
ioned creativity. Such an integral part of the G✳D✳ initiation scheme
need not be dismissed as a mere nineteenth century curiosity.

Theoi Megaloi: The Great Gods

There is a great deal of puzzling and conflicting information about the
Great Gods of Samothrace. The generic term *Kabeiroi* is used by several
ancient writers, but there is no evidence that the *Theoi Megaloi* were
referred to by this title at Samothrace itself. The actual Kabeiroi venerated at Lemnos and Thebes were possibly of Etruscan origin, and they
were often portrayed as drunken, buffoonish companions of Hephais-
tos, the god of metalworking. A real connection between the Lemnian
and Samothracian cults seems unlikely, but both the Kabeiroi and the
mythical founders of the Samothracian mysteries were seen as ante-
diluvian "primordial men." Because iron and magnetism played a
crucial role in Samothracian initiation, the association of the Kabeiroi
with the forging of metals may also have been an important link.

    We are indebted to Mnaseas, a third century B.C.E. traveler, for
preserving a series of names that are most probably those of the Great
Gods. He gives a triad of related names: *Axieros, Axiokersos*, and *Axiokersa*, as well as a fourth, *Kasmilos*. Various later authors have identified
these with other Greek divinities, but several different sets of genders
and attributions are known. It is most probable that the triad was composed of a central female deity (Axiokersa) accompanied by a male
pair of gods (Axieros and Axiokersos), and attended by a herald or
servant (Kasmilos).

    The linguistic meaning of the three similar names of the triad is
not currently known. The nineteenth century German philosopher F.
W. J. Schelling speculated that the root *Axier-*, in "Phoenician dialect,"
referred to hunger, poverty, or yearning—qualities of lonely primordial beings. The name *Kersa* might be related to Demeter (Ceres) or
Kore, goddesses of agriculture and the earth worshipped at Eleusis.
This pattern of three personages with identically prefixed names is
preserved in certain jurisdictions of Freemasonry, where the characters
Jubelo, Jubela, and Jubelum play a pivotal role in the Third Degree of
Master Mason. These names are usually assumed to be derived either
from the Latin *iubere*, "to command," or from the Biblical Jubal or

Tubal Cain, but they can also be interpreted as corruptions of the tripartite name of God, *IAO-BAAL-ON*, utilized in older versions of the Masonic Royal Arch Degree. Although there is now no explicit connection claimed between the ancient Greek mysteries and Freemasonry, it is still interesting to acknowledge the recurrent and syncretic themes that link the Great Gods to the present day.

Many have likened *Axiokersa* to a primeval Mother Goddess. Diodorus Siculus preserved a myth of the early colonization of Samothrace by Amazons, who were saved from a shipwreck and set up altars to the *Métera Theon* (Mother of the Gods). Samothrace itself is often referred to as "the island of Electra," the mother of the Dardanian (or Trojan) people. Electra was a daughter of the Titan Atlas and one of the Pleiades, which, as a constellation, traditionally rose at the season of safe sailing weather. The Great Goddess of Samothrace was also identified at various times with Rhea, Hecate, and Demeter. The Golden Dawn also attributed Isis, Nephthys, and the office of the Hegemon to this deity.

Closely connected to the Mother figure are the other two members of the triad, *Axieros* and *Axiokersos*. Often characterized as an opposing pair on either side of Axiokersa, common identifications were with sky and earth, "Zeus the elder" and "Dionysos the younger," and Osiris and Typhon (in the Golden Dawn 3=8 ceremony). The twin sons of Electra, Dardanos, and Ietion, also seem to be memorialized in these deities. Dardanos was known in myth for transporting the Samothracian mysteries to Troy, where his son Idaeus began the magical cult of the Dactyli on Mount Ida, which supposedly trained Orpheus. The family of Dardanos was also said to have founded the city of Troy around a temple set up to honor a "Goddess who fell from the skies"—possibly an iron meteorite. Ietion (or Iasion) married the priestess Cybele and had a son named Corybas, who began the tradition of the Corybantes: dancing wildly and noisily to flute music in worship of the Mother of the Gods. An anonymous Homeric Hymn from the seventh century B.C.E. asserts this relationship:

> *I prithee, clear-voiced Muse, daughter of mighty Zeus, sing of the mother of all gods and men. She is well-pleased with the sound of rattles and of timbrels, with the voice of flutes and the outcry of wolves and bright-eyed lions, with echoing hills and wooded coombes.*

The twin Samothracian gods were also sometimes identified with the well-known *Dioskouroi*, Castor and Polydeuces, the mythical twins immortalized in the constellation of Gemini. These rival brothers were the siblings of Helen and Clytaemnestra, and they eventually became embroiled in the bloody legacy of the royal house of Mycenae. The emblem of this family (and city) was the lion, an important symbol in Bronze Age Aegean culture. The twin lions represented the rising and setting sun, over which the Mother Goddess at center exercised her domain. A somewhat more concrete connection between the Dioskouroi and Samothrace was their popular aspect as saviors of shipwrecked sailors, via the sending of favorable winds.

The fourth Samothracian deity mentioned by Mnaseas was *Kasmilos,* most probably an attendant to the main triad. The common identification of Kasmilos with the god Hermes may have figured in the initiation ritual of *myesis*, where the candidate passed between two large statues of ithyphallic (erect) Hermes. The Golden Dawn 3=8 ceremony identifies this divinity with the candidate herself, as well as with the Egyptian god Horus. The name Kasmilos is etymologically similar to Kadmos, or Cadmus, the mythical grandson of Poseidon and founder of Thebes. Cadmus was an initiate of the Samothracian mysteries, and the myth of his wedding to Harmonia on Samothrace seemingly played a part in the annual public celebration of the priesthood of the *Theoi Megaloi.*

The Paths of Fire and the Sun

The Great Gods of Samothrace appear in two sections of the Golden Dawn 3=8 grade of Practicus: the 31st Path of Shin and the 30th Path of Resh. These two paths on the Tree of Life traditionally correspond to elemental fire and the sun, respectively, and thus may appear out of place in a grade mainly attributed to the element of water. Hopefully we can see how these apparent opposites can be reconciled in a larger context.

When the G✶D✶ candidate is admitted to the 31st Path, she is addressed as Kasmilos by the three "Kabiri," who read from the Chaldean Oracles (laden with Neoplatonic fire symbolism; see below) and identify themselves with a host of correspondences:

Kabir	Officer	Angel	Type of Fire	
Axieros	Hierophant	Michael	AUD	(life-giving solar fire)
Axiokersos	Hiereus	Samael	AUB	(volcanic and terrestrial fire)
Axiokersa	Hegemon	Anael	AUR	(vital astral light)
Kasmilos	Candidate	Arel	ASCH	(latent heat)

These relationships are symbolized by the "Solid Triangular Pyramid" or tetrahedron, which displays three visible faces and conceals one invisible (bottom) face at all times. The tarot key of the *Last Judgment* and the "Perpetual Intelligence" of the *Sepher Yetzirah* can be interpreted as reflecting the final manifestation of the Pillar of Severity (fiery and martial Gevurah) through Hod to Malkuth, the physical world.

Next, the candidate is given the Solar Greek Cross of thirteen squares, and is admitted to the 30th Path. Again the officers refer to her as Kasmilos, but now equate themselves (as Kabiri) to the sun at various times of the year. Axieros and Axiokersos represent the Summer and Winter Solstices—the sun at greatest elevation and depression with respect to the equator—and Axiokersa represents the two intervening Equinoxes. Thus the *Theoi Megaloi* become personifications of the Adeptus Minor keyword I.N.R.I., which can be imagined as a projection into the zodiac of the three primal forces: **I** (Axiokersa, ever-present "mighty mother"), **A** (Axiokersos, "destroyer" of winter), **O** (Axieros, "risen" in summer): **IAO**. The tarot key of *The Sun* portrays two children beneath the shining luminary, possibly corresponding to the twin deities Axieros and Axiokersos who bracket its yearly path. The Greek Cross and the astrologically-inclined "Collecting Intelligence" of the *Sepher Yetzirah* further symbolize the orderly progression of the seasons as a projection of divine Severity (law and rigidity) through Hod into the abstract and pervasive Foundation of Yesod.

Although the Samothracian *Theoi* are not explicitly mentioned hereafter in the ceremonies of the G✷D✷, further light can be found by examining one other path on the Tree of Life: the 23rd Path of Mem, which is normally traversed in the 6=5 Adeptus Major initiation. This path connects Hod to Gevurah and forms the bottom-most vertical support in the Pillar of Severity or Form. Mem is the "Spirit of the Mighty Waters" which transforms the incendiary strength of *Elohim Gibor* into the multitudinous *Elohim Tzabaoth*, which is likened to the plural Spirit of God which "moved upon the Face of the Waters of Creation." This transformative force (likened to the matronly *Shekhinah* or, equivalently, to Axiokersa) is a reflection of the sacrificial symbolism of *The Hanged Man*. The G✷D✷ Philosophus is warned of this powerful force when entering the Second Order:

> *Can your tears prevail against the Tide of the Sea, your might against the waves of the storm, your love against the sorrows of all the world?*

Finally, one can utilize the interpretive tool of *gematria* to elucidate any further links between the Samothracian Great Gods and the primarily Hebrew "pantheon" of the Golden Dawn. The phrase *Theoi Megaloi* itself adds by Greek gematria to 253, the sum of all integers from one to twenty-two, and a sort of totality of the twenty-two Paths on the Tree of Life. The names Axieros and Axiokersos add to 446 and 736, respectively. The former is the numeration of the Hebrew word *Maveth*, מות, or "death," alluding to the correspondence of Axieros with Osiris and the G∴D∴ Hierophant in the 3=8 ceremony. The latter is the numeration of *Aron ha-Edeth*, ארון העדת, the Ark of the Testimony, which was guarded in the Holy of Holies with no less resolve than the extreme west of the G∴D∴ temple is watched over by the Hiereus, representing Axiokersos. The name of the Great Goddess Axiokersa numbers 467, which Aleister Crowley's *Sepher Sephiroth* lists with the transliteration *GLGLThA*, גלגלתא, possibly *Golgotha*, the Aramaic name for the "place of skulls" of Christ's crucifixion (see *The Hanged Man* of the 23rd Path, above). Lastly, the name of the attending herald Kasmilos sums to 571, equivalent to both *Malakh*, מלאך, ("angel") and *Metheqela*, מתקלא, ("balance") in Hebrew. Does this fact assert the innate spiritual nature of the candidate, as well as the value in keeping to the Middle Pillar? It of course depends on how much validity one ascribes to this kind of manipulation. Gematria trains the mind to seek connections and relationships, but it is more than possible to begin mistaking this arbitrary "glass bead game" for something objectively accurate.

Myesis and Epopteia

In any case, it is virtually impossible to truly understand a mythical system without the tangible context of time and place. Let us then begin to fill in this vacuum with a brief tour of the island of Samothrace and the sanctuary of the *Theoi Megaloi*, and an archaeological overview of what is known about the initiations once performed there.

Sea-girt Samothrace is a small mountainous island, no more than twenty miles across at its longest. Its highest peak, Mount Phengari, commands the surrounding Aegean. In Homer's *Iliad*, Poseidon watched over the Trojan War from this crest, and indeed, Mount Phengari can actually be discerned on the horizon from as far away as Troy. The sacred area where the mysteries of the Great Gods were celebrated is in a valley on the northern coast of the island, and two rivers once cut through this valley on either side of the main buildings of the sanctuary.

There are ruins and buildings from many epochs, but most range from the fifth to third centuries B.C.E., the heyday of the mysteries. The primary structures that have been identified seem to form a four-fold symmetry in the four compass directions. In the north is the Anaktoron, a rectangular building with rows of benches for initiates, where the first degree of *myesis* is thought to have been conferred. In the south is a similar building called the Hieron, in which the second degree of *epopteia* was performed. The Hieron contained an enclosed circular apse at its southern end. It is interesting from a Golden Dawn (or Masonic) perspective that the degree of "secrecy" or "hiddenness" was celebrated in the north, while the degree of "sight" or "awakening" was in the south, these being symbolic directions of least and most light, respectively.

The east of the sanctuary was the traditional entrance point for candidates, where they were prepared for initiation. No buildings stood at this end of the valley until the Hellenistic era, when several votive areas were constructed by the family of Alexander the Great. Legend claimed that Alexander was conceived on Samothrace after his parents, Philip and Olympias, first saw each other across the Anaktoron during a celebration of the mysteries, and fell in love. The west of the sanctuary contained several long buildings seemingly designed to house and feed the many visitors to the island, and ancient writers mention festive torch-lit banquets here. Finally, the central area of the valley held a building now known as the Temenos, which probably contained the public sacrifices and dancing rites held annually on Samothrace.

Candidates for initiation into the degree of *myesis* would have entered the sanctuary from the east, sometime after sunset, and would have been ushered to the southern door of the Anaktoron. In the southeast corner of this building was a domed well-like structure, called a *bothros*, with an opening at the top. Pouring a libation into this deep pit, as well as a ceremonial disrobing and washing, was probably part of the preparation of candidates.

The ceremony then led into the large main chamber of the Anaktoron, in which benches for spectators lined the walls. Not much is known of the details of the ritual procedures performed here, but bronze shields and iron knives have been found in this chamber, suggesting the noisy and clanging dancing rites of the Corybantes. The paired ithyphallic statues of Hermes probably stood at the northern end of this room, and the Greek historian Herodotus connects them with the secrets of the ceremony: the meaning of sex and the origin of human life. The relationship between the Mother Goddess Axiokersa and the twin male deities Axieros and Axiokersos was probably communicated to initiates in this chamber.

Finally, the new *mystai* were given two items during this ceremony that signified their initiation, and possibly acted as signs of the nautical protection the ritual conferred. The first was a purple sash or belt, called a *porphyris*, which might have been put on after the ceremonial bathing. The second was a ring made of magnetized iron. This ceremonial token has been interpreted by many as evidence for a tradition of sympathetic magic based around a magnetic lodestone, possibly an iron meteorite that could have fallen to Samothrace in antiquity. The Roman writer Lucretius described a bronze basin used on Samothrace, inside which "iron rings dance and iron filings go mad." If this bronze surface (possibly related to the shields found in the Anaktoron?) was placed over a lodestone, such apparently miraculous effects would be seen. Even the sacred reputation of the entire island may be explained by the presence of this carefully guarded "magical" object.

The performance of the second, more advanced degree of *epopteia* was seemingly a rarer occasion than the first. Fewer than ten percent of the carved initiate-lists on Samothrace record names of *epoptai* rather than *mystai*. In 1951, archaeologist Karl Lehmann identified that the Hieron was where the second degree was celebrated, based upon an inscription barring those who had not experienced *myesis*. There was a special concern for the "purity" of the candidate in this rite. An important part of the preparation was an oath of secrecy, supplemented by a question that asked about the worst deed the candidate ever committed. Several ancient writers recorded the words of a particularly free-thinking candidate, who when asked this question, replied to the effect that if the priest let him in, he would give his answer directly to the Gods! Candidates also were probably purified by a washing or lustration; a large drain was found in the northern part of the Hieron.

Even less is known about the main ceremony of *epopteia* than is known about *myesis*. There is some evidence for a sacrifice of birds at a central platform in the Hieron. The enclosed apse at the southern end of the building was probably hidden by a curtain for most of the ritual, then opened at the end for some important revelation. Some archaeologists have suggested a connection between the Samothracian *epopteia* and various astral mysteries, either Mithraic or Orphic, and indeed, the Great Gods have been mentioned in many inscriptions in conjunction with the stars of the zodiac. However, even with the present textual and physical evidence, the actual secrets of the mysteries are still very much hidden.

The Chaldean Connection

The creative and syncretic authors of the Golden Dawn Cipher Manuscripts paired the Samothracian "Kabiri" with the Chaldean Oracles, or "Sentences of Zoroaster." We know today that this collection of Greek hexameter verses, rumored to be divinely inspired, hails from the late second century C.E., and probably never had anything to do with the mysteries of Samothrace. However, the Oracles had a strong impact on the development of Neoplatonic thought, which some have regarded as a virtual continuation (albeit filtered through Near-Eastern Gnosticism) of the ideas and cosmology of the ancient Greeks.

The theology present in the Chaldean Oracles has been compared with that of Middle Platonism, which represented a move away from the scholarly and purely philosophical schools of earlier Greek thought, and a move toward a more "underground" religious and theurgic magical system. As in Gnosticism, there is a duality in the Chaldean fragments between a transcendent Highest God and a lower Demiurge, the former being a self-contemplating formulator of Ideas, and the latter actually acting on and projecting these Ideas into the physical world. The Oracles also mention a third deity, a feminine mediating power *dynamis* between the First and Second "Fathers." While related to the Gnostic figures of Sophia and Ennoia, this goddess was often conflated with Hecate, the ancient Greek triple-goddess of crossroads and magic.

This certainly seems reminiscent of the Samothracian triad: the Great Goddess Axiokersa positioned between the opposing male deities Axieros and Axiokersos. It is also a similar formulation of the Kabbalistic Tetragrammaton *IHVH*, יהוה, which is woven into nearly every aspect of the Golden Dawn. The transcendent Supernal Father, or Macroprosopus, is encoded in the *Yod* of the Tetragrammaton, while the active Son, or Microprosopus, is encoded into the *Vav*. The intervening Great Mother, *Aima*, occupies the first *Heh*, while the created physical world is embodied in the second *Heh*. The Neoplatonic roots of Hermetic Kabbalah are well known, and it is certainly possible that these similar constructs came from a common source.

The most probable reason for the reading of the Chaldean Oracles in the G∴D∴ceremony of the 31st Path of Fire is the omnipresence of fire symbolism in the haunting phrases of the Oracles. The two primal male deities of the Chaldean system are often called the "First Transcendent Fire" and the "Intelligible Fire." Both the cosmogonic creation of the universe and the process of thought are likened to fire, as well as a very Kabbalistic lightning flash:

> *For Implacable Thunders leap from him [i.e., the First Transcendent God] and the lightning-receiving womb of the shining ray of Hecate, who is generated from the Father. From him leap the girdling flower of fire and the powerful breath [situated] beyond the fiery poles (fragment 35, Majercik).*

Fire was also seemingly used as a part of the theurgic rituals of the Chaldeans, as the traditional Golden Dawn purification and consecration texts (fragments 133 and 148, see ceremony below) imply.

The Chaldeans saw theurgy as the primary means for the salvation of the soul. While some authors attempt to distinguish between theurgy and "lower" forms of magic, or *goeteia*, there seems to be such a continuous array of practical and theoretical aspects to make such a dividing line meaningless. One of the primary ritual objects was the Iynx or Strophalos of Hecate, which was a spinning wheel or "turbine" that made sounds that were interpreted as magical vibrations or the "music of the spheres." The name Iynx was also applied to a class of lesser divine beings that represented binding forces between the human and the divine, and were metaphorically compared to such abstract concepts as names, prayers, and thoughts. Amulets and stones, such as the enigmatic *Mnizouris* stone mentioned parenthetically in the Oracles (and by the Hierophant in the G✳D✳ 3=8 ceremony) were also employed in a sacrificial or protective context.

The Ring of Iron

The curious reader, faced with the foregoing mass of archaeological and literary minutiae, may wonder about its actual usefulness in modern ceremonial magic. It is a credit to the unique syncretism set up by Mathers, Westcott, and Woodman that innovation need not end with the historical Golden Dawn. With this in mind I have attempted to integrate the infamous "iron ring" of *myesis* into the collection of standard magical implements, as a defensive counterpart to the more offense-oriented Magic Sword. Both items, Ring and Sword, are made primarily of the martial metal iron, but the Samothracian rings were said to often be covered in gold, here symbolizing adepthood.

The consecration ceremony that follows is written in the traditional style, which requires the celebrant to be at least a Zelator Adeptus Minor (5=6). It can easily be adapted, however, for use by members of the Outer Order—especially a Practicus (3=8), for which the symbolism of the *Theoi Megaloi* will resonate most strongly. I use Majercik's newer translations from the Chaldean Oracles in sections 4 and 5 below, and these can be replaced with the more traditional versions if desired. Finally, it may be advisable to align the northern axis of the temple with magnetic north, rather than geographic north, because the Earth is the true lodestone with which the Ring is being attuned.

Consecration of the Ring

1. Prepare a central altar, draped in black. Upon it arrange the red cross and white triangle as in the Neophyte grade. Surround it with the symbols of the four elements: rose and incense (air), cup (water), lamp (fire), and plate of salt (earth). Place the new Ring upon the triangle, along with the Magic Sword and Lotus Wand.

2. Stand at the west of the altar, facing east. Take up the Lotus Wand by the black band and say: *"Hekas! Hekas! Este Bebeloi!"* which calls the temple's wardens to service.

3. Perform the Lesser Banishing Ritual of the Pentagram, using the Lotus Wand to trace the signs.

4. Lay down the wand and purify the temple with water. Sprinkle from the cup in the four quarters, saying:

   Above all, let the priest himself who governs the works of fire, be sprinkled with the icy billow of the deep-roaring sea.

5. Consecrate the temple with fire, passing the incense around the four quarters, saying:

   But when you see the formless, very holy fire shining by leaps and bounds throughout the depths of the whole world, then listen to the voice of the fire.

6. Take up the Lotus Wand by the white band. Circumambulate the temple three times with the sun (clockwise), and return to the west of the altar. Face east.

7. Repeat the Adoration (either below or from the Neophyte grade ceremony), saluting with the 0=0 Sign of the Enterer at each line. At the end, give the Sign of Silence.

   O Thou, Ocean of Infinite Perfection! O Height, which reflectest Thyself in the Depth! O Depth, which exhalest into the Height! Lead us into the true life, through intelligence, through love!

8. Turn to face opposite the direction of the present position of Mars in the zodiac, standing to face the altar. Use the Sword to describe in the air the Invoking Pentagram of Fire, saying at each point:

Spirit point:	*"Ouranos"*	("heaven")
Fire point:	*"Chrysos"*	("gold")
Air point:	*"Argyros"*	("silver")
Water point:	*"Chalkos"*	("bronze")
Earth point:	*"Sidéros"*	("iron")
Spirit point:	*"Gé"*	("earth")

9. Perform the Supreme Invoking Ritual of the Hexagram of Mars, using the Magic Sword to trace the figures.

10. Lay down the Sword, and pick up the Lotus Wand. Stand to the west of the altar, facing east. Holding the wand by the Aquarius (violet) band, invoke over the Ring:

> *O Thou, most sublime Axieros, Thou strong and terrible ELOHIM GIBOR, I beseech Thee to bestow upon this Ring of Iron the Power of Truth to defend against the evil and weakness I may encounter. May Thy life-giving and light-producing Fire bring ripening heat to all things! May Thy Great Archangel MICHAEL and Thy Powerful Order of Synoches bestow upon me the courage to use this Ring aright in my search for True Wisdom and Perfect Happiness!*

11. Move to the north of the altar, facing south. Holding the wand by the Leo (yellow) band, invoke over the Ring:

> *O Thou, most sublime Axiokersos, Thou shining and fleet ELOHIM TZABAOTH, I beseech Thee to bestow upon this Ring of Iron the Power of Faith to defend against the evil and weakness I may encounter. May Thy raging and tormented Fire tear asunder the steely curtain of Matter! May Thy Great Archangel SAMAEL and Thy Powerful Order of Teletarchs bestow upon me the courage to use this Ring aright in my search for True Wisdom and Perfect Happiness!*

12. Move to the east of the altar, facing west. Holding the wand by the Scorpio (green-blue) band, invoke over the Ring:

> *O Thou, most sublime Axiokersa, Thou Mother of All, Thou Divine Presence SHEKINAH, vouchsafe upon this Ring of Iron a breath of Thine Ineffable Inspiration, the vital Power of Love. May it be a focus for Thy winding and corruscating fluid Fire! May all dwellers upon Earth*

remain safely under Thy Shadow! May Thy Great Archangel ANAEL and Thy Powerful Order of Iynges bestow upon me the fidelity to use this Ring aright in my search for True Wisdom and Perfect Happiness!

13. Move to the south of the altar, facing north. Holding the wand by the Taurus (red-orange) band, invoke over the Ring:

    O Thou, most sublime Kasmilos, Thou risen from the rock-hewn tomb, Thou great night of faith ZAUIR ANPIN, vouchsafe upon this Ring of Iron a tear from Thine Eyes of Lightning, the generative Power of Balance. May Thy latent heat aid the two smiths and the midwife to forge the stone Mnizouris, the stone which cometh forth from the abyss once every thousand years, from the abyss of the great firmament! May Thy Great Archangel ARAL and Thy Powerful Order of Hagioi Anaktes bestow upon me the reserve to use this Ring aright in my search for True Wisdom and Perfect Happiness!

14. Still facing north, hold the wand by the white band and trace over the Ring the sigils of the god-names invoked above.

15. Align the Ring and Sword along the north-south axis, and slowly describe (clockwise) a circle over them with the wand, saying:

    Sword of Dardanos! Ring of Ietion!

    Thrice blessed are those who have felt the binding power of the Great Lodestone, Star of the Dragon! Thrice blessed is he that goeth beneath the earth, for he knoweth the end of life! Thrice blessed is she that goeth into the firmament, for she knoweth the beginning given by the Light!

    Sword of Dardanos! Ring of Ietion!

16. Lay down the wand and purify the new Ring with water. Make a Rose-Cross over it with the cup.

17. Consecrate the new Ring with Fire. Describe a Rose-Cross over it with the incense.

18. Take up the Ring and put it on the second (middle) finger of your right hand. Give the 1=10 Sign of Earth, and vibrate the name of the Lord of the Great Lodestone: *"ADONAI HA-ARETZ."*

19. Perform the Supreme Invoking Ritual of the Hexagram of Mars, holding the Sword in the same hand as is wearing the Ring of Iron. Visualize the triad of Axieros, Axiokersos, and Axiokersa when analyzing the appropriate parts of the keyword: I.N.R.I.

20. With the cup, purify the temple as in the opening.

21. With the incense, consecrate the temple as in the opening.

22. Lay down the Sword, and take up the Lotus Wand by the black band. Circumambulate the temple three times in the reverse direction (counter-clockwise).

23. Standing at the west of the altar, face east, saying:

> *In the name of YEHESHUAH, the Redeemer, I do now suffer all Spirits bound by this ceremony to depart in peace unto their abodes. May the blessing of Yeheshuah Yehovashah be with you now and forever more, and let there be peace between me and you.*

24. Perform the Lesser Banishing Ritual of the Pentagram, using the Lotus Wand to trace the signs.

25. Remove the Ring and keep it wrapped in white or green-blue (the color of the Scorpio band of the wand) silk.

About the Author

Steven Cranmer is a professional astronomer who works in Cambridge, Massachusetts. He has been working with the Golden Dawn system since 1990, and participates in several Internet computer forums on magic, the occult, and Freemasonry. He is the author of the *Golden Dawn FAQ* (list of Frequently-Asked Questions), an online document that attempts to summarize the G✳D✳ system of magic, sketch out the history of the Order, as well as act as a worldwide directory of active Golden Dawn organizations. He lives in Pennsylvania with his wife and three cats.

Bibliography

Brown, Robert F. *Schelling's Treatise on "The Deities of Samothrace": A Translation and an Interpretation.* Missoula, Montana: Scholars Press, 1977.

Campbell, Joseph. *The Masks of God: Occidental Mythology.* New York: Penguin Books, 1964.

Cole, Susan Guettel. *Theoi Megaloi: The Cult of the Great Gods at Samothrace.* Leiden, Netherlands: E. J. Brill, 1984.

Ehrhardt, Hartmut. *Samothrake: Heiligtümer in ihrer Landschaft und Geschichte als Zeugen Antiken Geisteslebens.* Stuttgart, Germany: Urachhaus, 1985.

Evelyn-White, Hugh. G., trans. *Hesiod, the Homeric Hymns, and Homerica.* London: Loeb Classical Library. William Heinemann, 1914.

Graves, Robert. *The Greek Myths.* New York: Penguin Books, 1960.

Godwin, David. *Godwin's Cabalistic Encyclopedia.* St. Paul, Minnesota: Llewellyn Publications, 1989.

Lehmann, Karl, *Samothrace: A Guide to the Excavations and the Museum.* New York: New York University Press, 1955.

Lewis, Naphtali, ed. *Samothrace: The Ancient Literary Sources.* Vol. 1 of Bollingen Series LX, ed. Karl Lehmann. New York: Pantheon Books, 1958.

Majercik, Ruth. *The Chaldean Oracles: Text, Translation, and Commentary.* Leiden, Netherlands: E. J. Brill, 1989.

Regardie, Israel. *The Golden Dawn.* 6th ed. St. Paul, Minnesota: Llewellyn Publications, 1989.

Ronan, Stephen. "Hekate's Iynx: An Ancient Theurgical Tool," in *Alexandria,* ed. D. R. Fideler. Vol. 1. Grand Rapids, Michigan: Phanes Press, 1991.

The Ancient Ones of the Irish Faery-Faith.

The Ancient Ones
of the Irish Faery-Faith

Kisma K. Stepanich

As an *Ollamh* of the Irish Faery-Faith and a modern practitioner of its off-spring, Faery Wicca, I find much joy and sovereignty in the passing-on of the tradition to those believers who truly desire to live it. Faery Wicca, an ancient branch of Celtic Wicca, is an old religion, a way of life, earth-centered, in which Dana (God), the Great Mother of the Irish pantheon, is the primary deity. It is a very simple folk-faith, not overly adorned with paraphernalia; however, many skills are expected of those who involve themselves with this tradition, and initiation can only be acquired under the guidance of an Ollamh.

In this study I hope to shed light on the background of our pantheon, for like many of the Old Ones from ancient religions and spiritual belief systems, the Irish pantheon has suffered demotion, resulting in a new classification of imaginary and mythological beings. Through understanding their origins and demotion, as well as the Celtic division of the year, the four great festivals, the Otherworld universe, and our fundamental art of magickal visualization, you will receive enough information and guidance to begin exploring this rich pantheon and reconnecting with them. However, I must be fair in saying: journey with caution, for once you have been chosen to experience their world and energy and receive their gifts, your mortal life will be in danger; for your soul will long to ever return to their Land and share in their company!

Irish Pantheon

The Irish pantheon is richly abundant with goddesses mighty in magick, enchantment, and divination, and gods powerful in battle and wit. In the Faery-Faith, the gods and goddesses are known as the Ancient Ones, the *Tuatha De Danann* (Tribe of Dana), and even more commonly as the Faery.

Today, when one hears the word *"Faery"* (usually spelled *fairy*),[1] a fantasy creature comes to mind. Within their kingdom we find remnants of a magickal race of beings not of this world, as well as diminutive fairies, flower fairies with tiny wings, garden fairies, and elemental fairies, to mention only a few, each with their own virtues and traditions.

Over the past few centuries there have been many ideas about what the Faery are. Scholarly research brought forth many theories in regards to the ancient Irish Faery-Faith tradition; e.g., the naturalistic, pygmy, druid, mythological, and psychological theories, indicating almost all the essential elements. The advocates of such theories are adequate evidence that the Faery-Faith was a living tradition, and that it's chief characters, the Faery, were, on some level, in existence. Theirs became a study of human nature itself, proving that all the world over, human beings interpret visions pragmatically and sociologically, or hold beliefs in accord with their own personal experiences, and are forever unconsciously immersed in a sea of psychological influences. These influences may be explainable through the methods of sociological inquiry, which may sometimes be supernormal in origin and nature, and hence to be explained most adequately, if at all, through psychical research. Therefore, the most difficult problem of all, they surmised, was for human nature to interpret and understand its own ultimate essence and psychological instincts.

In modern psychology there is now a well-established interpretation of the Faery, as based on the psychological theory, which is that the Faery are inherent, either passively or actively, within the psyche, that they have no independent entity as actual living beings other than in human consciousness. In this school of thought, there are many psychological themes: the Faery are sexual images; they are archetypes, such as those of the classical gods and goddesses (interesting, because that's what they are); they are embodiments and projected images of our fear of the unknown; they are the remnants of an old nature religion. The usage of archetypes is perhaps the leading avenue of practice in the psychological theory. The fact that consciousness consists of many images endlessly relating to one another around a central core is by no means a modern discovery; it has long been taught in esoteric traditions.

In esoteric traditions, archetypes become the magickal images used to move the consciousness toward the goals that lie in directions normally ignored or unknown in daily habitual living patterns. Archetypes, or matrices, are higher-order patterns, and are traditionally taught as constants, or as undergoing changes of shape over vast periods of outer time. They appear as cosmologies, glyphs, maps, images, and portent symbols, enduring throughout magickal training from the exercises of the beginner to the adept's advanced use of energies for specific chosen ends.

In the beginning of a novice's training, the Ancient Ones present themselves through symbols. Symbols speak to our subconscious mind, remembering us to ancient truths, or forgotten events; for the world, with its events and objects, is not contained, but translated, into the realm of the mind. Symbols bring these memories, forgotten or ancient, into the subconscious mind, where through moments of intuition, deep thought, dreams, serious contemplation, or deep meditation they may be remembered.

Symbols are the language by which the unconscious speaks to consciousness. The choice of symbols with which one works is therefore a two-way process. On the one hand, one listens to the unconscious and tries to grasp the meaning of the symbols it puts forward. On the other, one tries out symbols that seem appropriate and numinously charged.

Symbols and images used in magick are derived from those shared by the collective imagination, and are found in myths and folk lore—the images that connect us to the natural cycles and rhythms of life. Such symbols are archetypes, but not in the modern sense of the word as dictated in psychology, although similar.

In Faery Wicca, we turn to Irish mythology to understand the archetypes of our pantheon. Mythology is, after all, a symbolic language that can be compared with our intuitive, subconscious level of memory, one that reveals the contents of the collective rather than personal unconscious. Mythology speaks to us in symbols, that is, in terms or pictures that may be familiar to us in everyday life and which nevertheless possess, in the mythological context, specific connotations in addition to conventional and obvious meanings.

A mythological symbol implies something hidden, unknown, difficult to describe in the temporal language. A mythological symbolism is more often beyond the reach of rational understanding, representing concepts that move our emotions in a rapture of psychological force. Our common use of symbolic language to describe the indescribable is evidence enough of humankind's unconscious tendency to create symbolic mythology.

The recorded mythology and literature of ancient Ireland has, very faithfully for the most part, preserved clear pictures of the Tuatha De Danann and their Mother Goddess Dana, so that, disregarding some Christian influence in the texts of certain manuscripts, much rationalization, and a good deal of poetical coloring and romantic imagination in the pictures, we can easily describe the People of Dana as they appeared in Pagan days, when they were more frequently seen by mortals, and from which we have the symbolic mythology.

Myth and fairy-tales can teach us many profound truths if we but. take the time to study the culture, people, time period, and esoteric traditions from which they originated. All religions birth from myth, and all esoteric traditions continue to be remembered through tales.

The mysticism, which is the backbone of the Faery tradition and the Celtic spirituality, is indeed part of the Irish heritage; for there was probably never a time when the Irish or Celt did not believe in the invisible Otherworld, or held the thought of not being able to travel there to discover the deep mystery of life. The Irish have kept this belief alive, even through the encroachment of new religions and the possibility of meeting death by holding the ancient views.

The Tuatha De Danaan survived through the folk-voice of the *fili*, Bardic poets, who were collectively known as *"aes Dana,"* servants of the Goddess Dana. The fili were experts in native learning (e.g., legal tradition, history, genealogy, and the science of natural phenomena, which are aspects woven into the tradition's divine myths).

Although the Tuatha De Danaan were denigrated by Iron Age warrior patriarchy, Christianity, and modern materialism, these Ancient Ones and the collective wisdom of the fili remain with us today, symbolizing through myth an endangered vital relationship— the cohesion of "culture-in-nature," and the sense of a sacred whole.

For the modern practitioner of Faery Wicca, the literate and oral traditions have remained almost as one. The Irish scholar, Patrick MacCana, speaks of the ancient Irish mind as having a "preference for the oral mode, both in their teaching and in their composition. Consequently," he tells us, "the Irish oral tradition embraced the literature of greatest social prestige as well as the common lore of the mass of the people. Thus Irish literary tradition is ideally the manifold oral tradition, which in a sense had no beginning—and has hardly yet ended...."[2]

In this tradition, the habitual gesture of mythic comprehensiveness—whether of a political nature or simply the art of compromise of a much-invaded people, living in an ancient land—the Ancient Ones did survive, albeit interbred with later gods, historical characters, and monotheistic saints.

Keeping this culture-in-nature connection in mind, a major theme connected to the goddesses of Ireland is an association to a particular body of water—usually a river, but at times a spring, a lake, holy well, or the ocean. Linking their goddesses with various bodies of water in turn appears to have linked the Celtic reverence for the Goddess as the Great Mare, for the white breakers of the ocean were described in Irish legend as the "white mane of the Morrigan's head."

If we ponder how the sea and horse draw a parallel in the Celts' mind, we may see a connection in the double use of the word *mare*. It means "sea" in Latin and Russian, and is the root of the English word *marine*. At the same time, it was used to designate a female horse. Both meanings of mare may have been derived from the same initial Indo-European source word, possibly the Sanskrit *mah*, meaning "mighty." This word may also be the foundation of the Goddess names: Morrigan and Morgen—the roots *gan, gin,* and *gen* meaning "birth," as in genesis and begin.

This interesting connection between the two words may suggest that the origin of the pantheon was not in Ireland itself, but came from across the sea, and that the symbol of the first God—Dana—may very well have been that of a horse.

An aspect of the Irish goddesses worth noting is their wonderful and magickal ability to shape-change, not only as animals, but alternating between an ugly hag-state and that of a beautiful, alluring woman. Dana, mother of all the gods, was noted to take different human-like forms known as Ainé and Brigid, as well as the shape of a horse. Several other goddesses were connected to the form of the horse, such as the Morrigan, Macha, and Cailleach Bera.

The Morrigan also became an eel, a wolf (as did Turrean), a heifer, a raven, and several diverse images of mortal women. The raven or Royston crow was the shape Neman, Macha, and Badb also took, each a triple aspect of the Morrigu.

Banbha, one of the three queens of the Tuatha De Danaan, and one of the three daughters of Dagda mor, who asked the Milesian bard, Amergin, to call Ireland after her, derives her name from the sow or piglet. Dechtire, mother of Cu Chulainn, was a swan, as was Ainé, Caer, Derbforgaille, and Finola.

Garbh Ogh alternated between a giant-state and becoming the winter storms. The Cailleach Bera was also known to become the winter storms, as were several other goddesses. Liban was the most famous mermaid, while Libanie (perhaps a derivative of) was a mermaid of a lake, and Logia a mermaid of a river.

Aige turned herself into a fawn, while Badbh was changed into a deer. Airmed became the herbs, and Druantia was a fir tree. The Ban Naomha was a fish. Bo Find was the white cow, as was Buana, as was Dil. Corra was a stork, while Muanna was the crane, and both Estiu and Uairebhuidhe could become birds. The great serpent of Ireland that St. Patrick supposedly chased away was the Goddess Caoranach.

In addition to these powers, there is the martial prowess of Irish goddesses, who often acted as ambassadors in battles and rivalries between the Celtic tribes, sitting in on peace councils when disputes were discussed.

Unlike the goddesses, many of the Irish gods did not shapeshift. Among those known to shapeshift were Cu Chulainn, who was known to become a hound, an eel, a wolf, and a bird. Lugh was connected to the raven, Midhir to cranes, and Oengus to a swan. Cernunnos, or Hearne, was a fox, a badger, a wolf, a wild boar, a stag. Moccos became a pig. Mullo was connected to the ass. Amergin, though a Milesian Bard, is perhaps noted as the greatest shapeshifter of all, for he not only shapeshifted into every shape, but was also a time traveler.

Irish gods were connected to trees and inanimate objects, many of which were powerful weapons and magickal tools. Lugh had a bloodthirsty spear that never missed its mark, and the Dagda mor, the primary father God, had a cauldron of abundance and was acknowledged as an oak and a living harp, which when strummed created the seasons.

Manannan mac Lir, who had a cloak of invisibility, was invisible one minute, in human shape the next, and shifted into a boat the next. Leucetios could become thunder. Mac Cecht could become a plough and the element earth. Mac Cuill could become the element water. Mac Greine could become the element fire.

Most importantly, these heroes of the Tuatha De Danann make up a warrior aristocracy, the major emphasis of what might be solar gods. This thought is attached to Newgrange, the great megalithic mound that overlooks the River Boyne, believed to have been built by a thriving agricultural community around 3000 B.C.E. Newgrange is often described as a passage grave. The whole structure covers an acre of ground, is estimated to contain about two-hundred thousand tons of stone, and was made without metal tools or the use of mortar.

Over the entrance is a stone-framed slit that is called the Roof Box. On the morning of the winter solstice, the rising sun throws a pencil of light the whole length of the passage and chamber to illuminate the central of the three recesses for approximately seventeen minutes.[3] This same effect is seen, though less strongly, from three mornings before the solstice to three mornings after. This structure lends strong consideration to the credence that the Irish gods may have been annually worshipped.

Solar gods are often referred to as war gods. War gods are ambiguous; sometimes they represent the hope of victory, sometimes pure destructiveness. To the Celt they represented both, to be invoked or propitiated accordingly.

A lesser-known aspect of the Celtic God is that of the Horned God, a fertility God. The Celtic God as a fertility god is rare. However, the Horned God's existence cannot be doubted, although no certain origin of name can be placed for him. He is portrayed in many Celtic artifacts, such as on the medieval market cross in the center of Kells, County Meath, and on a stone in the churchyard on Tara Hill. He is usually portrayed with horns and accompanied by animals. He either wears, or has looped on his horns, the torc (a circular necklace) of Celtic nobility (although the Horned God of animals, nature, and fecundity was primarily a God of the ordinary people). He is known by the names Cernunnos or Hearne.

Most of the gods are connected to a wife in their myth. This careful detail to polarity defines the Celtic view that man required woman to exist, recognizing his need for procreation and thus emphasizing that the masculine and feminine principles were not mutually exclusive; each contained the seed of the other; each required the expression of the polarity, otherwise they could not relate to each other.

The Ancient Ones of the Irish pantheon do exist; they ensoul the archetypes presented above. The aim of communicating, or making contact with an archetype through the act of meditation or invocation in the traditional esoteric way, is not to become the archetype, not even to identify with the archetype in a personal way. Such an overlapping of one reality with the next, such a superimposition, contains the danger of possible delusion.

True contact with an Ancient One is always accompanied by a disturbing echo of undeniable deep personal insight; it often indicates areas of weakness that require inner attention and development of re-balance. In this role alone, work such as mediation of advanced forms of consciousness or god- and goddess-forms is of immense value to us, though its resulting personal insight is only one of many side-effects and not a major aim.

The true aim is to surrender ourselves to the mystery of communion with the Ancient Ones, to allow the tuning to take place; thus allowing our own special creative flow to be unleashed into the earth's plane, into our lives, to enliven us and help us achieve a more perfect sense of balance.

The Celtic Division of the Year

The Irish tradition focuses on the balance of polarities. To everything there is a negative and a positive side. This fundamental duality can be expressed through the night and the day being the times of darkness and light.

The day (light) belongs to the physical world, the world made manifest. The night (dark) belongs to the Otherworld and those realms that cannot be seen in the stark light of day. The two most important times of the twenty-four hour cycle are the times of twilight and dawn. Dawn, or first light, is thought of as dispelling the darkness, and so is considered the "banisher of spirits to their abodes."

The other most important time of the twenty-four hour cycle is twilight, or two-lights. Twilight moves nearer the other realm, and so is considered the "invoker of spirits from their abodes."

The division of day and night, light and dark, is also applied to the Celtic year, which is divided in two parts: winter and summer. Winter is the season of night, dark, and cold; while summer, maintaining the alternation of opposites, is the season of day, light, and warmth.

In the Celtic year, the beginning of the new cycle or Wheel of the Year is celebrated on the eve of winter at Samhain (SOW-an), November 1, being the calend of winter. The second half of the year is summer, which begins on the eve of La Baal Tinne, May 1, being the calend of summer.

The four seasons each have a place in the division of the year. Winter and spring belong on the first half, which is the dark side of the year, known as the Time of the Little Sun, while summer and autumn belong on the second half, which is the light side of the year, known as the Time of the Big Sun.

The Time of the Little Sun, winter, contains the months of November through the end of April. Winter is the realm of the spirits and Faery. This is the negative polarity (not in the sense of good or evil). The doorway into night, twilight, is handled with extreme care, becoming the time at which we begin our ceremonies and perform our magickal enchantments.

Twilight, as the "invoker of the spirits from their abode," provides the necessary energy that aids us in our journeys to the Otherworld, as well as in dreamwork, contacting Faery allies, and all acts of magickal visioning. Dawn is then used to birth the information received during such journey, dreams, ally contact, and magickal visioning into our conscious mind.

The Little Sun refers to the moon, the natural light that shines brightest in the dark of night. Thus, the moonlight becomes a primary source of inspiration. In Faery Wicca, moon rituals are always important during the Time of the Little Sun.

During the winter half of the year, only the Ancient Ones who are connected to the seasons of winter and spring, the night, the moon, and the underworld are invoked (See Table One on page 110).

The second half of the year, the Time of the Big Sun, is comprised of the months May through the end of October. Summer is the positive time, when those things that are shown by the dark seem not to exist because of the abundant light. Sun rituals become more important during the Time of the Big Sun, and often we work our magickal enchantments at the time of dawn, opening to receive the full strength of the energy made naturally available to us via the sunlight. Our magick focuses on activity, planting of seed-goals, nurturing growth and transformation, harvesting, celebrating the bounty of our efforts, and giving thanks.

During the summer half of the year, we invoke only the Ancient Ones who are connected to the seasons of summer and autumn, the day, the sun, and the Heavenly Realm (See Table Two on page 111).

The Four Great Festivals

There are four major Sabbats with which we celebrate the Faery-Faith. These Four Great Festivals hold specific importance as based on the mythology of the tradition.

Two Great Festivals are held during the Time of the Little Sun: the Feast of Samfuim and Imbolc. The Feast of Sam-fuim (Samhain) occurs on October 31, the eve of winter. This is the time when the Big Sun dies to the Little Sun and the powers of darkness exercise great influence over all things. Because we are entering into the domain of spirits and the Fay,[4] it is a time of vulnerability, for we are standing at the boundary between two halves of the Celtic year. This boundary is considered as outside, or suspended from time, when the normal laws of the world are held temporarily in abeyance. With the barriers between the real world (as we believe it to be) and the supernatural dissolved, and with the Otherworld spirits and Faery moving freely from the sid to the land of the living, mortals can also penetrate the underworld quite easily.

In a traditional sense, Samhain marks a time of immense spiritual energy, when the Ancient Ones have to be accorded special rituals to appease them. The Cailleach is honored, for she is reborn each winter, and Cu Chullain is called upon to bring his spear of protection against all evil spirits that roam the winter nights.

Imbolc is the beginning of spring, dividing the Time of the Little Sun in half.[5] Traditionally celebrated on the evening of February 1,

Table One: The Ancient Ones of the Time of the Little Sun

(The following deities are often invoked at different times between November and the end of April.)

Goddesses:

Aoibhinn	Underworld
Bean Si	death
Biddy Mannion	death/rebirth
Black Annis	Underworld hag
Blathnat	Underworld
Boand	moon
Bronach	Underworld hag
Caer	shapechanger
Carravogue	winter
Cebhfhionn	wisdom
Echtghe Aughty	earth
Fand	Underworld
Flaithius	Underworld guide
Fodhla	earth
Gentle Annis	weather
Gyre-Carling	weaver
Moingfhion	winter
Morrigu	Triple Goddess
Muireartach	Underworld/stormy seas
Onaugh	queen of Faery

Gods:

Camulos	earth
Cernunnos	Underworld guardian
Dagda	earth
Donn	Lord of the Dead
the Holy King	waning year
Leucetios	god of weather magick
Lir	Underworld guardian
Mac Cecht	earth
Manannan mac Lir	king of Emhain/Underworld
Midir	king of Underworld
Nemed	moon god
Oberon	Underworld fairy king
Oisin	poet of Tir na nog
Tethra	king of Locklann/Underworld

Table Two: The Ancient Ones of the Time of the Big Sun

(The following list of deities are often invoked at different times between May and the end of October.)

Goddesses:

Adsullata	sun
Aeife	reflection
Ainé	the Bright Faery
Airmed	healer
Andarta	victory
Anu	fertility
Becuna Cneisgel	fertility
Bo Find	fertility
Canola	music
Cebhfhionn	inspiration
Eadon	poetry/inspiration
Finncaev	fair love
Gillagriene	daughter of the sun
Grain	sun
Iseult	fire
Liban	healing/pleasure

Gods:

Nuada	air
Oengus	love and beauty
Oghma	learning/writing
Credne	fire/smith
Diancecht	healer
Essus	agriculture
Gavida	fire
Goibniu	fire/smith
Herne	fertility
Mac Cuill	water
Mac Greine	son of the sun
Moccos	identified with Mercury
Mullo	identified with Mars
the Oak King	waxing year

today Imbolc is celebrated on February 2—the day that has also become known as the day of initiation for modern witches. The emphasis of this Great Festival is the marking of the ending of the time of darkness and the return of the light. With this holy day, the Triple Goddess Brigid is acknowledged as the Fiery Arrow of Inspiration, coming forth from the universe to remind us that the time of darkness is waning and soon we will move back into the Time of the Big Sun and full activity.

Two Great Festivals are held during the Time of the Big Sun: La Baal Tinne and Lughnasadh. La Baal Tinne is perhaps the most memorable and auspicious of the Four Great Festivals, for it is the holy day marking the arrival of the Tuatha De Danann on the shores of Erin. On the eve of May 1, the celebrations of Beltane begin and carry on until May Day, when it is believed that the Faery are at their jolliest and in the best of humors. Since this is the celebration of the "Bright Fire," Grainne and Lugh, both solar deities, are invoked.

When autumn begins on the eve of August 1, the Great Festival of Lughnasadh is celebrated in honor of the God Lugh, who put an end to the long war between the Fomorians and the Tuatha De Danann. We honor Lugh with games of skill, for he was a stealthy warrior.

On this day, Tailltiu, the Harvest Goddess, and step mother of Lugh, is also honored. Lammas towers are built out of corn stalks in honor of the Earth Mother who ensures the continuation of life through the rebirthing of the corn, as well as the future incarnations of the De Danann.

The Ancient Practice of Invoking the Ancient Ones

When the ancients invoked a particular Goddess, she was usually approached at her seasonal time through her symbolic animal form, rather than a human image. Votive offerings were taken to the body of water (usually her well) and left behind after the performing of a *pishogue* (ritual incantation), one that usually incorporated the swearing-in of the elements, such as:

> *I will keep faith*
> *until the sky falls upon me and crushes me,*
> *until the earth opens and swallows me,*
> *until the seas arise and overwhelm me!*

The custom of leaving a votive offering was an essential part of paying homage to the patron's holy well. This has certainly been the practice for hundreds of years in Ireland. Ordinarily, things left as votive offerings are simple personal possessions. As well as pieces of clothing, they include coins, buttons, brooches and other trinkets, pipes, hair pins, and many other types of pins, nails, screws, and fishhooks.

The most permanent votive offerings are the heaps of small stones—white stones or other specially colored ones—that are considered holy or endowed with some other supernatural power. Some of the stones have holes in them; these are often credited with strange powers and have an air of mystery about them. Since nobody has ever explained how the holes are made, they are believed to be Faery stones. Each stone in the heap, and some heaps are very large, has been added by a seeker as a gift to the Goddess who is in charge of the holy place, and while most other votive offerings gradually disappear, the stones remain as a permanent memorial to the piety of the seeker, and as a permanent reminder to the Goddess of the seeker's request.

This custom is more common along the west coast of Ireland. In some cases the stones are put in the well. The cult of the stones was so prominent in Ireland that even today one can find many "holy" stones still standing, as well as hear the natives discussing the myriad uses of stones; e.g., healing stones, stones that return home, floating stones, swearing stones, *bullauns* or basin stones in which water is always found, cursing stones, and God-stones.

However, the most usual objects left as votive offerings are small pieces of cloth that are hung on the holy tree near the well. Nowadays, the cloths may be any color, but the oldest remnants are recorded as being red.

As already discussed, many Irish gods are connected to trees, specifically the oak, symbolizing strength and longevity; its acorn is expressively phallic; its roots are said to extend as far below ground as its branches do into the air, thus showing that such a God had dominion over heaven, earth, and the underworld. The oak was central to Celtic religious symbology; it was the tree of the Dagda mor, the supreme Irish father God, but most importantly, it was also the Irish Tree of Trees upon which was found the entry points into the Land of Faery where the Ancient Ones resided. The wood of the ritual midsummer fire was always oak, as was the yule log.

Praying at special trees and walking around them is part of the pishogue ritual at many Irish holy wells. Sacred and special trees have always been important in the social and religious life of the Irish, and in our oldest records there are references to these special trees. Venerated trees were never to be cut down or harmed in any way, the result of which a tragedy would always befall the harmer. Considered possibly the oldest form of religion in Ireland, tree worship was connected to immortality and the Celtic Doctrine of Rebirth, through which the practitioner, with the aid of the God, could perform many miracles.

The Irish Tree of Trees and the Land of Faery

Faery-Faith practitioners travel up and down the Tree of Trees, the mythic synthesizing vegetable, which brings the world of the Ancient Ones and humanity together. The Irish Tree of Trees is believed located in Lough Gur in the province of Munster.

The Lough Gur tree stands for a divinely renewable prosperity. In Irish mythology it is connected to the *Cloch a bhile*, "The Stone of the Tree," which stands two meters high, gray, runnelled, and lichened on the west shore of the Lough as a sacred outpost to the magick tree, which was revealed beneath the Lough at seven-year intervals. The stone is a permanent reminder of the ideal World Tree, for lack of which—it is believed—all the forests of the world fall into danger. In myth, the divine tree has the power to en-green the entire earth.

This myth asks us to remember the sacred tree, the cosmological axis, and living force in the land. Because of this, believers of the Faith have a close relationship with nature; for we recognize the oneness and interconnectedness between all aspects of the creation. Just like women, children, and men, nature is a living, intelligent being, worthy of respect. Through our personal and mystical relationship with the land and the forces of nature, we know that it has its own personality, spirit, and yes, human characteristics. This knowledge becomes part of our magick, because we see, within nature and the life it nurtures, reflections of important truths about the human soul.

We come to know that the spirits of the Ancient Ones keep hidden within the shroud of nature, communing with the animals, plants, and elements, skirting the edges of the human's normal (or should I say, "average") field of sensory perception.

The Ancient Ones are non-human, supernatural beings, a part of nature, and to the Irish and Celts' minds, could be found by visiting a natural wildlife area. In ancient times it was not uncommon to find sacred woodlands running with dark springs, and grim-faced figures of gods "uncouthly hewn by the ax from the untrimmed tree-trunk, rotted to whiteness," as the Roman historian, Lucan, once described.[6]

Ascribing such tree trunks with faces was the seekers attempt to draw the hidden spirit out of nature, to commune with the power contained therein; thus, obtaining knowledge to be used for their own use or for those who asked for assistance, as well as for the larger community.

With such an understanding in mind, Faery believers regard the oak tree as the center, the doorway between the worlds. Therefore, the Irish word for oak, *duir*, is also the word for "door," and as already discussed above, the Irish Tree of Trees, the Lough Gur Tree, was oak.

Traditionally, the Lough Gur Tree is envisaged in poetic form (the language of the Ancient Ones), allowing us back into the primordial forest where the Tree of Life is synonymous with the Tree of Knowledge.

In myth, the magic tree is covered with a *Brat Uaine*, a green cloth or cloak. Often this cloak becomes the desired possession of many. Beneath the tree sits an old woman, watching, knitting under the cloak. When an attempt is made to steal the cloak she cries out:

> *Chughat, chughat, a bhuaine bhalbh!*
> *Marcach o' Thir na mBan Marbh*
> *A 'fuadach an bhruit uaine dhom bhathas.*
>
> *Awake, awake, thou silent tide!*
> *From the Mortal Women's Land a horseman rides,*
> *From my head the green cloth snatching.*

At these words, the waters rise and fiercely pursue the thief, and as the thief gains the edge of the lake, one-half of the steed (upon which the thief usually rides) is swept away, and with it the Brat Uaine, which the thief is drawing after him. Had the green cloak been taken by the thief, the enchantment of nature would be ended forever.[7]

The Otherworld Goddess, represented by the old woman, calls on the waters to return to protect her tree from a greedy human. Although she allows each thief to touch the green cloak, she must not allow him to remove Ireland's green mantle. *For to plunder Ireland of her green mantle would mean the final separation between the world of humans and that of the Otherworld—the world of the Ancient Ones.* The repetition of this myth, generation after generation, is a reminder that each generation needs to hear and to understand the message.

The physical world, or the realm of humans, in Faery Wicca is referred to as being the "Mortal Women's Land," reminding humankind that life is birthed from the womb of woman, thus generating a natural link to the reverence of feminine standard.

Michael Dames, in his study on Ireland, writes that "Throughout the world…[pre-historic] art is centered on the birth act, and serves to link human and divine parturition with sympathetic topographical events, such as the emergence of streams from caves, and of islands from lakes."[8]

In Faery Wicca, the features of the landscape are considered to be alive, and certain locations take on a supernatural intensity. Such locations become a revelation of the chief deity of the province. The trunk of the Irish Tree of Trees is known as Ainé, who is a later form of Dana, the Great Mother Goddess of all the gods; thus, Ainé, rising from the waters of parturition gives access to a hidden realm, an Otherworld realm, traditionally known as Tir na nog, which is accessible to the living and considered the esoteric Land of Women.

At Lough Gur entrance into both the Mortal Women's Land and the Otherworld Land of Women merge to make a primary world, from which earth is considered a derivative, and it is Tir na nog where:

> *A woman abides in this noble house*
> *Above all the women of Erin,*
> *With hair of gold she welcomes us*
> *In her accomplished beauty.*[9]

Ainé, as the old woman, watches and knits beneath the green cloak, and the "green cloth from my head" symbolically ranges from a head scarf to the leafy canopy of the tree under which she sits, to the green mantle of Ireland under which her realm exists, to the earth in her entirety. Deity radiates from local to the universe, and adds Dames, "This ambiguous scale is a feature of the task that all deities take on, in proposing microcosm and macrocosm as interchangeable terms."[10]

The Land of Faery is the dimension where the Ancient Ones dwell, which is comprised of the Otherworlds, plains, or realms of existence located on the Tree of Tree. Climbing the branches, spiraling up into what is called the Heavenly Realm, we move into sacred space and sacred time, where the planets orbit within, the stars are clustered, moon and sun shed their light, signaling night and day, winter, spring, summer, and autumn. In the deepest space of the branches dwells the origin of Spirit before its dissension into the physical plain.

It is from the Heavenly Realm that the origin of the universe as we know it was birthed. We work with the Heavenly Realm to learn about Spirit-light and dissension, as well as astral travel, connecting with the light source, universal energy, the concept of Father-Sky, and super-consciousness. Within this realm are found the Over-lords—the Archangels, the Christian God, the galactic brotherhood, and the beings from neighboring universes.

Many plains exist within the Heavenly Realm, such as:

Magh Ildathach—The Many Colored Plain
Magh Mor—The Great Plain
Magh Ciuin—The Gentle Plain
Sen Magh—The Old Plain

Traditionally, these are the plains from where the Tuatha De Danann dwelled before descending to earth. Sen Magh was the plain from where Dana gave birth to the Ancient Ones.

As we dwell in the trunk of the Tree of Trees, we spiral out into the Plains. The Otherworld of the Plains stretches in all directions and most prominently in the cardinal directions; thus, we must become deeply attuned to the land and oriented to the directions, of the natural world. Such orientation creates harmony and within this harmony, we work with the holism, bridging the split between body/mind/spirit, connecting the division between humans, animals, and vegetation, and keeping the worlds from further widening.

When one begins to work with the directions and the elements, they begin to align with the idea of the land as being sacred. These esoteric teachings revolve around reducing our separation from, and antagonism toward, the planet through cathartic meditative or visualization experiences. In doing so we make contact with our inner power.

Inner power allows us to begin undergoing personal transformation within our minds, emotions, and hearts. This involves bringing the outer and inner realities together. We begin to see ourselves as an extension of the land, other life-forms, and other humans. We also see the land, other life-forms, and other humans as extensions of self.

Within the Plains exists the waking world, in which humans dwell, and the beginning point of every witch and magician's training. The Plains is the level of the Otherworld that embraces the earth within its scheme. It is in this realm that the Tuatha De Danann dwelled at one time alongside humans. In fact, it is not uncommon to find myths from around the world telling us of the gods coming to earth and living with mortals.

In Faery Wicca, we work with the Plains to learn about physical activation, elemental compatibility, cycles, ego development, mind/body connection, functioning in physicality, the concept of Mother-Earth, and wakeful consciousness.

The earthly realm of the Land of Faery is known as Erin or Ireland, and her heart center, once called Cathair Crofthind, but today known as Tara, was the stronghold, the psychical center, of the Ancient Ones' power.

The compilation of opening self to the cosmic energies falling down from the Heavenly Realm into the Plains, and surrendering to the downward flow of Spirit, can help to gently ease one toward the underworld, the realm where the Ancient Ones now dwell.

The final direction we spiral in on the Tree of Trees is downward, down the roots, to the very tips of them and into the realm of the underworld, the primal land, the place where the true encounters with the Ancient Ones today take place.

In this realm, under the waves and in the hollow hills, resides the Horned God and the Great Earth Mother, the living fire, the beasts, the seven streams of wisdom, and the stars within the earth.

Most importantly, within the underworld resides the true Land of Faery, where the ancient teachings of the Ancestors are found, as well as the primal land and beings that make up the foundation of the tradition's beliefs.

The underworld teaches the release of ego, the rich darkness of creation, dissension into the world-soul, connecting to death without fear, initiation, hearth-source, and delving into the subconscious. At its deepest levels, the underworld leads us to a realization of universal consciousness within—not merely within our minds, but within this planet.

A number of lands exist within the underworld, such as:

Tir na nOg—Land of Youth
Tir na mBan—Land of Women
Tir Tairngiri—Land of Promise

Like the other two levels, the underworld exists according to its own laws, which are opposite to our own. Unlike our law of cause and effect, the underworld has no such law. Perhaps this is because of the difference in the time cycle. Theirs seems to be a realm that resonates beyond such cycles of energy as we know it. We are bound to the cycles of the moon, sun, and stars (although less powerfully than the former two). Since the Land of Faery does not contain, nor is lit by, the sun or moon, but by an inherent light within the primal land itself, the Ancient Ones and all in-dwelling beings are not governed by our time cycle.

Everything in the Otherworld is intensified, amplified, sometimes painfully or ecstatically real. The three-tiered universe of the Faery-Faith is not a fantasy land, not a child's imagination, but the primal land within, both within our consciousness and within our planet. We do not just imagine this realm, for it has a true nature and firm identity of its own, existing even if one never thinks of it. It is so real that once visited, one returns truly changed.

How the Celtic Tradition Lives in the Magick of Today

In the ancient Faery Tradition, magickal techniques were embodied in sagas or mythic cycles, in which poetry, song, music, dance, and ritual drama were employed to create visions that were shared by performers and audience alike. Such tales were attuned to the deepest levels of collective consciousness.

Today, in the specialized training of Faith practitioners, magickal techniques are employed with collective symbolism and esoteric images that were in ancient times reserved for only those persons who sought enlightenment beyond collective religion or superstition. We strive to journey into the Otherworld, especially the underworld, with the intent of making contact with the primal land, the Ancient Ones, the Ancestors, and other allies known as guardians, guides, companions, and helpers. This is done through the development of an inner discipline, or fundamental art.

In Faery magick, the technique of magickal visualization is used to consciously align ourselves with the natural harmony of the universe. We believe that what we create in our mind by imagination will polarize or organize loose energy in the universe, causing our heart's desire to eventually be manifested in objective reality. We know that we can visualize and attain goals on any level—material, emotional, spiritual, mental. Through visualization, we can channel the energy of the universe as it flows from one person to the next, enriching our lives.

The physical universe is energy. Everything is some form of energy. Thoughts are a light, an easily changed form of energy, while matter is a dense, less changeable form. This idea is borne out somewhat by modern physics, which is discovering that everything can indeed be considered some form of energy.

The Faery witch and the magician alike believe in the invisible realm and the unified powers, and seek to move into the alternate reality to which such a realm is connected. In our tradition, the invisible realm has been described countless times in the myths that today are known as fairy tales.

Fairy tales are rich with mortals encountering troupes of Faery, being abducted into the Land of Faery, where wild adventures await them, and where they might possibly be given a gift from a Faery Queen or King, or where they might find a lost treasure. Returning back to this world, the traveler always finds that time has passed, although they seem to have traveled in the Otherworld but a few minutes. The traveler always comes back with their life changed forever;

the traveler always comes back in an ecstatic state, desiring to return to the Otherworld and Ancient Ones left behind.

Magickal Technique:
The Inner Discipline of Magickal Visualization

We will explore the formulas and theories behind creating your own magickal visualization through which to contact an Ancient One. To begin practicing magickal visualization there are certain key elements to take into consideration regarding the structure of creating visualizations. Unlike meditation, visualization is a formulated structure, a story that guides the sojourner into a specific destination.

There are three types of visualization formulas important to understand; for each has a specific function in our magick.

Receiving Visualization

This form is closely connected to meditation, and is the technique of listening to your unconscious. In its purest form, you close your eyes, relax, and wait to see what comes into your mind. You might set a minimal scene first, or ask a question and wait for the answer. This kind of visualization is excellent for exploring resistance to change, uncovering true feelings when ambivalent, unearthing personal images or symbols of change, or for clarifying what you really want to do when faced with several confusing alternatives. The information that comes up during receiving visualization is sometimes vague, like dream images. It often requires some interpretation before the meaning becomes clear.

Receiving visualizations requires that you suspend judgment, take what you get, and trust yourself. Since visualization is a right-brain activity, meaning non-rational, non-linear, intuitive, you can expect the unexpected. As you try to uncover your deepest feelings about yourself, even though your intent is serious, you might get non-sensical images, such as a cartoon. Remaining non-judgmental allows you to "check" your rational, logical, left-brain self at the door, so that it will not cloud the experience with doubts and intellectual interpretations that can throw you off the track. By doing so, you allow your intuition to flow, bringing forward primitive images.

Intuition will push us toward areas that seem foreign. Yet, everything received in a visualization comes from some part of self. It's all genuine, all self. Trusting these images allows us to begin trusting self (intuition). The mind is connected intimately with the body, as well as our own personal history. Trusting self will allow our mind/body to speak to us.

Finally, creating an inner landscape is important for performing receiving visualizations for two reasons. The first is that it becomes our personal secret place where only we go. When we are there, we know that there will be no intruders, that it is created by self, for self, and that it is within our mind/body. Second, the inner landscape becomes a mental place of focus, one that will allow us to relax deeper into intuition.

Spellcraft Visualization

This is the technique of talking to your unconscious by creating what you want to see and hear and feel in great detail and manipulating it according to a predetermined script, while you stay in conscious control. Spellcraft visualization is used for creating a future goal or creating a physical manifestation, and is performed in addition to spells and affirmation. Affirmations function as reminders of our intentions. They have three elements—Desire: you must truly want the change or object; Belief: you must believe that the change, or obtaining the object, is possible; and, Acceptance: you must be willing to have the change take place, or do whatever is necessary to obtain the object.

These three elements add up to the intention of the affirmation or spell. Intention also means you are willing to take responsibility for whatever you create through the change, or in obtaining the object.

Visualization—no matter what form—is magick in the truest and highest meaning of the word. It involves understanding aligning yourself with the natural principles that govern the workings of the universe and learning to use these principles in the most conscious and creative way. Like affirmations, there are basic steps for effective visualization.

1. Set your goal. Decide on something you would like to have, work toward, realize, or create (e.g., job, house, relationship, change in self, increased prosperity, happier state of mind, improved health, beauty, deeper connection with Deity, etc.).

2. Create a clear idea or picture or situation exactly as you want it. Think of it in the present tense as already existing the way you want it to be. Picture yourself with the situation as you desire it now. Include as many details as you can. (You can make an actual physical picture of it as well if this will help you visualize it better.)

3. Focus on it often. Bring your idea or mental picture to mind often, both in quiet meditation periods, and also casually throughout the day when you happen to think of it. In doing so, it will become integrated as part of your life, becoming more of a reality. You will begin to project it successfully.

4. Give it positive energy. As you focus on your goal, think about it in a positive, encouraging way. Make strong, positive present-tense affirmations. See yourself receiving or achieving it.

Magickal Visualization

This technique is a combination of receiving and spellcraft visualization, and the method most used in Faery magick concerning the Otherworld and spiritual deepening. In this structure, a scene is described in detail, with certain elements left out so the subconscious can fill them in. Most often, an ally is contacted, becoming our guide into the Otherworld.

In this method there are certain guidelines to follow, which are general to the more complex and powerful visualizations used in magickal training.

Guidelines For Creating Magickal Visualizations

1. It is very important that all symbolism be synchronous to a specific tradition in order to gain skill in its more powerful workings. Through the symbols, we attune to parallel levels in the Otherworld. For example, in Faery Wicca, we work with Celtic sacred symbols, ogham, Irish alphabets, and magickal numbers; for each has a great deal of wisdom and energy connected to it. By working with our tradition's symbology, we move deeper into the Mystery teachings connected to the Circles of Existence and the Three Worlds.

2. The visualization is not regarded as complete or authoritative. The person writing or guiding the visualization need not attempt to make it all-inclusive. The imagination must be allowed to explore the world in which it is being guided. Therefore, a rigid structure will not allow the imagination much freedom. Secondary symbolism can be included in "storytelling" by indicating there are several paths to choose from, even if only one path is utilized. Including closed doorways will hint at future areas to explore when returning to the same world. Providing a sense of

"choice" or option allows the subconscious to bring forth the unknown elements hidden in the Otherworld.

3. Powerful visualizations are often riddled with antagonistic forces and challenges. "Airy-fairy" experiences are nothing more than entertaining and do little to arouse the many aspects of the psyche and bring forth a new energetic pattern or transformative forces.

4. Opportunities are allowed for silent meditation. These specially placed and periodic spaces of silence allow the traveler to receive inward visions or connect with Otherworld beings that have the potential of becoming guides, allies, helpers, and companions, providing a host of other functions.

5. The foundation of all magickal visualizations is better served if it is based on a traditional tale, song, poem, or personal experience that originated from traditional imagery. Fiction, while fun to create, will do little to develop the magickal or spiritual tradition and deeper levels of attunement the witch and the magician are striving to obtain.

In traditional magickal visualizations it is expected that the mediator (guide or narrator) has traveled to the inner landscape numerous times and become familiar with the symbols and beings one might encounter therein. The inner landscapes and beings narrated about in the old tales, which are based on the travels of others who have gone before us, are very much alive, and when endeavoring to journey into them, there are three simple laws that you may want to remember.

The Otherworld Laws

1. Keep to the way that leads you to whatever you seek.
2. Never fear distractions and never follow them.
3. Respond to those who give you love, and respect those who act as guardians.

When following the first law, know that those who have gone before you have left their light in the stones and pathways that will lead you to whatever you seek.

Distractions will try to take you away from the mediator's direction, creating a sense of need to suddenly abandon the path of energy flow you are being guided down and follow your own. Distractions such as these hinder the traveler, and you are strongly warned against following them. The individual who always follows the distraction usually accomplishes little in their magickal workings and mundane living.

Difficulties may also be seen as distractions, if given into; however, when you do meet with difficulties, it is important to remember they come from within yourself and not from anywhere else. Be aware of them. Check to see why you hold resistance to the experience and expel the resistance through your next out breath.

The third law should be easy to understand. Move away from antagonistic or threatening beings. Never follow them if you are afraid of them. The guides who come to you will be loving, but not always gentle. They will exude an aura of concern for your safety and best interest. Gifting your guides and Otherworld beings is most important, for this simple act portrays your willingness to join in the exchange of inner and outer worlds and energy.

Respect is of the utmost importance and is to be shown to such beings. Do not back talk them, yell at them, or ignore them, lest you jeopardize the success of your journey, as well as future contact with them. The sidhe are quite sensitive and will close you out of their realm faster than saying *"Sha gadda galot!"*

Magickal visualizations have an operational process consisting of four stages that correspond to the four province/quarters of the Great Circle:

1. Opening of the Way—*Instructional East*
2. Magickal Travel—*Magickal South*
3. Mystical Contemplation—*Mystical West*
4. Active Giving Release—*Creating North*

Instructional East

Preceding the Otherworld journey, the narrator begins with instructional information that prepares each traveler mentally. The travelers are reminded that they have decided to take the trip and that they will be carried on by their own awareness and will; if difficulties arise, they are to check their resistance to the experience and release it; the three laws are recited; and the signal for return is given (e.g., a bell, whistle, drumbeat). It is important to note here that return from the Otherworld is unlike other forms of visualizations where the travelers retrace their steps. In magickal visualization, the traveler is able to gently return to their physical body the moment the signal is given. Finally, the travelers are instructed to breathe deeply and fully, relaxing into the rhythm by closing their eyes.

As the narration of the tale begins, it is the responsibility of the narrator to open the way for the travelers by taking them to the portal between the worlds and walking them through. Once they have stepped into the Otherworld, the travelers turn from the east to...

Magickal South

The moment the journey begins and the travelers have stepped into the Otherworld, there is a directional opposition that takes place: The inner action now begins to move in another direction (which shall be discussed below).

Mystical West

Within every magickal visualization, it is very important to have periodic pauses in the narration to allow integration, and a time of silence after the travelers are left alone when the guiding action of the narrator stops. From this point the travelers must continue on alone to contact the inner power and receive the information that will prepare them to make an outer dedication as they move toward the...

Creating North

The vision has provided each traveler with details that will most likely be shared in common by everyone, if in a group experience, without prior preparation or information. This is what is known as the occult secrecy, and is information that the group must agree to keep among themselves and not share with others until they too have experienced the inner power and received the vision details that indicate they have walked the *Secret Path*. After walking the Path, the return journey is quite automatic at the vision's conclusion. The traveler has culminated their dedication and when returning to the outer world locks the energies into the material world in specific ways to be manifested. This "locking" in is also enhanced by the narrator's ritual pattern of keywords when ending the journey after everyone has returned.

Let us return to the *Magickal South* and the inner action that moves the traveler in a reversal of direction. As soon as the narrator opens the way and puts everyone into the Otherworld, the inner landscape described is that of the North, in winter.

The journey moves through the holy elements from Earth to Water, and then inwards and downwards to the center, the beginning point, the breath of origination, where the elements originate in the heart of all Being.

From here the journey continues. The traveler emerges to the dawning light of the east, taking the breath of origination, the holy element of Air. They continue into the maximum light in the south, the holy element of Fire, where they become illuminated with the inner power.

At this point the traveler is left on their own by the narrator. The journey continues to the west, where the traveler is given the vision and receives details that are to be contemplated. Here their dedication is culminated and the fulfillment of the Great Circle is completed when the traveler moves to the north, bridging the gap between inner and outer consciousness. The traveler then gives the dedication to the Earth, which allows the traveler to emerge back into the east, back into the outer world; thus, the magickal working has moved inward and outward.

Such a map also connects the journey with the phases of the moon, starting at dark moon and moving to full moon. Interestingly enough, this is not a journey that moves us from darkness to light, but is the way of light to darkness. As we move into the darkness, we traverse the secret way to the Mother, which has been known to activate the light energy within each of us. This metaphysical cycle is a realization of the unity of the female and male powers within and without as one.

In magickal visualization, the principle that is found in all metaphysics is portrayed in the holy elements and related powers through the specific cycle of the four province/quarters around the Great Circle. This principle is also especially important for the practice of effective magick.

The folk tale or myth used for the magickal visualization will, of course, dictate the landscape you enter, as well as the features, Ancient Ones, and Otherworld allies you will encounter. Suggested myths to explore are:

The Quest of the Children of Tureen
Midir and Etain
The Fate of the Children of Lir
The Boyhood Deeds of Cu Chulainn
The Battle Raid of Cooley
The Story of Deirdre
The Pursuit of Diarmid and Grainne
Oisin in Tir na nog
Connla and the Faery Maiden
The Sea-Maiden

And, of course, all the magickal visualizations narrated in my books: *Faery Wicca, Book One* and *Book Two*, which are based on the Otherworld realms located on the Tree of Trees. May your *immrans* (journeys) be successful.

About the Author

Kisma K. Stepanich was born July 4, 1958, in Santa Ana, California. Of Irish and Romanian Gypsy descent, Kisma is a leading expert in the field of Faery Wicca, and a traditionally initiated Ollamh (High Priestess) of the Faery-Faith Tradition. She is the author of several best selling books, including *Sister Moon Lodge: The Power and Mystery of Menstruation, Faery Wicca, Book One: Magick & Theory, and Faery Wicca, Book Two: The Shamanic Practices of the Cunning Arts.* Kisma resides in Southern California where she teaches apprentices and celebrates the Faery-Faith with her covens.

Endnotes

1. I use the spelling *Faery* when referring to the Tuatha De Danann, and *fairy* for the literary fairy.
2. Patrick MacCana, *The Irish Mind*, 35.
3. This event is so highly valued that the tourist center is booked until 1999.
4. Another term for the Faery.
5. Another traditional name for this festival was Oimelc, or the First Milk of the Lamb. After Ireland was Christianized it became known as Bride's Day or St. Brigit's Day.
6. Stuart Piggot, *The Druids*, 80.
7. D. Fitzgerald, *Popular Tales of Ireland*, 1879.
8. Michale Dames, *Mythic Ireland*, 88.
9. Leagh's description of the palace in *Magh Mell*, trans. Elinore Hull, *The Poem Book of the Gael*, 151.
10. Dames, *Ibid.*, 78.

The three Norns: Urd, Verandi, and Skuld (Past, Present, and Future; painting by C. Ehrenberg).

The Incomplete Mythological Pantheons of the Golden Dawn

Pat Zalewski

In the series of tabulations that Crowley published as 777, we will find that for the main part these were a portion of a Golden Dawn manuscript called the "Book of General Correspondences." There were two pantheons that the Golden Dawn worked on that have not yet seen the light of day. The first is the Irish-Celtic pantheon of gods and all related epics of Irish mythology. This was explored by Mathers and Yeats. According to Ithel Colquhoun in her book Sword of Wisdom, a full or partial manuscript of the Mather/Yeats collaboration does exist, though it has not yet been published.

Some years ago, wanting to appease my Irish lineage[1] (through my maternal grandfather), I embarked upon my own research of Celtic mythology as applied to the Tree of Life and the tarot, with the results now being published for the first time in *The Golden Dawn Journal*. I used Charles Squire's *Celtic Myth and Legend*[2] as the main reference text in this portion of the work, and it has been like an old friend who has introduced me to long lost ancestral myth. I would also recommend Peter Ellis's *Dictionary of Irish Mythology*, which works in very well with Squire's book.

Another area that the Golden Dawn referred to quite often (in their A. O. temples) was the Norse pantheon of mythology. An incomplete version of this pantheon appears in Column 33 of 777. This time I tried to appease the paternal Nordic side of the family[3] and worked it into a complete Kabbalistic Tree. For the main part of this study I used Donald Mackenzie's *Teutonic Myth and Legend*[4] and Crossley Holland's *The Norse Myths*. I would also refer readers to the works of Freya Aswynn and Kveldulf Gundarsson.

Unfortunately, both the Irish and Norse pantheons of mythology have not gained the spotlight they deserve in Western magic. Although some authors have recently made inroads into both systems, it is still a weak area overall as far as magical research and acceptance goes, especially in the United States, Australia, and New Zealand.

What I have tried to present here is a reference point for both these pantheons so that readers can do their own research. When I first discussed mythology associated with the Golden Dawn Tree of Life with my old mentor Jack Taylor some fifteen years ago, he told me to be flexible—to not take what is suggested as "gospel," and try to find my own way with the associations.[5] It is a suggestion that I would like to pass on to the reader, since very little in this world is hard and fast by way of associations, especially mythology. One of the things I have tried to avoid is the use of gods that overlap their domain. Unfortunately, this is very evident in some of the early Golden Dawn associations, with the same deity appearing in more than one path or Sephirah.

One of the first uses of magical pantheons is to form some type of archetypal imagery, but it takes time and effort to construct your personal viewpoint of a mythological godform. As a suggestion, try to draw the godforms for both the Irish and Norse pantheons, and create two sets of twenty-two tarot keys, using the Golden Dawn color scales as a guide. As your study increases in this area, slowly build additional cards to each of the decks until you reach a full complement of seventy-eight cards. These can be utilized for both meditational and divinatory workings. Above all, we must remember that magical godforms are there to be *used*. They will give back as much as they receive.

THE IRISH PANTHEON
AS APPLIED TO THE KABBALAH

The Sephiroth

Kether: *Nauda (of the Silver Hand)*

Nauda was said to be the son of Danu, and king of the Tuatha De Danann. In his fight against the Fir Bolgs, he forced them to a truce and a set of rules to fight by, which were more advantageous to his people who were outnumbered by their foes. He got them to fight against equal numbers only, and in individual battles to try and decide the outcome. The champion Sreng fought a single combat with Nauda and was defeated, though the king lost his hand. (This was replaced with one of silver, made by Diancecht the physician.)

Eventually, Nauda offered his enemy a fifth of all Ireland to live in—a peace offering they accepted.

Because Nauda had a blemish (the silver hand), tradition said that he could not be king. The Tuatha De Danann needed a king and asked for Bres, the son of the Fomoron king, to rule over them and offered Bridget (daughter of Dagda) as a bride. Bres told the Tuatha De Danann that he would abdicate if the people ever wanted him to leave. After a reign of tyranny under Bres, the people sought out Nauda to be returned as king, providing his blemish could be eliminated. Two physicians, who felt they were equal to the task, came forward and restored his original hand. Bres abdicated, but returned to his father and asked him to raise an army so that he could take the crown back by conquest. Nauda vacated the throne to Lugh, and he and his wife, Macha, were killed during the battle.

Chokmah: *Lugh*[6]

Lugh,[7] son of Cian and Ethnia (daughter of Balor), was brought up by Manannan Mac Lir, and was hidden from his grandfather, Balor of the Evil Eye, who tried to kill him as an infant, for it was foretold that Lugh would eventually kill his grandfather. Lugh was trained in all the arts by his foster parent. He favored the use of the rod-sling and the magic spear, which constantly thirsted for blood and could only be kept under control by the use of a draught of poppy leaves. The spear was released only at the time of battle, and it never stopped slaying the enemy. (Lugh also possessed a magic hound.)

When the time came to leave his foster parent, Lugh dressed like a king and came to the celebration of Nauda's return to the throne at Tar, which only master craftsmen could attend. Lugh then listed his crafts as a carpenter, smith, warrior, harpist, poet, bard, sorcerer, physician, cup bearer, bronze worker, and chess player. As an example of his powers, Lugh tested his strength against Ogma, the champion, and easily bested him. He then started to show the king all of his talents. Nauda thought to exploit Lugh by helping his kingdom in a war with the Fomors. Nauda decided that Lugh should sit in the "Sage's seat," which was kept for the wisest man, since Lugh had outwitted everyone present. He then gave Lugh his throne for thirteen days while Nauda took the seat beside him.

Lugh summoned all the Tuatha De Danann to a council of war. He started his war on the hill of Balor where he destroyed most of the Fomoron tax gatherers. Nothing could stop him. It was here that his father was killed by Brian and his two brothers. In revenge, Lugh sent them on impossible tasks to the ends of the earth as a means of repayment. When they returned, bringing with them the impossible gifts, Lugh sent them to self-destruction.

During the battle with the Fomors, Lugh killed his grandfather with a magic stone, which turned the tide of the battle. When the Fomors approached Lugh with a peace offering, he used his wisdom to gain many advantages for his people from the Fomoron gods of the sea. The Fomors taught the science of ploughing, and presented the Tuatha De Danann with a good wheat harvest every year, as well as increased the milk yield for the cows. Lugh married Dechtire and was the father of Cuchulainn, who fought at his side in battle.

Binah: *Dagda*

The Dagda[8] is considered Father of the gods as well as the god of the earth. He possessed a Cauldron[9] that was said to satisfy every man who ate from it. Dagda possessed a harp that called forth the seasons in their correct order. He is described as a man wearing a brown leather hooded tunic that reached down to his hips, along with boots made of hairy horse hide. He had a large war club[10] that was so big it took eight men to lift it. (It was usually carried in a cart, the tracks of which formed a territorial boundary.) The Dagda's wife was Boann, who gave him several children: Bridget, Angus, Mider, Ogma, and Bodb the Red.

In the "Second Battle of the Moytura,"[11] Dagda visited the camp of the Fomors.[12] They forced him to drink gigantic portions of food, or else face death. During the following battle, Dagda chased the Fomors, who had stolen his magic harp. He played a weeping tune, a laughing tune, and a sleeping tune on the harp, putting the Fomors to sleep. He returned all the cattle they had stolen, and then forced the Fomors to sign a peace treaty with the Tuatha De Danann.

Some dispossessed gods approached the Dagda to live in the various hillocks and barrows[13] (sidhs). Dagda was tricked out of the one he assigned to himself by Angus.

Dagda eventually resigned his kingship, which was taken up by his son Bodb the Red.

Chesed: *Lir*

Lir was a sea god who was the patron saint of sailors. Lir, along with Mider, refused to accept Bodb the Red as king (when Dagda renounced the crown). They refused to pay tribute, and left to stay in another part of the country. Bodb declared war on Mider but did not attack Lir because of his affection for the old god. When Lir's wife died, Bodb tried to be conciliatory by offering one of his foster daughters to take the place of the lost wife. Lir relented and chose Aebh. He took her back to Fionnachaidh (sidh) where together they had four children: Finola, Aed, and the twins Fiachra and Conn. (Aebh died in childbirth of the twins.)

Bodb offered another of his foster daughters, Aeife, who was childless and envious of Lir's children. In a fit of jealousy she took a druid's wand and changed Lir's children into swans, and told Lir the children had drowned. The sea god was suspicious, and when confronted with the swans, he found that neither he nor Bobd the Red had enough magic to change them back. When brought before her foster father, Aeife was asked what form she feared the most. Forced to reply truthfully, she told her foster father that what she most feared was the air demon. Bobd promptly changed her into an air demon.

Lir was later killed by Caoilte.

Geburah: *Fergus*

Fergus, son of Roy, was an Ulster king and champion of the Red Branch. He fell in love with Nessa, widow of his half brother. She promised to marry him if he gave up the throne for a year and allowed her son, Conchobar, to rule. When he did so, he found that King Conchobar, who was strongly supported by the people at Ulster, would not give back the throne. Fergus then decided to remain at Ulster and support the new king.

King Conchobar decided to send Fergus to Alba to bring back the exiled sons of Usnach. The king secretly pined for Deirdre, the woman who rejected him, and who was married to one of the sons, Naoise. Fergus took his sons, Illann and Buinne, by galley to the shore of Loch Etive. Fergus gave his word that nothing would happen to the group, but Deirdre had visions of death. The sons agreed that they would go with Fergus because his word was good. When he arrived at Borrach with the Sons of Usnach and Deirdre, he was told to attend a feast. This meant that he could not watch over them, and by law he was forbidden to refuse an invitation to a feast. He decided to go to the feast and sent the sons of Usnach, under the protection of his sons, to Emain Macha of Conchobar.

The king decided to kill the Sons of Usnach when they arrived by setting their dwelling on fire. However, Fergus' sons foiled the attempt and killed the attackers. The siege lasted for a while, and the Sons of Usnach were killed. Deirdre died soon after. When Fergus returned and found out what had happened, he slew the king's sons and joined with the king's enemies, Ailill and Medb.

Fergus found himself facing his old friend, Cuchulainn, during the war of the Tain. He made a pact never to fight him. Because of this, Ailill and Medb lost the battle. Soon after, Ailill killed Fergus as he swam in a lake.

Tiphareth: *Cuchulainn*

Cuchulainn was the grandson of Dagda and the son of Lugh. He was also the grandson of Angus. He was a Sun god that few could bear to look at—his countenance could melt snow and boil water. He was conceived when his mother, Dechtire, swallowed a May fly. Lugh then came to her in a dream and told her that she was pregnant. Some months later she gave birth to a boy (in miraculous circumstances) whom she called Setanta.

While still a youth, Setanta bested all those of his age in sporting events at Emain Macha. He was noticed by King Conchobar and invited to follow him to a banquet hosted by Culann the Smith. Once they were all in the banquet (save Setanta), Culann asked the king's permission to release his ferocious watchdog. When the hound saw the boy, he rushed at him. However, Setanta killed the beast with his bare hands. The youth promised to take the place of the hound (while he looked for another to train). He was then called Culann's Hound—Cuchulainn.

A short while later, Cuchulainn heard Cathbad the Druid say that a boy who took up arms on a certain day would be the greatest heroes of the land—but that his life would be short. Cuchulainn went to the king and demanded armour and a chariot. The king gave in to him and later that day he returned with the heads of three champions who had killed many Ulster warriors.[14]

Pressure was put on Cuchulainn to find a wife, but all the women he saw he refused. He fell for Emer, daughter of Forgall, the Wily; but she saw him only as a boy, and refused him. She reluctantly agreed to marry him if he could take her away from her warlike relations. Forgall tried to trick Cuchulainn from taking his daughter. He approached King Conchobar and asked to see the youth perform all of his feats. Forgall dared the youth to go to train with Sacathach, the Amazon, in the east of Alba—for no one could stand up to her. After an amazing journey, he found her and she started to train him in her skill at arms. In return for this, he helped conquer a rival queen called Aoife.

On returning to Ireland, he went to Forgall's fortress and asked for his daughter's hand. Forgall refused. Cuchulainn went berserk and slew everyone around, including Forgall, for no one was a match for him. He then married Emer.

Cuchulainn's deeds of fighting culminated during the War of the Tain, when Ireland, headed by Ailill and Medb (king and queen of Connaught), declared war on Ulster to get the Bull of Cualagne. Cuchulainn killed over a hundred men a day with his sling. He was approached by the Morrigan, a goddess of war, who offered her love and help. He rejected her love, and she then vowed to be his enemy. During the battle, he killed his friend Ferdiad. Eventually Cuchulainn was killed.

Netzach: *Fand*

Fand was wife of Manannan Mac Lir. When she was abandoned by her husband, she sent her sister, Liban, to go to Cuchulainn and tell him of her love for him.[15] He refused Fand's love at first, but then sent Laeg (along with Liban) to see what Fand, and the kingdom she ruled over, looked like. Laeg returned with glowing reports, and this made Cuchulainn go and see for himself. He stayed for a month in her kingdom, and worked out a scheme where he could be with Fand from time to time. When Emer found out about it, she tried to kill Fand. When she approached her husband to try and shame him, she was unsuccessful. Eventually she offered to give up her husband to Fand. Cuchulainn decided that he wanted both of them. In the meantime, Manannan heard what was going on and intervened. He asked Fand to forgive him and to remember the happy times they had together. He also gave her the option of choosing between him and her new lover. She decided to go back to the sea god, who then shook his magic mantle and made Cuchulainn forget all about Fand.

Hod: *Ogma*

Ogma (also called Cermait) is the god of literature and eloquence. He was a son of Dagda and husband of Etan (Diancecht's daughter). His children included Tuirenn, Cairpre, Mac Cuill, and Mac Cecht. Ogman was the inventor of the Ogman alphabet. He was also noted for his feats of great strength. During the war with the Fomors, he killed Indech, son of the goddess Domnu. He then claimed the sword of Tethra, one of the Fomor kings. Ogma retired to the Sidh Airceltran.

Yesod: *Bridget*

Bridget was a triple goddess (of healing, smithing, and poetry). Bridget was said to have been born at sunrise. The house where she was born was suddenly emgulfed with a huge pillar that reached the heavens. It is said that as a healer, Bridget's breath gave life to the dead. She was married to Bres and was the daughter of Dagda. Her sons were Ruadan, Brian, Iuchar, and Iucharba.

Malkuth: *Danu*

Danu (Anu) was the mother of the gods who represented the earth. It is from this goddess that her people, the Tuatha De Danann, got their name.

The Paths

The 11th Path, The Fool: *Demna — Young Finn*

Demna was the son of Cumal, a royal bodyguard to the high kings. Finn was born in isolation due to the elopement of his father with Murna, daughter of the Druid Tadhg and descendent of Nauda and Balor. Murna's father had Cumal killed, so she fled to the forest of Slieveboom where she gave birth to Demna. The boy grew up in the forests under the care of Bodhmall and Liath Luachra. He was kept away from others so that he was safe from the vengeance of Tadhg. One day he met Finn the Soothsayer, who was camped beside a pool (for seven years) in the hope of catching the Salmon of Knowledge. Demna caught the fish and handed it to Finn to eat. The old man refused and told the youngster to eat it instead. Demna thus obtained instant knowledge and later took the name of Finn.[16]

The 12th Path, The Magician: *Cathbad*

Cathbad, the Druid, was to King Conchobar what Merlin was to Arthur. He prophesied Cuchulainn's fame and also guided the Champion when the daughters of Calatain tried to make magic on Cuchulainn during the Tain War. For the most part, he supported his king, but when Conchobar let his personal lust for Diedre get in the way, the Druid had to obey the wishes of the king in helping to slay the sons of Usnach with magic. He then cursed Conchobar and his kingdom for his lust and left the king.

The 13th Path, The High Priestess: *Caer*

Caer, daughter of Etal Ambulel, was a swan maiden who drove Angus crazy by appearing to him in his dreams. She sang and played the harp for him, but when he went to embrace her, she vanished. Angus waited a year for her, and when he approached her (while she was still in the form of a swan), he asked her to marry him. Caer promised to wed him only if he consented to become a swan. Angus agreed. She then turned him into a swan, and they flew to his sidh where they changed back into human form for their lovemaking.

The 14th Path, The Empress: *Aine*

Aine, a goddess of love and fertility, was the daughter of Eogabail. She was Queen of the Fairies of South Munster. Her gifts were prosperity and abundance.[17] She was raped, or at least coerced, into marriage by the Fourth Earl of Desmond. He had seen her bathing, so he took her cloak and said that he would not return it until she married him. They had a son, Gerald, who was a magician—he performed many extraordinary feats. Aine warned her husband that she would leave him (in accordance with fairy law) if he showed surprise at any feat performed by their son. When the Earl broke his promise, she left him and lived with her son until his death. Gerald was then accepted to live in the fairy kingdom with his mother.

The 15th Path, The Emperor: *Conchobar*

Conchobar was the son of the king of Ulster, Fachtns Fathach, and the lady Nessa. When his father died, the kingship went to Fergus, the king's brother. Fergus fell in love with Nessa, who agreed to marry him on the condition that her son, Conchobar, would be king for a year. When the time elapsed, the people of Ulster refused to support Fergus, and so Conchobar remained on the throne. His reign was good, and he was well supported by the people and the heroes. But in his later years, his lust for Deirdre got the better of him. Deirdre fled with her lover, for she could not wed an old man like the king. Conchobar sent Fergus to bring back Deirdre. The king went back on his word and had all those he had previously pledged to protect, killed. The king was ambushed by Cet, who fired a sling-shot at him. The shot remained in his head for seven years. During this time he was told not to get excited or travel in chariots because the motion would kill him. Unfortunately, he got into a rage one day and it did kill him.

The 16th Path, The Hierophant: *Amairgen*

Amairgen (of the fair knee) was a druid of the Milesians (possibly from Spain), who accompanied Milesius on his conquest of Ireland after his nephew, Ith, was killed by the three sons of Ogma. Unfortunately, Amairgen lost his wife on the journey. Through the use of magic, the druid was able to duplicate Ith's landing spot on Ireland and immediately prophesied victory for the travellers. Considering the long list of achievements attributed to the Amairgin, he must have indeed been a master druid. On his journey inland, Amairgin met the goddesses Banba and Folta, who asked that the land be named after them.

When they arrived at Uisnech, the centre of Ireland, they were greeted by the goddess Eriu, who made them welcome. She also asked that the land be named after her, and the druid agreed—it was called Erinn. The Tuatha De Danann complained that invaders came without any prior notification (as the rules of war were at that time), and Amairgin was given the task of arbitration. He decided that his people should attack the now-prepared Tuatha De Danann. After two fierce battles in which the three main kings were killed by the Milesians, the gods retired beneath the earth and Ireland was given to the invaders.

The 17th Path, The Lovers: *Baile and Ailinn*

Baile, son of Buain, and prince of Ulster, fell in love with Ailinn, daughter of Fergus, and granddaughter of the king of Leinster. These kingdoms were enemies. The aspiring lovers had arranged to meet at Dundealgan. When Baile arrived there, he was met by a stranger who told him that the lovers' plans for a rendezvous were discovered by the people of Leinster, and thus Ailinn was prevented from coming. Baile died of a broken heart. The messenger then went to tell Ailinn that her beloved had died. On hearing this news, Ailinn fell dead with grief. A tree arose from each grave. The fruit that grew on Baile's tree resembled Ailinn, while Ailinn's tree bore fruit that resembled Baile. Eventually the two trees were cut down and turned into wands. Once they were brought together in the Hall of Tara, they sprang together and could not be separated.

The 18th Path, The Chariot: *Laeg*

Laeg, son of Rangabur, was the charioteer for Cuchulainn from the start of the hero's battles to his final one at the Pillar of Stone, where Laeg died for his master. It was Laeg who commanded Cuchulainn's two famous horses, Grey Macha and Black Sainglend. When Fand declared her love for Cuchulainn, it was Laeg (whose judgement he trusted), who went to Fand's Kingdom and reported of the wonders he had seen there.

The 19th Path, Strength: *Macha*

Macha was a triple goddess, as well as a goddess of battle. During the war with the Fir Bolgs, she teamed up with other goddesses (Morrigan and Badb) and took an active part in the battle by using her magic. In one story, Macha was said to be one of the wives of Nauda of the Silver Hand, and was slain by the Formor leader Balor during the battle of the Northern Moytura.

She was also said to be the wife of Crunnic of Ulster. In this story, Macha came to Crunnic, took the place of his dead wife, and became pregnant by him. When attending the king's court, Crunnic declared that his pregnant wife could outrun the king's fastest horses. The king wanted to see this and so he told Crunnic's wife that if she refused, he would have her husband killed. She immediately identified herself as Macha, daughter of Sainraith Mac Imbaith. During the race, she gave birth to twins. In labor, she uttered a curse—all who heard her cry would suffer from childbirth pains for five days and four nights during Ulster's hours of trouble. Only women, boys, and Cuchulainn were exempt from the curse.

As Macha of the red tresses, daughter of Aedh Ruadh, she built Emain Macha and ruled Ireland with her father's brothers. When her father died, she quarrelled with her uncles over the throne (which was left to her). She killed one uncle and took his sons captive. She married the other uncle.

The 20th Path, The Hermit: *Brian*

Though not a hermit in the true sense of the word, it was Brian who travelled (along with his brothers) on a special spiritual quest to kill the father of Lugh. To do this they had to perform the following tasks:

1. Obtain three apples from the garden of Hespridies.
2. Obtain a magical pigskin from the king of Greece.
3. Obtain a poisoned spear from Pisear of Persia.
4. Obtain two horses from the king of Scilly's chariot.
5. Obtain two pigs from the Golden Pillars.
6. Obtain the hound from the king of Ioruiadh.
7. Obtain the cooking spit from the Fianchubhe women at the bottom of the ocean.
8. Give three shouts on the hill of Miodchaion.

Brian and his brothers were killed on the final quest, but the treasures taken during the voyage were given to Lugh.

The 21st Path, The Wheel of Fortune: *Manannan*

Manannan was the son of Lir, and like his father, he was the patron saint of early sailors. When this god rose to full prominence, he over-took over his father's stature. He was the god of merchants. He was also the god of Irishmen living in foreign parts—he had the ability to bring them safely home. Manannan also could cause good crops and favorable weather. His boat, which could go anywhere, was called "Wave Sweeper." He had a horse called "Splendid Maine," which could travel over both water and land. His two spears were called "Fury" (Greater and Lesser), and he wore impenetrable mail. He was also a shape-shifter, and his mantle was invisible. Of all the gods, Manannan appeared the most blessed. He had numerous affairs with many goddesses, but he settled down finally with Fand.

It was Manannan who shipwrecked the invaders of Ireland when the Tuatha De Danann called upon him. He led a full life for a god, and after a time withdrew into seclusion from the main part of Celtic myth. Some say he went to live in Scotland, and others say he returned to his home on the Isle of Man.

The 22nd Path, Justice: *Cormac*

Cormac was the king of Ulster and was referred to as the "Gaelic Solomon." He won the friendship of the sea god Manannan, and was lured into the Otherworld where the sea god gave him a magic silver branch that bore golden apples. When the branch was shaken, the sick and wounded forgot their pain and went into a deep sleep. The king had an eye put out by Aonghus's spear when he tried to save his son, Cellach, from death at the hands of Aonghus. Cormac was forced to abdicate the throne, since no one who had a disfigurement could be king.

The 23rd Path, The Hanged Man: *The Children of Lir*

This path relates to the myth about the Children of Lir: Finola, Aed, Fiachra, and Conn, who were changed into swans by Aeife when they went to bathe in Lake Darva. The curse kept them as swans for a period of nine hundred years in three different locations. It was during their stay on the Sea of Moyle that their fate was most difficult, and they suffered greatly from it. When they were released to go back to their home, they found it deserted—St. Patrick had banned the gods from Ireland. There were no gods left to change them back into human shape. They retired to live on the island of Glora, and were changed back into human form when St. Caemhoc baptized them.

The 24th Path, Death: *Bile / Donn*

Bile was the god of death (and some say the husband of Danu). His feast day was celebrated on the first of May. Donn was also a Celtic god of death. He gave his son to Angus Og, the god of youth, to be looked after. Donn's wife betrayed him to Roc, Angus Og's steward. When Roc's son was born, the god of death crushed him and gave the body to the hounds. Roc used magic to transform the dead child into a boar to await the death of his real son under the care of Angus Og.

The 25th Path, Temperance: *Goibhniu*

Goibhniu was a smith god who made the weapons for the Tuatha De Danann. At the feast of Fled Giobhenn, he also supplied them with an elixir that made the people of the Red Branch invulnerable to death and disease. In the war against the Fomors, he replaced every broken lance of his people with a new one, and each new lance would never miss its mark. Goibhniu had two brothers, Cian and Samhain. During the war with the Fomorians, he was stabbed by Rauduan. However, he survived through the healing waters of Dian Cecht, god of medicine.

The 26th Path, The Devil: *Cromm Cruaich*

Cromm Cruaich ("bowed one of the mound"), was a golden idol that the Celts worshipped above all others. He was closely allied to Pan, though not as harsh. He was a greedy god who had children sacrificed to him so that battles could be won and crops would grow. When Patrick of Macha (St. Patrick) came to Ireland and saw the golden idol, he destroyed it and watched as the demon god fled back to his mound beneath the earth.

The 27th Path, The Blasted Tower: *Balor*

Balor was one of the main leaders of the Fomorians who came from the Otherworld. The Fomorians were said to be misshapen, and Balor had one huge eye that killed anything he looked at. It was prophesied that he would be killed by his grandson, and therefore he took almost every measure possible to prevent this. He placed his daughter, Ethlinn, in isolation in a crystal tower. Her lover, Cian, asked the druidess, Birog, for help. Birog managed to get Cian into the crystal tower. Ethlinn slept with Cian and gave birth to Lugh, who later killed Balor with a magic stone that knocked his eye out.

Also associated with the Tower is the fortress of Aileach, built by the Tuatha De Danann, which was the royal residence of Ulster. It was here that Ireland was divided up between the goddesses Banba, Fotla, and Eire. It was later destroyed by the king of Munster in revenge for the destruction of Kincora.

The 28th Path, The Star: *Boann*

Boann means "she of the white cattle." In this version of the myth, Boann is a water goddess who was married to Nechtan, a water god. Legend has it that there was a well that was surrounded by nine Trees of Knowledge that bore red hazel nuts. Eating the nuts would give one instant knowledge of everything. Since the trees were very close to the well, only the salmon that lived in the well were allowed to eat the nuts that dropped from the tree. One day Boann approached the well, but its waters suddenly rose up and drove her off. She had, in fact, created a flood—the waters of the well formed the Boyne river.

The 29th Path, The Moon: *Maeldun*

Maeldun was the bastard child of Ailill and a nun. When he grew to manhood, he was told the truth about his parentage and the death of his father, who was killed by overseas raiders. Maeldun (along with sixty others), set out to find his father's killers. He underwent a series of adventures that can only be compared with the "Odyssey." After being away for many years, he managed to catch up with his father's killers near the end of his journey. However, his experiences taught him that revenge was useless, and so he made peace with them.

In many ways, Tarot Key 18 depicts this journey—the crayfish crawls past the towers and the jackals. It does not deviate from the journey's path, no matter what the hardships are.

The 30th Path, The Sun: *Red Branch Cycle*

Veneration of the Sun was the main form of Celtic worship. The spring equinox was called Beltane; the autumn equinox was Samhain. The two celebrations together effectively marked the beginning and end of summer. The Solstices were also celebrated, but not as enthusiastically as were the Equinoxes. There were a number of solar deities in the Celtic religion—Cuchulainn and Lugh being two prominent examples. The whole of Ireland was called the "land of the setting Sun."

The 31st Path, Judgment: *Mider*

Mider, son of Dagda, was the Celtic Pluto. His home was in the Isle of Falga, where he kept the "three cranes of denial and churlishness," along with three cows and a magic cauldron. Mider married Etain, but she was stolen from him by Angus, son of Young, who kept her prisoner in a glass enclosure, which always he carried with him. When Mider was about to recapture her, a rival of his wife lured him away and set Etain free, but in doing so changed her into a fly. Seven years passed. Etain found herself in a golden cup of liquid and was swallowed. She was reborn as the daughter of Etair. Twenty years passed and she grew into a beautiful woman who married the high king, Eochaid. Mider saw her and knew who she was; but when he told her, she refused to give up the life of a queen. Mider then challenged the king to a game of chess, which Mider lost. A year later, he came back and challenged the king again. This time the king lost, and Mider won Etain back. She lived with Mider in his Sidh until the king marched on it and started to destroy it. Mider reluctantly gave Etain back to the king. All did not go well for the king, however. His male heirs all died violent deaths.

The 32nd Path, The World: *Morrigan*

Although Morrigan ("Great Queen"), was often cited as the goddess of death, her nature was very Saturnian. She was often represented as going into battle with two spears. There is evidence that she was also a former Moon goddess. In battle, she often changed sides. She fought with Cuchulainn for a while, and later she fought against him. She did

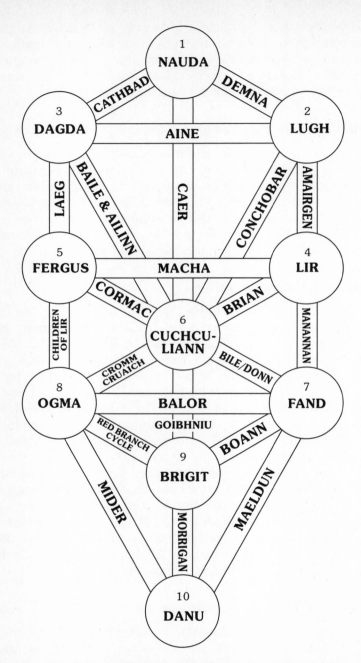

The Celtic Pantheon applied to the Tree of Life.

help the Tuatha De Danann against outsiders on numerous occasions. She also pitted friend against friend in the civil wars of the Red Branch.

Path	Godform
1. Kether	Nauda
2. Chokmah	Lugh
3. Binah	Dagda
4. Chesed	Lir
5. Geburah	Fergus
6. Tiphareth	Cuchulainn
7. Netzach	Fand
8. Hod	Ogma
9. Yesod	Brigit (Bridget)
10. Malkuth	Danu
11. Uranus/The Fool	Demna
12. Mercury/ The Magician	Cathbad
13. Moon/The High Priestess	Caer
14. Venus/Empress	Aine
15. Aries/The Emperor	Conchobar
16. Taurus/ The Hierophant	Amairgen
17. Gemini/The Lovers	Baile and Ailinn
18. Cancer/The Chariot	Laeg
19. Leo/Strength	Macha
20. Virgo/The Hermit	Brian
21. Jupiter/The Wheel of Fortune	Manannan
22. Libra/Justice	Cormac
23. Neptune/Hanged Man	Children of Lir
24. Scorpio/Death	Bile and Donn
25. Sagittarius/Temperance	Goibhniu
26. Capricorn/Devil	Cromm Cruaich
27. Mars/Blasted Tower	Balor
28. Aquarius/Star	Boann
29. Pisces/Moon	Maeldun
30. Sun/Sun	Red Branch Cycle
31. Pluto/Judgment	Mider
32. Saturn/World	Morrigan

THE TEUTONIC (NORSE) PANTHEON
AS APPLIED TO THE KABBALAH

The Nine Worlds of Yggdrasil

Kether, Chokmah, and Binah: *Asgard*

Asgard was the celestial city of the Asa-gods, situated at the top of the World Tree. It had twelve palaces or halls: Thrudheimer (Thor), Ydal-plains (Ullr), Valaskjalf (Odin), Sokvabekk (Saga), Valhalla (all gods), Thrymheimer (Skadhi), Briedhablik (Baldor), Himinbjorg (Heimdal), Folkvanger (Freya), Glitnir (Forseti), Noatun (Njord), and Vithi (Vidar).

There was only one entrance into this world—through Odin's gate. Asgard was an island surrounded by a large wall, river currents, and mists, from which lightning (vafer-flame) erupted. To approach the gate of Odin, one would have to cross the Bifrost, or flaming bridge. This was guarded by Heimdal,[18] "Watchman of the gods." There was a trap set into the door, which was rigged to crush the uninvited who tried to get past Heimdal.

Daath: *Alfheimer*

Alfheimer was the home of the Air Elves and was ruled by Frey. There were various subdivisions of this world. Delling, the Red Elf of the Dawn, is often referred to as an inhabitant of this world. His hall is called Heljar-ran. This was a world where both gods and humans met. The gods occupied the upper half of this world, while humans dwelt in the lower half.

Chesed: *Vanaheim*

Vanaheim relates to the element of Water and, to a limited extent, the element of Air. Within this world was the hall of Aeger, god of the ocean. This world was ruled by Honor, brother of Odin, who was sent to keep the peace in a type of exchange program after the wars of the gods were over. Vanaheim was a place of wealth, fertility, and prophesy. The Vanirs were gods of both fertility and death. Their duties approximated some of the functions of the Greek Charon, who ferried the dead across the river.

Geburah: *Muspelheim*

Muspelheim, a world of Fire, was said to be the first created world. Only those who were born there could survive there. Muspelheim was guarded by Surt and his flaming sword, who waited to rise up and take over the other gods in conquest. Muspelheim is a world of both creation and destruction.

Tiphareth: *Midgard*

Midgard, or "middle ward," was the central world on the Tree. It is where man first sprang from (from the ash tree came man, and from the alder tree came woman). This world was the main focal point of the Tree, for it was here that everything was held together. Midgard was protected by Thor.

Netzach: *Svartalheim*

Svartalheim was the "home of the dark elves," and was very earthy by nature. It was the world where the transmutation of metals (the conversion of base metals into gold and silver) took place, and where precious gems were hidden. This, too, was a world of both creation and destruction.

Hod: *Jontunheim*

Jontunheim was the "land of giants." This most violent of worlds was ruled by the giant, Thrym. It was a world of ice, and the roads that led both in and out of it were difficult to travel. To a certain extent, this was very much an isolated world.

Yesod: *Hel*

Hel was ruled by Hel or Hela, a daughter of Loki. She was depicted as a monster who was half white and half black. Hel is the hall of the dead.

Malkuth: *Nifelheim*

Nifelheim, the "misty" or "dark Hel," was a world of its own, though some have described it as the lower reaches of Hel. It was the place where the evil souls went. Those who lived a good life resided in Hel after their death, but those who led an evil life were taken first to Hel, then to Nifelheim. This was a world where the soul experienced a second death.

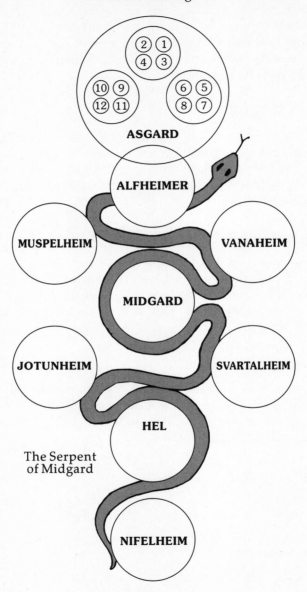

12 Palaces of Asgard

ASGARD

② ①
④ ③

⑩ ⑨
⑫ ⑪

⑥ ⑤
⑧ ⑦

ALFHEIMER

MUSPELHEIM

VANAHEIM

MIDGARD

JOTUNHEIM

SVARTALHEIM

HEL

The Serpent
of Midgard

NIFELHEIM

*The Nine Worlds of Yggdrasil
applied to the Kabbalah.*

The Gods and the Sephiroth

Kether: *Odin*

Odin, whose name meant "fury" or "inspiration," was the father of the gods and son of Bestla, the giantess, and Bor. Odin's brothers were Ve and Vile. In his youth, Odin approached the wise god, Mimer, who received his wisdom from the draught of egg-white mead that he drank daily from his Gjallar-horn. Odin paid the price of the ale by forfeiting an eye. From that time on, he became the ruler of the gods. The lesson that Odin learned was that nothing could be accomplished without sacrifice. After drinking the mead, he learned the wisdom of the runes. He later searched all nine worlds of the Tree of Yggdrasil.

A type of civil war erupted between the gods and their various worlds. The Moon god was killed and his son, Hyuki, suffered a bad wound. The song-mead, a magical drink that bestowed powers of prophesy was taken by Sviddur, one of the main instigators of this war. Sviddur fled to the cave of the giant Sutting, who gave him his own daughter Gunlad as a reward for the song-mead. The first task Odin accepted, was to recapture the stolen song-mead. He went to the hall of Suttung (beyond Hel), where he got the support of the guardians of the world of the Frost Giants, Heimdal, and the dwarf. Odin entered the hall of Suttung during a feast. He took on the guise of Svigdur and was consequently married to Gunlad. When the real Svigdur turned up and discovered Odin in his place, he rushed at him. The dwarf, though, had produced an illusion—and Svigdur killed himself by charging at a rock wall that did not exist. Gunlad spent her wedding night with Odin, who she assumed was Svigdur. When Gunlad found out who he really was, she gave him the precious song-mead. Odin turned into an eagle and flew back to his world.

Odin used his two pet ravens, Hugen ("reflection") and Munin ("memory"), to give him information about what was going on in the world of men. He also had two wolf-dogs, Freke ("the voracious") and Gere ("greedy"), which he fed with food of the heroes.

Odin's children were Thor (whose mother was Jord), Bragi, Hodur, Tyr, Hremod, and Balder (whose mother was Frigga).

Chokmah: *Bragi*

Bragi, whose name meant "best," was a son of Odin. He was the god of wisdom, poetry, and eloquence. Bragi's wife was called Indun. One of Bragi's functions was to record the deeds of warriors. He was kept young with the apples of youth supplied by his wife. It was Bragi who spoke up against Loki at a feast of the gods, and who told the trickster god that he was not wanted. Bragi was about to fight Loki, but he was restrained by Odin.

Binah: *Frigga*

Frigga was wife of Odin, the daughter of Nat, and the sister of Njord. She is a goddess of marriage and is sometimes referred to as "Mother of the Gods," "Queen of Asgard," and "Goddess of the Fruitful Earth." She had the gift of prophesy and thus she knew all things. Because of this, she was very reluctant to discuss her gifts with any of the gods. Frigga was the goddess of the cloud threads (allied with the fates and karma), which she spun from her jewelled wheel. She was very protective of her son, Balder, and she extracted a promise from all her servants that no living thing could hurt him. Loki went to Frigga in the guise of a woman and inquired as to what could hurt Balder. Frigga replied that all living things vowed not to hurt Balder, save the mistletoe—for this plant was slender and weak, and could harm no one. However, the mistletoe did eventually kill Balder.

While the body of Balder was burned on a Viking's pyre, the god Hermond (brother of Balder) journeyed to the world of Hel where Balder's spirit was kept. Frigga had urged him to go there with the intended task of bringing Balder back to the highest world in order to join all those who mourned him. Balder refused, but sent gifts to his mother to pacify her. It was at a feast shortly after Balder's death that the truth of her son's demise, and how she had unwittingly caused it, was revealed to Frigga.

Chesed: *Freya*

Freya, a triple goddess, had many attributes. She was considered a goddess of fertility and of wealth, but also a goddess who went to the land of the dead (or underworld), in the guise of a falcon. She would return from the underworld with prophecies. From a Kabbalistic perspective, the journey of Freya resembles the journey through Daath. Though she has some Venusian qualities, she also has some Jovian traits as well. She was the guardian of feminine magic who was always ready to unleash magical forces if it pleased her. Freya was a skilled warrior, as well as a goddess of love. This seems to correspond well with the name for Chesed-Gedulah (Greatness).

Geburah: *Thor*

Thor, the god of thunder, was considered the strongest of the gods. He had control of the magic hammer (Mjolnir), the iron gloves needed to wield it, and the a of threefold strength. All of these implements were used by the god with great effect in battle. One of the stories associated with Thor tells that when the god of thunder travels between worlds, especially to Hel, he must wade across the four great rivers (for his chariot of fire might destroy the bridges between the worlds). It was Thor who killed the Frost Giant with his hammer of stone when the creature threatened the safety of the gods. Thor's final battle was with the Midgard serpent. Thor killed the beast, but unfortunately died as a result of the venomous fumes it threw at the god of thunder.

Tiphareth: *Balder*

Balder was called "the Beautiful." He was gifted with wisdom and great eloquence, and he was the most loved among the gods. He was the son of Odin and Frigga, and brother of Hodur. He and his wife, Nanna, the Moon goddess, often rode into battle together. His horse, called "Billow Falcons," blinded the opposition with its brilliance. Balder was blessed with invulnerability (except for the mistletoe). It was during a trip to the forest with his father, Odin, that Loki's magic arrow, made of mistletoe, was unleashed by Hodur—eventually killing Balder. Balder's spirit was taken by the Valkries to Hel. At the time of Ragnarok (the twilight or fatal destiny of the gods), Balder returned to Valhalla, and the world of Asgard brightened at his homecoming.

Netzach: *Sif*

Sif was a fertility goddess, and a goddess of the harvest, who was associated with corn, because of her golden-colored hair. She was a goddess of the family and a former wife of Thor. She was also a goddess of health and wealth. The evil Loki shape-changed in order to trick Sif. He cut off her hair while she slept. Loki was forced to replace it when threatened by Thor's anger.

Hod: *Hermod*

Hermod was the son and messenger of Odin. He rode to Hel on his father's steed, Sleipnir, to find the spirit of his dead brother, Balder. For nine nights (one for each of the nine worlds of Yggdrasil), Hermod searched until he came to the maid, Modgud, on the bridge. After he identified himself, she gave him directions. He finally arrived at the hall of Eljudnir, where he met the Hel herself. Hermod implored her to return his brother to Asgard. Hel told him that if every living thing in all the nine worlds wept for Balder, she would let him return to Asgard. Odin put the word out to all the inhabitants of the nine worlds that everyone should weep for Balder. One messenger went to the cave of the giantess, Thokk, who said she would not weep for Balder, and thus prevented his return. For Thokk was, in reality, Loki in disguise. Hermod was sent by Odin to capture the children of Loki. Hermod was also sent to the underworld to fashion a cord of strength called "the devourer" to be used against Fener.

Yesod: *Nanna*

Nanna was a Moon goddess, daughter of Nep (or Gewar—depending on the version of the story), and wife of Balder. In her early youth, she was wooed by her foster brother, Hother (son of Hodbrodd), until Balder saw her bathing and lost his heart to her. Hother became jealous and asked the Valkyries for help in winning Nanna's affections. They told him the whereabouts of a magic sword that would help him fight Balder. A war then erupted between Balder and Hother. Nanna eventually married Balder, but died of a broken heart when she saw her husband's body. She accompanied him to Hel. She and Balder both greeted Hermod when he went to the house of the Dead in the world of Hel.

Malkuth: *Jord*

Jord was the earth goddess, wife of Odin, and mother of Thor. The power of Jord, fused with that of the sky god, Odin, is that universal force that produces offspring. It thus refers to growth and fertility. Jord is a very old goddess. Not much is known about her.

The Paths

The 11th Path, The Fool: *Sigmund*[19]

Sigmund was the son of King Volsung. During a voyage to the land of Siggeir, Volsung was killed and his sons were taken to a forest where they were bound to a tree. One of the sons was killed by a wolf. When Sigmund's sister heard of this, she sent messengers to ensure that the only surviving son, Sigmund, was smeared with honey. Instead of killing him, the wolf started to lick him with her tongue. Sigmund grabbed her tongue between his teeth and bit it off. He then managed to escape unhurt. The wolf was actually the mother of King Sigger, who had the power to shape-shift. Sigmund swore vengeance against King Sigger. He lived for many years in the forest and trained his nephew in the art of warfare.

The 12th Path, The Magician: *Ull*

Ull, the "brilliant one," was the son of Orvandel and Sif, husband of Skadi, and stepson of Thor. He was one of the early deities and was considered to be god of snowshoes, archery, and the runes. It was Ull who went with his stepbrother Svipdag to Jotunheim to rescue Frey and Freya from the giants. A dispute erupted and Ull killed one of the giant's sons. They managed to rescue an enchanted Freya and take her back home with them.

Ull was the god Thor conferred with in his hour of need, for he was a planner as well as a warrior.

The 13th Path, The High Priestess: *Idun*

Idun was the daughter of Ivalde and wife of Bragi. She was keeper of the golden apples that gave the gods perpetual youth. Idun was taken away from Asgard by Loki because of a threat imposed on him by Thyasse. The gods found that they started to grow old when Idun's apples were forbidden them, and they immediately conducted a search for Idun. Loki confessed to Odin that he had taken her. The loss of Idun threw all nine worlds out of balance—the cold of the frost giants began climbing up the World Tree. Loki promised to find Idun and return her, which he did. Thjasse followed Loki, but was eventually slain by Thor on the rainbow bridge outside the very walls of Asgard itself.

The 14th Path, The Empress: *Skade*

Skade's father was Thjasse, brother of Idun and shaper of the "Sword of Victory." When Skade learned that her father had been slain by the gods, she journeyed to Asgard with her spear and poisoned arrows, and demanded vengeance. The gods had a meeting and decided that her cause was a just one. They tried to pacify her because of her righteous motive and great beauty. She gave the gods two conditions on which she would put away her thirst for vengeance. The first requirement was to make her laugh. This was done when Loki danced before her with a goat. The second requirement was that she could choose a husband from among them. Though she wanted Balder, she was faced with the task of choosing her husband from his feet alone. Skade's eyes were partly veiled so that she saw only the feet of her potential mate. Unfortunately, the most beautiful feet belonged to Njord. She decided to keep her part of the bargain and went to live in Noatun, Njord's kingdom. It was Skade who was instrumental in deciding Loki's eventual punishment for his misdeeds. Though she dwelt in the Water realm, she was originally a goddess of the forests and plains. She eventually returned to live in the forest apart from her husband.

The 15th Path, The Emperor: *Njord*

Njord was known as the "blameless ruler of men." Although he was a Water god, his fiery nature was revealed by his role as the leader of the Vanas in their war against the gods of Asgard. During the war, the Sword of Victory was lost and the Hammer of Thor was broken. Without either, the gods of Asgard found the fight to retain their homeland difficult indeed. The Vana crossed the great bridge without hindrance from the vafer-flames. Njord was the first to put his great axe through the door of Asgard and enter the highest kingdom. Frey, Ull, and Svipdag gave their loyal support to Njord in the attack. In fact, Njord was the highest leader in all nine worlds when he conquered Asgard.

The 16th Path, The Hierophant: *Mimer*

Mimer was created by Ymer. He was considered a god of wisdom and guidance. In addition, he was king of the dwarfs of Midgard and also of the world of men. It was Mimer who gave Odin a draught each morning from his magic well. Mimer was eventually killed by the Vana gods and his head was sent to Odin as a present. Odin preserved the head, which spoke words of wisdom and guidance to Odin when he conversed with it.

The 17th Path, The Lovers: *Frey and Gerd*

Frey once ascended the throne of Odin, where he saw visions of all things happening in each of the nine worlds. He saw a beautiful woman whom he fell instantly in love with. She was Gerd, daughter of the giant, Gymer. Unfortunately, Frey's vision suddenly ceased and he became lovesick for Gerd, but would not tell anyone what was the matter. Frey's friend, Skirner, eventually found out what was wrong with Frey and told the other gods. Odin gave Skirner the Sword of Victory and other gifts in order to go and seek out Gerd. She refused every offer from Skirner until he threatened her with the Sword of Victory. Eventually, thanks to the effort of Skirner, Frey and Gerd were married and the Sword of Victory was given to Gymer as payment for his daughter.

The 18th Path, The Chariot: *Dietrich*

Dietrich was the son of the king of Bern. He was taught by the warrior, Hildbrand, in the ways of war. With the magic sword, Naglering, he fought a number of successful battles, especially against the giants. Dietrich's uncle, King Ermenrich, came under the evil influence of Sibeche, who had the king's sons either banished or killed. Sibeche even turned the king against his beloved nephew, Dietrich, and started a war between them. Dietrich eventually went into exile for thirty years while continuing to fight and win against his enemies. Dietrich passed on into immortality by climbing on a magical horse that would not stop its journey—forever pursuing an elusive stag across the heavens.

The 19th Path, Strength: *Halfdan*

Halfdan, the god of knowledge and strength, was the son of Thor. He had knowledge of his father's runes, which he used wisely. He understood the speech of the animals around him, and thus always knew when danger approached. Halfdan was an almost unstoppable opponent. He married the swan maiden Signe-Alveig ("nourishing drink"), and became a furious fighter of frost giants—especially when they tried to invade Midgard. During one fight, he killed his wife's father and made her sister, Groa, prisoner. (Groa's family had joined the frost giants in the war against Midgard). Groa's son, Svipdag, sought revenge on Halfdan and took him prisoner with the help of the ghost of his mother. Halfdan eventually died of his wounds in the war with Svipdag—betrayed by the magic of Groa.

The 20th Path, The Hermit: *Hother*

Hother was the son of Hodbrodd. He was a gifted athlete, archer, and musician. The association with The Hermit comes from his escape from Balder and his subsequent exile to Sweden and Jutland. There he forfeited all comforts and travelled alone through the forests and solitary places where he was given magical assistance and armor from some maidens. They urged him to go back to war with Balder.

The 21st Path, The Wheel of Fortune: *Norns*

The Norns were a triad of goddesses: Urd, Verdana, and Skuld. They wove the fates and karmic patterns for all the gods (including Odin) on their golden wheels. Urd controlled the past, Verdana governed the present, and Skuld ruled the future. In relationship to the Golden Dawn concept of the *Wheel of Fortune,* Urd (from Erda meaning earth) is the Sphinx because she was the oldest of the trio. The ape (who helps turn the wheel) is analogous to the youthful Skuld (who is closely related to Hel and the mysteries of death and the underworld). The present, Verdana, is the *Wheel* itself, which is constantly unfolding.

The 22nd Path, Justice: *Forseti*

Forseti was the son of Balder and Nanna, and was given the title of the "God of Justice." Very little is known of this god other than his title; but we are told in the myths handed down to us that Forseti is often found in the hall of Glitnir presiding over justice and solving strife. Because of his eloquence and persuasive manner, the gods accepted his judgments.

The 23rd Path, The Hanged Man: *Hadding*

Hadding, son of Halfdan, was cursed by Freya. He was eventually cast into the raging seas. Freya told him that tempest would forever follow him over all the seas in which he travelled. It took a great deal of time (including a journey to the underworld) and sacrifice (to Frey) before the curse of the Vana-gods was removed from him. Only with Odin's help did he eventually slay his enemies.

The 24th Path, Death: *Hel*

Hel was the daughter of Loki. She was in charge of Eljudnir—the hall of the Dead. Hel was originally a goddess who displeased Odin. He threw her into the underworld and gave her the task of welcoming the dead.

The 25th Path, Temperance: *Bil and Menja*

Bil and her brother, Hyuki,[20] came out of the night (Vidfinner) to the mountain in order to fetch the song-mead that had overflowed from Mimer's fountain. On their way back, they were seized by Mani, the Moon god. The skalds invoked Bil so that she might sprinkle the song-mead on their lips from her lunar home. There is a certain Hermaphrodite quality of the figure of Temperance in the Golden Dawn trump. The giantess, Menja, can also be associated here. Both Menja and her sister, Fenja, were daughters of mountain giants and were needed to turn the huge World Mill. From this they ground gold, rich harvests, peace, and prosperity. However, when their talents were abused, Menja sang and brought disaster by fire and sword. With the help of Mysinger, the sisters took the World Mill into the ocean where they grind it to this day.

The 26th Path, The Devil: *Loki*

Loki was the son of Laufey and Farbauti. Although he was descended from the giants, he was given access to Asgard. To call Loki a trickster and mischief maker is being too kind, for he was a god who got progressively more evil, and corrupted all those he came into contact with. He deliberately caused the death of Balder and prevented him from returning to Asgard after his death. In the tales of Loki, there is very little evidence of an overall malicious plan—he seemed to have committed atrocious acts just for the pleasure of it. Loki was to suffer the fate of being bound to some rocks by chains. Venom was poured on him repeatedly, giving him eternal torment. Loki had three children: Fenris, the wolf, the Midgard serpent, and Hel.

The 27th Path, The Tower: *Tyr*

Tyr, a son of Odin, is very closely allied to Mars, the Roman god of war. Tyr is associated with battle and the sword. He gives strength and courage when invoked. Tyr alone had the courage to feed the captured wolf, Fenris, who eventually bit off his right hand. It was on a journey with Thor that Tyr first came across his grandmother, a giantess.

The 28th Path, The Star: *Saga*

Saga lived in the hall of Sokvabek ("deep stream") where Odin often came to listen to the stream that came from a fountain—possibly the fountain of Mimer—that told of the great deeds of the past. It was here that Odin was often found with the goddess, Saga. Both would listen to tales of past glories while the stream increased in size and strength.

The 29th Path, The Moon: *Ymer*

Ymer is one of the creation gods who was formed from drops of vapor. When he felt his first pangs of hunger, he went forth in search of food amongst the darkness and whirlwinds. More vapor came and a gigantic cow was formed. From it gushed forth milk, which Ymer drank. The whole concept here shows the journey of the crayfish on its path of evolution in the tarot trump of *The Moon*.

The 30th Path, The Sun: *Yggdrasil and Frey*

This is the creation of the Tree, Yggdrasil, and the formation of the nine worlds. It is an extension of the creation myth, and it shows the expansion of creation past the existing boundaries, like the tarot trump of *The Sun*.

The god Frey can also be associated here. Frey was a solar god who rode his chariot across the heavens each day, giving bounty and a good harvest. Frey is also a god of war, who could cause havoc when angered. He was sometimes called "God of the World."

The 31st Path, Judgment: *Ragarnok*

This is the "dusk of the gods"—a time when all the nine worlds of the gods would vanish, and a new Tree and pantheon would come to take their place. The gods would then fight each other to the death. Evil would have ended. It would be the end of misery and a time of plenty.

The 32nd Path, The World: *Hag of Iarnvid*

The Hag of Iarnvid was sometimes called the "Mother of Evil," although she presented herself as a young beautiful woman. She was initially responsible for the Fall of Asgard. While the trump of The World is not an evil card, it is a card that shows the casting off of the old order. This is where the association to the Hag and her Saturn-like nature comes in. She was the catalyst for the new world order of the gods.

Path	*Godform*
1. Kether	Odin
2. Chokmah	Bragg
3. Binah	Frigga
4. Chesed	Freya
5. Geburah	Thor
6. Tiphareth	Balder
7. Netzach	Sif
8. Hod	Hermond
9. Yesod	Nanna
10. Malkuth	Jord
11. Uranus/The Fool	Sigmund
12. Mercury/ The Magician	Ull
13. Moon/The High Priestess	Idun
14. Venus/Empress	Skade
15. Aries/The Emperor	Njord
16. Taurus/The Hierophant	Mimer
17. Gemini/The Lovers	Frey and Gerd
18. Cancer/The Chariot	Dietrich
19. Leo/Strength	Halfdan
20. Virgo/The Hermit	Hother
21. Jupiter/The Wheel of Fortune	Norns
22. Libra/Justice	Forseti
23. Neptune/Hanged Man	Hadding
24. Scorpio/Death	Hel
25. Sagittarius/Temperance	Bil and Menja
26. Capricorn/Devil	Loki
27. Mars/Blasted Tower	Tyr
28. Aquarius/Star	Saga
29. Pisces/Moon	Ymer
30. Sun/Sun	Yggdrasil and Frey
31. Pluto/Judgment	Ragarnok
32. Saturn/World	Hag of Iarnvid

About the Author

Pat Zalewski by his own admission was a South Sea island adventurer in his early youth, living in New Guinea as a gold prospector. He has also lived in Australia and Southeast Asia. In India, he studied Tantric Yoga under Master Vivandatta in the late 1960s. In 1975, he represented

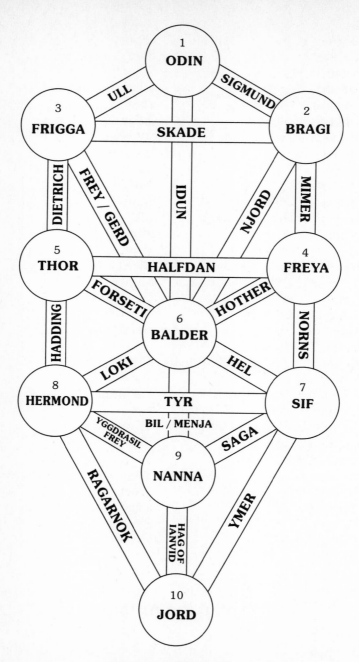

The Norse Pantheon applied to the Tree of Life.

New Zealand in karate at the IAKF World Karate Championships in Los Angeles. He, along with his wife Chris, were initiated into the Golden Dawn through members of its New Zealand temple *Whare Ra* in the late 1970's. He has authored a number of best-selling books on the Golden Dawn, and is in the process of completing books on the Golden Dawn rituals, the Tarot of the Golden Dawn, and on Golden Dawn Talisman and Evocation techniques. A self-confessed fitness fanatic, he lives in Wellington, New Zealand with his wife Chris and daughter Selena, where he is presently a radionic therapist.

Endnotes

1. The Cahill's and Prendagast's from County Clare.
2. First published in 1905.
3. Polish-German and Danish.
4. My Gresham edition is undated, though I suspect around 1912. A possible earlier edition may exist.
5. The reader should keep in mind that these are not the only possible Qabalistic associations of the Celtic and Norse deities.
6. Though Lugh was considered a Sun god. His feats of wisdom far exceed those of anyone else in the Tuatha De Danann.
7. The name means "long-handed" or "far-shooter."
8. His name means "Good God."
9. Called "The Undry."
10. It could both slay and heal at a touch.
11. Translated by Dr. Whitley Stokes (from Harleian, 5280) and published in Revue Celtic, Vol XII, and M. de Jubainville in *L`Epopee Celtique en Irlande.*
12. These evil gods were undersea dwellers with limited eyes and limbs. Balor (of the Evil Eye-Death) is considered their leader.
13. Each of these was a door to an underground kingdom.
14. He was said to be seven years old at the time.
15. Some sources say she sent for the hero after her kingdom was attacked by the Formors.
16. In the Golden Dawn version of *The Fool,* the divine child is brought up in the forests and appears to be reaching toward a blossom from the Tree of Knowledge.
17. Her time of ritual is St. John's Eve.
18. He is depicted as having silver armor and a helmet with ram's horns. His steed is called "Gull-top." His hall is called Himinbjorg "ward of heaven." He is a god who virtually never sleeps, and can see as well in the night as he can in the daylight hours.
19. I have chosen Sigmund here, rather than Loki, because the Golden Dawn version of *The Fool* differs considerably from the standard concepts of the wandering youth or vagabond. The Golden Dawn version touches more on the "divine child" myth—one who survives in the wilderness more than anything else.
20. Possibly the origin of the Jack and Jill myth.

St. John's vision of Christ and the Seven Candlesticks.
(Woodcut by Albrecht Dürer.)

In the Beginning was the Word

Harvey Newstrom

hen the prophet Elijah stood alone on Mt. Carmel against four hundred and fifty prophets of Baal and four hundred prophets of the Asherah, he attempted to convince them of the merits of his belief system of deity over theirs. He reasoned that "If YHVH is the Elohim, go after Him; but if the Baal is, go after Him."[1] He then proposed a test between the two systems. He suggested, "And you shall call on the name of your Elohim; and I will call on the name of YHVH; and He will be the Elohim who answers by fire."[2] Although Elijah was obviously promoting his religion over others, the basic technique is valid for us today. The modern theurgist should question and test each system. If one finds that a particular system works, one should pursue it, but if one finds that a particular system does not work, one should look for another system.

Different Names for the Divine

There are many different pantheons utilized by human beings to represent various aspects of deity. It is this ineffable light that we seek via the Golden Dawn and other systems. Immediately upon being admitted into the 0 = 0 grade of Neophyte of the Hermetic Order of the Golden Dawn, the Hierophant directs the Hiereus to pronounce a short address to the new initiate. After reminding the initiate of the obligation to secrecy, the Hiereus makes the first pronouncement to the new initiate, which is to "Remember that you hold all Religions in reverence, for there is none but contains a Ray from the Ineffable Light that you are seeking."[3]

For the modern practitioner of Western magic there are numerous pantheonic systems for the expression of deity. The Golden Dawn system draws upon well over a dozen Western pantheons of divine names which represent these aspects. The Assyrian, and Assyro-Babylonian divine names are presented to the student along with those deriving from the earlier Sumerian legends.[4] The later Babylonian divine names and Canaanite divine names are included as well.[5] The Egyptian divine names and how they relate to the Neophyte Hall are described in various order documents such as the "Z" documents.[6] The Coptic divine names are likewise explained in these documents.[7] The Hebrew divine names utilized in rituals and associated with the ten Sephiroth are described in the knowledge lectures given to the initiate at each grade.[8] The Samothracian divine names of the Kabiri, the deluge gods, are represented during the initiatory rituals.[9] The Greek divine names are frequently used as archetypes within the Order,[10] while the Roman divine names are referenced as deities in addition to being names of various planets.[11] The Christian divine names and titles of Jesus, Christ, Son of God, Son of Man, and the Holy Spirit, are utilized.[12] Gnostic divine names are found in footnotes to Regardie's *The Golden Dawn*, and the supreme Gnostic divine name of IAO is extensively used in ritual.[13] The Teutonic divine names are available for use by the initiate, along with their later Germanic forms.[14] The Celtic divine names are also available for use by the student.[15] The alchemical divine names are taught during the Zelator grade,[16] and the Qabalistic divine names are taught during the Philosophus grade.[17] The Enochian divine names, including the "Three Great Secret Holy Names of God," associated with each element are established on a tablet in each quarter of the Neophyte Hall.[18] These are sequentially revealed to the initiate at the rate of one per grade after the grade of Neophyte.[19] Even artificial divine names and words derived by early practitioners have been adopted by the Order, such as the contractive notariqons of INRI, Agla, and Ararita.[20] The Golden Dawn makes use of universal archetypes that transcend all religions, such as the Mother Goddess, the Father God, the Holy Child, the Heavenly Consort, the Cosmic Consciousness or Higher Self, and the Divine Spark in each of us that is the individual soul.[21] The Golden Dawn pulls all these representational pantheons together with the universal archetypes to form a unified and consistent system by which the initiate can seek the Divine.

Although the Order utilizes these many different pantheons of divine names, the Hebrew divine names are the most prominent within the system. The term "divine name" in the Golden Dawn specifically refers to the Hebrew divine name associated with each Sephira on the Tree of Life. This usage stems from the evolution of ceremonial Qabalah from its roots in Jewish mysticism, and not from any preference for one pantheon over another. The Jewish mystic would naturally use the Hebrew names for the Divine, and the writings of those early mystics would naturally reflect this usage. Since the concepts of the ten Sephiroth and the Tree of Life are derived from the Hebrew sources, it is natural that the Hebrew terminology would be the primary mode for representing the deity therein. Other pantheons can be applied to the Tree of Life, but they lack the historical and evolutionary basis for their usage and are open to more interpretation by each practitioner. For the purpose of investigation into the sources of the divine names, this article will focus on the ancient Hebrew divine names and their origins.

The Names of Creation

The Gospel According to John tells us that:

> In the beginning was the Word, and the Word was with God, and the Word was God. He was in the beginning with God. All things through Him came into being, and without Him came into being not even one thing that came into being. In Him was life, and the life was the light of the world, and the light shines in the darkness, and the darkness comprehended it not.[22]

It was the word of the Divine that was utilized to create the universe. Each and every act of creation was accomplished through the divine word.

The *Sepher Yetzirah*, or the Book of Formation, tells us that "Ten are the ineffable Sephiroth. Twenty-two are the Letters, the Foundation of all things...."[23] The text makes an association between the ten Sephiroth of creation and the Hebrew formative letters of words. It then goes on to say that:

> Ten is the number of the ineffable Sephiroth, ten and not nine, ten and not eleven. Understand this wisdom, and be wise in the perception. Search out concerning it, restore the Word to its creator, and replace Him who formed it upon his throne.[24]

Here we see that the word of creation has come from the Divine and must return to the Divine. The text goes on to state that:

> The ten ineffable Sephiroth have the appearance of the Lightning flash, their origin is unseen and no end is perceived. The Word is in them as they rush forth and as they return, they speak as from the whirlwind, and returning fall prostrate in adoration before the Throne.[25]

The divine word is manifest in each of the ten Sephiroth as they originate. Every sphere that has been created has been created through the power of these manifestations of the word. As the text states:

> The twenty-two sounds and letters are the Foundation of all things.... He hath formed, weighed, and composed with these twenty-two letters every soul, and the soul of everything which shall hereafter be.[26]

Finally, we see that the word manifest in each of the ten Sephiroth is the power of the divine name as it is revealed in each sphere. The text summarizes that the Divine:

> ...(B)y the power of His Name made every creature and everything that is; and the production of all things from the twenty-two letters is the proof that they are all but parts of one body.[27]

Thus, we can see that in the Qabalistic system of the Tree of Life, the Word of creation is the divine name, and it is by the divine name that everything was created. The word *Sephira* comes from the Hebrew root meaning to speak, to write, or to enumerate. The ten divine words are the ten divine names of deity, which are proclaimed in the ten spheres of creation that are the Sephiroth on the Tree of Life.

This view of creation is supported in the *Sepher Bahir,* or the Book of Brilliance, which tells us that all was created by the Tree, which consists of ten "sayings." The Blessed Holy One says "I am the One who planted this tree in order that all the world should delight in it. And in it, I spread All."[28] The text tells us that "We have learned that there are Ten Spheres and Ten Sayings. Each Sphere has its Saying...."[29] The ten sayings of creation are then described, obviously corresponding to the ten Sephiroth on the Tree of Life. The *Sepher Bahir* represents an early understanding of the same ten Sephiroth as on the modern Tree of Life, although there are a couple of minor differences. Malkuth is "supported" above Yesod, which is elevated higher than Netzach and Hod (the second Netzach).

Ten Sephiroth (Sayings) of Creation in the *Sepher Bahir*[30]

Saying 1. "The first is the Highest Crown (Kether)…who is unified in all His Names."

Saying 2. "The second one is Wisdom (Chokmah)…the fear of YHVH."

Saying 3. "The third one is the quarry of the Torah, the Treasury of Wisdom, the quarry of the spirit of YHVH."

Saying 4. "The fourth is the charity of YHVH, His merit, and His Kindness (Chesed) to all the world."

Saying 5. "The fifth is the Great Fire…the Left Hand of the Blessed Holy One."

Saying 6. "The sixth one is the Throne of Glory, crowned, included, praised and hailed."

Saying 7. "What is the seventh? It is the firmament of Arabhoth (Plains)."

Saying 8. "What is the eighth one? …(A) single Righteous One (Tzadiq)…. It is the Foundation (Yesod) of all souls."

Saying 9 and 10. "The ninth and tenth are together, one opposite the other."

"There is a single Victory (Netzach)…. It is the one that inclines toward the west. … And what is secondary to it? This is the one that inclines toward the north."

This view of creation meshes well with the creation sequence found in the book of *Genesis*. Here, too, we find ten declarations of the Divine successively manifesting the different domains of creation in sequence. The ten iterations of the phrase "And God said…." that occur in the first chapter of Genesis are undoubtedly the inspiration for the ten sayings as described in the *Sepher Bahir*.[31] Although the sequencing of the ten Sephiroth are not as clearly recognized in the Genesis account, what does seem to be more evident are the examples of the four stages of manifestation between the divine archetype and the material product of creation. These stages correspond to the four worlds of Qabalah. Upon examining the *Genesis* account, we find that each of the ten statements of creation is enacted through four stages of manifestation. Firstly, there is the archetypal proclamation by the Divine directing that the creation occur. This is the action of the Yod of the Tetragrammaton acting in the world of Atziluth. Secondly, there is the creative act of manifestation by the Divine that produces that which is created. This is the action of the Heh of the Tetragrammaton acting in the world of Briah. Thirdly, there is the formative reconciliation of the creation into the duality of two contending forces. This is the action of the Vav of the Tetragrammaton acting in the world of Yetzirah. Finally, there is the material analysis in which the results of creation are observed to be "good." This is the action of the final Heh of the Tetragrammaton acting in the world of Assiah.

The Ten Sephiroth (Sayings) and Four Worlds of Creation in *Genesis*[32]

	YOD 1. Atziluth *(World of Deity)*	HEH 2. Briah *(World of Creation)*	VAV 3. Yetzirah *(World of Formation)*	HEH 4. Assiah *(World of Action)*
Saying 1 (Day 1)	"Let there be light"	and there was light	Elohim divided the light from the darkness	Elohim saw the light, that it was good[33]
Saying 2 (Day 2)	"Let there be a firmament in the midst of the waters"	and Elohim made the firmament	Elohim...divided the waters that were under the firmament from the waters that were above the firmament	Elohim called the firmament Heaven[34]
Saying 3 (Day 3)	"Let the dry land appear"	and it was so	Elohim called the dry land Earth and ...the waters Seas	Elohim saw that it was good
Saying 4 (Day 3)	"Let the earth bring forth" grass"	and the earth brought forth grass	and herb yielding seed after its kind, and tree yielding fruit...after its kind	Elohim saw that it was good
Saying 5 (Day 4)	"Let there be lights in the firmament"	and it was so	Elohim made two great lights; the large light to rule the day, and the small light to rule the night	Elohim saw that it was good

Saying 6 (Day 5)	"Let the waters be filled with many kinds of living creatures and birds"	Elohim created...	every kind of creature that lives in the waters and every kind of winged bird	Elohim saw that it was good
Saying 7 (Day 6)	"Let the earth bring forth all kinds of living creatures..."[35]	and it was so	Elohim made the beasts of the earth after their kind, and everything that creeps upon the earth after its kind	Elohim saw that it was good
Saying 8 (Day 6)	"Let us make man in Our image"	Elohim created man	Elohim created them male and female	And Elohim blessed them
Saying 9 (Day 6)	"Be fruitful and multiply... ....subdue...rule..."	-	-	-
Saying 10 (Day 6)	"Behold..."	-	"I have given you... and where there is life, I have given [them]..."	And Elohim saw everything that was made and behold, it was very good

The Evolution of the Names

Qabalistic texts describe the divine source descending from the highest sphere in Kether to the lowest sphere of Malkuth. The earliest of these texts do not differentiate the names for the Divine from the name of each sphere. In *Genesis*, the early writer was concerned with describing what was created by each statement. In the *Sepher Bahir*, the early writer was concerned with describing the attributes expressed by the deity in each statement. In the *Sepher Yetzirah*, the early writer was concerned with the Tree as representing paths toward deity. There was not a division between the Divine in each sphere and the sphere of the Divine until later in Qabalistic development. The *Zohar* reflects this when it states of the Sephiroth, "He is They and They are He."[36] To the early Qabalists, the Sephira Abba literally *was* the Father God and the Sephira Aima literally *was* the Mother Goddess. It was not until later that the spheres were seen as locations separate from the divinity that embodied them.

Originally, the same divine name was applied to all of the Sephiroth. Genesis describes Elohim as performing all ten of the creative statements. The *Sepher Bahir* describes YHVH or "The Blessed Holy One" as manifesting all ten of its creative statements. As the study of the different spheres developed, there probably would have been references to "YHVH, the Elohim," "YHVH in Geburah," "YHVH, the Deity of Knowledge," or "YHVH, the Deity of Hosts" and the like. The use of distinguishing titles for the Divine in each sphere probably led to the development of more consistent terminology. Eventually, this would have led to the standardized list of divine names that we use today.

A possible example of this can be seen in the Pirkei *Hekhaloth*—specifically the chapters on the Palaces. The text describes the ascent to the *Merkabah* (chariot) through seven Palaces of deity. Entry is gained into each Palace by the presentation of two seals, one of which is for the YHVH of the Palace. The YHVH of the Palace represents the Hebrew divine name of the YHVH as manifested down into the different spheres. In this text, however, we see the name of YHVH prefixed with a different name within each Palace.[37] This may be an example of a text describing a single deity within all spheres, but trying to differentiate which aspect of the Divine is manifested in each.

Of all the divine names used for deity in the Hebrew language, YHVH is the most exact and personal. This name alone represents a specific divinity, while the other terms are more generic. The word Elohim, for example, is used by the Hebrews not only to represent *their* god, but also *other* gods, new gods, and even strange gods.[38] It is used to describe the Egyptian gods and goddesses, the goddess Ashtoreth, and even idols.[39] In many descriptions of calamity, the writings state that each person prayed to their own Elohim.[40] The same applies to shorter forms of the word such as Eloah and El. Other terms such as Adonai, which means ruler, and Shaddai, which means mighty, are euphemisms that describe the Divine, but they are also used of people and are not personal names. Only YHVH represents the personal and actual name of the divinity in the Hebrew language.

YHVH, therefore, was probably the original name that was utilized in all the spheres. The formula of YHVH is believed to be the root and foundation of all the divine names.[41] We also see YHVH being transliterated into Greek as the all-important IAO of the Gnostics. Many ancient writers state that IAO was the name of the Hebrew deity.[42] It seems very likely that the divine names all derived from the supreme name of YHVH.

An additional aspect of the evolution of the divine names might have come from the traditional Hebrew practice of not pronouncing the Tetragrammaton when merely repeating sentences aloud. This was done to avoid invoking the divine name in vain. For this purpose, the traditional Hebrew would pronounce the word "Adonai" in place of YHVH.[43] They would write the modern vowel marks for "Adonai" under the consonants of YHVH to remind them to do this. This lead later scholars to misread the name as "Jehovah," which was never pronounced in any case.[44] An exception to this pronunciation would be where the phrase already contained the word Adonai, in which case the word Elohim would be substituted instead.[45] Thus, the name "Adonai YHVH" would be pronounced "Adonai Elohim" instead of "Adonai Adonai."[46] In this case, the vowel marks for "Elohim" were written under the consonants of YHVH, again causing confusion among later scholars.[47] It is possible that these variations in the oral representation of the names may have contributed to the differing references to the Divine. Many of the divine names containing "Adonai" or "Elohim" may have in fact originally been more direct references to the Tetragrammaton.

The Names of the Spheres

The ten divine names of creation became standardized into the ten Sephiroth that we know today. Their arrangement varied as the understanding of the Divine evolved, but the common arrangement has become a virtual standard for modern Qabalah. The Tree of Life is arranged with the most high Kether at the top of the Tree. Under Kether we find Chokmah and Binah, the Supernal Father and Mother. Under these we find Chesed and Geburah, the archetypal Mercy and Severity. Under this, in the place of perfect balance at the center of the Tree, we find Tiphareth, the Throne of Glory. Below Tiphareth, we discern Netzach and Hod, representing the Lord of Hosts in two dualities. Beneath this, situated on the Middle Pillar, we find Yesod, which corresponds to the Akashic just above our physical world. And finally, at the bottom, we find our own Mother Earth, Malkuth.

Kether

Kether is the first appearance of deity, which is described as embodying "The Crown."[48] This masculine[49] Hebrew name is pronounced "KEH-ther."[50] It means a circlet, a diadem, or a crown.[51] The name derives from the Hebrew root verb meaning to surround or to environ, and to wait.[52]

Other names include *Existence of Existences, Concealed of the Concealed, Ancient of Ancients, Ancient of Days, The Smooth Point, The Primordial Point, The Most High, The Vast Countenance, The White Head, The Head Which Is Not,* and *Macroprosopus.*[53] Kether can be represented by the symbols of the point, the point within a circle, the crown, and the swastika or fylfot cross. The Ultimate is seen as being colored with brilliance in Atziluth, a pure white brilliance in Briah and Yetzirah, and white flecked with gold in Assiah.

The *Sepher Yetzirah* describes this divinity as being:

> ...(T)he Admirable or Hidden Intelligence because it is the Light giving the power of comprehension of the First Principle, which hath not beginning. And it is the Primal Glory, because no created being can attain to its essence.[54]

The *Sepher Bahir* describes this divinity as being:

> ...(T)he Highest Crown. Blessed and praised be its name and its people. Who are its people? They are Israel. It is thus written 'Know that the YHVH is God, He has made us, and not we ourselves.' We are to recognize and know the Unity of Unities, who is unified in all His names.[55]

The Golden Dawn relates Kether to the source of all things and the highest divine essence of which we can conceive.[56]

Eheieh is the grand word used as the divine name of Kether.[57] This Hebrew name means "I Am" and has no gender associated with it.[58] It is pronounced "ay-HAY-yay." The name derives from the Hebrew root verb meaning to be, to exist, to become, to be made, to be done, to come to pass, and to experience.[59] It is not defined as masculine or feminine, nor is it a word that can be defined in terms of other words. It just is what it is.

In *Exodus*, this is the name given to Moses by the Divine:

> And Elohim said to Moses, I am (Eheieh) who I am (Eheieh); and He said, You shall say this to the children of Israel, I am (Eheieh) has sent me to you. ...(T)his is My Name forever, and this is My Title from generation to generation.[60]

This name is often used in connection with the communion aspects of deity.

In *The Key of Solomon*, the conjuration takes place:

> ...*(B)y the Power, Wisdom, and the Virtue of the Spirit of God, by the uncreate Divine Knowledge, by the vast Mercy of God, by the Strength of God, by the Greatness of God, by the Unity of God; and by the Holy Name of God Eheieh, which is the root, trunk, source, and origin of all the other divine names, whence they all draw their life and their virtue, which Adam having invoked, he acquired the knowledge of all created things.*[61]

Chokmah

Chokmah is the second appearance of deity, which is described as embodying "Wisdom."[62] This feminine[63] Hebrew name is pronounced "khok-MAW."[64] It means skill, dexterity, and wisdom.[65] The name derives from the Hebrew root verb meaning to be wise, to judge, and to rule.

Abba is an alternative name, which is described as embodying the Supernal Father.[66] This masculine Hebrew name is pronounced "AWB-bah."[67] It means father, ancestor, founder, author, maker, nourisher, master, teacher, and possessor.[68] The name derives from the Hebrew root verb meaning to produce fruit, to be verdant, and to germinate.

Other names include *Power of Yetzirah, Tetragrammaton,* and *Yod* of Tetragrammaton.[69] He can be represented by the symbols of the phallus, the letter Yod, the Inner Robe of Glory, the standing stone, the tower, the uplifted Rod of Power, and the straight line. Chokmah is seen as being colored pure soft blue in Atziluth, gray in Briah, pearl gray iridescence in Yetzirah, and white flecked with red, blue, and yellow in Assiah.

The *Sepher Yetzirah* describes this divinity as being:

> ...*(T)he Illuminating Intelligence. It is the Crown of Creation, the Splendor of Unity, equaling it. It is exalted above every head, and is named by Qabalists, the Second Glory.*[70]

The *Sepher Bahir* describes this divinity as being:

> ...*Wisdom. It is thus written 'YHVH possesses me in the beginning of His way, before His works from then.' A beginning is nothing other than Wisdom (Chokmah), as it is written 'The fear of YHVH is the beginning of Wisdom (Chokmah).'*[71]

The Golden Dawn relates Chokmah to the Supernal Father and the root essence of masculine or dynamic force.[72]

Yah or *Jah*, shortened from YHVH, is the grand word used as the divine name of Chokmah.[73] This Hebrew name is pronounced "YAW."[74] It is derived from the beginning of the Tetragrammaton.[75] The full Tetragrammaton formula of YHVH represents the ultimate formula of balance. It embodies the interplay of masculine and feminine, past and future, above and below. The four letters of the Tetragrammaton are ascribed to Father, Mother, Son, and Daughter, or Fire, Water, Air, and Earth. It represents all of the elements of creation. The Digrammaton represents the beginning of the YHVH formula in this sphere, which finds its completion in the next sphere. Sometimes this name is abbreviated to the Monogrammaton or Yod of YHVH, again representing the beginning of the formula. The Digrammaton is also used as a suffix on Hebrew names ending in "-iah" or "-jah" and represents their connection to the Divine.[76] Some texts give the full Tetragrammaton in this sphere, probably considering this to be the beginning of the formula of YHVH Elohim, which finds its completion in the next sphere.

In *The Key of Solomon*, the conjuration takes place:

> ...(B)y the Indivisible Name Yod, which marketh and expresseth the Simplicity and the Unity of the Nature Divine, which Abel having invoked, he deserved to escape from the hands of Cain his brother.[77]

Binah

Binah is the third appearance of deity, which is described as embodying "Understanding."[78] This feminine[79] Hebrew name is pronounced "bee-NAH."[80] It means understanding, intelligence, and skill.[81] The name derives from the Hebrew root verb meaning to distinguish, to separate, to discern, to perceive, to counsel, to understand, to regard or know, to be prudent, to be intelligent, or to perceive.

Aima is an alternative name, which is described as embodying the Supernal Mother.[82] This feminine[83] Hebrew name is pronounced "am-MAW."[84] It means mother, grandmother, a parting, and metropolis.[85] The name derives from the Hebrew root verb meaning to join together, to be near, and to be related.

Khorsia is another name which is described as embodying the Throne.[86] This masculine[87] Hebrew name is pronounced "kor-see-YAH."[88] It means throne, tribunal, and seat.[89] The name derives from the Hebrew root verb meaning to cover, to cover over, and to conceal.

Marah is yet another name which is described as embodying the Great Sea.[90] This feminine[91] Hebrew name is pronounced "maw-RAW."[92] It means bitter water, acrid water, bitterness, sadness, sorrow, and fierceness.[93] The name derives from the Hebrew root verb meaning to flow, to drip, to distill, to be embittered, to irritate, to provoke, to sadden, and to weep.

Other names include *Aima, the bright fertile mother*, and *Ama, the dark sterile mother*.[94] Binah is also called the *Supernal Mother* and the *Heh* of Tetragrammaton. She can be represented by the symbols of the vesica piscis, the cup or chalice, and the Outer Robe of Concealment. She can also be represented by the symbols of the womb, the triangle, and the letter Heh. Binah is seen as being colored crimson in Atziluth, black in Briah, dark brown in Yetzirah, and gray flecked with pink in Assiah.

The *Sepher Yetzirah* describes this divinity as being:

> ...(T)he Sanctifying Intelligence, the Foundation of Primordial Wisdom; it is also called the Creator of Faith, and its roots are in Amen.[95] It is the parent of faith, whence faith emanates.[96]

The *Sepher Bahir* describes this divinity as being:

> ...(T)he quarry of the Torah, the treasury of Wisdom, the quarry of the spirit of YHVH."[97] It goes on to expand upon Her by stating, "This teaches us that YHVH carved out all the letters of the Torah, engraved it with spirit, and with it made all Forms. This is the meaning of the verse 'There is no rock like our YHVH.' There is no former like our YHVH.[98]

The Golden Dawn relates Binah to the Supernal Mother and the great negative polarity. It is a feminine, watery force.[99]

YHVH Elohim is the grand word used as the divine name of Binah.[100] It represents the completion of the YHVH formula. It also represents another formula, that of Elohim. The Hebrew name Elohim is a masculine plural of a feminine noun.[101] With such construction, the name also represents both the active and passive dualities of the universe. The Hebrew name is pronounced "el-o-HEEM."[102] It means deities and divinity, and is used to represent gods, goddesses, and even idols.[103] Some authors tend to associate the YHVH more with the masculine deities because of its initiating actions on the masculine pillar, while associating Elohim more with the feminine deities because of its completing actions on the feminine pillar. The combined formulas of YHVH and Elohim are used to represent not only Binah, but the completion of the Supernal Triad as well.

In the first chapter of Genesis, it is the Elohim who are the creators. "In the beginning Elohim created the heavens and the earth."[104] Ten times we find the phrase "And Elohim said…." All humanity was created in the image of the Elohim. "And Elohim said, Let Us make man in Our image, according to Our likeness."[105] In the first chapter, they are Elohim. In the second chapter, they are YHVH Elohim. These names are often used in connection with the creating aspects of deity or the highest aspects of deity.

In *The Key of Solomon*, the conjuration takes place:

> …(B)y the Name Tetragrammaton Elohim, which expresseth and signifieth the Grandeur of so lofty a Majesty, that Noah having pronounced it, saved himself, and protected himself with his whole household from the Waters of the Deluge.[106]

Chesed

Chesed is the fourth appearance of deity, which is described as embodying "Mercy."[107] This masculine[108] Hebrew name is pronounced "KHEH-sed."[109] It means desire, ardor, zeal, love, kindness, benignity, benevolence, piety, grace, favor, and mercy.[110] The name derives from the Hebrew root verb meaning to love, to desire, to emulate, to envy, and to be gracious.

Gedulah is an alternative name, which is described as embodying Glory.[111] This feminine[112] Hebrew name is pronounced "ghed-oo-LAW."[113] It means magnitude, greatness, and magnificence.[114] The name derives from the Hebrew root verb meaning to twist together, to bind together, to become great, to grow, to be greatly valued, and to be praised.

Other names include *Majesty* and *Magnificence*.[115] This sphere can be represented by the symbols of the tetrahedron or pyramid, the orb, the wand, the scepter, and the crook. Chesed can also be represented by the symbol of the square. Chesed is seen as being colored deep violet in Atziluth, blue in Briah, deep purple in Yetzirah, and deep azure flecked with yellow in Assiah.

The *Sepher Yetzirah* describes this divinity as being:

> ...(T)he Cohesive or Receptive Intelligence because it contains all the Holy Powers, and from it emanate all the spiritual virtues with the most exalted essences. They emanate one from another by virtue of the Primordial Emanation, the Highest Crown, Kether.[116]

The *Sepher Bahir* describes this divinity as being:

> ...(T)he charity of YHVH, His merit, and His Kindness (Chesed) to all the world. This is the Right Hand of the Blessed Holy One.[117]

The Golden Dawn relates Chesed to "the builder" and the matrix upon which the archetypal ideas will be built into tangible form.[118]

El is the grand word used as the divine name of Chesed.[119] This masculine[120] Hebrew name is pronounced "ALE."[121] It means might and strength.[122] It derives from the Hebrew word for a mighty one, a leader, a noble, and a robust one. This name may also be seen as the beginning of the Elohim formula. This Digrammaton is also used as a suffix on Hebrew names ending in "-al" or "-el" and represents their connection to the Divine, but in a somewhat lower fashion than those with the suffix deriving from Yah.[123]

In Exodus, it is El who is served by Melchizedek, the righteous king of Salem who came to Abraham.[124] It was in the name of El that Melchizedek pronounced the blessings on Abraham. This name is often used in connection with the merciful and benevolent aspects of deity.

In The *Key of Solomon*, the conjuration takes place:

> ...(B)y the Name El Strong and Wonderful, which denoteth the Mercy and Goodness of His Majesty Divine, which Abraham having invoked, he was found worthy to come forth from the Ur of the Chaldeans.[125]

Geburah

Geburah is the fifth appearance of deity, which is described as embodying "Severity."[126] This feminine[127] Hebrew name is pronounced "gheb-oo-RAW."[128] It means strength, fortitude, military virtue, power, and victory.[129] The name derives from the Hebrew root verb meaning to be strong, to prevail, to bind, to strengthen, to be proud, and to be insolent.

Din is an older name, which is described as embodying Judgment.[130] This masculine[131] Hebrew name is pronounced "DEEN."[132] It means judgment, strife, controversy, justice, and penalty.[133] The name derives from the Hebrew root verb meaning to rule, to regulate, to subdue, to subjugate, to judge, and to contend.

Pachad is alternative older name, which is described as embodying Fear.[134] This masculine[135] Hebrew name is pronounced "PAKH-ad."[136] It means fear and terror.[137] The name derives from the Hebrew root verb meaning to tremble, to be in trepidation, to hasten, to be timid, and to be cautious.

Other names include *The Great Fire* and the *Left Hand of the Divine*.[138] Geburah can be represented by the symbols of the pentagon, the five-petalled rose or Tudor Rose, the sword, the spear, the scourge, and the chain. Geburah is seen as being colored orange in Atziluth, scarlet red in Briah, bright scarlet in Yetzirah, and red flecked with black in Assiah.

The *Sepher Yetzirah* describes this divinity as being:

> ...(T)he Radical Intelligence because it resembles Unity, uniting itself to Binah, Understanding, which emanates from the primordial depths of Chokmah, Wisdom.[139]

The *Sepher Bahir* describes this divinity as being:

> ...(T)he great fire of the Blessed Holy One. Regarding this it is written 'Let me not see this great fire any more, lest I die.' This is the Left Hand of the Blessed Holy One.[140]

The Golden Dawn relates Geburah to the energy that burns away all that is useless or outmoded.[141]

Elohim Gibor is the grand word used as the divine name of Geburah.[142] This phrase means Elohim of Geburah. The name Elohim may be seen as completing the Elohim formula, which was begun in Chesed, much in the way the YHVH formula is begun in Chokmah and completed in Binah.

In *The Key of Solomon*, the conjuration takes place:

> ...(B)y the most powerful Name of Elohim Gibor, which showeth forth the Strength of God, of a God All Powerful, Who punisheth the crimes of the wicked, Who seeketh out

and chastiseth the iniquities of the fathers upon the children unto the third and fourth generation; which Isaac having invoked, he was found worthy to escape from the Sword of Abraham his father.[143]

Tiphareth

Tiphareth is the sixth appearance of deity, which is described as embodying "Beauty."[144] This feminine[145] Hebrew name is pronounced "tif-EH-reth."[146] It means ornament, splendor, and glory.[147] The name derives from the Hebrew root verb meaning to be beautiful, to be ornamented, to be proud, to be adorned, to be honored, to be glorified, and to boast.

Other names include *Zoar Anpin, The Lesser Countenance, and Melekh* (the King).[148] Tiphareth was originally called the *Throne of Glory.*[149] Tiphareth is also called the *Vav* of Tetragrammaton. Tiphareth can be represented by the symbols of the lamen, the Rose Cross, the Calvary Cross, the truncated pyramid, and the cube. Tiphareth is seen as being colored clear rose-pink in Atziluth, yellow in Briah, rich salmon pink in Yetzirah, and golden amber in Assiah.

The *Sepher Yetzirah* describes this divinity as being:

> ...(T)he Mediating Intelligence, because in it are multiplied the influxes of the Emanations; for it causes that influence to flow into all the reservoirs of the blessings with which they themselves are united.[150]

The *Sepher Bahir* describes this divinity as being:

> ...(T)he Throne of Glory, crowned, included, praised and hailed. It is the house of the World to Come, and its place is in Wisdom. It is thus written 'then Elohim said, let there be light, and there was light.'[151]

The Golden Dawn relates Tiphareth to the Mediator, Reconciler, or Redeemer, which reconciles "that which is above to that which is below."[152]

YHVH Eloah ve-Daath is the grand word used as the divine name of Tiphareth.[153] The Hebrew name Eloah is pronounced "el-OH-ah."[154] It is a longer form of the name El found on the masculine pillar, and can also be seen as being a shorter form of the name Elohim found on the feminine pillar. In this case, it is a singular form of the name for deity. The full name also contains the YHVH, which is the complete formula of the Divine descending down through the four worlds. Therefore, this phrase can be seen as representing the balance of YHVH and Elohim, residing between the left and right, and residing between that which is above and that which is below. The full phrase means "YHVH, Deity of Daath (Knowledge)." The reference to Daath indicates the combination of Aima and Abba, which is seen as the top point of the hexagram, representing the Supernals. It probably indicates the Reconciler as being the child of the Mother Goddess and Father God, as indicated in the YHVH formula, as Tiphareth is associated with the Vav in that formula.

In *The Key of Solomon*, the conjuration takes place:

> ...(B)y the most holy Name of Eloah ve-Daath, which Jacob invoked when in great trouble, and was found worthy to bear the Name of Israel, which signifieth Vanquisher of God; and he was delivered from the fury of Esau his brother.[155]

Netzach

Netzach is the seventh appearance of deity, which is described as embodying "Victory."[156] This masculine[157] Hebrew name is pronounced "NEH-tsakh."[158] It means splendor, glory, faith, confidence, perpetuity, eternity, perfection, and completeness.[159] The name derives from the Hebrew root verb meaning to shine, to be bright, to be pure, to be chaste, to be sincere, to be faithful, to superintend, to be perfect, and to be complete.

Other names include *Firmness* and *Valor*.[160] Netzach can be represented by the symbols of the lamp, the girdle, and the rose. Netzach is seen as being colored amber in Atziluth, emerald in Briah, bright yellow green in Yetzirah, and olive flecked with gold in Assiah.

The *Sepher Yetzirah* describes this divinity as being:

> ...(T)he Occult Intelligence because it is the refulgent splendor of the intellectual virtues which are perceived by the eyes of the intellect and the contemplations of faith.[161]

The *Sepher Bahir* describes Netzach as being related to Hod:

> They are like two wheels. One inclines toward the north, while the other inclines toward the west. They reach down

> *to the lowest earth…. The Victory (Netzach) of the world is*
> *there. It is thus written '…(F)or victory of victories (Net-*
> *zach Netzachim).' What is the meaning of victory of victo-*
> *ries? There is a single victory (Netzach). What is it? It is the*
> *one that inclines toward the west.*[162]

The Golden Dawn relates Netzach to the emotions of the Right Brain and the group mind that expresses art, music, dance and poetry.[163]

YHVH Tzabaoth is the grand word used as the divine name of Netzach.[164] The Hebrew name Tzabaoth is pronounced "tzah-baw-OTH" and is a plural form of the Tzabah.[165] It is a masculine name but occasionally is used with the feminine form of the verb.[166] It means armies and hosts, usually referring to the hosts of angels.[167] It derives from the Hebrew root verb meaning to go forth and to muster. Netzach and Hod are associated with the Yetziratic world of angels. At this level, the divinity is referenced as being the Deity of hosts. The use of YHVH Tzabaoth for Netzach is again indicative of the use of YHVH for the initiating actions of the masculine pillar. Here the initiating actions of the YHVH Tzabaoth are in conjunction with the completing actions of the Elohim Tzabaoth in Hod.

In the *Old Testament*, it is the Lord of Hosts who directs the armies of angels to do battle. This description is used to reference the intervening aspects of deity. The YHVH Tzabaoth form is used most frequently, often before or during a battle or conflict directed by the Divine. It is the YHVH Elohi Tzabaoth form of Hod that is often used when describing the conclusion or outcome of such a conflict.

In *The Key of Solomon*, the conjuration takes place:

> *…(B)y the most potent Name of El Adonai Tzabaoth, which*
> *is the God of Armies, ruling in the Heavens, which Joseph*
> *invoked, and was found worthy to escape from the hands of*
> *his Brethren.*[168]

This text uses the name El Adonai Tzabaoth instead of the usual YHVH Tzabaoth, and may be an example of where the Tetragrammaton is replaced by the name Adonai. In other places the conjuration uses the term Tetragrammaton instead of spelling out YHVH.

Hod

Hod is the eighth appearance of deity, which is described as embodying "Glory."[169] This masculine[170] Hebrew name is pronounced "HODE."[171]

It means beauty, comeliness, excellency, glory, honor, and majesty.[172] The name derives from the Hebrew root verb meaning to shine, to give light, to be glad, and to rejoice.

Hod can be represented by the names of power, the versicles, and the Masonic apron.[173] Hod is seen as being colored violet purple in Atziluth, orange in Briah, red russet in Yetzirah, and yellowish black flecked with white in Assiah.

The *Sepher Yetzirah* describes this divinity as being:

> ...(T)he Absolute or Perfect Intelligence because it is the mean of the Primordial, which has no root by which it can cleave or rest, save in the hidden places of Gedulah, from which emanates its proper essence.[174]

The *Sepher Bahir* describes this divinity as being "the second victory (second Netzach)" and "the left foot of the Blessed Holy One." It describes Hod as being related to Netzach by stating:

> They are like two wheels. One inclines toward the north, while the other inclines toward the west. They reach down to the lowest earth.... There is a single victory (Netzach).... And what is secondary to it? It is the one that inclines toward the north.[175]

The Golden Dawn relates Hod to the intellect of the Left Brain and the individual mind, which expresses writing, language, communication, science, and magic.[176]

Elohim Tzabaoth, shortened from YHVH *Elohi Tzabaoth*, is the grand word used as the divine name of Hod.[177] The Hebrew name Tzabaoth is used here in the same manner as seen for Netzach. Again, the divinity is referenced as being the Deity of Hosts. The use of Elohim Tzabaoth for Hod again represents the use of Elohim for the completing actions of the feminine pillar. Here the completing actions of the Elohim Tzabaoth are in conjunction with the initiating actions of the YHVH Tzabaoth in Netzach.

In the *Old Testament*, it is the Lord of Hosts who directs the armies of angels to do battle. This description is used to reference the intervening aspects of deity. The YHVH Elohi Tzabaoth is used less frequently, often when describing the conclusion or outcome of a battle or conflict directed by the Divine. It is the YHVH Tzabaoth form that is used most frequently, often before or during such a conflict.

In *The Key of Solomon*, the conjuration takes place:

...(B)y the most potent name of Elohim Tzabaoth, which expresseth piety, mercy, splendor, and knowledge of God, which Moses invoked, and he was found worthy to deliver the People Israel from Egypt, and from the servitude of Pharaoh.[178]

Yesod

Yesod is the ninth Sphere of deity, which is described as embodying "the Foundation."[179] This masculine[180] Hebrew name is pronounced "yes-ODE."[181] It means foundation, beginning, or base.[182] The name derives from the Hebrew root verb meaning to found, to set, to constitute, to establish, to support, to lean, to rest, to appoint, and to ordain.

Tzadiq is an older name, which is described as embodying "the Righteous."[183] This masculine[184] Hebrew name is pronounced "TSEH-dek"[185] It means straightness, rightness, justice, rectitude, right and just.[186] The name derives from the Hebrew root verb meaning to be right, to be straight, to be stiff, to be just, to be righteous, to have a just cause, to speak the truth, and to be upright.

Yesod is also called the *Treasurehouse of Images*.[187] Yesod can be represented by the symbols of perfume and sandals. Yesod is seen as being colored indigo in Atziluth, violet in Briah, very dark purple in Yetzirah, and citrine flecked with azure in Assiah.

The *Sepher Yetzirah* describes this divinity as being:

> *...(T)he Pure Intelligence because it purifies the Emanations. It proves and corrects the designing of their representations, and disposes the unity with which they are designed without diminution or division.*[188]

The *Sepher Bahir* describes this divinity by stating:

> *The Blessed Holy One has a single Righteousness (Tzadiq) in His World, and it is dear to Him because it supports all the world. It is the foundation (Yesod). This is what sustains it, and makes it grow, increasing and watching it. It is beloved and dear on high, and beloved and dear below; fearsome and mighty on high, and fearsome and mighty below; rectified and accepted on high, and rectified and accepted below. It is the foundation (Yesod) of all souls.*[189]

The Golden Dawn relates Yesod to the astral light and Akashic matrix upon which the entire universe is built and wherein all magical operations take place.[190]

Shaddai El Chai is the grand word used as the divine name of Yesod.[191] The masculine[192] Hebrew name Shaddai is pronounced "shad-DAH-ee."[193] It means the most powerful and the mightiest.[194] It derives from the Hebrew root verb meaning to be strong, to be powerful, to oppress, and to destroy. The Hebrew name El Chai is pronounced "ALE KHAH-ee."[195] It means the deity (El) who is alive, living, lively, vigorous, flourishing, prosperous, reviving, and fresh.[196] The Hebrew name Chai derives from the Hebrew root verb meaning to live, to breathe, to continue, to revive, to be healthy, to be refreshed, to enliven, and to give life. These two deity names are combined to give us the full modern phrase.[197] Altogether, the phrase can be understood as the Mighty Deity of Life.

In the book of *Job* can be found most occurrences of the name Shaddai. Both Shaddai and El Chai refer to the supporting aspects of deity, and by contrast the undermining aspect of deity when that support is withdrawn. As Job responds to Bildad, the Shuhite, "El Chai has taken away my judgment, and Shaddai has embittered my soul."[198]

In *The Key of Solomon*, the conjuration takes place:

> ...(B)y the most potent Name of Shaddai, which signifieth doing good unto all; which Moses invoked, and having struck the Sea, it divided into two parts in the midst, on the right hand and on the left." and "by the most holy Name of El Chai, which is that of the Living God, through the virtue of which alliance with us, and redemption for us have been made; which Moses invoked and all the waters returned to their prior state and enveloped the Egyptians, so that not one of them escaped to carry the news into the Land of Mizraim.[199]

Malkuth

Malkuth is the tenth appearance of deity, which is described as embodying "the Kingdom."[200] This feminine Hebrew[201] name is pronounced "mal-KOOTH."[202] It means kingdom, dominion, and palace.[203] The name derives from the Hebrew root verb meaning to reign, to rule, and to consult.

Malkah is an alternative name, which is described as embodying "the Queen."[204] This feminine[205] Hebrew name is pronounced "mal-KAW."[206] It means queen and counsel.[207] The name derives from the same Hebrew root as does Malkuth.

Kalah is similar to Malkah as an alternative name, which is described as embodying The Bride.[208] This feminine[209] Hebrew name is pronounced "kal-LAW."[210] It means bride, betrothed maiden, or daughter-in-law.[211] The name derives from the Hebrew root verb meaning to complete, to perfect, and to crown.

Shaar is another name, which is described as embodying "the Gate."[212] This feminine[213] Hebrew name is pronounced "SHAH-ar."[214] It means gate, entrance, and measure.[215] The name derives from the Hebrew root verb meaning to cleave, to divide, to open, to dismiss, to set free, to estimate, and to set a price.

Other names include *the Gate, Gate of Death, Gate of the Shadow of Death, Gate of Tears, Gate of Justice, Gate of Prayer, Gate of the Daughter of the Mighty Ones, Gate of the Garden of Eden, The Inferior Mother* and *The Virgin*.[216] Malkuth is also called the final *Heh* of Tetragrammaton. She can be represented by the symbols of the equal-armed cross, the magic circle, and the triangle of evocation or triangle of art. She can also be represented by the final letter Heh. Malkuth is seen as being colored yellow in Atziluth; citrine, olive, russet and black in Briah; citrine, olive, russet and black, all flecked with gold in Yetzirah; and black rayed with yellow in Assiah.

The *Sepher Yetzirah* describes this divinity as being:

> …(T)he Resplendent Intelligence because it is exalted above every head and sits upon the throne of Binah. It illuminates the splendors of all the Lights, and causes an influence from the Prince of Countenances, the Angel of Kether.[217]

The *Sepher Bahir* describes this divinity as being:

> …(T)he last of seven earths below. The end of the Divine Presence of the Blessed Holy One is under His feet. It is thus written 'Heaven is my throne, and the earth is my footstool.' [218]

The Golden Dawn relates Malkuth to the completion and stability of the final manifestation where solid, liquid, gas, and energy are combined into a physical universe.[219]

Adonai ha-Aretz or *Adonai Melekh* is the grand word used as the divine name of Malkuth.[220] The masculine[221] Hebrew name Adonai is pronounced "ad-OH-nah-ee" when combined with other words.[222] It means lord, master, possessor, and ruler.[223] It comes from the Hebrew root verb meaning to judge, to command, and to domineer, hence to lord, to own, and to master. The Hebrew name ha-Aretz is pronounced "HA EH-rets."[224] It means the earth, the land, the ground, and the element of earth.[225] The full phrase can be understood as the Ruler of Earth or the Ruler of Malkuth. The masculine[226] Hebrew name Melekh is pronounced "MEH-lek."[227] It means king.[228] It derives from the Hebrew root verb meaning to reign, to possess, to rule, and to consult. The meaning of the latter phrase can be understood as "Ruler and King." This comes from the legendary imagery of Malkuth being the kingdom with a divine king.

In the *Old Testament*, the term Adonai is used to mean any ruler or master, whether it applies to deity or not. Similarly, the term Melekh is used to indicate any ruler or king, whether it applies to deity or not. Often these terms are combined as Adonai ha-Melekh, meaning Lord and King. The name Adonai YHVH is used to indicate the divine ruler. This term is often used in reference to the ruling aspects of deity as being over the kings and lords of the earth.

In *The Key of Solomon*, the conjuration takes place:

> ...(B)y the most holy Name of God Adonai Melekh, which Joshua invoked, and stayed the course of the Sun in his presence.[229]

The Names in Practice

These holy names are not mere words to the magician. These are expressions of the divine powers that can be invoked and directed, with great or dire results. The researcher must carefully learn the meanings of the names. They must be practiced and pronounced carefully. They must be vibrated and intoned correctly so that their powers and potentials are properly revealed. These are the goals of the practitioner. This is why the ritual is practiced.

In the basic Qabalistic Cross ritual, the magician invokes Kether while intoning "Atah." The divine light is drawn down all the way to earth while pronouncing "Malkuth." The forces within the magician are balanced while manifesting "ve-Geburah" and "ve-Gedulah." The powers are commanded when he declares "le-Olam." The magician must set the work into being with the final "Amen." Merely projecting these names without actually performing the work implicit in each would be like telling someone that a job had been completed when in fact nothing had been done. Such actions would merely be the telling of a story about magical workings. The names must not be confused with the actions themselves.

In the Greater Rituals of the Pentagram, the magician works with YHVH Eloah ve-Daath to manage the powers of Air. The magician works with Elohim Gibor to manage the powers of Fire. The work is with El to manage the powers of Water and with Adonai ha-Aretz or Adonai Melekh to manage the powers of Earth. In the Rituals of the Hexagram, the magician can call upon other divine names found on the Tree of Life.

These names have come down through the ages until they have become standardized into the system that we use today. They represent the archetypal divine forces that existed from the beginning. Our understanding of these forces is still evolving and growing today. To the modern theurgists these spheres of knowledge not only represent sources of power from which to draw, but they also represent directions for growth and unlimited potential. Perceiving these powers as mere batteries is to ignore the unlimited frontiers for human expansion. Perceiving these universes as merely cosmic locations is to ignore the unlimited applications for practical living. The careful practitioner balances these understandings until they are perceived as both the creature and the creator, the mundane and the sublime. When "that which is below" becomes "that which is above" in the mind of the magician, that is when real magic begins!

About the Author

Harvey Newstrom was introduced to magic in 1982. In 1986 Harvey became a priest of Wicca. He discovered the *Hermetic Order of the Golden Dawn* in 1989 and began work with that group. Harvey has written articles, given lectures, taught classes, and done private research in the area of magic and religion. He holds degrees in computer science and business administration, with minors in biology and psychology. His professional career includes over a decade as a computer engineer, designing nationwide networks and publishing technical manuals describing operating systems software and telecommunications security. His nutritional research includes the development of dozens of formulae for a supplement manufacturer. The completion of his *Nutrients Catalog* (McFarland, 1993) describing hundreds of dietary components, was his first extensive project. Harvey lives in Florida, where he is continuing his magical work and research.

Endnotes

1. *I Kings* 18:21.
2. Ibid., verse 24.
3. Regardie, *The Golden Dawn*, 129.
4. Cicero and Cicero, *Self-Initiation into the Golden Dawn Tradition*, Tammuz, 168; Vul, 283; Ishtar, 289, 538; Nammu, 395; Ea or Hea, 289, 395; Dannes, 395; Nanshe, 395; Nabu, 401; Tashmetum, 401; Marduk, 404; Adad, 404; Nusku, 535; Gibil, 535.
5. Ibid., Anu, 282, Enlil, 283, Adad, 383, Marduk and Baal, 476, Apsu, Tiamat and Mummu, 395, 476; Lahmu and Lahamu, 476; Anshar and Kishar, 476; Anu, 476; Enki, 395, 401, 476; Baal, 477; Anath, 477; Yamm or Nahir, 477; El, 477; Leviathan, 477.
6. Regardie, *The Golden Dawn*, 330–400.
7. Ibid.
8. Ibid., 53, 62, 64, 67, 73, 80, 105.
9. Ibid., 87, 169–71, 172, 343, 357.
10. Ibid., Atlas and Hercules, 163; Castor and Pollux, 548; Dionysus, 588; Here (Hera), 550; Hermes, 188, 162, 340, 477–8, 588; Pan, 212–3; Persephone, 172; Perseus and Andromeda, 589; Zeus, 172, 667.
11. Ibid., Ceres, 172, 550; Diana, 549; Icarus, 592; Jupiter, 76, 626, 628; Mars, 424; Mercury, 476–8; Minerva, 549; Neptune, 600; Proserpina, 550; Pluto, 172; Sol, 169, 600; Venus, 272, 276, 589.
12. Ibid., Jesus, 94, 214, 240; Christ, 56, 80, 83, 150, 223, 229, 230, 236, 311, 359, 477, 478, 479; Son of God, 657, 635; Son of Man, 413, 429, 445, 449; Holy Spirit, 232, 272, 407, 410, 431, 432, 635.
13. Ibid., 207 note, 375 note, Ibid., 224, 229, 261, 375 note, 429, 437, 445, 448, 566, 668.
14. Cicero and Cicero. *Self-Initiation into the Golden Dawn Tradition*, Gefjon, 170; Nerthus, 170; Thor or Donar, 284; Aegir and Ran, 399; Mimir, 399; Nix 400; Odin or Woden, 403; Freya or Frigg, 539.
15. Ibid., Danu or Dana, 170; Brigit, 170; Epona, 170; Cernunnos, 292; Manannan, 399; Llyr, 399; Lug or Lugh, 403.
16. Regardie, *The Golden Dawn*, 60–1.
17. Ibid., 77–8.
18. Ibid., Earth Tablet, 143, 152–3; Air Tablet, 155–6, 164–5; Water Tablet, 167–8, 179–80; Fire Tablet, 182–3, 195–6.
19. Ibid., Earth Tablet, 147–8, Air Tablet, 163–4, Water Tablet, 178, Fire Tablet, 194, Tablet of Union, 217.
20. Cicero and Cicero, *Self-Initiation into the Golden Dawn Tradition*, 392.
21. Regardie, *The Golden Dawn*, Mother Goddess, 72, 73, 76, 77, 78, 100, 150, 177, 188, 193, 276, 331, 375, 409, 423, 428, 436, 447, 507, 510, 543, 588, 592, 693, 695; Father God, 72, 77, 78, 100, 331, 375, 415, 422, 655, 693, 695; Child, 60, 72, 74, 77, 78, 79, 101, 103, 193, 655; Concort, 60, 72, 77, 150, 159; Higher, 67, 100, 101, 103, 105, 106, 110, 345, 365–8, 417, 424; Within, 67, 74–6, 101, 102, 105, 110, 365–8, 417, 616–7.
22. *The Gospel According to John* 1:1–5.
23. *Sepher Yetzirah* 1:2.
24. Ibid., verse 4.
25. Ibid., verse 6.
26. Ibid., 2:1–2.
27. Ibid., verse 6.
28. *Sepher Bahir* 1:22.

29.   Ibid., verse 179.

30.   *Sepher Bahir* 1:141–170.

31.   Wilson, p. 147 note.

32.   *Genesis* 1:1–31.

33.   In this first case, the text describes the Elohim declaring the light to be good before dividing out the darkness.

34.   The text does not describe a specific declaration that Heaven was good.

35.   The text does state that "Elohim blessed them, saying….", but the Hebrew wording is not the same as the ten sayings that begin, "And Elohim said…."

36.   *Zohar* 3:11.

37.   The names given in the *Pirkei Hekhaloth* are *Tutroseah-YHVH, Adiriron-YHVH, Tzurtak-YHVH, Zavudiel-YHVH, Tutrabiel-YHVH, Adastan Iran Adastan Kafino Shamnush Akhshene-YHVH*, and "*Ayir, Suber, Metzugeyah and Beshpitash-YHVH*" for the first through seventh Palaces, respectively.

38.   Other Gods *Exodus* 18:11, 22:19; New Gods *Deuteronomy* 32:17; Strange Gods *Genesis* 35:2, *Deuteronomy* 29:18.

39.   Egyptian Gods and Goddesses *Exodus* 12:12; Goddess Ashtoreth *1 Kings* 11:5; Idols *Exodus* 32:1, *2 Kings* 1:2, 3, 6, 16.

40.   *Genesis* 17:7–8, 28:21, *Jonah* 1:5, *Ruth* 1:16.

41.   Lévi, *The History of Magic*, 99 note.

42.   Gesenius, *Gesenius' Hebrew and Chaldee Lexicon*, 337.

43.   Ibid.

44.   Barthel, *What the Bible Really Says*, 28.

45.   Gesenius, *Gesenius' Hebrew and Chaldee Lexicon*, 337.

46.   Ibid.

47.   Barthel, *What the Bible Really Says*, 28.

48.   Regardie, *The Golden Dawn*, 51.

49.   Gesenius, *Gesenius' Hebrew and Chaldee Lexicon*, 421.

50.   Strong, *The Exhaustive Concordance of the Bible*, 58.

51.   Gesenius, *Gesenius' Hebrew and Chaldee Lexicon*, 421.

52.   Ibid.

53.   Knight, *A Practical Guide to Qabalistic Symbolism*, 65.

54.   *Sepher Yetzirah* supplement.

55.   *Sepher Bahir* 1:1141 quoting from *Psalms* 100:3.

56.   Cicero and Cicero, *Self-Initiation into the Golden Dawn Tradition*, 61.

57.   Regardie, *The Golden Dawn*, 64.

58.   Strong, *The Exhaustive Concordance of the Bible*, 32.

59.   Gesenius, *Gesenius' Hebrew and Chaldee Lexicon*, 221–2.

60.   *Exodus* 3:13-15.

61.   Mathers, *The Key of Solomon the King*, 26.

62.   Regardie, *The Golden Dawn*, 51.

63.   Gesenius, *Gesenius' Hebrew and Chaldee Lexicon*, 278.

64.   Strong, *The Exhaustive Concordance of the Bible*, 39.

65.   Gesenius, *Gesenius' Hebrew and Chaldee Lexicon*, 278.

66.   Regardie, *The Golden Dawn*, 77-8.

67.   Strong, *The Exhaustive Concordance of the Bible*, 7.

68. Gesenius, *Gesenius' Hebrew and Chaldee Lexicon*, 1–2.

69. Knight, *A Practical Guide to Qabalistic Symbolism*, 76.

70. *Sepher Yetzirah* supplement.

71. *Sepher Bahir* 1:142 quoting *Psalms* 8:22 and 111:10.

72. Cicero and Cicero, *Self-Initiation into the Golden Dawn Tradition*, 62.

73. Regardie, *The Golden Dawn*, 64.

74. Strong, *The Exhaustive Concordance of the Bible*, 47.

75. Gesenius, *Gesenius' Hebrew and Chaldee Lexicon*, 335.

76. Regardie, *The Golden Dawn*, 487.

77. Mathers, *The Key of Solomon the King*, 26.

78. Regardie, *The Golden Dawn*, 51.

79. Gesenius, *Gesenius' Hebrew and Chaldee Lexicon*, 115.

80. Strong, *The Exhaustive Concordance of the Bible*, 20.

81. Gesenius, *Gesenius' Hebrew and Chaldee Lexicon*, 115.

82. Regardie, *The Golden Dawn*, 77–8.

83. Gesenius, *Gesenius' Hebrew and Chaldee Lexicon*, 55.

84. Strong, *The Exhaustive Concordance of the Bible*, 13–14.

85. Gesenius, *Gesenius' Hebrew and Chaldee Lexicon*, 55.

86. Knight, *A Practical Guide to Qabalistic Symbolism*, 87.

87. Gesenius, *Gesenius' Hebrew and Chaldee Lexicon*, 407.

88. Strong, 57 gives the root "kor-SAY," Gesenius, 415 gives an example with the "-iah" ending.

89. Gesenius, *Gesenius' Hebrew and Chaldee Lexicon*, 415.

90. Knight, *A Practical Guide to Qabalistic Symbolism*, 87.

91. Gesenius, *Gesenius' Hebrew and Chaldee Lexicon*, 407.

92. Strong, *The Exhaustive Concordance of the Bible*, 72.

93. Gesenius, *Gesenius' Hebrew and Chaldee Lexicon*, 505, 508.

94. Knight, *A Practical Guide to Qabalistic Symbolism*, 87.

95. The Hebrew root *AMN* means "faith."

96. *Sepher Yetzirah* supplement.

97. *Sepher Bahir* 1:143.

98. Ibid., quoting *1 Samuel* 2:2.

99. Cicero and Cicero, *Self-Initiation into the Golden Dawn Tradition*, 63.

100. Regardie, *The Golden Dawn*, 64.

101. Godwin, *Godwin's Cabalistic Encyclopedia*, 52.

102. Strong, *The Exhaustive Concordance of the Bible*, 12.

103. Gesenius, *Gesenius' Hebrew and Chaldee Lexicon*, 49–50.

104. *Genesis* 1:1.

105. Ibid., verse 26.

106. Mathers, *The Key of Solomon the King*, 26.

107. Regardie, *The Golden Dawn*, 51.

108. Gesenius, *Gesenius' Hebrew and Chaldee Lexicon*, 293–4 and *1 Kings* 4:10, used for a proper name of a male.

109. Strong, *The Exhaustive Concordance of the Bible*, 41.

110. Gesenius, *Gesenius' Hebrew and Chaldee Lexicon*, 293–4.
111. Regardie, *The Golden Dawn*, 53.
112. Gesenius, *Gesenius' Hebrew and Chaldee Lexicon*, 158.
113. Strong, *The Exhaustive Concordance of the Bible*, 25.
114. Gesenius, *Gesenius' Hebrew and Chaldee Lexicon*, 158.
115. Knight, *A Practical Guide to Qabalistic Symbolism*, 113.
116. *Sepher Yetzirah* supplement.
117. *Sepher Bahir* 1:144.
118. Cicero and Cicero, *Self-Initiation into the Golden Dawn Tradition*, 64.
119. Regardie, *The Golden Dawn*, 64.
120. Gesenius, *Gesenius' Hebrew and Chaldee Lexicon*, 45.
121. Strong, *The Exhaustive Concordance of the Bible*, 12.
122. Gesenius, *Gesenius' Hebrew and Chaldee Lexicon*, 45.
123. Regardie, *The Golden Dawn*, 487.
124. *Exodus* 14:18-20.
125. Mathers, *The Key of Solomon the King*, 26.
126. Regardie, *The Golden Dawn*, 51.
127. Gesenius, *Gesenius' Hebrew and Chaldee Lexicon*, 154.
128. Strong, *The Exhaustive Concordance of the Bible*, 25
129. Gesenius, *Gesenius' Hebrew and Chaldee Lexicon*, 154.
130. Wilson, *The Golden Dawn Journal Book II: Qabalah: Theory and Magic*, 148.
131. Gesenius, *Gesenius' Hebrew and Chaldee Lexicon*, 197.
132. Strong, *The Exhaustive Concordance of the Bible*, 30.
133. Gesenius, *Gesenius' Hebrew and Chaldee Lexicon*, 197.
134. Wilson, *The Golden Dawn Journal Book II: Qabalah: Theory and Magic*, 148.
135. Gesenius, *Gesenius' Hebrew and Chaldee Lexicon*, 671.
136. Strong, *The Exhaustive Concordance of the Bible*, 94
137. Gesenius, *Gesenius' Hebrew and Chaldee Lexicon*, 671.
138. *Sepher Bahir* 1:145.
139. *Sepher Yetzirah* supplement.
140. *Sepher Bahir* 1:145 quoting *Deuteronomy* 18:16.
141. Cicero and Cicero, *Self-Initiation into the Golden Dawn Tradition*, 65.
142. Regardie, *The Golden Dawn*, 64.
143. Mathers, *The Key of Solomon the King*, 26.
144. Regardie, *The Golden Dawn*, 51.
145. Gesenius, *Gesenius' Hebrew and Chaldee Lexicon*, 871.
146. Strong, *The Exhaustive Concordance of the Bible*, 125.
147. Gesenius, *Gesenius' Hebrew and Chaldee Lexicon*, 871.
148. Knight, *A Practical Guide to Qabalistic Symbolism*, 137.
149. Wilson, *The Golden Dawn Journal Book II: Qabalah: Theory and Magic*, 148.
150. *Sepher Yetzirah* supplement.
151. *Sepher Bahir* 1:146 quoting *Genesis* 1:3.
152. Cicero and Cicero, *Self-Initiation into the Golden Dawn Tradition*, 66.
153. Regardie, *The Golden Dawn*, 64.

154. Strong, *The Exhaustive Concordance of the Bible*, 12.

155. Mathers, *The Key of Solomon the King*, 26.

156. Regardie, *The Golden Dawn*, 51.

157. Gesenius, *Gesenius' Hebrew and Chaldee Lexicon*, 562.

158. Strong, *The Exhaustive Concordance of the Bible*, 80.

159. Gesenius, *Gesenius' Hebrew and Chaldee Lexicon*, 562.

160. Knight, *A Practical Guide to Qabalistic Symbolism*, 150.

161. *Sepher Yetzirah* supplement.

162. *Sepher Bahir* 1:169 quoting *Isaiah* 34:10.

163. Cicero and Cicero, *Self-Initiation into the Golden Dawn Tradition*, 67.

164. Regardie, *The Golden Dawn*, 64.

165. Strong, *The Exhaustive Concordance of the Bible*, 12.

166. Gesenius, *Gesenius' Hebrew and Chaldee Lexicon*, 699.

167. Ibid.

168. Mathers, *The Key of Solomon the King*, 27.

169. Regardie, *The Golden Dawn*, 51.

170. Gesenius,*Gesenius' Hebrew and Chaldee Lexicon*, 218–9 and *1 Chronicles* 7:37, used for a proper name of a male.

171. Strong, *The Exhaustive Concordance of the Bible*, 32.

172. Ibid.

173. Knight, *A Practical Guide to Qabalistic Symbolism*, 164.

174. *Sepher Yetzirah* supplement.

175. *Sepher Bahir* 1:169–170.

176. Cicero and Cicero, *Self-Initiation into the Golden Dawn Tradition*, 68.

177. Regardie, *The Golden Dawn*, 64.

178. Mathers, *The Key of Solomon the King*, 27–8.

179. Regardie, *The Golden Dawn*,51.

180. Gesenius, *Gesenius' Hebrew and Chaldee Lexicon*, 353.

181. Strong, *The Exhaustive Concordance of the Bible*, 50.

182. Gesenius, *Gesenius' Hebrew and Chaldee Lexicon*, 353.

183. Godwin, *Godwin's Cabalistic Encyclopedia*, 126, 134, 210, 275, 309.

184. Gesenius, *Gesenius' Hebrew and Chaldee Lexicon*, 702.

185. Strong, *The Exhaustive Concordance of the Bible*, 98.

186. Gesenius, *Gesenius' Hebrew and Chaldee Lexicon*, 702–3.

187. Knight, *A Practical Guide to Qabalistic Symbolism*, 175.

188. *Sepher Yetzirah* supplement.

189. *Sepher Bahir* 1:157.

190. Cicero and Cicero, *Self-Initiation into the Golden Dawn Tradition*, 69.

191. Regardie, *The Golden Dawn*, 64.

192. Gesenius, *Gesenius' Hebrew and Chaldee Lexicon*, 806.

193. Strong, *The Exhaustive Concordance of the Bible*, 113.

194. Gesenius, *Gesenius' Hebrew and Chaldee Lexicon*, 806.

195. Strong, *The Exhaustive Concordance of the Bible*, 38.

196. Gesenius, *Gesenius' Hebrew and Chaldee Lexicon*, 273.

197. Regardie, *The Golden Dawn*, 98.

198. *Job* 27:2.

199. Mathers, *The Key of Solomon the King*, 26–7.

200. Regardie, *The Golden Dawn*, 51.

201. Gesenius, *Gesenius' Hebrew and Chaldee Lexicon*, 478.

202. Strong, *The Exhaustive Concordance of the Bible*, 67.

203. Gesenius, *Gesenius' Hebrew and Chaldee Lexicon*, 478.

204. Regardie, *The Golden Dawn*, 77–8, 150.

205. Gesenius, *Gesenius' Hebrew and Chaldee Lexicon*, 478.

206. Strong, *The Exhaustive Concordance of the Bible*, 67.

207. Gesenius, *Gesenius' Hebrew and Chaldee Lexicon*, 478.

208. Regardie, *The Golden Dawn*, 77.

209. Gesenius, *Gesenius' Hebrew and Chaldee Lexicon*, 478.

210. Strong, *The Exhaustive Concordance of the Bible*, 55.

211. Gesenius, *Gesenius' Hebrew and Chaldee Lexicon*, 399.

212. Regardie, *The Golden Dawn*, 152.

213. Gesenius, *Gesenius' Hebrew and Chaldee Lexicon*, 843.

214. Strong, *The Exhaustive Concordance of the Bible*, 119.

215. Gesenius, *Gesenius' Hebrew and Chaldee Lexicon*, 843.

216. Knight, *A Practical Guide to Qabalistic Symbolism*, 189.

217. *Sepher Yetzirah* supplement.

218. *Sepher Bahir* 1:169 quoting *Isaiah* 66:1.

219. Cicero and Cicero, *Self-Initiation into the Golden Dawn Tradition*, 70.

220. Regardie, *The Golden Dawn*, 64, 143, 152.

221. Gesenius, *Gesenius' Hebrew and Chaldee Lexicon*, 806.

222. Strong, *The Exhaustive Concordance of the Bible*, 8.

223. Gesenius, *Gesenius' Hebrew and Chaldee Lexicon*, 806.

224. Strong, *The Exhaustive Concordance of the Bible*, 17.

225. Gesenius, *Gesenius' Hebrew and Chaldee Lexicon*, 81.

226. Ibid., 477.

227. Strong, *The Exhaustive Concordance of the Bible*, 67.

228. Gesenius, *Gesenius' Hebrew and Chaldee Lexicon*, 477.

229. Mathers, *The Key of Solomon the King*, 27.

Bibliography

Archer, Gleason A. *The Encyclopedia of Bible Difficulties*. Grand Rapids, Michigan: Zondervan Corporation, 1982.

Barrett, Francis. *The Magus*. Secaucus, New Jersey: The Citadel Press, 1967.

Barthel, Manfred. Translated by Mark Howson. *What the Bible Really Says*. New York: William Morrow and Company, 1982.

Charlesworth, James H., editor. *The Old Testament Pseudepigrapha*. Vols. 1-2. Garden City, New York: Doubleday and Company, Inc., 1983.

———. Unpublished correspondence to Harvey Newstrom. Princeton, New Jersey: Princeton Theological Seminary, July 21, 1988.

Cicero, Chic and Sandra Tabatha Cicero. *Self Initiation into the Golden Dawn Tradition*. St. Paul, Minnesota: Llewellyn Publications, 1995.

D'Olivet, Fabre. Translated by Nayán Louise Redfield. *The Hebraic Tongue Restored*. York Beach, Maine: Samuel Weiser, Inc., 1921.

Forrest, Adam P. "This Holy Invisible Companionship: Angels in the Hermetic Qabalah of the Golden Dawn." *The Golden Dawn Journal Book II: Qabalah: Theory and Magic*. Chic and Sandra Tabatha Cicero, editors. St. Paul, Minnesota: Llewellyn Publications, 1995.

———. Unpublished correspondence to Harvey Newstrom. April 27, 1995.

———. Unpublished correspondence to Harvey Newstrom. May 17, 1995.

Forrest, M. Isidora. "The Equilibration of Jehovah: A Ritual of Healing." *The Golden Dawn Journal Book II: Qabalah: Theory and Magic*. Chic and Sandra Tabatha Cicero, editors. St. Paul, Minnesota: Llewellyn Publications, 1995.

Gaster, Theodor H. *The Dead Sea Scriptures*. 3rd ed. Garden City, New York: Anchor Press/Doubleday, 1976.

Gesenius, Dr. William. Translated by Samuel Prideaux Tregelles, LL.D. *Gesenius' Hebrew and Chaldee Lexicon*. Grand Rapids, Michigan: Baker Book House, 1979.

Godwin, David. *Godwin's Cabalistic Encyclopedia*. St. Paul, Minnesota: Llewellyn Publications, 1989.

Green, Jay ed. and trans. *The Interlinear Hebrew-Greek-English Bible*. Vols. 1-4. Lafayette, Indiana: Associated Publishers and Authors, Inc., 1984.

Haley, John W., M.A. *Alleged Discrepancies of the Bible*. Grand Rapids, Michigan: Baker Book House, 1982.

Harrison, R.K., Ph.D., D.D. *Teach Yourself Biblical Hebrew*. Chicago, Illinois: NTC Publishing Group, 1993.

Kaplan, Aryeh., translator. *The Bahir*. York Beach, Maine: Samuel Weiser, Inc., 1979.

Knight, Gareth. *A Practical Guide to Qabalistic Symbolism*. Vol. 1. York Beach, Maine: Samuel Weiser, Inc., 1978.

Lévi, Eliphas. *The History of Magic*. York Beach, Maine: Samuel Weiser, Inc., 1988.

Mansoor, Menahem. *Biblical Hebrew*. 2nd ed. Grand Rapids, Michigan: Baker Book House, 1980.

Marshall, Alfred, Rev. "The Nestle Greek Text with a Literal English Translation" *The New International Version Interlinear Greek-English New Testament*. Grand Rapids, Michigan: Zondervan Publishing House, 1976.

Mathers, S. Liddell MacGregor, translator. *The Key of Solomon the King*. York Beach, Maine: Samuel Weiser, Inc., 1974.

Milgram, Jeff. *The Old Testament for Macintosh*. Software Version 2.0. New York: Bible Land Software, Inc., 1994.

Regardie, Israel. *The Complete Golden Dawn System of Magic*. 1st ed. Scottsdale, Arizona: New Falcon Publications, 1984.

Regardie, Israel. *Foundations of Practical Magic*. Great Britain: The Aquarian Press, 1979.

Regardie, Israel. *The Golden Dawn*. 4th ed. St. Paul, Minnesota: Llewellyn Publications, 1982.

————. *The Golden Dawn*. 6th ed. St. Paul, Minnesota: Llewellyn Publications, 1989.

————. The Tree of Life. First paperback edition. York Beach, Maine: Samuel Weiser, Inc., 1972.

Reich, Ronny, Dr., Israel Antiquities Authority. *The Dead Sea Scrolls Revealed*. Software version 1.0. Tel Aviv: Pixel Multimedia, London: Aaron Witkin Associates, 1994.

Robinson, James M., General Editor. *The Nag Hammadi Library in English*. San Francisco, California: Harper and Row, Publishers, 1981.

Robinson, James M., General Editor. *The Nag Hammadi Library in English*. Revised edition. San Francisco, California: Harper Collins, Publishers, 1988.

Schonfield, Hugh J. *The Original New Testament*. New York: Harper and Row, Publishers, 1985.

Stirling, William. *The Canon*. 3rd ed. Great Briton: Research Into Lost Knowledge Organisation, 1981.

Strong, S.T.D., LL.D., James. "Hebrew and Chaldee Dictionary," *The Exhaustive Concordance of the Bible*. Peabody, Massachusetts: Hendrickson Publishers, 1923.

Suarès, Carlo. "The Cipher of Genesis." *The Qabala Trilogy*. Boston & London: Shambhala Publications, Inc., 1985.

————. "The Song of Songs" *The Qabala Trilogy*. Boston & London: Shambhala Publications, Inc., 1985.

————. "The Sepher Yetsira." *The Qabala Trilogy*. Boston & London: Shambhala Publications, Inc., 1985.

Thayer, Joseph Henry, D.D., translator. *A Greek-English Lexicon of the New Testament*. Grand Rapids, Michigan: Zondervan Publishing House, 1979.

Vermes, G. *The Dead Sea Scrolls in English*. 2nd ed. New York: Viking Penguin, Inc., 1986.

Westcott, W. Wynn., translator. *Sepher Yetzirah: The Book of Formation*. 3rd ed., New York: Samuel Weiser, Inc., 1980.

Whiston, William, A.M., translator. *Complete Works of Flavius Josephus*. Grand Rapids, Michigan: Kregel Publications, 1981.

Wilson, George. "The Evolution of the Medieval Kabbalistic World-view." *The Golden Dawn' Journal Book II: Qabalah: Theory and Magic*. Chic and Sandra Tabatha Cicero, editors. St. Paul, Minnesota: Llewellyn Publications, 1995.

Young, L. L. D., Robert. "Index-Lexicon to the Old Testament," *Analytical Concordance to the Bible*. 22nd American ed. Grand Rapids, Michigan: William. B. Eerdmans Publishing Company, 1970.

The Divine Mystery.

Hebrew Hierarchical Names in Briah

James A. Eshelman

f all magical "pantheons," none is employed more commonly by Hermetic-Qabalistic magicians than are the classic Hebrew hierarchies. The familiar lists of divine names, archangels, choirs of angels, etc. are standard fare for the student of magick, and certainly form the practical basis of the traditional Golden Dawn system.

It is less commonly known, however, that these familiar and standard name lists comprise but one of the Hebrew magical hierarchies.

A magician who has long learned and applied the knowledge that the divine name of Netzach is *Yod Heh Vav Heh Tzabaoth*, its archangel *Haniel,* and its choir of angels the *Elohim,* may be surprised to learn that—in another way of approaching the matter—Netzach's divine name is *Elohim,* its archangel is *Ussiel,* and its choir of angels is the *Melakim.*

Buried in obscurity—and in the little-consulted columns 84 through 87 of Aleister Crowley's *Liber 777*—are lists of Hebrew "words of power" identified as divine names, angels, choirs of angels, and "palaces" of the world of Briah. These lists derive from classical Hebrew Qabalistic writings. They do not appear (so far as we know) in any of the published instructions of the Hermetic Order of the Golden Dawn, but were, apparently, subjects of interest and of study for at least some of its leading Qabalistic minds.

These names open an entire new world for mystical and magical exploration—specifically, the world of Briah, the natural abode of the Adept's magical consciousness. Although not the highest nor most rarefied of the four worlds of the Qabalah, Briah is, to most people, the plane of "spiritual consciousness." It is, as well, the natural level of the awakened or spiritually fulfilled human being, the primary target of spiritual aspiration.

The four worlds of the Qabalah are: *Assiah,* the world of action, which encompasses all matter and energy, as these are usually understood, and all perceptions of the same general type as are received by our five physical senses; *Yetzirah,* the world of formation, the "astral plane" proper, manifest in the microcosm as the human personality and, especially, its elements of intellect, emotion, and imagery; *Briah*, the creative world, discussed immediately below; and *Atziluth*, the archetypal world, which is the world of unconditioned divinity, the essential truth behind the highest intuitive and philosophical perceptions of "God" that humanity has created.

Although Qabalists associate the world of Briah with the element of Water, this is not the turbulent water of troubled emotions, but the serene embrace of the Great Mother, the "passionate peace" or "peace profound" *(pax profunda)* of a great inner vital stillness. In describing this level, we can employ the analogy of water in two ways. First, in contrast to the divisive, excited, and tumultuous characteristics of the human intellect and emotions (in the human personality, or microcosmic world of Yetzirah), Briah represents a tranquil and clear lake that has become capable of reflecting sunlight, brilliantly, even blindingly, without diminishment or distortion. Second, in relationship to the unconditioned essence of divinity of the world of Atziluth still beyond, Briah is like a chalice that becomes filled by divine inspiration, a womb that has become fertilized by a sacred seed, and, again, a lake lucidly reflecting the One Light of the spiritual Sun. It is a consciousness beyond emotion, beyond thought and word, even beyond image—although all of these are necessarily employed by the human mind in its continuing effort to give form and expression to Briatic perceptions.

In contrast, the more familiar Hebrew hierarchical lists are classified as names in the world of Assiah. Assiah, the world of action, is the densest of the four worlds, the world of the physical senses. It may be that these names (employed as they are in the operation of astral and other related magical phenomena) are better called names in Yetzirah; but, historically, they have not been so labeled. We don't make the rules, we just report them!

These explanations will prove no problem for the advanced student. For the beginner, the matter can be simplified considerably, as follows: The usual Hebrew god-names, archangels, angels, etc., are called "names in Assiah." Those on the variant list, discussed in the present article, are called "names in Briah." These "names in Briah" refer to a significantly different and more advanced level of operation than the more familiar "names in Assiah."

Unfortunately, the available lists in *Liber 777* contain errors that have gone uncorrected for the more than eight decades since they were published. Some detective work was required to reconstruct and correct these tables. The primary lists can be found in *Maseketh Aztiluth*, reprinted in *Ozar Midrashim* (Grossman's Hebrew Book Store,

New York, 1956). A similar list—but attributing the angelic names to the Sephiroth, for the most part, in *reverse order*—is reportedly given in *Berith Menucha* (published in Amsterdam in 1648, and quite hard to find). It is not clear from what source Crowley (or, perhaps, his mentor Allan Bennett) extracted the lists later published in *Liber 777*, but, with some judicious corrections for apparent transcription errors, they are quite authentic.

Like most students, the present writer ignored these Briatic hierarchies for a couple of decades. The main reason is that no one seemed to know what they were for! How does one use them? Why do they differ from the more familiar "names in Assiah?" What could it possibly mean that these are "names in Briah?"

The last question was the most troublesome. Contemporary magical theory teaches (very successfully and workably) that god-names exist in Atziluth, archangels in Briah, and angels in Yetzirah. This is one of the most functional definitions of the Qabalistic worlds. William Gray's excellent book *Ladder of Lights* is structured entirely in conformity with these definitions, and his approach is correct. Is it not a contradiction in terms to say we have a "divine name in Briah" or "choirs of angels in Briah?"

After a little meditation on these questions, a basic answer arose. It is that these names do not represent God, archangels, and angels "in Briah" themselves. Rather, these Briatic hierarchies describe the Qabalistic structure of the inner universe as it appears to a *Qabalist whose consciousness is in Briah.*

This key opened the way to an exciting new area of work. These Briatic hierarchies are disclosed as a natural area of exploration by the full Adept especially, and also by aspirants at an earlier stage who are undertaking very deep aspirational work. Both theory, and subsequent practice, confirm that the Briatic work is much more deeply mystical than magical—to the extent that mysticism and magick can be differentiated from each other.

That differentiation can, of course, never be complete. Magick is the tool of mysticism, the *modus* of undertaking the Great Work. The ways of working with these names, it has been found, are identical to the familiar methods of invocation or evocation of elements of the Assiatic lists. The same type of Pentagram and Hexagram rituals, hierarchical invocations, and all the rest, may be employed with these names as well.

DIVINE NAMES

Kether, Chokmah, and Binah

אֵל *El* ("[Mighty] God"). Attributed to the first palace of Briah—that is, to the three Supernal Sephiroth—is the divine name *El*. It means, simply, "God."

El is more correctly the *word* "god" than the *name* "God," at least in prosaic constructions; but in poetic passages, where it is much more frequently encountered in scriptural Hebrew, it usually carries the raw force of a single and supreme deity. Literally, it also means "strong, mighty," and thus conveys (as the Hebrew scholar William Gesenius phrased it) "the notion of strength and power."

In the world of Assiah, where it is attributed primarily to Chesed, Qabalists are less accustomed to associating *El* with such ideas of strength, preferring to reserve these for the complementary Sephirah, Geburah; but these ideas are very much a part of the basic implication of the name. Nor will the Thelemite have the slightest difficulty recognizing the highest idea of deity in Briah in this name *El*; for it is the esoteric title of the Thelemic *Book of the Law*, also titled *Liber* אל *vel Legis*.

The other familiar attribution of *El* in Assiah is to the element of Water. This, of course, derives from its correspondence to Chesed, which is reflected into Hod in the First Order. Even in this we find an important symbolism, for the world of Briah corresponds primarily to the letter ה in the Tetragrammaton, and thus to Water. Therefore, from this point of view as well, the name *El* is rightly the highest expression of divinity in this penultimate of the four worlds.

Perhaps the subtle flavor of this particular name was best captured by Melita Denning and Osborne Phillips, discussing *El* in terms of Chesed in Assiah. They observed that the Greek name of Jupiter, Zeus—the correct pronunciation of which, in ancient Greek, was *Zdeus* (*zd* as in 'Mazda')—is merely *deus*, "god." The Latin name Jupiter is but *deo-pater*, "god-father." Similarly, *El* just means "god." Here, they noted, is shown repeatedly the simple idea of "god," the word, taking on the practical characteristics of "God," the name, in the same fashion that a young child believes that "Daddy" is his or her father's actual name.

Of course, while Chesed in Assiah carries this particularly paternal characteristic, *El* as the divine name of all three Supernals in Briah demands the appellation "parent" rather than "father." Both Chokmah and Binah must be captured in this deity idea, as well as that Crown that transcends them. This is implicit in the name אל itself, where Aleph is the ox and Lamed its goad, Tao and Teh respectively.

Finally, in the gematria of this name we find some of its purest symbolism. *El* enumerates to 31. The 31st Path of the Tree of Life is attributed to ש, Shin, a symbol among Qabalists of transcendent Spirit, of transforming Fire, and of deity as Three-that-are-One. By reversing the order of the two letters, we obtain לא, *lo*, "not, nothing"—fulfilling the idea of deity by denying it, that is, by invoking the idea of the zero that lies even beyond the Supernal unity. Here, indeed, is that "Lord of the Universe who works in Silence and whom Naught but Silence can express."

Perhaps as important as these facts are the ideas hidden in the number 496. This is the "Theosophical extension" of 31 (the sum of all positive integers through 31). Among other things, it is the value of מלכות, Malkuth. The Kingdom, the full manifestation of the primal God-idea, is thus seen by gematria to be the natural completion or fulfillment of the number 31, which is this name אל.

Chesed

מצפץ *Matzpatz*. This strange-looking word is far more familiar in meaning than may appear at first. It is a temurah (essentially, a substitution-cipher) of the Tetragrammaton, יהוה.

The method employed in this letter substitution is called *Ath Bash* (את בש) to cue us that Aleph is substituted for Tav, Beth for Shin, etc. From these two keys, the entire cipher can be reconstructed. Thus, Mem is as far from the end of the alphabet as Yod is from its *beginning*. Similarly, Tzaddi swaps with Heh, and Peh with Vav.

The essential significance of this name is, therefore, that of the Tetragrammaton. There are, in fact, tables of attributions that give יהוה as a divine name of Chesed, the fourth Sephirah, because this Tetragrammaton is a solid representation of the number four.

However, it is evident that we are to pay special attention to the gematria of this name for the following reason: The name *Matzpatz* is also attributed to Hod in Briah, but with one difference. In relation to Hod, the name is naturally spelled with a final Tzaddi at its end; but in relation to Chesed, it is not. Atypically, the medial (or nonfinal) Tzaddi is used at the end. There can be no good reason for this other than to point out the differing and distinctive numerical values of each form.

מצפצ enumerates to 300. This is the value of the letter Shin. All of the symbolism of Shin mentioned above, under *El*, may be applied here as well. But the number 300 particularizes the significance even more carefully. It is the value of רוח אלהים, *Ruach Elohim*, "the Spirit of God," the phrase signifying the initial inseminating Breath, which in *Genesis* is said to have moved upon the face of the waters and inaugurated creation. Additionally, 300 is the value of אור בפאהה, *Or be-Pe'ahah*, Hebrew for "Light in Extension."

Three hundred is also one form of the great name *Elohim* spelled in plenitude, אלף למד הה יוד מם. (This will take on added significance when we later note that *Elohim* is the divine name of Netzach in Briah, that Sephirah at the base of the Pillar of Force into which the consciousness of Chesed directly descends). *Elohim* is the divine name associated especially with the Mother; along with שכינה, *Shekinah*, it represents the divine feminine by a pentagrammaton that precedes the formula יהשוה by centuries. It is perhaps significant that, in Assiah, *Elohim* is the divine name used to govern elemental Fire, further confirming the Shin symbolism of this name.

As the sanctifying Fire, Shin is also that "third thing" that transcends and completes the opposing polarities of Sun and Moon, and all of their cognate symbols. It is Apophis to Isis and Osiris, or Sushumna to Ida and Pingala. Appropriately, its value of 300 is also the sum of the values of Qoph (100) and Resh (200), the two letters attributed, respectively, to *The Moon* and *The Sun* in Tarot. By related symbolism, in the Greek Qabalah it is Σ.Ρ., the notariqon of σταυρος ροδιον, "the Rosy Cross."

In summary, *Matzpatz* is an expression of the holiest name in the Qabalah, the Tetragrammaton, but in such a way that it enumerates to 300, a number representing sanctifying Spirit, transforming Fire, Light in extension, and that samadhic completion—represented in countless ways by the triangle of Shin—which is effectuated by the union of opposites.

Geburah

יְהֶוִֹה *Yehevid*. This name differs from יהוה only in its final letter, and only by a numerical value of one. That is, the concluding Daleth—which, being *The Empress* of the Tarot, would surely represent the Daughter in a letter-by-letter analysis—changes the value of the Tetragrammaton from 26 to 25.

We need look no further for the significance of this name. Its value, 25, is the square of five, the number of Geburah. By all appearances, *Yehevid* is a way of rendering *Yod Heh Vav Heh* so that it specifically refers to the fifth sephirah.

However, this simple observation discloses a captivating pattern. As we shall see immediately below, *Yod Heh Vav Heh* itself—"classic Tetragrammaton"—is the divine name attributed, in Briah as in Assiah, to Tiphareth. We saw just above that *Matzpatz*, the divine name of Chesed in Briah, is this same Tetragrammaton viewed through a Qabalistic substitution cipher. Thus, all three divine names given in this middle triad of the Tree of Life are, in fact, יהוה, the central formula of Tiphareth. All three of these Sephiroth represent grades of Adepthood; and, in a sense, they are but three aspects of one idea, as much as Binah and Chokmah are integral aspects of Kether.

Incidentally, with different pointing (dagesh), the word יְהוּד is the Chaldean name for the land of Judea. However, the word יִהוּד *yihud*, means "conversion to Judaism," *i.e.*, Judaization.

Tiphareth

יהוה *Yod Heh Vav Heh* ("That Which Was, Is, and Shall Be"). There is no mystery concerning the significance of this name in this place. The Tetragrammaton, יהוה, the "Unpronounceable Name," is the name of deity corresponding to the Sephirah Tiphareth in all of the four worlds.

This last statement may be somewhat surprising to those whose instruction in Qabalah has been primarily from the basic books of the contemporary Western Mystery Schools such as those of the Golden Dawn tradition. Usually to Tiphareth in Assiah we find attributed the longer name יהוה אלוה ודעת, *IHVH Eloah va-Daath*. However, the contemporary preferred divine names in Assiah are often composites of multiple names, which in earlier times were individually attributed to the Sephirah. Thus, where most contemporary Western magicians employ the full name *Shaddai El Chai* for the Sephirah Yesod, in earlier centuries the name *Shaddai* alone, or *El* alone, or *Chai* alone, or combinations such as *El Shaddai* and *El Chai* were all variously attributed to Yesod. Similarly, to Tiphareth has often been attributed *Eloah*, or *Eloah va-Daath*, as well as the full form, *IHVH va-Daath* (the notariqon of which is יאו, *i.e.* IAΩ). Yet in the earliest written Qabalistic works (such as the thirteenth century *Sha'ari Orah*) it is יהוה alone, pure and simple, which is attributed to Tiphareth.

As mentioned above, IHVH is called "the Unpronounceable Name." When it is encountered in scripture, the name *Adonai*—a name attributed to Malkuth that literally means "my Lord"—is said in its place. (This is at least true in most instances; there are certain additional rules for special cases.) In this sense, *Adonai* is the "substituted word," to borrow a Masonic phrase. That is, it is the adopted pronunciation or, rather, vocalization, that is used when IHVH is encountered in print.

Such is the conventional knowledge. However, in these phonetic details is an important symbolism that we have not seen discussed anywhere before. We have long felt that the Tetragrammaton represents the unique "Unpronounceable Name"—of God or of oneself—that each of us may come to know within his or her own heart in the climactic fulfillment of the Great Work. That is, it is representative of the name of the Holy Guardian Angel, or of the inarticulate inner Knowledge of one's God (hence its cognomen, *Eloah va-Daath*). In contrast, *Adonai* is commonly used among Qabalistic magicians as a generic title for the Holy Guardian Angel. Divinity witnessed in Malkuth is the outer, tangible expression of that which, in Tiphareth, is not-to-be-said.

Netzach

אֱלֹהִים *Elohim*. To understand the names attributed in Briah to Netzach and Hod, we must first look back to the conventional attributions of the Supernals in Assiah.

The two most common words for "God" in the Old Testament are *IHVH* and *Elohim*. (For the inquiring minds that want to know, אלהים appears 2,249 times, and יהוה 5,521 times in the Hebrew scriptures.) It is not always (nor even usually) possible to differentiate their meanings on a purely linguistic basis, both meaning roughly "God" or "the Lord." *Elohim* is also translated "judge" in modern Hebrew, a meaning that likely evolved from its early attribution to Geburah in Assiah, as the Lord of Justice. *Elohim* is the sole divine name employed in *Genesis* prior to the Garden of Eden story; yet its real significance has barely been explored in modern Qabalistic primers.

Even the tyro usually knows that *Elohim* is the masculine pluralization of the feminine noun *Eloah*. For this reason some Qabalists have chosen to interpret *Elohim* as a male-female blend, an emblem of the divine Father-Mother in union. However, the same Qabalists usually disregard the fact that the internal Father-Mother-Son-Daughter formula of the Tetragrammaton is also gender-balanced.

In practice, IHVH has long been employed as a formula for the Father, and *Elohim* as a formula for the Mother. As such, they are traditionally attributed to Chokmah and Binah (of Assiah) respectively, as if to represent the "roots" of two vast "families" of names in the Qabalistic tradition. As is written in the *Zohar*, "יהוה, the nature of the male, אלהים, the nature of the female" (*Sepher Dtzenioutha*, III:24); and, "seeing that יהוה denoteth the masculine, and אלהים the feminine" (*Idra Rabba Qadisha*, v. 795).

In our present study, we see *Elohim* attributed to Netzach in Briah and (as discussed below) *Matzpatz*—a temurah of IHVH—to Hod in Briah. These are reflections of these great names downward: יהוה being reflected from Chokmah (through Chesed) unto Hod, and אלהים being reflected from Binah (through Geburah) unto Netzach. As such, they continue to represent this pair of majestic and holy names in their balance.

The name *Elohim* is not foreign to Netzach even in the world of Assiah. Besides being a name of deity, it is also the name of the choir of angels attributed to Netzach in Assiah. It is also the divine name attributed to Fire, of which Netzach is the primary expression in the personality.

Hod

מַצְפָּץ *Matzpatz*. The formation of this name was discussed above, with respect to Chesed. Its importance as a reflection of the Tetragrammaton, יהוה, and in balancing the presence of *Elohim* at Netzach, was discussed immediately above in connection with Netzach. Both of those sections should be reviewed as part of understanding the significance of this divine name for the Sephirah Hod.

There is a natural reflection of consciousness from Chesed into Hod. As is written in the familiar passage from *The 32 Paths of Wisdom* wherein Hod is identified as the Perfect Consciousness: "It is the Plan of the Primordial. It has no root where it can abide except in the hidden chambers of Gedulah [Chesed] from which its own essence emanates."[1]

There is, however, one significant difference in the forms of *Matzpatz* attributed to Chesed and to Hod. Whereas the medial form of Tzaddi is used at the end of *Matzpatz* with respect to Chesed, this is not so with the form credited to Hod. We must consider that the numerical value is of particular significance. מצפץ, valuing Tzaddi-final as 900, enumerates to 1,110. This is immediately seen to be 10 x 111, or a "super-scale" of ideas related to the number 111, and especially the letter-name Aleph. The development of these ideas is potentially very involved and lengthy, and is therefore best left to the individual reader.

Yesod and Malkuth

יָה-אֲדֹנָי *Yah-Adonai* ("Lord God" or "God, my Lord"). This name is attributed to the seventh palace, and thus to Malkuth and Yesod together. Its significance will be different in each of these two Sephiroth.

The composition of this name is very intriguing. It is composed of the joining of two great divine names, *Yah* and *Adonai*. The first of these, *Yah*, is best known to us, among the hierarchies of Assiah, as the divine name attributed to Chokmah, and thus to Will; the latter, *Adonai*, is the oldest divine attribution to Malkuth itself, in any known Qabalistic scheme.[2]

Yah is variously and inconsistently described as a primitive (that is, earlier), or as a truncated (that is, later), form of the Tetragrammaton. However, among Qabalists it has come to have its own distinctive implications. It is, especially, the union of the letters representative of the divine Male and Female, Father and Mother, י and ה. This has an especial significance for Yesod, corresponding to the sexual organs of the archetypal humanity, and to the union of the polarities therein.[3] Gesenius apparently considered יה nothing more than an abbreviation for the Tetragrammaton; and, all things considered, this present name, *Yah-Adonai*, may well have originated as the more common יהוה אדני.

Where *Yah* is probably best translated "God," *Adonai* literally means "my Lord." Especially if this composite name is an adaptation of *IHVH Adonai*, it is best translated "Lord God" (following the translators of the *Torah*), or "God, my Lord." Of the longer form, tens of thousands of words have been written by Qabalists over the last eight centuries; but our concern is, at the moment, for the shorter form now before us. Perhaps the most important feature of the name *Adonai* is that it is used as the "substituted word" for the Tetragrammaton. This was discussed extensively above, under Tiphareth. Divinity witnessed in Malkuth is the outer, tangible expression of that which, in Tiphareth, is not-to-be-said.

Yah-Adonai is, therefore, a most suitable expression of the nature of deity in Yesod and Malkuth for those who are in Briah. It implies many things, the chiefest of which are best discovered by each mystic independently and personally, but which surely include the balanced union of *Yod* and *Heh*, Yang and Yin, Will and Love, Sun and Moon, and all such cognate ideas as central to the veiled God-Reality.

Why are we given the shorter form, יה אדני, instead of the more common יהוה אדני? Most likely, this answer is to be found in the numerical value of the name, 80 rather than 91. Eighty is the value of the word *Yesod* itself. It is also the value of the letter Peh, attributed to the planet Mars, the significance of which is summarized in the 16th Trump, *The Tower*. Upon first entry unto this outermost aspect of the Tree of Life in the world of Briah, one would hardly be expected to maintain, intact, one's prior intellect-bound view of the world. On the contrary, the Adept's entry into Briatic consciousness (in Malkuth of Briah) can rightly be expected to overthrow the prior world view. Of this, *The Tower* is an apt symbol. More importantly, however, is that the purely divine aspect of Malkuth and Yesod, in this Briatic world, is presented to us as an aspect of the force of the planet Mars.

This is an astonishing confirmation of the symbols; for both *Yah* (= 15) and *Adonai* (= 65) have, as their values, numbers sacred to Mars. *Yah*, in fact, is also the traditional password of the Adeptus Major Grade attributed to Mars. The Thelemite will especially see in this that the martial god Horus in that distinctive form called Ra-Hoor-Khuit is "the visible object of worship," the outermost aspect of deity, even as אל is the inmost aspect. The non-Thelemite, as well, may draw much significance from this Qabalistic symbolization of the Lord of Initiation by the fiery and transforming power of the planet Mars.

ARCHANGELS

Listed as "angels" in the usual tabulations, these spiritual entities appear to serve an archangelic function with respect to the divine potencies above them and the choirs of angels below them. Also, most of them are well-known and readily recognized archangelic names. Historic distinctions between "angels" and "archangels" have been rather vague until very recent times. We have treated them all as archangels herein.

In contrast to the divine names, a separate archangel is attributed to each of the ten Sephiroth.

Kether

יְהוּאֵל *Yehoel*. This name is formed by appending the determinative אֵל- to the Trigrammaton, *Yod Heh Vav*, forming a name of tremendous majesty, power, and beauty. We have not attempted a literal translation; but the essential idea expressed is that the power of the holy name is manifest through an angelic or archangelic medium. In *The Apocalypse of Abraham*, this angel is quoted as saying, "I am called Yehoel...a power by virtue of the ineffable name dwelling in me."

According to the *Sepher Yetzirah*, it is by six permutations of this Trigrammaton, יהו, that God created the universe as we know it, sealing the six directions.

Yehoel enumerates to 52, a number having many important correspondences. Perhaps most significant for this angelic name, which is founded on the Father-Mother-Son formula of the Trigrammaton, are the following: 52 is בן, *ben*, "son"; it is אימא, *aima*, "mother"; and it is יוד הה וו הה, the simplest way of spelling the Tetragrammaton in full, a representation of the Father.

What is surely most important about this angelic name is that, according to Gustav Davidson, *Yehoel* is an alternate name for Metatron! Metatron is, of course, the archangel attributed to Kether in Assiah; and, as will be seen, under variant names and appearances, he is manifest on most, or possibly all, of the Middle Pillar of the Tree of Life in this Briatic scheme.

Chokmah

רְפָאֵל *Raphael* ("Healer of God") -*or*- אוֹפָנִיאֵל *Ophaniel* (Chief of the Ophanim). Raphael is one of the three great archangels whose offices traditionally bear a special protective and instructional relationship to humanity. His legends and attributions are varied and legion. He is, for example, the only archangel to have an entire book of the (Catholic) Bible devoted to him.

His name means "healer of God." Healing is whole-making. We are most accustomed, in the world of Assiah, to relate him to the Sephirah Tiphareth and to the Sun, along with the primary healer-gods (most of whom are also Sun-gods) of many lands. Even ignoring this explicit Tipharic association, Raphael is broadly regarded in tradition as the regent of the Sun; and an intrinsic solar connection is also implied by his earlier name, *Labiel*, "the Heart of God."

Furthermore, we are wont to think of Raphael as something of a Solar-Mercurial entity, due to the *angel* (not archangel) named Raphael being angel of the planet Mercury. This is one of numerous cross-relationships between Solar and Mercurial attributions.

The resultant idea of Raphael as archangel of Chokmah in Briah is not unlike that of the Egyptian god of wisdom and magick, Thoth, combined with (or emphasizing) the Solar-phallic quality characteristic of Chokmah.

As a direct result of this attribution to Chokmah in Briah, Raphael is identified in some classic Qabalistic texts as the chief of the order of Ophanim. Alternately, the name of the archangel fulfilling this function is given as *Ophaniel*. This is clearly a categorical name designating the generic governor of Chokmah's angels. Nonetheless, some independent doctrine has arisen around the name Ophaniel.

Davidson, for example, quotes *3 Enoch* as depicting him with sixteen faces, one-hundred pairs of wings (two-hundred wings implies, once again, the power of the Sun), and 8,466 eyes, a fact mentioned for those who place great weight on traditional descriptions of such beings. We think, rather, that Ophaniel is best regarded, in the present context at least, as a cognomen or attribution of Raphael, and that the full name *Raphael-Ophaniel*—Raphael, chief of the Ophanim—may be employed in addressing this archangel in this particular office.

Binah

כְּרוּבִיאֵל *Kerubiel* (Chief of the Kerubim). This designation simply identifies the angel so named as chief of the Kerubim, the nature of which will be discussed later. However, a magical anecdote concerning this archangel may be of interest to demonstrate the magical applicability of these names. When the present author began working seriously with these Briatic hierarchies, one of the first experiments was with Kerubiel. Invoking this archangel by the divine name *El* (which is that of all three Supernals), and employing the Hexagram Ritual of Binah, a vision was obtained that included a meeting with a representation of Kerubiel. The chief details of this vast and majestic archangel's appearance were as follows: a figure of indiscernible gender, but seemingly feminine essence, robed in scintillating and pulsing crimson (which was interpreted as the King Scale color of Binah); about the head, a fully luminous orb of the Sun, burning with the naked splendor of a close-viewed star in open space; just below the throat and across the shoulder-line, a broad and narrow Lunar crescent, opening upward, of silvery-white light. At the time, this was interpreted as a symbol of the union or balance of the Sun and Moon within a distinctly Binah theme. It was filed away with the rest of the diary entry.

However, a few weeks later, when researching fine points of this article in Gustav Davidson's *A Dictionary of Angels*, I was startled to find a quotation from 3 *Enoch* that described Kerubiel's body as "full of burning coals...there is a crown of holiness on his head...and the bow of the Shekinah is between his shoulders."

Even the most experienced magician is likely, in the face of such a confirmation, to commence at least a brief struggle with the demon Pride, for which the greatest aid is to invoke whole-heartedly the angels Wonder and Amazement. Yet the wonderful confirmation does not end here; for, on consideration of the traditional description, it was noted that Kerubiel strikingly resembles the traditional image of *Aima Elohim*, the Great Mother at Binah, whose chief characteristics are the bow of the Moon, the glow of great luminescence about her body, and the crown upon her head.

Since that time, there has been no difficulty for me in relating this particular archangel to the sephirah Binah.

Chesed

צָדְקִיאֵל *Tzadqiel* ("Righteousness of God"). *Tzedeq* is also the Hebrew name for the planet Jupiter; therefore, this name could as well be translated, "the angel of Jupiter." Because *Tzadqiel* (often written *Zadkiel*) is the familiar name of the archangel of Chesed in Assiah, little need be added concerning this familiar messenger of benevolence, mercy, and majesty.

Geburah

תַּרְשִׁישׁ *Tarshish* ("Precious Stone," Chief of the *Tarshishim*). As the name implies, this archangel is the governor of that body of angels called the Tarshishim, discussed below. We will reserve most of our discussion of this name for that later section.

Tarshish should not be confused with *Tharsis* (תרשים), the Ruler of the element of Water. This name similarity has resulted in numerous authors attempting to translate *Tarshish* in terms of the sea. In fact (as will be discussed more fully later), the word means some variety of precious stone, probably of a golden or luminous yellow variety. The present author has seen this archangel appearing in bright raiment of a topaz or luminous amber color that subjectively "rang true" despite its apparent incongruence with any of the usual formal attributions of Geburah.

Note that these golden or yellow qualities normally associated with Tiphareth and the Sun are not entirely out of place in Geburah. To a very great extent, the grade of Adeptus Major (6=5) fulfills and completes that of Adeptus Minor (5=6). It is written in the *Zohar* (and echoed in the Practicus grade) that in Geburah there is gold, even as the red color most often associated with Mars is the heraldic representation of gold. And the word *Geburah* itself (גבורה) enumerates to 216, or 63, the "solid" (materialization) of sunlight. (Or it may simply be—based upon the usual techniques for formulating telesmatic images—that Tarshish's observed robe colors were but the reflection of the letter Resh, which is the second letter of this archangel's name.)

Tiphareth

מְטַטְרוֹן *Metatron* ("About Thy Throne") *-or-* חַשְׁמָאֵל *Khasmæl* (Chief of the *Khasmalim*). We have previously noted that *Yehoel*, the name of the archangel of Kether in Briah, is actually an alternative name of the archangel *Metatron*. Now, on the second Sephirah of the Middle Pillar, we find the name *Metatron* itself.

Metatron is clearly not a Hebrew word, although it is rendered, by Qabalists, in Hebraic form. But its form, is most likely Greek in origin; and we have long accepted William Gray's proposal that it is a contraction of some phrase such as μετα τον θρονον, "About Thy Throne," an appropriate descriptive phrase for this archangel. "Throne" is, additionally, a distinctive attribution of the world of Briah in general.

Whether attributed to Kether (in either Assiah or Briah) or to Tiphareth, *Metatron* is unquestionably given the highest regard and dignity by tradition. As is true of others of the greatest of the angels, the legends, attributions, and sobriquets of *Metatron* are legion and varied. Nearly all of these are readily recognizable as some Tipharic aspect.

The lengthy article on this angel in Davidson contains a wealth of information. *Metatron* is called King of Angels, Prince of the Divine Face (or Presence), Chancellor of Heaven, Angel of the Covenant,

Chief of the Ministering Angels, and even the Lesser Tetragrammaton. He is charged with the sustenance of humanity. An especially Tipharic quality is reflected in his being called the link, or mediator, between humanity and the divine. When invoked, he is said to appear "as a pillar of fire, his face more dazzling than the sun." This "pillar" may well be the Tree of Life's Middle Pillar itself, and especially the Sushumna, which is its microcosmic aspect.

Additionally, the name *Khasmael* is attributed to Tiphareth in Briah. This indicates an angel who is chief of the Khasmalim, the angelic choir assigned here. As with Ophaniel at Chokmah, *Khasmael* would appear to be more of a title of office than a distinctive name. It is quite interesting to note that Louis Ginzberg, in *The Legends of the Jews*, says that Khasmæl "surrounds the throne of God"—since "about thy throne" is likely the literal meaning of the name *Metatron*. Additionally, like *Metatron*, *Khasmael* has been historically associated with forth-pouring consuming fire, the sobriquette "fire-breathing angel" reminding one of the climactic line in *The Bornless Ritual*, "I am He, whose mouth ever flameth!"

Netzach

וּסִיאֵל *Ussiel* ("Splendor of God"). This has been a difficult name to track and translate. Almost no words in Hebrew begin with the letter Vav, and none that give a clue to the meaning of this angelic name. Nor did it prove fruitful to consider the initial letter, ו, a conjunction, and seek for a further meaning from the rest.

However, the angel itself is adequately known. *Ussiel*, or *Uzziel*, appears in diverse Qabalistic works over the ages. She is specifically cited in the *Maseketh Atziluth* as chief of the Melakim, which confirms the present office of the archangel of Netzach in Briah.

But what does the name mean?

I suspect that וסי is a prefixed, shortened form of an underlying root such as ציה (*tziyah*). There is an unused Hebrew root of this form that, by comparison to other regional languages, means "sunny, arid." The form existent in Hebrew is צחה (*tzahah*), meaning "to be white, shining"; hence derivative meanings such as "to be sunny, shone upon, dried up by the sun," etc. Now, this is interesting in its relationship to Netzach alone, since the proper name of Venus, in Hebrew and in other ancient languages, means "shining, splendor, burning," etc. The mode of consciousness attributed to Venus-as-Daleth in *The 32 Paths of Wisdom* is the Luminous Consciousness (*Sekhel Meir*), "because it is the essence of that brilliant flame which is the instructor in the Secret Foundations of Holiness."

But, even more interesting, is that this צהה is the root of *Zion* (more properly, *Tzion*, ציון). The place-name *Tzion* literally means "a sunny place," it being the southern hill on which Jerusalem rests. The name, of course, became equated with Jerusalem itself, as the perfected "Holy City," or representative of that ultimate state toward which humanity was progressing and perfecting. (In Latin, the name *Hierosolyma* enumerates to 124, as does *Magnum Opus*, "the Great Work." In Hebrew, ירושלים is 596, the value of *Shekinah* (שכינה) spelled in plenitude, and of the spelling in plenitude of *Aleph, Beth,* and *Gimel,* the letters of the three paths by which one ultimately returns to the Crown.) *Tzion,* enumerating to 156, is equivalent to the name *Babalon,* and is intimately connected thereby to Venus and Netzach. A multitude of Binah ideas are reflected herein, even as the divine name attributed to Netzach in Briah is *Elohim.*

I therefore strongly suspect that the name *Ussiel* is derived from the ancient Hebrew root meaning "to be white, shining, sunny, shone upon," etc. We propose the tentative translation, "Splendor of God," or "Luminosity of God." This angelic name should be understood as referring to all of the luminous, fiery, passionate, life-affirming, fulfilling aspects of female divinity such as Venus, Elohim, Shekinah, Babalon, etc.

Hod

הפניאל *Hophniel* ("Turning to God"). *Liber 777* gives this name as הסניאל, usually rendered *Hosaniel*. This is incorrect. In both the *Maseketh Atziluth* and the *Berith Menucha,* the name is given as *Hophniel,* who is listed as the chief of the Beni Elohim. We have translated this name as "Turning to God." Several words beginning with הפנ- share a common meaning of "turning," including: *hiphnah* (הפנה), "to direct, to cause to turn"; *haphnayah* (הפניה), "turn"; and *haphnamah* (הפנמה), "introversion." The second of these is almost exactly the name with which we are here dealing, but ending in -יה instead of -אל. The root appears to be פנה, "to turn (oneself)," which Gesenius stated is always intransitive. That is, it means to turn oneself, rather than to turn a thing.

Yesod

יְהוֹאֵל *Yehoel* -or- זְפָנִיאֵל *Zephaniel*. *Yehoel* is also given as the archangel of Kether. As seen earlier, the chief characteristics of the name are: 1) that it is formed from the Trigrammaton, יהו, and 2) that it is one of the names of Metatron. Metatron is the archangel of Tiphareth in Briah. Therefore, the same great archangel, in one or another aspect, is explicitly attributed to every Sephirah so far encountered on the Middle Pillar! (We shall presently see that after a fashion—he is attributed to Malkuth as well.)

The previous sections discussing Kether and Tiphareth should be reviewed for more pointed and extended discussion of this archangel.

With respect to Yesod specifically, Yehoel is traditionally stated to hold Leviathan in check. In this is a subtle symbolism, with at least four levels of interpretation immediately evident.

First, Leviathan (literally, "twisted serpent") is one of the four great Princes of Darkness, represented especially in serpentine form. Thus, the holding of Leviathan in check is the controlling of the Nepheshic energies associated with Yesod. *Second*, this name usually rendered "twisted serpent" is also, literally, the *coiled* serpent, the Kundalini. *Third*, לויתן, *Leviathan*, enumerates to 496, the same as מלכות, Malkuth; much can be learned from meditating on this archangel of Yesod holding the essential nature of Malkuth in check. *Fourth*, this same 496 is the sum of the first 31 numbers, or the full extension, or manifestation, of the name אל, *El*, the divine name of the Supernals in Briah (including Kether, of which *Yehoel* is also the archangel). By "holding these powers in check" is meant that the conscious represented by *Yehoel* is holding the original divine impulse, or fundamental Will, true to its original nature while adapting it to the exigencies of manifestation in Malkuth. It is the same function that is described when Yesod is called the Purifying Consciousness, because, "It purifies the essence of the Sephiroth. It proves and adapts the design of their patterns, and establishes their unity. They remain united, without diminution or division."

According to the *Maseketh Atziluth*, the archangel of Yesod and chief of its angels is *Zephaniel*. (*Berith Menucha* gives this as *Zephaniah*.) I have been unable to confirm the translation of this name, although it appears to derive from the root זפה, *zaphah*, which has reference to flowing or pouring, as with sap. *Zephaniel* enumerates to 178, as does *Ophaniel*, and can be profitably studied in terms of that number, especially in the Hebrew and Latin Simplex Qabalahs.

Malkuth

מִיכָאֵל _Mikhæl_ ("Who is Like Unto God") is one of the very greatest of all archangels, and one of the three who appear to have an office of special relationship to humanity. Like *Raphael, Gabriel*, and others of comparable importance, his attributions, sobriquets, legends, and titles are legion and varied, and far beyond the scope of this short article to elaborate.

Of particular interest at the moment is the tradition that *Mikhael*, evolving further, became *Metatron*. This is most likely a metaphor for the illuminated self-realization at Tiphareth ultimately evolving into the purified selfhood of Kether. Nonetheless, if taken seriously, it means that every archangel attributed to a Briatic Middle Pillar sephirah is some form of *Metatron*, the "Prince of the Divine Presence."

From earliest times, *Mikhael* was considered virtually a god. Almost in the fashion of Prometheus and others, he has been viewed as teacher, defender, and caretaker of humanity, providing instruction, guardianship, and sustenance. Like Prometheus, he is traditionally related to the powers of fire and of the Sun, symbols that encapsulate heaven's greatest gifts to its children. *Mikhael* is depicted as warrior and "the Prince of Light"; and, after the legendary "fall" of Satan, he inherited the title "Viceroy of Heaven." As archangel of Hod in Assiah, he is especially the leader of the *Elohim Tzabaoth*, the "heavenly hosts"; and there is no reason to doubt that similar characteristics belong to him in Briah.

In short, the Adept should have little difficulty recognizing the aptness of *Mikhael's* attribution in this place. Additionally, "He Who is Like Unto God" (the literal meaning of מיכאל) is the perfect veil, or messenger, of *Yah-Adonai*, even as the commander of the heavenly hosts is the sure viceroy of that divine name of Malkuth, which we have already interpreted as embodying the nature of the planet Mars.

CHOIRS OF ANGELS

In the *Sepher Yetzirah* (I:10, Westcott translation) we read that God "made for Himself a Throne of Glory with Auphanim, Seraphim and Kerubim, as his ministering angels; and with these three he completed his dwelling, as it is written, 'Who maketh his angels spirits and his ministers a flaming fire.'"

The Hebrew words that Brother Westcott translated "Auphanim, Seraphim and Kerubim" are שרפים ואופנים וחיות הקדוש, *seraphim ve-ophanim ve-chaioth ha-qadesh*. Westcott, in his endnotes, explains his translation choice of "Kerubim" for the *chaioth*; and, perhaps as significant, is that rabbinical writings not uncommonly interchange the Seraphim, the Kerubim, and the Chaioth ha-Qadesh.

Our reason for sighting this passage at all is that, despite the great familiarity of these three classes of angels, they are not actually grouped together in any of the usual tabulations or categorizations of Qabalistic attributions. For example, in the world of Assiah, the Seraphim, Ophanim, and Kerubim are, respectively, the angels of Geburah, Chokmah, and Yesod. Yet in the list we are now examining, of angelic attributions for those in Briah, they are, respectively, the angelic choirs of Kether, Chokmah, and Binah. In the passage from *Sepher Yetzirah* quoted above, *Elohim Chayim* is stated to have placed these three varieties of "ministering angels" about his *Throne of Glory*. The word "throne," as mentioned previously, is a distinctive title of the world of Briah. Further, it is by these three— which we now know to be the angels of the Supernal Sephiroth in Briah—that "he completed his dwelling."

Many of the angelic names that follow are fairly familiar. When this is so, we have devoted proportionately less space to their discussion.

Kether

שְׂרָפִים *Seraphim* ("Fiery Serpents"). These angels are usually envisioned as winged, fiery serpents, or angelic representations of brilliant living flame. Although magicians know them best as the angels of Geburah in Assiah, their correspondence to Kether is assured by the frequency with which rabbinical writings seem to confuse them with the *Chaioth ha-Qadesh*, the "Holy Living Creatures" who are the angelic choir of Kether in Assiah. It is likely no coincidence that 630, the value of *Seraphim*, is also the value of רוחא קדישא, "the Holy Spirit."

In *Isaiah 6*, the Seraphim are described as standing above the "throne of the Lord," and as having six wings: "with twain he covered his face, and with twain he covered his feet, and with twain he did fly. And one cried unto another, and said, Holy, holy, holy *is* the LORD of Hosts [יהוה צבאות]: the whole earth is full of his glory."

They are the "fiery serpents" of *Num*. 21 upon which a significant teaching of the traditional Philosophus grade is based; likewise, the "fiery serpents" of *Deut*. 8:15, and the "fiery flying serpent" of *Isaiah* 30:6.

Chokmah

אוֹפַנִּים *Ophanim* ("Wheels"). These are the familiar angels of Chokmah already known to us from the world of Assiah. They bear the same significance in Briah.

Binah

כְּרוּבִים *Kerubim* ("Cherubs"). Far from the sweet baby-plump "Cherubs" prominent in the Gospel According to Hallmark, the Kerubim are mighty Sphinx-like guardians of the inner sanctuary. Even as they were charged with the outer security of the Garden of Eden after the legendary fall, so do we encounter them at the threshold of the most significant inward steps along the path of initiation. They are represented sacramentally as guardians of the 32nd Path of Tav, of the Portal of the Vault of the Adepti, and of the threshold of the Abyss. It is entirely fitting, therefore, that they should be attributed to guard the outermost veil of the Supernal Triad in the world of Briah.

As will be seen a little later, to the Briatic Supernals corresponds the Holy of Holies; and, in the Tabernacle of the Wilderness (upon which the first three grades of the Golden Dawn system are based), it is with images of the Kerubim that the veil guarding this inmost sanctum is adorned.

Although the ancient word *kerub* is well known, it has never been possible to definitively trace its origin or its fundamental meaning. William Gesenius was at a loss to translate it, saying only that it was, "in the theology of the Hebrews, a being of a sublime and celestial nature, in figure compounded of that of a man, an ox, a lion, and an eagle." (At one time, Gesenius thought *kerub* was related to an older word for "strength." Once this opinion emanated into scholarly circles, it has been repeated frequently despite the fact that its author was later forced to reject and withdraw the idea himself.)

Davidson stated that, "in name as well as in concept," they are "Assyrian or Akkadian in origin." In Assyrian art, they were depicted as huge, winged creatures with leonine or human faces, bodies of bulls or sphinxes, eagles, etc., usually placed at entrances to palaces or temples as vigilant guardians. Thus, even if the name cannot be translated literally, we can comfortably assume that we know what it means in practice.

Chesed

שִׁנְאָנִים *Shinanim* ("Shining Ones"). This name is wrongly given in *Liber 777* as שיככים, probably as a scribal distortion (somewhere along the way) of שירנים. Yet the correct spelling is שנאנים. Though not among the best-known angels, S. L. Mathers attributed them to Tiphareth (presumably of Assiah) in his Introduction to *The Kabbalah Unveiled*.

The singular noun שנאן, *shinan*, means "iteration, repetition," from the root, שנה, "to repeat, to do the second time." But the same Hebrew root also means, "to shine, to be bright." There are many puns and interlocking ideas here that become visible when reviewing the legends attributed to these angels.

Sources from Gesenius to Mathers wrongly cite this word as being used in *Psalms* 68:18. It is, instead, in *Psalms* 68:17, in the phrase "thousands upon thousands." Davidson quotes the *Pesikta Rabba* as saying that millions of Shinanim descended from heaven to be present at the revelation on Sinai. Also, per the *Zohar*, "myriad of thousands of *Shin'an* are on the chariot of God." The name is also literally connected to the letter-name *Shin*, and there is passing reference in at least one text to "the *shinanim* of fire." Thus, the Shinanim have typically been represented as appearing in vast multitudes, and the name seems intimately connected to that very idea of multiplicity; but the workable basic translation in practice should probably be, "the Shining Ones." ("God's Repeaters" stimulates less than reverent images.) These descriptions all paint an image not tremendously different from that implied by the name *Khasmalim*, "Brilliant Ones," the angels attributed to Chesed in Assiah and to Tiphareth in Briah.

Geburah

תַּרְשִׁישִׁים *Tarshishim* ("Precious Stones"). No angelic name has been so widely attributed by so many competent sources to so many different parts of the Tree of Life. Mathers attributes them to Netzach, Crowley to Tiphareth, the Aurum Solis to Hod; and here we find the Tarshishim ascribed to Geburah in Briah. Although the *Tarshishim* are not among the primary attributions employed in the most common hierarchies generally in use, it seems that there has been a strong and persistent desire on the part of Qabalistic magicians to have them show up *someplace*!

Mathers, in *Kabbalah Unveiled*, calls the *Tarshishim* the "brilliant ones." This is a rather figurative rendering of the literal meaning, which is probably best rendered as "precious stones."

Gesenius ventured that *tarshish* (תרשיש) probably means "breaking," or "subjection," and refers to a "subjected region"; for it is, in any case, the name of a city and area in Spain (Tarsis) that was a flourishing Phoenician colony mentioned repeatedly in the Old Testament. However, the same name is given to a precious stone from the same Tartessus area. Most scholars translate the word as *some* variety of gem, but with negligible agreement as to which one is precisely meant. In *Daniel* 10:6 it is usually translated "beryl." Other scholars (among the more modern) have rendered it as "chrysolite" or "topaz" and the topaz and many forms of chrysolite share a yellow or golden color. Godwin interprets it as "chrysolite" or, more broadly, "precious stones." I am persuaded of the wisdom of this conservative translation, and have adopted it. (Further discussion of the magical manifestation of these angels has already been given above while discussing their eponymous governor, Tarshish.)

Tiphareth

חַשְׁמַלִים *Khasmalim* ("Brilliant Ones"). *Khasmalim* is usually translated "Brilliant Ones." (Mathers called them "Scintillating Flames.") We should not be blinded, by our habituation of relating these angels to Chesed in Assiah, from seeing how obviously appropriate such an appellation is to those who would be angels of the Sun.

Gesenius interpreted the word חשמל, *hashmal*, as "polished brass" (that is, "brass made smooth"). It seems to be a contraction of the Hebrew נחושת, "brass," and the Chaldean מללא, "gold." The syllable מל, furthermore, carries the significance "not only of softness [malleability], but also that of *smoothness* and *brightness*." We have, then, a picture of brass that has a smooth, polished, bright quality, perhaps like that attributed to gold. Hence the idea of "brilliant ones"—which is even more solar, or golden, than usually thought.

Davidson quoted from *Berashith Rabb*, that the river Dinur ("fiery river") was created "out of the sweat of those animals [the Khasmalim] who sweat because they carry the throne of the Holy and Blessed God." This is an excellent description of those angels that pull the chariot of the Sun, under the dominion of the beneficent chief, Metatron-Khasmael.

Netzach

מְלָכִים *Melakim* ("Kings"). The word means "kings," and these angels are also attributed to Tiphareth in Assiah.

I must admit a blind spot with respect to these angels; for the idea of kings is, in the present author's psyche, so firmly attached to Tiphareth that it has been difficult so far to draw more than the most superficial conclusions regarding an alternative attribution. As usual in such work, conclusions should be based not on theory but on ceremonial work, astral vision, and the various *practical* tools with which a magician may explore magical realities.

It is possible, by the way, that a slightly different word was intended here. Perhaps the angelic choir intended are the *Malakim*, מלאכים, which means simply "messengers" or "angels." If this is so, the idea would be similar to the "Seven Elohim" (usually interpreted as the seven planetary angels) being those angels attributed to Netzach in Assiah.

Hod

בְּנִי אֱלֹהִים *Beni Elohim* ("Sons of God"). These "Sons of Elohim" are the same angels that are attributed to Hod in Assiah, but the significance is surely somewhat different. In Briah, they are under the rule of Hophniel, which means "Turning to God"; and it is surely this archangelic guidance that fulfills the Beni Elohim's "sonship" of the divine.

Ironically, the name Beni Elohim has the same value, 148, as the word *Netzach*, and other words related thereto. Similarly, the "palace of Briah" here attributed is *Hekel Nogah*—the name of the planet Venus!

Yesod

יֹשִׁים *Ishim* ("Sainted Souls"). We must, at the start, side-step a potential confusion with this name. The *Ishim* should not be confused with the אשים, *Eshim* (often written "Ashim"), which are the angels of Malkuth in Assiah. This is a tempting confusion, since some Qabalistic writers have attempted to swap the Kerubim of Yesod for the Eshim of Malkuth, generally based (ultimately) on mistaking the latter for the Ishim. The *Eshim* are "flames." The *Ishim*, though their name is a little harder to translate, are about to be discussed.

Ish, in Hebrew, means "being, existence," etc., and thus a being. Ish particularly refers to a human being. The word has a complex allegorical significance in the rabbinical writings, and absorbs considerable attention in the *Zohar* itself.

Ultimately, *ishim* came, in context, to mean "great beings" or "sainted souls." Gustav Davidson declares that, "Their duty, since Creation, has been to extol the Lord." Ironically—just as we have carefully differentiated them from their common confusion with the fiery Eshim—we also note that the name *Ishim* enumerates to 360, the value of *Shin* spelled in full, and they appear, in their own right, to be sometimes characterized as beings of brilliant flame. In consideration of the method of composing telesmatic images, we note that the two letters forming the name יש are those two most associated with fire.

Malkuth

אֶרְאֶלִים *Arelim* ("Thrones"). These angels are well-known to Qabalists, especially as the choir attributed to Binah in Assiah. Their name is most often translated "thrones." This is of considerable interest, since, besides Binah, only Malkuth (the daughter of Binah) is traditionally represented as enthroned.

Despite its familiarity and frequent mention, this translation of *Arelim* as "thrones" is highly controversial. The usual Hebrew words for "throne" are כרסיא, *korsia*, and כס, *kes*. In contrast, *arel* (the singular of *arelim*) is a perfectly recognizable Hebrew word. *Ar* (like the longer *ari* and *aryeh*) means "lion," probably from the Chaldean אר, "light" (like the Hebrew אור). Gesenius translates אראל as "lion of God" and then, derivatively, as "hero." (It is, perhaps, in response to this literal meaning that Godwin has translated *Arelim* as "Mighty Ones.") The word occurs in the *Torah* as the proper name Areli, one of the sons of Gad, and is variously translated as "lion of God" or as "son of a hero."

Nonetheless, the attribution of the *Arelim* to Malkuth in Briah surely results from the established tradition that the name means, or at least signifies, "Thrones." This is important for many reasons. We have already alluded to the fact (mentioned in *The 32 Paths of Wisdom*) that Malkuth "is exalted above every head, and sits on the throne of Binah." Furthermore, from Briah's distinct relationship to Binah, the world of Briah is called "the world of Thrones," and the entrance to it, we see, is distinguished by angels so characterized. The Throne is the identifying hieroglyph of Isis, and is closely identified in both the Hebraic and Egyptian systems with the divine feminine in many aspects; and if we accept the common interpretation that Isis' "throne" is a birthing chair, it lends considerable meaning to the attribution of the *Arelim* (under any claimed meanings of the name) to Malkuth in this world.

Finally, according to Davidson, the *Arelim* are composed of white fire and are appointed to the governance of grass, trees, fruit, and grain—a comfortable agricultural correspondence that actually fits Malkuth even better than it would Binah.

PALACES OF BRIAH

Supernals: *Hekel Qadesh Qadeshim*, היכל קדוש קדשים, "Temple of the Holy of Holies"

Chesed: *Hekel Ahavah*, היכל אהבה, "Temple of Love"

Geburah: *Hekel Zekuth*, היכל זכות, "Temple of Merit"

Tiphareth: *Hekel Ratzon*, היכל רצון, "Temple of Delight"

Netzach: *Hekel Etzem ha-Shamaim*, היכל עצם שמים "Temple of the Essence of Heaven"

Hod: *Hekel Nogah*, היכל נוגה, "Temple of Luster (or Splendor)"

Yesod-Malkuth: *Hekel Livnat ha-Sappir*, היכל לונת הספיר, "Temple of the Pavement of Lapis Lazuli"

The "palaces of Assiah" are given according to the *seven palaces* model and are, in fact, one basis of that familiar diagram.

We will not discuss these individually. One reason is that there is controversy about their attribution. They are sometimes given in the reversed order, or in a different order. See, for example, Kaplan, *Sepher Yetzirah in Theory & Practice*, chapter 4. The traditional list given above seems to stand up to both intellectual scrutiny and the limited practical work we have performed with them; but greater confidence can only be placed on them after they are subject to much more work by a wider circle of initiates. In hierarchical invocatory work, we recommend that the word *hekel* be dropped, and that only the remainder of the name be employed as a fourth "word of power"; but that the entire name, either in Hebrew or in English, be employed in any other expository or descriptive language that is employed during the invocation.

These "palaces" all begin with the word היכל, usually translated "palace." However, the word may also mean "temple"; and its most important Biblical usage, היכל יהוה, referred to the temple at Jerusalem. We have, therefore, substituted the more evocative translation "temple" for practical purposes.

Often, other translations will be given than what we have provided here. These are usually translations not of the Hebrew names themselves, but rather of the Latin translations often given in their place. Thus, *Hekel Nogah* is given as the Latin *Palatium Serenitatis*, "Palace of Serenity," whereas the correct meaning of nogah is "luster" or "splendor." Similarly, *Hekel Etzem ha-Shamaim*, was rendered into Latin as *Palatium Substantiæ Coeli*, "Palace of the Substance of Heaven"; but the correct translation of *etzem ha-shamaim* is exactly the opposite, "*essence* of heaven."

We will close this section with one example, and that of the most interesting and practical of the seven. To Malkuth and Yesod, the entry points to the Tree of Life for the advancing aspirant are attributed *Hekel Livnat ha-Sappir*. Its Latin title, *Palatium Albedinis Crystalinæ*, "Palace of Crystaline Whiteness," is misleading; the Hebrew would usually be translated, "Temple of the Pavement of Sapphire."

It is almost certain, however, that the word translated "sapphire" in old Hebrew (and appearing throughout the Old Testament) actually means the blue stone we know as lapis lazuli. Notwithstanding the more usual translation "sapphire," it is this word *sappir* that is used in *Ezekiel* I:26, which may be translated, "And above the firmament that was over their heads was the likeness of a throne, as the appearance of lapis lazuli"; and in *Ezekiel* 10:1, "Then I looked, and, behold, in the firmament that was above the head of the kerubim there appeared over them as it were lapis lazuli [lit., *blue stone*], as the appearance of the likeness of a throne." Compare also the revealing use of the same word in *Exodus* 24:10, which may be read, "And they saw the God of Israel: and there was under his feet as it were a paved work of lapis lazuli, and as it were the body of heaven in its clearness."

If we did not already recognize the implications of this "Temple" name, then this passage from *Exodus* would surely open our eyes. Malkuth in Briah, the initial opening of the way unto the world of creation, is depicted as a temple of a pavement of lapis lazuli, "as it were the body of heaven in its clearness." To step into such a temple on earth, with its dark, midnight blue substance and its golden veins and flecks, would be, seemingly, to step into the infinite starry heavens. Here are the Arelim, the angelic Thrones that mark the attainment of the world of Thrones. Here Mikhael stands ready to escort us as we see-hear-feel-perceive the thunderous and mighty essence that is Yah-Adonai. In this image we gain new insight—perhaps a Briatic perspective—into the attribution to Malkuth of the Resplendent Consciousness, which according to *The 32 Paths of Wisdom*, "is illuminated with the splendor of all the lights, and…causes an influence to flow forth from the Prince of Countenances."

About the Author

James A. Eshelman has been a noted author and teacher of occult and metaphysical subjects for twenty-five years, originally in the field of astrology and then in magick, mysticism, Qabalah, tarot, occult psychology, and related subjects. He was a member of Ordo Templi Orientis (O.T.O.) for thirteen years, serving as a senior officer before resigning in 1992 to devote his energies to other responsibilities. He accepted ordination in the Gnostic Catholic Church (Ecclesia Gnostica Catholica) in 1979, and was consecrated a Gnostic bishop in the Vilatte succession in 1985.

Mr. Eshelman is presently Deputy Executive Director and a faculty member of the College of Thelema. He serves as a Grand Chief of the Temple of Thelema, which he cofounded in 1987 with Anna-Kria King and Phyllis Seckler. He is also a former Grand Imperator of Fraternitas LVX Occulta (Fraternity of the Hidden Light), which he continues to serve in a Grand Lodge position. He lives in Los Angeles, California, and is author of The Mystical & Magical System of the A∴A∴, and of *776½, Tables of Correspondences for Practical Ceremonial.*

Endnotes

1. *The 32 Paths of Wisdom*, translated by James A. Eshelman. College of Thelema, Los Angeles, 1994. In the present article, all quotes from *The 32 Paths of Wisdom* are from this edition.

2. In working with these Names meditatively and reflectively, it sometimes seems that *Yah* is distinctly attributable to Yesod, and *Adonai* to Malkuth. This is, however, solely an intuitive, and perhaps personal, observation that, so far as we know, is not substantiated by any of the source literature.

3. The corresponding doctrine is very complex, but of so great an importance that it should be stated here even if only in outline form: The Mystic Number of Yesod, and a number otherwise significantly related to the world of Yetzirah, is 45, the value of the Hebrew אדם, *Adam*, "humanity." Similarly, 45 is the value, in the Latin Qabalah Simplex, of both *deus*, "god," and *homo*, "man" (humanity). *Deus* = 45 = *homo*. God is Man. אדם, *Adam*, is a temurah (by the Qabalah of Nine Chambers) for אמת, *emeth*, "Truth." Humanity, which is "God," is Truth. אמת = 441 or 21²; it is thus an expression as well of the number 21, which is not only the value of אהיה, *Eheieh*, but also of the Trigrammaton יהו, the Great Name expressed only to the level of Yetzirah. 21 is the sum of the first 6 numbers, resolving to Tiphareth, the Son; 6 is the sum of the first 3 numbers, resolving to Binah, the Mother; 3 is the sum of the first 2 numbers, resolving to Chokmah, the Father, thus retracing the extended Trigrammaton to its root in Yod. The net effect is to declare that humanity is God and that humanity is TRUTH; and that this mystery is keyed to the Sephirah Yesod and to the world of Yetzirah in general, rooted in a primal seed-Will. The problem each person must solve is to discover what this means in each of the four worlds, and then to carry out the resultant formula without confusing the planes all over again. The union of the genitals in the world of Assiah is only the outermost veil of the whole.

Osiris.

Osiris and Christ

Powers of Transformation in Golden Dawn Ritual

John Michael Greer

One aspect of Golden Dawn ritual that can easily baffle the modern student of the tradition is the fusion of Christian, Jewish, and Pagan imagery, which takes place constantly within all levels of the Order's ritual structure. Egyptian gods, Neoplatonic powers, and even such oddities as the Samothracian Cabeiri stand cheek by jowl with Cabalistic names of God and mythic structures from Christian esotericism. Sometimes these various things are presented as different names or symbols for the same reality; more often, though, they simply coexist within the ritual work, and the connections between them are nowhere spelled out.

Some scholars, writing about the Golden Dawn from an academic perspective, have interpreted this habit as simple eclecticism, the same Victorian mania for clutter that produced so much atrocious art and architecture in the same period. To those who have worked with the Golden Dawn system, though, it's clear that deeper unities underlie the whole structure of the Order's ritual and magic. The system is effective and consistent in ways which a purely eclectic approach rarely achieves.

One of most important of these unifying patterns, one that runs through the entire labyrinth of Golden Dawn ritual, is the interaction between the images of Osiris, the Egyptian lord of the dead, and Jesus Christ, the Christian savior. These two figures both belong to the class of so-called "dying gods," deities whose deaths and resurrections are central to many religions. Some esoteric traditions have simply identified all such figures with one another. The Golden Dawn's approach, though, was subtler.

Both Osiris and Christ are used in Golden Dawn ritual, but in different places and in different ways. Neither one is an object of worship; in the Order's rituals, the only divinity who is actually invoked or worshiped is the abstract One of traditional Western magical philosophy, represented by the various names of God used in the Cabala. Rather, Christ and Osiris both represent a pattern of forces—in the

229

Order's terminology, a formula—which is used to structure consciousness in various ritual contexts.

In the rituals of the Outer Order, from Neophyte to Philosophus, Osiris is the primary figure; this is true in the magical work of these rituals as outlined in the Golden Dawn documents, but also, as we'll see, on a deeper level as well. The Portal Grade marks a transition, however; the symbolism of Osiris is central to its first half, but in the second, the figure of Christ takes over. This and the Adeptus Minor Grade are not Christian in any ordinary sense of the word, but the legends and imagery of Christ provide the dominant symbolism and much of the incidental detail for these ceremonies.

Understanding the role and meaning of these two figures will involve a journey down some strange by-paths. The Golden Dawn's use of Osiris and Christ rose from certain older patterns in the history of Western spirituality and magic; as with so many other things in the Order's work, the symbolism we'll be exploring has deep roots. To understand that symbolism, it's necessary to turn back to ancient ways of looking at the world. In the process, some common assumptions that have structured the magical community's approach to questions of religion may prove to need revising, and some familiar images and ideas may take on an unexpected meaning.

The Way of Sacrifice

Osiris and Christ, as mentioned above, belong to a class of traditional divine figures that can be labeled "dying gods." At the root of the whole complex of these traditions is the concept of sacrifice, one of the oldest and most constant of all human spiritual ideas. Though it takes a bewildering array of forms, sacrifice centers on a single principle; its essence is exchange. This comes across most clearly, perhaps, in the sacrificial formula of Roman paganism: *do ut des*, "I give so that you may give."

In every sacrifice, something is sent from the visible world of everyday life into the hidden world of powers beyond, so that something else may pass by the same channel out of the Unseen. Consider the sacrifices offered for fertility across the ancient world. Livestock of various kinds died before the altar, and certain portions of their bodies went up in fire to the local gods; the rest, sensibly enough, was cooked and shared out among the priests and worshippers. In exchange for the offerings, the powers behind the natural world sent sun and rain in season and kept disease from the livestock and the crops.

The same principle was used in less concrete ways.

Sacrifices at the founding of a city, the naming of a child, or the coronation of a king brought forth a guardian spirit to give protection during vulnerable beginnings. More subtly, sin, disease, or ritual impurity—the three were not sharply differentiated, and modern research into the role of emotions in disease suggests that this seeming confusion has a point—were often understood as forces that drew the one affected by them out of the human world into the borderlands of the Unseen. Caught between the worlds, such people were seen as dangerous to themselves and the community alike, and had to be brought back into the human world; one common way to do this was by sacrifice. This is the origin of the sacrifices of purification that have such a large role in the Hebrew sacrificial rites, among many others.

To the modern mind, these ways of thinking about the world are likely to sound bizarre or worse. The principle behind sacrifice, though, is a principle of balance; the act of exchange between the worlds was seen as a way of maintaining the balance of the universe, and the rituals of sacrifice were thus central to the balance of the ancient world on many levels. The priests and philosophers of that world were by no means blind to the deeper implications of this principle, and some of the highest intellectual achievements of the ancients drew on it in ways we can only begin to trace today.

One role of the idea of sacrifice, though, is central to our theme. While the process of exchange central to sacrifice was not measured out on a tit-for-tat basis—one sacrificed a few cows in exchange for the birth of many more—the concept does imply that different scales of offering were needed to bring about different scales of divine response. From this came the idea that the most important divine actions, such as the creation of the world, could only have resulted from the sacrifice of a divine victim. Many creation myths—Norse, Babylonian, and Hindu, among others—thus came to tell of the origin of the world out of the sacrifice of a primal being; a tale of the same sort lies behind the Cabalistic account of Adam Cadmon.

Seed as Sacrifice, Sacrifice as Seed

The traditions of sacrifice also made particularly deep connections with agriculture, the economic basis of ancient society. Time and the coming of new discoveries have both tended to blur the tremendous impact that the discovery of agriculture made on ancient cultures. At once a complex and evolving technology and a profoundly magical act, farming reshaped philosophy and spirituality just as it revolutionized the cycle of everyday life. In turn, traditional ways of thinking shaped the way that agriculture itself was understood.

The seed buried in the earth, then, was seen as a sacrifice, and—by the same principle of exchange that governs all sacrifice—it brought forth a response from the Earth. But that response, in turn, had to be brought all the way into the human world by a second sacrifice, the harvesting and threshing of the grain. This double sacrifice, in which the grain was both victim and reward, was bound to the seasons of the year by the nature of the agricultural cycle; around it gathered calendar-lore and early astronomy, as well as an enormous amount of magical and ritual practice.

The thought of the ancient world tended to clothe itself in myth, and so this cycle of seed and sacrifice appears in one form or another throughout mythology and folklore. One example, drawn from Celtic sources, can be followed in the Scots ballad of John Barleycorn:

> There were three kings come from the East,
>   Their fortune for to try,
> And they ha' ta'en a solemn vow
>   John Barleycorn should die.
> They took a plough and plough'd him down,
>   Cast clods upon his head,
> And they ha' ta'en a solemn vow
>   John Barleycorn was dead.
> But when the Spring came kindly on,
>   And show'rs began to fall,
> John Barleycorn got up again
>   And sore surpris'd them all.
> The sultry suns of Summer came,
>   And he grew thick and strong;
> His head well armed wi' pointed spears,
>   That none should do him wrong.
> The sober Autumn enter'd mild,
>   And he grew wan and pale;
> His bending joints and drooping head
>   Show'd he began to fail.
> His colour sicken'd more and more,
>   He faded into age;
> And then his enemies began
>   To show their deadly rage.
> They took a sickle, long and sharp,
>   And cut him at the knee;

Then tied him fast upon a cart,
  Like a rogue for forgery.
They laid him down upon his back,
  And cudgell'd him full sore;
Then hung him up before the blast,
  And turned him o'er and o'er.
They next filled up a darksome pit
  With water to the brim;
They heaved in poor John Barleycorn
  And let him sink or swim.
They roasted o'er a scorching flame
  The marrow of his bones;
But the miller us'd him worse than that,
  And ground him 'twixt two stones.
And they ha' ta'en his own heart's blood,
  And drank it round and round,
And still the more that they ha' drunk
  Their joy did more abound.
So let us toast John Barleycorn,
  Each one wi' glass in hand,
And may his great posterity
  Ne'er fail in old Scotland![1]

This ballad presents the mythic image of the agricultural cycle in its most obvious form—seemingly, a form far removed from either the Golden Dawn rituals or the ancient myths on which those rituals drew. Appearances deceive, though. The story within this ballad, beneath its rustic clothing, is identical—in outline, and in many of its details—to the ancient Egyptian legend of Osiris.

The Myth of Osiris

According to classical accounts, Osiris and his sister-wife Isis were King and Queen of Egypt in the earliest of times, the founders of Egyptian civilization and the inventors of farming. Osiris' brother Set, however, envied his brother, and set out to kill him and seize the kingship for himself. He secretly arranged to learn the exact measurements of Osiris' body, and had a richly decorated coffin made precisely to fit. Then, at a banquet, he offered to give the coffin to anyone who fit its measure. All the guests lay in it, one after another, but everyone was too large or too small. Finally Osiris lay in the coffin, upon which Set and his henchmen shut the lid, nailed it, sealed it with molten lead, and cast it into the Nile.

Isis, grieving, went in search of the body of Osiris, and after wandering the world discovered that it had floated all the way to Byblos in Syria. There it had lodged in the branches of an acacia tree, which had then grown around it, lifting it into the air; the tree had been cut down and made into one of the pillars of the local king's palace. After various adventures, Isis reclaimed the body and returned with it to the Nile delta. There, with the help of Thoth the god of magic, she restored Osiris to life, and by him conceived a son, Horus.

Set, however, discovered their hiding place, and he and his henchmen attacked Osiris again, cutting him into fourteen pieces, which he then scattered across Egypt. Isis searched for them and found all of him but his penis, which had been eaten by a fish. Because of this lack, Osiris could not be restored to life, but instead was mummified and went into the otherworld to become lord and judge of the dead. Horus, however, grew to manhood, finished off the story (and Set) in the traditional manner, and became king.[2]

To describe this legend as "just" an agricultural myth is a little like describing *Romeo and Juliet* as a play about puppy love gone wrong. Much that is finest in Egyptian literature and art centers on this story. At the same time, the agricultural side of the myth cannot be doubted. The first death by burial amid the irrigating waters of the Nile is followed by the raising up of the body of Osiris and the birth of Horus, who in this context—Horus is one of the most complex of the Egyptian gods—represents the seed grain for the next season; the penis of Osiris has the same significance, and is swallowed up in the waters of the Nile just as Osiris himself had been. Thereafter, the body of Osiris is broken apart and passes into the otherworld. Many of the rituals of the cult of Osiris have to do directly with the plowing and harvesting of the fields, and devout Egyptians molded little statues of Osiris from earth and barley seed, watered these, and watched the resurrection of Osiris unfold as the seeds sprouted and grew. A number of these statues were found, withered but intact, in the tomb of Tutankhamen.

Symbols of the Dying God

The same pattern of sacrifice can be found in the myths of many other ancient cultures, more or less garbled by the transition from oral to written cultures, and thus from myth to literature. One version that played an important role in the traditions ancestral to the Golden Dawn was the Greek myth of Orpheus, the divine musician. The versions that have survived were rewritten for literary effect, but the tale still shows the marks of the older pattern: Orpheus descends into Hades, the realm of Death, and returns from it alive; later, he is killed and torn to pieces, though his head continues to sing and becomes an oracle of the gods.

The severed head that speaks is an important feature, one that came to Greece from the Greeks' Indo-European ancestors. Other Indo-European peoples use the same image quite often; the severed head of Bran son of Llyr, in the second branch of the Welsh *Mabinogion,* spoke for eighty-seven years after it was cut off its body; the severed head of Mimir, in the Norse *Ynglingasaga,* was kept by Odin as an oracular source of wisdom. It is an image we will see again in this essay.

Some of the Indo-European myths of divine sacrifice also give a different manner of death for the sacrificed god. Instead of being cut or torn apart, he is suspended in the air and pierced by a spear; typically, too, he dies once, rather than twice, in these legends. This probably derives from a symbolism of hunting or the slaughter of livestock rather than farming. The Norse god Odin's self-sacrifice on the world-tree Yggdrasil is a famous example:

> *I know that I hung*
> *   on the windy tree*
> *Nine full nights,*
> *   Wounded with the spear,*
> *sacrificed to Odin,*
> *   Myself offered to myself,*
> *On the tree,*
> *   where its roots run*
> *No one knows.*[3]

The Welsh, with a typically Celtic delight in the bizarre, had their sacrificial hero Llew Llaw Gyffes meet his death by the spear in a bath-house beside a stream, with one foot on the back of a goat and the other on the rim of a cauldron. Other Celtic legends, not to be outdone, have their victims suffer three different deaths at once.[4] While this level of weirdness was equaled by few other mythologies, the spear and the suspended death are also themes that will appear again in our exploration.

A final image that is often found in Indo-European myths, although it has very ancient sources and can be found worldwide, focuses on the burial of the seed as a pattern of the transcendence of death. This image, which hearkens back to archaic customs of mound burial, has given rise to countless legends of sleeping kings and gods buried beneath the earth, waiting out the turning of the cycles of time to come forth again. The legend of the fate of Arthur, the "Once and

Future King," is part of this complex of legends; so, critically, is that of Merlin sleeping in his cave. This, too, is an image we will see again.[5]

The Astronomical Sacrifice

The natural relationship mentioned above between the agricultural cycle and the seasons drew the symbolism of sacrifice into another of the major intellectual adventures of the ancient world. Astronomy and astrology, the twin quests to understand the movement of the bright points in the heavens and to interpret their meaning to dwellers on Earth, had a profound effect on ancient thought, shaping attitudes toward time and destiny, and quite possibly giving rise to the entire concept of natural law. What the ancients lacked in telescopes and other equipment, they made up in patience and careful record-keeping; the entire structure of modern astrology, and more of current scientific astronomy than modern scientists like to admit, are both founded on the knowledge gained over several thousand years by Chaldean scholar-priests who watched the heavens from mud-brick towers.[6]

Their discoveries, true to the ancient way of thought, were preserved in myths. The twelve labors of Hercules or his many equivalents—the Samson of Biblical myth, whose name comes from the Hebrew word for "sun," is one—represent the twelve signs of the Zodiac, through which the Sun moves in the course of the year. Other tales of Mars and Venus, Jupiter and Mercury—to this day, the names of planets as well as gods—tracked other movements across the sky. Many of these myths had the practical function of preserving calendar-lore, so that farmers could tell by a glance at the dawn, dusk, or midnight sky when it was time to plant crops or move herds.

One particular movement is of some importance in this context. The precession of the equinoxes, that slow wobble of the Earth's axis that causes the points of the equinoxes and solstices to creep slowly backward around the Zodiac, makes the stars and the seasons shift with respect to one another over long periods of time. Theoretically, the Sun stands at the beginning of the sign Aries on the day of the spring equinox; in fact, it is now much of the way through Pisces on this date. Four thousand years ago, when many of the myths we now read were taking shape, it stood near the beginning of Taurus.

This gradual shift in the heavens had a profound impact on ancient myth and philosophy. The passage of the spring equinox through each of the constellations was held to mark an age of the world, at the end of which the whole pattern of time shifted. The passing of each age was marked in myth by the legendary sacrifice of the symbol of its sign; thus the age in which Aries held the equinoctial point saw myths of bull-sacrifice, which marked the passing of the age of Taurus, play an important part in mythology.

Perhaps the clearest expression of this is to be found in the religion of Mithraism, one of the mystery religions that rose toward the end of the classical world. The great mythic event of the Mithraic faith, and one of the most common images in Mithraic art, was the *taurobolium* or bull sacrifice, in which Mithras is shown killing a great bull while various other figures and creatures stand nearby. This image baffled scholars until recently, when it was shown to be a precise star map of the constellations around Taurus. It has been suggested, quite plausibly, that Mithras was identified with the hidden power that was seen as driving the process of precession, the unmoved mover behind the visible cosmos who slew the Bull of Heaven by ending its long reign at the primary station of the skies.[7]

The Mystical Sacrifice

The development of an astrological symbolism of sacrifice was far from the only transformation of the pattern we've been examining. Another was the development of a mystical dimension of mythology—that is, a way of understanding myth in which the death and resurrection of the god become the model for the transformation of the individual self. In terms of the Western tradition, the most important name in this context is that of Orpheus, the divine musician mentioned earlier.

In Greek tradition, Orpheus was the founder of a tradition of mystical knowledge and initiation, the Orphic mysteries. Very little is known for sure about these today, but classical writings preserve some of the teachings of the tradition. To the Orphics, *soma*, Greek for "body," and *sema*, Greek for "tomb," were one and the same; the human spirit was trapped in matter and could only regain its true stature by escaping from the physical world. Their teachings included number symbolism and traditions about the immortality of the soul, and focused on the idea that knowledge of the real nature of the self was the key to redemption from the material world. In a way, their beliefs represented a rejection of the old theory of sacrifice, for the Orphic vision sought not to balance the worlds of spirit and matter but to separate them once and for all.

A surviving Orphic myth expresses the same thing in symbolic language. According to this, Dionysus was the child of Zeus, the king of the gods, and Persephone, the queen of the underworld. He was hidden away in a cave from Hera, Zeus' jealous wife. However, Hera learned of the child and incited the Titans—the primal powers of creation, who existed before the gods—to kill him. They disguised themselves by whitening their bodies with gypsum, crept up on the child, distracted him with toys and a mirror, and then killed and dismembered him and ate the body. Zeus, learning of this, burnt the Titans to ashes with a thunderbolt. From their ashes were created the first human beings.[8]

In this myth, most of the elements of the agricultural cycle can be traced out, at least in outline: the first death has been reduced to hiding in an underground cave, but the second appears in its full form, complete with the eating of the body, which has its mundane image in the baking and eating of bread. This is not the main point of the myth, however. To the Orphics, Dionysus represented the primal human soul, distracted by the toys and mirrors of the senses and then consumed by material life; the Titans represented matter, and the ashes from which humanity was born, partly Titanic, partly Dionysian, were the mixture of spirit and matter that makes up the human individual—and the human predicament.

The Orphic tradition is of critical importance for two reasons. First, it represents the first point of emergence in the West of the idea of individual spiritual transformation. The rites and theologies of the older sacrificial system were focused on the community, not the individual, and ideas such as personal freedom and the value of the individual had no role in them. The liberation sought by the Orphics, on the other hand, was a liberation of the individual, motivated by the same ways of thinking that made Greece the birthplace of the concept of democracy.

The second reason for Orphism's importance is that most of Western spirituality has grown up from Orphic roots. Pythagoras, the first major esoteric teacher in the recorded history of the West, was an Orphic initiate, and classical accounts state that he took the basis of his system of mystical geometry and mathematics from Orphic sources. Orphic and Pythagorean influences, in turn, play important roles in the thought of Plato, and the whole range of Neoplatonic, Gnostic, and Hermetic traditions, which became the basis for Western magic, can best be seen as further developments on Orphic themes. So can—despite a long history of sometimes strident denials—another Western spiritual tradition that emerged in the same era: Christianity.

The Christian Synthesis

For most of the last two thousand years, the barrier between Christianity and paganism has been a kind of Berlin Wall through the middle of

Western spirituality. Christians have defined their faith as uniquely good, and insisted, loudly, on the differences between their religion and every other religion in the world. In turn, modern pagan revivalists have too often simply reversed the equation; one can read any number of Christian-bashing diatribes in the current pagan and magical press, in which all non-Christian religions are seen as good while Christianity is uniquely evil.

What makes both these attitudes particularly misleading is that the supposed rigid barrier between Christianity and other religions simply isn't there. Despite the claims made for it, Christianity—even at its oldest and most basic levels—has roots in a wide range of classical pagan sources, roots that are at least as significant as Christianity's connections with Judaism. Nor are these pagan materials simply borrowed and tacked on to a non-pagan structure; they are central to the entire structure of Christian myth and theology, and they are worked together in a manner common to many other religions of the time. In fact, it would not be going too far to describe Christianity as the best surviving example of late classical paganism.

In Christianity, practically every major theme of classical pagan tradition appears, woven together into a single many-layered mythological structure. The births of two miraculous children, John and Jesus, are announced by angels; one is born to a woman past menopause, the other to a virgin; John is born at the summer solstice, Jesus at the winter solstice. John, the elder, goes out into the wilderness, baptizes his followers with water, and speaks of one who will come to baptize with fire. Jesus appears, is baptized, goes into the wilderness to contend with the powers of evil, and embarks on his own career as a holy man. Meanwhile, John is seized by an evil king and beheaded in a dungeon; the traditional date for this is August 29. Jesus travels about, performs miracles, and at Passover celebrates a meal in which he says that the bread is his body and the wine is his blood. He is then crucified and pierced with a spear; he dies, is resurrected, and ascends into heaven thereafter.

The old agricultural pattern is one of the more obvious elements of this myth. Here the two deaths have been divided between two figures. John, born at midsummer and sacrificed just before the beginning of fall, the planting season in the Middle East, is the seed. Jesus, born at midwinter as the new crop grows, and sacrificed at the harvest just after the beginning of spring, is the ripe grain. It is thus the body of Jesus that is eaten in the bread—one does not eat seed grain, after all. (The name of Bethlehem, the town where Jesus was born, literally means "house of bread" in Hebrew.)

Onto this a second, astronomical and calendrical level of symbolism has been built. John, born of an old woman at midsummer, is the waning half of the year, and he descends into the Earth to die as the Sun descends in the heavens; "I must decrease," he says comparing himself and Jesus, "but he must increase."[9] Jesus, born of a young virgin at midwinter, is the waxing half of the year, and meets his death raised up above the Earth as the Sun ascends in the heavens. Jesus in the midst of the twelve apostles is also the Sun amid the signs of the Zodiac, while Mary and Martha—Mary comes from the Hebrew for "sea," and Martha means simply "lady" or "mistress"—are Venus, sea-born goddess across the ancient world, as the evening and the morning star.

On a broader scale, Virgo the Virgin and Pisces the Fishes—the constellations of the equinoctial points in the age that began about the time of the life of Jesus—appear in Christian myth as the Virgin Mary, on the one hand, and the constant fish-symbolism of the New Testament, on the other. Jesus himself is Aries, the sacrificial Lamb of God, the former place of the spring equinox that was sacrificed at the turning of the ages. Christians who are "washed in the blood of the lamb" rarely realize the roots of that phrase in the astronomical symbolism of the Mithraic mysteries, where initiates were quite literally doused with the blood of a freshly sacrificed bull; still, the connection is there.

Christian Mysticism and Magic

Along with the agricultural and astronomical levels, a mystical level to Christian myth seems to have been present from the beginning. Trying to grasp the nature of this part of the symbolism, though, leads quickly into regions marked "off limits" for a very long time. The core of the problem is that most of what survives of early Christian mysticism has been given a label—Gnosticism—which means almost nothing, but which has become an excuse for a remarkable level of scholarly shoddiness.[10]

Consider the case of the Gospel of Thomas, one of the documents of the "Gnostic" library uncovered in 1945 at Nag Hammadi in Egypt. A collection of sayings attributed to Jesus, it has been generally been assigned to a date in the second century, comfortably distant from the life of Jesus, and labeled a "Gnostic" forgery. Unfortunately for this claim, sayings collections are recognized as the earliest form of Christian writings, replaced as early as 80 C.E. by the first narrative Gospels, and the sayings in the Gospel of Thomas are in many cases more complete and (according to modern "form criticism" methods) more authentic than their equivalents in the official Gospels. What makes this especially uncomfortable is that the Jesus of the Gospel of Thomas explicitly rejects the idea of an apocalyptic end of the world, the cornerstone of much later Christian theology, and teaches the essentially Orphic doctrine that knowledge of the self's true nature—not faith—is the key to salvation.[11]

Another discovery in Egypt offers an even more startling perspective on the question of Christian mysticism. The distinguished Biblical scholar Morton Smith has pointed out that the closest equivalents to many of the most basic elements of Christian faith and practice are to be found in Greek magical papyri that were discovered in Egypt at various times in the nineteenth century. One example is the formula of the Eucharist, in which the participants ritually eat the body and drink the blood of Christ in order to become part of the body of Christ. The closest equivalent to this formula outside of Christian contexts is to be found in the magical papyri, where magicians did exactly this to incorporate into themselves the power of a god. Based on these connections, and a great deal of other ignored data, Smith showed that the historical Jesus of Nazareth may well have been not a prophet, not the expected Jewish messiah, but a magician pure and simple.[12]

The exact form of the original mystical interpretations of Christianity is a matter for guesswork, despite these clues. One thing that does seem clear, though, is that the basic Orphic theme of the spirit as a prisoner in matter, and the Orphic rejection of sexuality and physical existence, were present in the Christian tradition from the beginning. At the same time, as we've seen, sacrificial imagery played a critical part in the symbolism of Christianity, and some of the ideas central to the new faith—particularly the dogmas of the Incarnation, which held that the creator of the universe was capable of inhabiting a human body and soul, and the Resurrection, which held that the physical body of Jesus had taken on immortality and divine power, bridging the two worlds Orphic thought sought to separate—pulled Christianity in a very different direction.

While the Orphic current remained dominant, these other patterns of thought were taken up by mystics, particularly in the Eastern Orthodox Church. There, even at present, one of the major points of church teaching is the idea of attaining the "resurrection body" or "glorified body"—a transformed body, material but without the limits of matter, equivalent to the body Christ was believed to have had after his resurrection—during one's life through mystical practice. The primary practice used to achieve the resurrection body was a system of mystical prayer known as the Heart Prayer, which combined special methods of breathing and posture with the constant repetition of some variation on the words "Christ have mercy on me, a sinner;" this is still an extremely common practice among Eastern Orthodox monks and lay-people. The experiences of heat and light within the heart center, which this practice can generate, have led some scholars to compare it to kundalini yoga.[13]

In addition to this material, an enormous body of pagan magical practices and beliefs were absorbed into Christianity from the earliest times. Some of these were eliminated when the Christian church became respectable and took on the Roman government's hostility toward magic and magicians, but a great deal more came in later, in the early Middle Ages, when the church carried out what amounted to an immense salvage operation on what remained of classical pagan culture.[14] From this period date many of the Christian "saints" who were lightly disguised pagan gods and goddesses, and a whole range of overtly magical practices reworked to call on Christian names and powers. All of this remained part of the Christian synthesis until the magical Christianity of the Middle Ages was crushed between the twin wheels of Reformation and Counter-Reformation at the beginning of the modern age.

The Middle Ages thus mark the last flowering of mythological thought in the Western world. The ways of thinking and speaking about the world, which shape the myths of all ages, move through medieval culture, but those ways became increasingly closed to the West, shut first by the Aristotelian rationalism of the late medieval schoolmen and then, more completely, by the rise of materialist thought in the early modern period. The awareness of that loss runs through the culture of the Renaissance, showing clearly in its cult of the "ancient wisdom" of the *Corpus Hermeticum* and its obsessions with classical myth. After the scientific revolution ushered in the first versions of what could be called modern thought, these interests (and the awareness behind them) were largely consigned to the cultural underground of magic, where the remnants of Renaissance occultism mixed with radical religious beliefs and fringe science.

And it was from this underground, finally, that the Hermetic Order of the Golden Dawn emerged near the end of the nineteenth century.

The Golden Dawn

In the year 1887, three English Freemasons—Dr. William R. Woodman, Dr. W. Wynn Westcott, and Samuel Liddell Mathers—founded the Hermetic Order of the Golden Dawn. According to the official history of that Order, this action followed on the discovery of mysterious "cipher manuscripts" by Westcott, a correspondence with a Rosicrucian Adept in Nuremburg, and the granting of a charter by that Adept for the founding of the Order.[15]

This tale, with its heavy borrowings from Masonic legend and popular occult fiction of the time, has been more or less conclusively shown to be a fraud, and the manuscripts themselves date from 1875–80 at the earliest.[16] Still, the dubious origins of the Order don't invalidate its system of magic, a system that combines and synthesizes in a fairly coherent manner nearly the whole body of traditional Western high magic.

The rituals of the Order have very much of the same quality. Their basic framework is derived from the traditional structure of fraternal lodge ritual, a topic I have explored elsewhere.[17] Their final form is a sometimes clumsy collage of tag-ends of occult wisdom, in which (to give just one example) figures in Egyptian robes representing the Samothracian Cabeiri quote lines from the Chaldean Oracles as they symbolically climb the Cabalistic Tree of Life! In between these two levels, though, is a third level of ritual meaning, and at this level something very different from either of the first two is happening.

Many lodge initiations, fraternal or magical, are constructed around the reenactment of a myth or a legendary story. In an obvious sense, this is true only in the Adeptus Minor Grade of the Golden Dawn, where the rediscovery of the tomb of Christian Rosencreutz as described in the *Fama Fraternitatis* forms the center of the ritual. Other rituals within the Golden Dawn structure seem, at least on first glance, to be either a simple hodgepodge of symbols or repetitious climbings and reclimbings of the Tree of Life. Again, appearances deceive. The mythic structure of the Golden Dawn rituals exists on the level of the entire sequence of grade ceremonies, rather than that of individual grades, and the myth around which the whole structure is built is precisely the one we've been exploring. Nor are the connections between this myth and the rituals simply a matter of imagery; as the Golden Dawn's papers show, they were consciously developed into tools of transformative magical work on every level, in a manner few Western magical traditions have been able to achieve.

The Journey of the Candidate

The best way to outline this process is to follow the candidate through the whole sequence of the Golden Dawn's initiations. Here Osiris and Christ are the central powers, symbols of transformation around which the candidate's journey from Neophyte to Adept is directed.

In the Neophyte Grade, the candidate is brought into the hall blinded and bound. He—the male pronoun will be used here purely for the sake of convenience—is brought to the altar and pledges himself, and then the sword of the Hiereus is brought against the back of his neck in a symbolic beheading. This phase is also a dismemberment; in the words of the Z-3 paper:

> ...(T)he Aspirant of the Mysteries is now, as it were, divided. That is, his Neschamah is directed to the contemplation of his Higher Self attracted to the Hegemon. His natural body is bound and blinded, his Ruach threatened by the simulacrum of the Evil Persona attracted by Omoo-Szathan, and a species of shadow of himself thrown forward to the place of the Pillars, where the Scales of Judgement are set.... Rarely in his life has he been nearer death, seeing that he is, as it were, disintegrated into his component parts.[18]

The candidate then enters the Path of Darkness to begin his search for light, and the rest of the Neophyte Grade centers on that search, the discovery of the light, and the establishment of the light once it is found. The whole pattern relates closely to that of physical death and near-death experiences, as well as to that of birth; in both cases the breaking of an established pattern results in a journey from darkness to light.

The same pattern can be traced out, however, in the burial and germination of the seed, the first stage of the mythic pattern we've been following. The seed is separated from the plant on which it has grown, cast into the darkness of the soil, and from there strives upward into the light. The symbolism of beheading, dismemberment, burial, and quest, which we've seen in other myths of the type, is present here in detail.

As a reenactment of the Osiris myth, however, this sequence starts halfway through the tale. The first death of Osiris is not part of the Golden Dawn ritual pattern; rather, like the Orphic myth of Dionysos or the Christian legend of John the Baptist, the first death is the beheading/dismemberment. In one sense, then, the formula of the first half of the ritual sequence might best be called the Formula of Dionysos, rather than that of Osiris. Still, there is another sense in which the entombment of Osiris does indeed play a role. The candidate in the Neophyte Grade, the "Inheritor of a Dying World," enters the hall blinded and bound, and thus already symbolically dead. His tomb is the body, and more generally the world of material existence: as with the Orphics, *soma* equals *sema*.

In the four Elemental Grades that follow, the candidate sets out—in the words of the Zelator Grade—"to analyze and comprehend that light" which was revealed in the Neophyte Grade. In large part, these Grades simply extend and complete the symbolism of the Neophyte

Grade; they play only a small part in the symbolism we are following here. Still, that part has an echo in the myths. The keynote of these Grades is journeying, and in them the candidate travels through the realms of the four elements and of the lower half of the Tree of Life. These rituals are marked by a series of "admission badges," most of them crosses, which are given to the candidate as he travels; counting the three badges given to the candidate in the Portal Grade, there are fourteen badges in all, the same number as the parts of the body of Osiris. Like Isis, then, the candidate must wander the world in search of the fragments of Osiris—but here Osiris is also the candidate himself.

This is made clear in the first half of the Portal Grade, when the candidate recapitulates each of the elemental grades, and from the realm of each element brings a token to lay on the central altar. These tokens represent the candidate himself, in terms taken straight from the myths: "Equated and equilibrated," the Hiereus says at this point, "here lie the Four Elements of the body of Osiris slain." The knowledge lecture on the work between the Portal and Adeptus Minor Grades expands on this:

> As the unborn child, stage by stage, grows through the ances-
> tral history of the race so the Candidate in the Portal by a sin-
> gle circumambulation for each, recalls his past Grades and, at
> the end of the first point regards their symbols on the Altar as
> parts of his body, and contemplates them as coming together
> in one place—the unity of his person.[19]

The scattered portions of the candidate's symbolic body, then, are gathered up in the Elemental Grades and brought together in the Portal. Placed on the altar, though, they are brought into equilibrium by the symbol of the cross. Freud was far from the first person to envision the cross as a phallic symbol—such ideas filled a whole literature of underground scholarship in the Victorian period—and in this sense the presence of the cross allows Osiris to be reassembled completely, as the Osiris of Egyptian myth could not be.

The cross, however, is also the defining symbol of Christianity, and its appearance here marks a change in symbolism. Up to this point the imagery of the rituals has been linked with Osiris, but now the imagery of Christ comes to the fore.

In the second part of the ritual, the body of Osiris is taken to the Altar of Spirit beyond the Veil—the Veil, which itself, in the words of the Portal ritual, is "the Veil of the Four Elements of the Body of Man, which was offered on the Cross for the service of Man." On that Altar, the elements of the body are offered up in fire, along with a paper bearing the magical name of the candidate, who thus offers himself up wholly to Spirit. It is at this stage, finally, that the symbol of the Rose Cross—core symbol of the Inner Order and synthesis of the entire magical tradition of the Golden Dawn—is first revealed to the candidate.

As the Neophyte Grade represents birth and death, the sequence of initiation from Zelator to Portal thus can symbolize both the process of growth by which the newborn child becomes an adult, and (in Western magical lore of that period) the process of purification in the after-death state, by which the soul between lives learns from its experiences.[20] For our purposes, though, these ways of approaching the rituals are less important than the archaic agricultural pattern we've been tracing. The seed that sprouted in the Neophyte Grade roots in earth in the Zelator Grade, and through air, water and the fire of the sun grows to maturity in the Portal Grade. Next, in the ancient cycle, follows the harvest.

This is represented in the Adeptus Minor Grade, amid the framework of a symbolism we've already discussed. The candidate here is judged, condemned, and crucified, and his body is marked five times with the point of a dagger. He is then taken down from the cross and brought into a tomb. All of this corresponds exactly to the Biblical legend of Jesus, as well as to the sacrificial myth behind it. At this point, though, a different element appears, for in the tomb is the figure of the Chief Adept as Christian Rosencreutz, who speaks to the candidate and exchanges implements with him before bidding him leave the tomb. It is the Chief Adept, in the third point of the ritual, who rises from the dead and proclaims the triumph of life.

The legend of Christian Rosencreutz is an example of the mythology of burial discussed earlier; like Merlin in his tower of glass, the founder of the Rosicrucian Order is at once dead and present, having passed from physical activity into another, deeper order of being. Still, this element of the ritual is an addition to the basic pattern, not a departure from it. After the Adeptus Minor Grade comes the Adeptus Major, the last Grade apparently worked in the original Golden Dawn system, and there the myth has its proper conclusion.

The original version of the Adeptus Major Grade, which was apparently written by Samuel Mathers, has not been published and may have been lost. Two later versions, one by A. E. Waite and the other by Robert Felkin, have survived.[21] These differ in details, but the basic pattern (which probably dates from Mathers' own work) is the same in both. The candidate, bound to silence, is brought into the Vault and there laid in the Pastos like a corpse in the tomb. A vigil is kept outside, and at intervals a gong sounds and sentences are spoken. Finally—after six hours, in Waite's version—the candidate is raised from his symbolic death and receives the secrets of the Grade.

Here the candidate takes the place of the Chief Adept of the Adeptus Minor ritual, and completes his passage through the myth of Christ. The imagery used in both versions of the ritual has much to do with light and darkness, just as in the Neophyte Grade, and this connection is not accidental. If the Neophyte Grade is taken as birth, the two Adept Grades discussed here are death and burial; if the Neophyte is death, these Grades are incarnation and birth. A circle is formed from planting to harvest and from harvest to planting.

The Way of Transformation

In the Golden Dawn system, then, the old mythology of the agricultural sacrifice is taken over and used as a framework for initiation. Some elements of the ancient synthesis are lacking—for example, despite the importance of the Equinoxes in the Golden Dawn, and despite the attention given to astrology and the celestial sphere in the Order's papers, the astrological symbolism we've seen in other sources seems to have made little impact on the Order's system. Nonetheless, the connections are clear and point out important parts of the process of ritual.

In this process, the figures of Osiris and Christ mark two phases of the initiatory work. They also represent, in turn, two stages in that path of inner transformation, which is the focus and goal of the Golden Dawn system. The first stage, corresponding to Osiris, is marked by the dissolution of the self, while the second is the reintegration of the self in a higher form: the *solve* and *coagula* of alchemy, in which the keys to the Great Work are said to be contained. More precisely, in alchemical language, the Neophyte Grade is the *nigredo* or "black phase" of corruption and disintegration; the Elemental Grades correspond to the *cauda pavonis* or "peacock's tail," in which various colors (Cabalistically, the colors of the bow Qesheth) mark the different aspects and transformations of the *materia*; the Portal Grade, when the white sash is received by the candidate, is the *albedo* or "white phase," the coagulation of the Stone, while the Adept Grades represent the *rubedo* or "red phase," when the Stone takes on the attributes of the Sun.

All this can be understood in a psychological sense, as a process of change in the psyche through self-knowledge. Such an interpretation is a valid one, backed by many of the Golden Dawn documents, and it forms the basis for a range of more or less Jungian readings of the rituals. There's another way in which these symbols can be read, though. This second way deals not with the psyche alone but with the total human being on all levels, including the physical, and the transformation it seeks touches on every part of human experience and existence.

The clearest expression of this broader way of thinking about the rituals is found in a Golden Dawn paper entitled Flying Roll X, written by Samuel Mathers and circulated among the Adepti of the Order. Subtitled "Concerning the Symbolism of Self-Sacrifice and Crucifixion contained in the 5=6 Grade," this dense and often murky paper touches on a range of themes we've seen already, and applies them to the work of the magician in some startling ways.[22]

Central to this interpretation is the relationship between the different levels of the self: the *nephesh* or vital self, the *ruach* or ordinary conscious self, the *neshamah* or higher spiritual self, and the transcendent aspects of the self beyond the neshamah. Normally, in Golden Dawn teaching, the ruach is cut off from the higher levels of the self, and the chief task of the magician is to restore this connection.

This, according to Flying Roll X, is the chief practical meaning of the myth of the dying god. The ruach, the ordinary self, must perfect itself through self-knowledge, and then offer itself up to the neshamah as a vehicle for the Higher. The center of the personality, in other words, must shift from the conscious self to a higher, spiritual self of which ordinary consciousness knows nothing. The prospect is a terrifying one—such a surrender of the self to the unknown is perceived as death, and often involves states like those of near-death experience—but this act of self-sacrifice on the part of the ruach brings about the rebirth of the wholeness of the self. Again, this acts on all levels:

> ...(O)nly after incurring that physical death, as it were, could the other divine parts suddenly come down and make it the resurrected or glorified body, which, according to the description, had after the Resurrection, the apparent solidity of the ordinary body, and the faculties of the Spirit body. Because if you can once get the great force of the Highest to send its ray clean down through the Neschamah into the mind, and thence, into your physical body, the Nephesch would be so transformed as to render you almost like a God walking on this Earth.[23]

The stress on the body of the resurrection in this passage points to one of the more unexpected of the Golden Dawn's borrowings, but it is not the only reference to Eastern Orthodox mystical techniques in the Golden Dawn material. In the Adeptus Minor ritual itself, the Chief Adept makes what may be an explicit reference to the Heart Prayer technique mentioned above:

And let the humble prayer of thy heart be: 'God, be merciful to
me a sinner, and keep me in the pathway of truth.'

It's possible that these things were borrowed from the Eastern
Church at some earlier point in the development of the tradition that
gave rise to the Golden Dawn. The core symbols of the Rosicrucian
movement of the late Renaissance—the heart as Sun, the phoenix in
flames, the pelican wounding its own breast, the central image of the
rose on the cross itself—can be read as references to the experiences
caused by work with the Heart Prayer, but there doesn't seem to be any
evidence that the Golden Dawn itself used this interpretation, or taught
or practiced the methods involved. Nor, it's worth noticing, does the
path of transformation outlined in Flying Roll X seem to have received
much practical attention in the Order; as happened so often in the
Golden Dawn's history, the deeper possibilities of the system were all
but ignored in favor of play-acting and power politics.

Still, the approach to Christian myth and symbolism used
throughout the Golden Dawn's magical system reaches toward a reso-
lution of many of the conflicts and confusions surrounding Christianity
at present. To the founders of the Golden Dawn, the myths of Christ
were wholly compatible with those of Osiris, as well as those of other
pagan divinities, and the whole structure of Christian religion was
understood as a variation on a set of themes common in the religions of
the Western world. This understanding enabled the Golden Dawn to
draw on useful features of Christian spirituality while discarding many
of the less valid elements of that tradition—a project that might well be
worth carrying on in the present.

In addition, the path of transformation illuminated by the
Order's rituals offers a valid way for the modern magician. It blends
the perspectives of the Orphic tradition with those of the older way of
sacrifice, using Christian and non-Christian myth alike as the instru-
ments of fusion. The work of inner transformation is described, in
Golden Dawn materials, in ways that sound very much like the Orphic
quest to transcend physical existence; when the Hierophant in the
Neophyte Grade speaks of "earthly or material inclination, that has
bound into a narrow place the once far-wandering soul," or when the
new Hierophant in the Equinox ceremony describes the purpose of the
Golden Dawn's work as "so to lead the Soul that it may be withdrawn
from the attraction of matter," they use the language of more than two
thousand years of Western esotericism. The answer that is offered by
these rituals to the problems of human existence, though, is not the

abandonment of the material world, but the transformation of matter through interaction with spirit: the ancient way of sacrifice made new.

In place of the blood sacrifices of an earlier time, the Golden Dawn Adept offers up his or her own self, transmuting matter into spirit and spirit into matter within the temple of the body, restoring the ancient pattern of exchange while opening up the higher possibilities of his or her being. This vision is not unique to the Golden Dawn system—the Order's founders were pack rats rather than creators, and very little in their system is unique in any sense—but there are few places in the magical traditions of the West where the possibilities of this approach to the world have been as thoroughly set out for those who are willing to look.

About the Author

John Michael Greer first encountered the Western esoteric tradition in 1975 and has been involved in it as student, practitioner, and teacher ever since. An active member of several fraternal lodges, he co-edits *Caduceus*, a quarterly journal of the Hermetic tradition. He has recently written two books, *Paths of Wisdom: Cabalah in the Golden Dawn Tradition*, and *Circles of Power: Ritual Magic in the Western Tradition*. He lives in Seattle.

Endnotes

1. This version of *John Barleycorn*—as with any folk song, there are scores of them—was collected at the Seattle, WA Folklife Festival in May, 1992.
2. I have adapted this account from Plutarch's version in *De Iside et Osiride*.
3. The Elder Edda, *Havamal*, 139.
4. Llew's death is recounted in the Tale of Math ap Mathonwy in the *Mabinogion*. The triple death is found in a number of Scottish and Irish legends; see Stewart, R. J., *The Mystic Life of Merlin* (London: Routledge & Kegan Paul, 1986).
5. See R. J. Stewart's fascinating essay "The Tomb of a King" in Stewart, R. J., *The Under-World Initiation* (Wellingborough: Aquarian, 1985), 261–266.
6. The seminal work on ancient astronomical symbolism is De Santillana, Giorgio, and von Dechend, Hertha, *Hamlet's Mill* (rep. Boston: David Godine, 1977), a masterly book weakened only by the authors' inablility—epidemic among modern scholars of mythology—to realize that myth can have more than one purpose and speak of more than one part of human experience.
7. See Ulansey, David, *The Origin of the Mithraic Mysteries* (New York: Oxford UP, 1989).

8. The Orphic tradition is discussed in Warden, John (ed.), *Orpheus: The Metamorphoses of a Myth* (Toronto: Toronto UP, 1982), and explored sympathetically in Fideler, David, *Jesus Christ Sun Of God: Ancient Cosmology and Early Christian Symbolism* (Wheaton: Quest, 1993).

9. *John* 3:30.

10. See Davies, Stevan L., *The Gospel of Thomas and Christian Wisdom* (NY: Seabury, 1983) for a discussion of the scholarly evasions surrounding the catch-all category "Gnosticism," which serves essentially as a dumpster for unpopular evidence concerning the early years of Christianity.

11. The Gospel of Thomas may be read in Robinson, James M. (ed.), *The Nag Hammadi Library* (NY: Harper Collins, 1988), 126–138. See also Davies, op. cit.

12. Smith, Morton, *Jesus the Magician* (San Francisco: Harper & Row, 1978).

13. The classic text of this tradition in Eastern Orthodoxy is the Philokalia. See *The Philokalia: The Complete Text* (London: Faber and Faber, 1983). See also Matus, Thomas, *Yoga and the Jesus Prayer Tradition* (Ramsey: Paulist, 1984), a capable summary by a practitioner of both the Heart Prayer method and Hindu yogic traditions.

14. See Flint, Valerie, *The Rise of Magic in Early Medieval Europe* (Princeton: Princeton UP, 1991) for an eye-opening study of the absorption of magic into Christianity. Meyer, Marvin (ed.), *Ancient Christian Magic* (NY: HarperCollins, 1994) is another useful source.

15. The official version of the history of the Order is discussed in Gilbert, R. A., *The Golden Dawn Companion* (Wellingborough: Aquarian, 1986), 1–29.

16. See Howe, Ellic, *The Magicians of the Golden Dawn* (London: Routledge & Kegan Paul, 1972).

17. Greer, John Michael, "The Hall of Thmaa: Sources and Transformations of Golden Dawn Lodge Technique," in *The Golden Dawn Journal* Vol. 3 (St. Paul: Llewellyn, 1995) edited by Chic Cicero and Sandra Tabatha Cicero.

18. Regardie, Israel, *The Golden Dawn* (St. Paul: Llewellyn, 1971), Vol. 3, 135.

19. Regardie, *The Golden Dawn*, Vol. 1, 185.

20. Compare, for example, this section of the initiatory sequence with material on reincarnation by Golden Dawn member W. B. Yeats; see Yeats, W. B., *A Vision* (NY: Collier, 1966).

21. The Waite version of the Adeptus Major ritual is in Regardie, Israel, *The Complete Golden Dawn System of Magic* (Phoenix: Falcon, 1984), Vol. 7, 127–158. The Felkin version is in Zalewski, Patrick, *Secret Inner Order Rituals of the Golden Dawn* (Phoenix: Falcon, 1988), 100–125.

22. Flying Roll X is included in Mathers, S. L., et al., *Astral Projection, Ritual Magic and Alchemy* (Rochester: Destiny, 1987), 131–140.

23. Ibid., 136.

24. Regardie, Israel, *The Golden Dawn* (St. Paul: Llewellyn, 1971), Vol. 2, 227. I am indebted to Carl Hood Jr. for pointing out the Eastern Orthodox references within the Golden Dawn material.

Do the Gods Exist?

Do the Gods Exist?

Donald Michael Kraig

On the other pages of this book you will find discussions of various pantheons of deities. You will, no doubt, see how the deities of these pantheons relate to one another, how they correspond to the Sephiroth on the Kabalistic Tree, of Life and how they can be used in rituals. Such discussions make the assumption that the gods and goddesses of these pantheons have some degree of existence.

But is this a valid assumption? Do we actually have any way of proving that these pantheons, or, for that matter, *any* deity, exists? Do we have any way to prove that they are not simply a creation of our minds? Can it be shown that the deities predate humanity (although the *forms* in which they appear in any society may be created by people)?

One of the initial problems that develops in any sort of philosophical discussion such as this is related to the meaning of the words we are using. Specifically, what a certain word means to one person may not be what it means to another. For example, imagine two people arguing over the value of capitalism. For for one person capitalism means freedom and a chance to get ahead through cleverness and hard work. For the other it means exploitation and necessitates imperialism. As long as they only *use* the term "capitalism," and never *define* the term, they will be speaking about two different things. They could argue forever and never come to an agreement because even though they are using the same words, they are talking about two different concepts. This, by the way, is the basic problem dealt with in the study known as General Semantics.

In order for these two arguers to truly understand each other they need to define the words they are using. It may be that both of them are in favor of freedom and getting ahead through hard work and against exploitation and imperialism. If they defined what they meant, things would quickly clear up for them.

Similarly, to answer the question about the existence of the gods, we must first define our terms so that our meanings are absolutely clear.

Existence, Personal Existence,
Cartesian Rationalism & Sartre's Existentialism

The definition of the word "exist," according to *The American Heritage Dictionary (Deluxe Electronic Edition)* is "to have actual being; be real." But before we can determine if anything else is real, we must first *prove* personal existence, our own reality. On the surface, this seems absurd. Of course I'm real! But the problem of proving personal existence has been a major issue of philosophy, perhaps *the* major issue of philosophy, for centuries.

The most common proof of personal existence comes in the simple and famous statement by one of the fathers of rationalism, René Descartes (1596–1650): "I think, therefore I am."

Some have attempted to refute this method of proving personal existence by asking, "How do you know that you're not simply a creation in the mind of another being?" This, in turn, has been refuted by the notion of free will—we can make any choice we desire, therefore, we must be in control of our own mind.

This proof, using the concept of free will, is countered by the argument that what we conceive of as "free will" may simply be the will of another being, a being who wishes us to have the impression that we have free will.

Let's step back for a moment. These arguments are quite convoluted. Further, they also imply that another being exists before we have even proven that we exist! Proving the existence of other beings, of course, seems easy. It is obvious to our senses: we can see, hear, touch, etc. them. But tricks such as optical illusions show us that our senses can be deceived. On a philosophical level, we can't trust our senses and must find another way of proving that others exist. And to do that, we first have to prove personal existence, that "I" exists.

This brings us back to Descartes' rationalism and the idea that we can, at first, only put our trust in our own mind. After all, it could be that everything else in the universe is of my mind's creation, and the moment I am not paying attention, everything disappears. Some philosophers have even argued that everything outside of your view ceases to exist until you want to see it again! In other words, nothing behind your back, beneath the surface of the ground or outside the range of your peripheral vision is real until you turn and perceive it. Outside the purview of your immediate senses is a vast nothing.

Descartes had a way to get around this. He proposed that we are all creations of God. Others exist because God wills it and God wouldn't fool us as it is not in His nature.

As an answer to the question of existence of self, others, the physical world, and Deity, this a weak answer, and I remain surprised that the rationalist Descartes came up with it as his only answer. It is based on the supposition of God's existence with no proof of that existence. Perhaps it was necessary for him to do this due to the religiopolitical structure of the time. A belief in God (at least in public statements) was necessary for one's very survival. Galileo (1564–1642), a contemporary of Descartes, was imprisoned and threatened with death by the Inquisition in 1633 for the heresy of disagreeing with the Catholic Church by daring to believe, and publicly stating, that the Earth orbits the Sun. (It is said that while on the stake, about to be burned alive, he retracted his claim. However, as he was being freed, he was heard to mutter about the earth, "Still, it moves." A short time ago he was finally officially forgiven by the Catholic Church for his "sin.")

Three centuries later, Jean Paul Sartre (1905–1980) tried to solve the riddle of the proof of personal existence and the existence of others in his classic book, *Being and Nothingness* (1943). This book is one of the key works of the philosophical school known as existentialism. It is a rather difficult book for many to study because of the words and terms Sartre invented and the new use he gave to traditional words. Most copies of this book have a glossary to explain how Sartre uses words and phrases such as "being-in-itself" as opposed to "being-for-itself." Also, this technical, philosophic work was originally written in French, so English readers such as myself are only getting a version of the book as filtered through the mind of a translator. Still, it is worth the study of anyone interested in philosophy or the history of philosophy.

Being and Nothingness covers a variety of topics. Sartre's discussion of personal existence, as with Descartes', begins with the concept of "I think, therefore I am." To this, however, Sartre added the concept of *object* and *objectifier*. If you look at another thing, including another person, you will notice the sensation that you are looking at (objectifying) that thing or person. You are the objectifier. If it is a person who looks at you, you may remain with the sensation of being the objectifier, making an "object" of the other person. However, you may feel as if the other person is making an object of you. This feeling of being looked at, being an object, may occur even if no one is looking at you. At one time or another we have all had the feeling of being watched, although no one is doing so.

This is a very important point to Sartre. *Unless others existed, you would never, could never, have the feeling of being an object.* Without the existence of others, such a feeling would be beyond anything in your experience. Therefore, others must exist, and since you are aware of them, you must exist too. The fact that we agree on the appearance of the physical world (what has been called, "consensus reality") shows that it also must exist.

As a logical proof of personal existence, as well as the existence of others, these concepts seem much more complete, logical, rational, and reasonable than having to resort to Descartes' *deus ex machina*, the introduction of a being, God, whose existence is accepted, not proven. Now that we have philosophically proved that I, you, and the universe around us exists (Did you ever doubt that we would?), we at least have a starting place for our exploration.

Can We Prove the Existence of Deity?

To be blunt, it is impossible to prove or disprove the existence of a god or gods through logic alone. For every argument that would "prove" such an existence there is a counter-argument. For every argument that "disproves" such an existence there is also a counter-argument.

As an analogy, let's say I claim that there are little green people on Mars. The counter argument to this is that we haven't seen them. This, I counter, by saying that we haven't looked everywhere on Mars. Until we have examined every square inch, you cannot prove I am wrong. Similarly, until every square inch of Loch Ness is thoroughly searched we cannot deny the possibility of the existence of Nessie, the so-called Loch Ness Monster. Further, we have to examine the entire Loch or all of Mars at the same time, because Nessie, or the little green men, might move to another location when we weren't looking. These arguments, based on logic, can never be resolved.

So if we can't use simple logic or our senses to prove the divine exists, what can we do? I think that just as Sartre was able to give a proof that others exist by the effect of others on ourself, so, too, should we be able to prove or disprove the existence of deity by whether or not a deity or deities have an effect on us.

Do Deities Affect Us?

There are several different schools of thought, here, and I would like to look at some of them.

Materialists: According to the materialist, a deity or deities could not possible affect us because they do not exist. The materialist would say that nothing that is non-physical exists. There is no soul, no deity, no spiritual entities, no non-physical worlds. While this philosophy (which, I contend, reached it's nadir with Ayn Rand's [1905–1982] modern version of social darwinism known as Objectivism) may satisfy its adherents, I see it as simply the reverse of Descartes' philosophy: "I don't believe, therefore it doesn't exist." Descartes would have you believe in a deity with no proof that such a deity exists. The materialist would have you disbelieve in a deity with no proof that such an entity does not exist.

The basis of what is known as "philosophical argument" is the presentation of a series of statements, called *premises,* which lead through a set of rules according to the practice known as "formal logic" to a conclusion. This is known as a logical proof. Perhaps the most famous, simple version of this works this way:

First Premise:	All men are mortal.
Second Premise:	Socrates is a man.
Conclusion:	Socrates is a mortal.

In formal logic the words are converted to mathematics-like expressions: "All men" becomes A. "Mortal" becomes B. "Socrates" becomes C. "Is" becomes =. Thus we have the following:

First Premise:	$A = B$
Second Premise:	$C = A$
Conclusion:	$C = B$

Notice that in many cases the rules of formal logic are identical with those of mathematics.

In this technique, all of your premises must be true or your conclusion is unproven. For example, perhaps there is one man who can be shown to be immortal. Therefore, the simple proof above is false. This is not to say that the conclusion is wrong—Socrates may, in fact, be mortal—only that the logical argument does not prove it.

Both Descartes and the materialists use a premise—the existence or non-existence of deity—known as a *tautology:* a vacuous statement without adequate proof that the premise is true. Thus, even though either position may be correct, neither the Cartesian rationalists nor the materialists have proven their point through the basic laws of philosophical logic.

Therefore, when looking at the question as to whether or not deities exist and can affect us, we must discard both Descartes and the materialists. They present conclusions (the existence or non-existence of deity) without a series of premises that support their claims. Because of this failure, they prove nothing and their unproven statements are of no value whatsoever in this discussion.

Chaos Magicians: The acknowledged leader (at least for Chaos Magic theory), is Peter J. Carroll (1953–). He has been involved with this system since its inception. Many would say that he is the founder, and he is certainly the most published and well-known writer on the subject. His writings were published in England in the 1980s, and vastly increased in popularity with the republication in America of two of his books, *Liber Null* and *Psychonaut*, in one volume. Perhaps his clearest explication of Chaos Magic appears in his book *Liber Kaos* (the title of which brings up unfortunate comparisons with the bumbling antagonists in the old TV sitcom, *Get Smart!*).

While Chaos Magic, as its many adherents can attest, is a viable system of magic, I contend that it is not as unique or original as many of its followers claim. For example, one of the reasons that the name "Chaos Magic" was chosen for this system is the concept that the source of everything was the original chaos that existed before order came into the universe. Therefore, to tap into that original chaos is to tap into the original power that is the basis for everything in the universe. In traditional forms of ceremonial magic, this original source of power is the unknowable deity, the *Ain*, which existed before the Demiurge that created the world. While the names and conceptions of the original sources may be different, the results are the same. For all practical purposes, Chaos Magicians have simply renamed the *Ain* as Chaos.

This is not meant as a criticism. I believe that calling this source-of-all "Chaos" is as limiting as calling it "Ain" or anything else. The Source is truly beyond names or definitions. But if calling it Ain, Chaos, or anything else helps the magician operate more efficiently, so much the better. The paradigm and technique is not as important as the result. As is stated in Crowley's *Book of the Law*, "Success is your proof."

What does this neo-paradigm, Chaos Magic, hold concerning the idea that the gods do or do not exist? In *Liber Kaos*, Carroll presents several ideas as to his notions about the gods. Concerning the nature of non-physical entities, he uses the term *Ether*: "Ether acts as though it were a form of information emitted by matter that is instantaneously available everywhere and has some power to shape the behavior of other matter…. The etheric pattern associated with any phenomenon can be regarded as its spirit…." He also states that the deities are not separate from humans, nor do they predate us: "Humanity creates gods, not vice versa, but once created they can have profound effects so long as they continue to be "worshiped" by deed and memory." When invoking gods, what you are doing is "…(C)alling the gods, the archetypal forces, up out of yourself and from the collective etheric of the human race."

So his contention is that the gods do not, initially, exist separate from us. Nor do they predate humanity. Yet, he encourages us to work with them: "…[C]hannel up the genius of whatever is invoked…throw yourself wholeheartedly into it with a supreme effort of method acting…. The real awesomeness lies in the range of things we can discover ourselves capable of, even if we may temporarily have to believe the effects are due to something else in order to be able to create them…. Fake it till you make it…." And finally, he says: "The gods are dead. Long live the gods."

As I interpret it, Carroll means that there are no gods, but we can *pretend* that gods exist to such a level that they actually end up existing for us. Carroll identifies the gods with which we are familiar with etheric manifestations of various parts of our psyches. By his definition, of course, there is no need to work with the traditional deities, we could create our own. But working with the familiar ones can be advantageous.

As I understand it, I would have to contend that Mr. Carroll ends up with the same problem as the materialists. He denies the existence of the gods (as pre-existent and originally separate from humanity) because he can find no proof that they exist. His problems multiply over those of the materialists, however, because unlike the materialists, he still wants to be able to use the traditional gods within the Chaos Magic paradigm. Since the gods don't exist, you have to pretend they do until they develop a reality for you. As he puts it, "Fake it till you make it."

To me this seems like a tremendous waste of time and effort. Why spend the time to develop the atheistic attitude that the gods don't exist, then spend more time to invent them? Would it not be simpler and more direct to simply accept the reality of the gods? Considering that Chaos magicians pride themselves on doing things more simply than traditional ceremonial magicians, I find this question particularly problematic for the entire paradigm. I'm not denying that Chaos Magic works, but it seems to me that this aspect of it seems contradictory to its basic theme of directness and simplicity.

While the materialists simply deny the gods, the Chaos magicians in the school of Peter Carroll deny the gods but want to use them. This seems to be a midway position between pure materialism and pure belief, neither of which can prove the existence or non-existence of the gods. Chaos Magic does not answer our basic question any more than does materialism.

Pop psychology and Jungian psychology: The birth of modern psychology coincides with the birth of the modern occult movement, which started in the last quarter of the nineteenth century. (Although some say that the modern occult movement began earlier with the French Occult Revival and its leading light, Eliphas Levi, I am more inclined to date it to the founding of the Theosophical Society by H. P. Blavatsky and others in 1875. It is believed that the Society's *Esoteric Section* was involved in the study of magic, and several of its members, including William Butler Yeats and S. L. M. Mathers, were vital to the Golden Dawn.) Although Sigmund Freud (1856–1939) despised occultism, there are those who believe that he was influenced by the Kabalah of his birth religion. The Kabalah has long held the notion of a subconscious, but it was only with Freud that this began to become an accepted principle of psychology. One of his followers, Carl Jung (1875–1961), even did his college thesis on a cousin who acted as a spirit medium in seances. When Jung was able to produce strange "spirit knocks" for Freud, Freud "freaked out" and split with Jung for good.

One of the principles that Jung popularized is the idea of the archetype. Unfortunately, some of those who have only a superficial understanding of Jung's theories misunderstand Jung's notion of the archetype. To those followers of the "pop" version of Jung, an archetype is an ideal from our minds. Each person creates his or her own archetypes and the archetypes then continue to exist until the person who created them wishes them to cease. If this were an accurate interpretation of Jung it would be fine. In reality, Jung's theory goes much deeper.

Before looking at Jung's archetype, however, I want to illustrate an unusual phenomenon that concerns the occult. While there are many dedicated people involved in occultism, for centuries the allure of the occult for some people has been to get something—money, power, sex partners, etc.—with no work. Actual occultists know, however, that mastering occult practices takes many years of hard work. That is why, while some alchemists tried to turn lead into gold very quickly, others tried the much longer process of turning the base metal of their non-spiritual self into the gold of spirituality.

It seems that with each new generation there is a new scientific paradigm to explain the nature of the individual and metaphysics. I have seen books with titles such as *Your Magnetic Body,* which probably related to Franz Mesmer's (1734–1815) theories of animal magnetism (which have been wrongly portrayed as nothing more than a precursor to therapeutic hypnosis). Other books I've seen have titles such as *Your Atomic Body* and *Your Nuclear Body*. Each one of these books represents a new generation trying to find a paradigm for understanding the spiritual aspects of our species.

These titles show something else, too. Some writers who are occultists are actually embarrassed by their occultism. They try to claim that their beliefs are actually based on scientific ideas that are just now being explored. Problems can develop, however, when the writer is not conversant with the full depth of both the science and the occult. (While Chaos Magicians fall into the category of claiming that Chaos Magic is based on scientific ideas, most of the theoreticians in this system are not only highly intelligent and well-read, but also quite talented and experienced occultists. I do not believe for a moment that they are in embarrassed in the slightest by their beliefs.)

Such is the case with a common misunderstanding of Jung's theory of archetypes. Jung postulated that although humanity is the source for an archetype, it manifests within the *collective unconscious*, a non-physical link between all members of a species. Thus, whether you, as an individual, work with an archetypal image is irrelevant to the existence of that archetype. Such an archetype "needs" us to exist, but it exists independently of any individual. That is why, according to Jung, there are similar myths and deities around the world in cultures that never communicated with one another—the people tuned into the collective unconscious and drew on the archetypes that waited there for manifestation in some manner. By doing so they also added to the strength of the archetype.

But to the pop "psycholo-occultist," such is not the case. The deities are simply creations of our minds. They identify this with Jung's theory of archtypes, but they do so only because of their misunderstanding of his theory.

I refer to this as the *psychologization of magic*. Magic treated this way, is nothing but mind games. Gods, goddesses, rituals, and other time-tested techniques and beliefs are irrelevant. All you have to do is some sort of mental masturbation and the magic takes place. I should add that any success they experience also occurs only in their minds, but the mind and subconscious can be a powerful worker of magic. Thus, although the pop psychology paradigm is based on a misunderstanding, those who psychologize magic can be quite effective as magicians.

So here we have a split decision as to the existence of the gods. To the pop psychologist, the gods are simply manifestations of an aspect of ourselves. When we stop working with them, they cease to be. To a true Jungian, however, the gods have an existence that is separate from any individual, although the way the deity/archetype manifests may be different from culture to culture, person to person. In short, the gods are alive, real, and can affect us. Some ceremonial magicians hold either the pop psychology or Jungian position. Others hold the position of the "believer."

The Believer: The believer assumes that the gods exist with no proof. And just as the materialist cannot prove the gods do not exist, so, too, the believer cannot prove that the gods do exist.

And here we've made our way back to Descartes' "proof" of personal existence, a proof that requires the assumption of the existence of god and that, I think, is incomplete at best. This has been a long trip to get…where?

Where Do We Stand?

Ah, what a tangled web this is! Descartes and the Believers contend that the gods do exist, separate from the individual and pre-existent to humanity, but have no proof to support their arguments. Chaos magicians, as represented by the writings of Peter Carroll, contend that the gods do not exist, but we should pretend they do in order to use them. This is similar to the argument of the pop psychologists who, like Carroll, contend that we create the gods, but they may exist separate from us. It is only in the psychology of Jung and his theory of the archetype that we find a proof of the existence of gods: since different cultures tap into the same archetype/god/goddess, but give the manifestation a different name and appearance, the entity must exist independent of the individual culture. Jung also gives us a methodology to understand the origination of these archetypal entities: They are created by needs of individuals but form a complex in the collective unconscious that allows the entity to be independent of any particular individual or group.

In Jung, however, there are two things that separate his archetypal gods from the traditional image of gods. First, the gods do not predate humanity. Second, the "proof" of these gods and goddesses is not complete. We infer their existence by our interpretation of the results of their perceived actions. We cannot see or measure them.

Do the Gods Pre-Exist Us?

As I will show in a moment, I do think it is possible to prove the existence of deity and the manifestation of the Godhead in the forms of various gods and goddesses. However, I do not think it possible to prove whether deities pre-date us or are the results of our effect on the divine. For every "proof" of the pre-existence of deity that anyone can come up with, there is another person who has an argument that disproves it.

One person could say that a deity must have predated us to be the creator of the universe and humanity, for it would be impossible for us to spring into creation *ex nihilo*, from nothing. This is countered by an explanation of how cosmology and evolution created the physical plane and humans over a period of billions of years.

The "Pre-existing God" argument might then say that if you look at a wristwatch you do not think that it came from nothing. You know it had a maker. We are far more complicated than a watch, so we must have had a maker, too. This is opposed by the argument that the comparison between humans and watches is a comparison between "apples and oranges." A human is a biological organism while a watch is a mechanical instrument. The bottom line is that there is no way to logically prove whether or not gods and goddesses existed before humanity.

In actuality, this makes sense. One of the definitions of deity is that for an entity to be a deity, it must be eternal. Our common notion of this term is "something that lives forever." In actuality (according to *The American Heritage Dictionary Deluxe Electronic Edition*) it means, "Being without beginning or end; existing outside of time." This does not mean that the gods and goddesses came before us, after us, or with our birth. If the Godhead is eternal, "existing outside of time," such notions of before and after are meaningless. Eternal deities live before us, after us, and along with us *simultaneously*. It is no wonder that we cannot determine whether they existed before us: for deities, time is meaningless.

This compares with the Kabalistic idea of deity being a combination of opposites. We, as humans, think only in terms of opposites. What is up? The opposite of down. What am I? Not you. What is fast? Anything that is not slow.

We make comparisons of this sort frequently. It is in our nature. The problem is that the definitions become meaningless because they are circular. What is up? Whatever is not down. What is down? Whatever is not up. When two words are used to define each other they are said to have a circular definition, which means they have no definition at all.

But to the divine such opposites do not exist. This is exemplified by the very nature of the holiest name in Judaism, the unpronounceable Tetragrammaton, YHVH, the *Yud Heh Vahv Heh* commonly mispronounced Yahweh or Jehovah. The first letter, *Yud* (**ı**), represents archetypal positive (traditionally called "male") energies. The second letter, the first *Heh* (✳), represents archetypal negative (traditionally called "female") energies. (Please note that the terms "positive" and "negative" are related to the idea of polar opposites, such as the positive and negative sides of a battery, and do not represent any qualities commonly called "good" or "bad." In this sense it is just as "good" to be negative as it is to be positive. And remember, too, that Hebrew is read from right to left.) The third letter, the *Vahv* (✿), represents physical positive energy while the last letter, the second *Heh* (✳), represents physical negative energies.

Thus, you could say that the nature of the divine is the union of all opposites, both physical and archetypal. Since we always conceive of things in terms of opposites, we cannot truly know this ultimate divinity, the Godhead. Likewise, since our nature is to exist in time, we cannot truly know an entity that is eternal and exists outside of time.

So did the gods and goddesses exist before us? Yes. And no. And both. All three answers are correct. This, of course, is meaningless to us because we are not eternal. I know that this is hardly a good answer, but if the deities are eternal, then it's the best I can give. That is, if deity exists.

Can We Prove that the Gods Exist?

For thousands of years, people far wiser than I have debated whether or not the gods exist. For me to make a claim that I can actually prove or disprove the reality of the gods is not just egotistical, it's damn egotistical. I have no doubt that what I have written so far will draw some howls of agreement or disagreement. However, I'm going to go further out on a limb, take a controversial chance, and say that there is a way to prove the existence of the divine.

So how can I have the audacity to claim to be able to do what thousands, perhaps tens-of-thousands of people who lived before me attempted to do, yet failed? Who am I compared to the great minds of the past, great minds who, in my opinion, still failed in making their proof of the existence of the divine inarguable?

Well, I certainly don't put myself on the level of any of those great thinkers who debated the reality of the gods. I can, however, point to the fatal flaw in virtually all of their pro and con arguments:

deity, by definition, is non-physical. Yet all of the proofs try to give objective evidence. Such objectivity exists only in the physical world. Trying to prove that the Godhead exists on the physical plane using only physical proofs is like two beings existing on the astral plane and trying to prove that a chair (which exists on the physical plane) exists on the astral through strictly non-physical, subjective arguments. It just won't work. We need to go to the plane where whatever it is we are trying to prove is supposed to exist and deal with the realities on that level. To answer the question of whether deity exists, we have to look to the non-physical and present a subjective proof or disproof so clean, obvious, and simple that it cannot be refuted.

Unfortunately, we exist on the physical plane where we are used to dealing with objective arguments. Subjective arguments tend to be based on emotions and can usually be easily countered or disproved. But there is one model that can, I believe, allow us to answer the question at hand. By making an analogy to this model we can obtain a criterion, once and for all, that should allow us to prove or disprove the existence of the divine.

As I already described, Sartre was able to prove the existence of others by showing that we had feelings that could not even be conceived of, let alone experienced, if there were not others to cause this feeling. I think that this is a great proof in that it's clever, direct, and simple. However, it is not objective. It is based on an emotion or inner response, a feeling, that could never exist if others did not exist. This is a valid proof in spite of the fact that it is based on a subjective experience that is not quantifiable or capable of reproduction in a laboratory.

The next step, and one that others may have taken, but that I have not seen before, is simply an adaptation of Sartre's proof of the existence of others, which I presented earlier:

> *If we can experience a sensation of the Divine, a feeling we could not conceive of or experience without there being a Deity, we must assume that, in fact, there is a Deity.*

All we have to do is come up with something as direct and simple as Sartre's idea of object and objectifier.

We can't use Sartre's proof of the existence of others in a way that says, "If I am confronted with an entity which is not human it must be a deity." Since he has already shown that others exist, such an entity may simply be our notion of a powerful other being. There has to be "something else," something that moves us beyond the experience of a powerful other being, God-as-superman, to a sublime deity. In other words, this deity must subjectively alter us in a way that could not happen if a deity—separate from us and independent from us—did not exist.

I call this something else, *Divine Effulgence.* By this term I mean a sensation of unity with an entity whose knowledge and love is beyond anything that any human or non-divine, non-physical entity can exhibit. To experience Divine Effulgence means that you are feeling something that, if there were no deity, you could neither conceive of nor participate in.

The word *effulgence* means, "A brilliant radiance." I use it here because such a radiance, beyond anything of which we, as human beings, can conceive, frequently accompanies such an experience. This experience has many names: enlightenment, cosmic consciousness, etc. But unlike Sartre's common sensation of object and objectifier, Divine Effulgence is something that is not only rarer, but is something that does not merely happen. It must be sought.

Perhaps this rarity, this necessary seeking, is part of our nature as humans. It is an incredible show of hubris for us to think that, although we may be at the peak of current evolutionary development, evolution itself has ceased. Evolution continues at its own rate and in its own manner. Perhaps we are evolving to a state where Divine Effulgence will be as common as Sartre's sensation of the other. Until that time, we must go the extra step to experience this sensation. It is we who must seek it.

One school of Kabalah gave a good description of this search. It was said that God is always there, but we have established veils between ourselves and the divine. It is as if we are in a room lit with one candle, but we have put up veils so that we suffer in spiritual darkness. The candle is always there, it is simply that we do not see it's flame because of these veils—blocks we have set up to seeing it. Likewise, we cannot see and experience the divine—the veils we have created block the view. Until our evolution allows us to naturally destroy the veils, or at least see through them, we live in a state of spiritual darkness.

But we can choose to *rend the veil* and seek the Divine Effulgence, or as the Golden Dawn eloquently says in the Neophyte Initiation Ritual:

> *Inheritor of a Dying World, we call thee to the Living Beauty.*
> *Wanderer in the Wild Darkness, we call thee to the Gentle Light.*
> *Long hast thou dwelt in darkness—*
> *Quit the night and seek the day.*

In this interpretation, the "Dying World" represents the current evolutionary state of humanity. Our current level, whatever it is, is always ending, dying, as we move to a new level. The "Wanderer in the

Wild Darkness" is the person (candidate for initiation) who is looking for a more spiritual life. "Long hast thou dwelt in darkness" means that the person has spent a long time in a non-spiritual state, the darkness of being separated from the divine. The expressions "Living Beauty," "Gentle Light," and "day" refer to the Divine Effulgence.

While there are many methods and systems that will allow a seeker to search for, find, and experience the Divine Effulgence—and thus produce for himself or herself the proof of the existence of the divine—I can think of none that is faster or finer than that which is contained within the *traditional* system of the Hermetic Order of the Golden Dawn.

Anyone can tap into the "magical current," or spiritual energy, that empowers the Golden Dawn either as a group or as an individual who follows the system. Unfortunately, there are some groups that claim to be the Golden Dawn (probably to get money, power, sex, etc. for the leader[s] of the group) and have so altered the teachings that they bear little relationship to the tradition. One sells lessons that I believe are simply taken from my book, *Modern Magick!* This is in spite of the fact that *Modern Magick,* while in the tradition of the Golden Dawn, was never meant to be a replacement for the teachings of that Order and has many differences from the traditional Golden Dawn system. Some groups are performing Neo-pagan or Thelemic rituals *as part* of their pseudo-Golden Dawns. While Neo-pagan and Thelemic rituals can be wonderful and powerful, they are not part of the tradition of the Hermetic Order of the Golden Dawn.

In order to determine if a group you are involved with is real, look for three things. First, is it following the tradition as shown in the books, *The Golden Dawn or The Complete Golden Dawn System of Magic* by Israel Regardie?

Second, while I think that change is vital and important, do they have valid reasons for making changes? After all, the Golden Dawn system has worked excellently for those who have followed the training for well over a century. If it works it should not be changed without extraordinary reasons. Third, if the leader(s) left the group, would the group continue? If you can say, "No," to any of the above questions, while what the group is doing may be wonderful, it is not the Golden Dawn.

The Proof That Gods and Goddesses Exist

As I wrote in *Modern Magick,* merely repeating what others have done before is nothing but hero worship. Really working a system, no matter what that system is, requires that you take what has gone before and expand upon it. The technique to experience the Divine Effulgence, and thus prove the existence of the Godhead, expands on Golden Dawn concepts. Specifically, it works with two of the most basic rituals of the Order, the Lesser Banishing Ritual of the Pentagram (LBRP) and the Banishing Ritual of the Hexagram (BRH). If you practice the following instructions, you should be able to have the sublime experience of Divine Effulgence within a few weeks.

Step One

Spend one week memorizing the Lesser Banishing Ritual of the Pentagram and Banishing Ritual of the Hexagram if you do not already know them. (For full information on these rituals see The *Golden Dawn* by Israel Regardie and *Modern Magick* by Donald Michael Kraig.) You may combine this with step two below.

Step Two

For one week, take a bath at the same hour each evening. Spend at least one hour in the *bath* (not a shower). During the hour, spend time memorizing the LBRP and BRH if you have not already done so. However, spend at least half of the time contemplating what you are going to do and the spiritual nature of the project. If you have some books that you consider especially spiritual, you might wish to read them, too.

When the hour is over, pull the plug and let the water drain *while you remain in the bath.* As the water slowly drains past your body, visualize all of your daily cares going down the drain with the water. The physical world is departing, leaving room for the spiritual to enter.

For those who want to increase the effect of this work, do the above practice starting with the waning moon, the time from just after the full moon as it decreases in size (Hint: when the moon is waning, the "horns" of the crescent point to the right). This way the departure of the physical is amplified by the effects of the shrinking of the moon. Repeating the techniques at the same hour has the effect of making your interest and desires known to the spiritual, non-physical entities that surround us.

Step Three

During the next week, before taking your ritual bath, physically clean the area where you will be doing your rituals. This means vacuum, dust, wash, etc., as necessary. Assemble any magical tools and props you wish to use and put them into the area. Also have ready the robe or special clothes you will wear for the ritual. (For instructions on the building and use of magical tools, altars, and robes see *Secrets of a Golden Dawn Temple* by Chic Cicero and Sandra Tabatha Cicero and *Modern Magick*). If you are going to use elemental tools or "weapons," I suggest you either have all of them for use or do not use any of them. In this way, the balance that is a natural part of the LBRP and BRH will not be compromised by an energy imbalance indicated by the use of some, but not all, of the elemental tools.

Take your cleansing bath (it should start at the same time as the previous nights). However, you need not spend a full hour in the water. Twenty minutes of meditation and contemplation should suffice. When you finish, dry yourself and put on your robe or magical clothing. Anoint yourself with the scented oil of your choice if you wish.

Spiritually cleanse the area using incense and/or water. Although it is not traditional, I have discovered that this preliminary work can also be completed using other spiritual systems. The shamanic technique of smudging works well, as does the Tantric banishing of loudly shouting the "Thunderbolt mantra," *Tophat*, at the quarters (east, south, west, north), half-way between the quarters, above and below.

Perform the LBRP. Before the Repetition of the Kabalistic Cross, spend five or ten minutes visualizing and communing with the archangels. If your arms get tired (they are extended to the sides during this part of the LBRP), allow them to slowly fall to your sides. At the end of this period, thank the archangels for attending and bid them goodbye. Finish the ritual.

Close down your temple and put your tools away if your situation does not allow you to leave them out. If you can leave your physical temple set up, so much the better. Be sure to change into your regular clothes. Be sure to record your experiences in your magical diary. (If you have never done such a diary, instructions are given in *Modern Magick* for how to keep one, or you can get a copy of *The Magical Diary* by Donald Michael Kraig, which gives instructions, examples, and has room for keeping records on over one hundred rituals with plenty of space for all appropriate entries.)

Step Four

During the following week (by now the moon should be waxing and leading up to the full moon), repeat step three, but do not spend the extra five or ten minutes dwelling on the archangels. After you have fully visualized them, move on to the Repetition of the Kabalistic Cross.

Then go directly into the performance of the BRH. After the Formulation of the Hexagrams, repeat the Analysis of the Key Word, but during this phase of the practice it is important that you do not say the phrase, "Let the Divine Light descend." At this stage you are only preparing yourself to experience the Divine Light, the Divine Effulgence. The exclamation of this statement earlier in the BRH sets you up for what is to come and informs the spiritual entities that surround you of the purpose of this magical opus.

Repeat the LBRP and close as in step three. Keep a record of what you did and what you experienced in your magical diary.

Step Five

On the day before the full moon, repeat step four. However, before repeating the Analysis of the Key Word, do the following.

a. Face east. Stand erect. Bring your hands next to your ears as you inhale. Your fingers should be flat, next to one another, and pointing forward. Your thumbs should be lined up with your fingers and your palms face the floor. Step forward with your left foot and simultaneously thrust your hands forward as you look down your hands past your thumbs and say, *"Holy art Thou, Lord of the Universe!"*

b. Repeat this, only instead say, *"Holy art Thou, Whom Nature hath not formed!"*

c. Repeat, saying, *"Holy art Thou, the Vast and the Mighty One!"*

d. Stand erect and say, *"Lord of the Light, and of the Darkness!"* Then stamp your left foot as you simultaneously touch the tip of the forefinger of your left hand to your lips.

(NOTE: I would like to add here that some people consider the use of the term "Lord" to be sexist and patriarchal. Nothing could be further from the truth. The term "Lord" is a title and should be thought of as being neither male nor female. Similarly, the ancient Egyptian title, *Pharaoh,* referred to the ruler, not merely a man. The Pharaoh could be male or female. As a sign of rulership, the Pharaoh would glue on a beard colored gold. Both males and females who were rulers wore this sign of authority. Thus, to change the title "Lord" to "Lord and Lady," "Source," or some other term would, I believe, invalidate the entire purpose of the above adoration.)

e. Now it is time to "rend the veil" between the planes. Still facing east, step forward with your left foot as you thrust your hands, palms together with the thumbs up, forward in front of you. While in this position, rotate your hands so that the are palms are out, then slowly separate your hands. It is as if you have forced your hands through some sealed curtains and then ripped them apart.

Spiritually, that is exactly what you have done. Your entire practice, up to this time, has helped to lead you to the point of being able to rend the veil. Now you can move from the physical to the spiritual.

Take two steps forward through the veil between the planes, through the split you have just made. Understand that you are moving into a new realm. If you can see on the astral plane, do not be surprised if you start to experience wonderful visions of beauty and light.

f. Now repeat the Analysis of the Key Word. This time, however, be sure to say, "Let the Divine Light descend!" Visualize that amazingly bright light coming to you from above. As you slowly lower your arms, allow the light to rain down upon you, cover you, merge with you. Let it fill you until you think you must burst. You may actually feel as if your mind is expanding or the universe is contracting until you both are one. There may also be physical sensations including heat, cold, breezes, sounds, and involuntary shaking. Allow this state to last as long as you desire.

g. Take two steps backward, thus re-entering the physical plane. Reverse the physical actions of step (e) above, thus closing the veil. Complete the ritual with the LBRP, closing the temple and making an entry in your magical record.

As with anything worthwhile, success comes with diligence, determination, and practice. Many, if not most, magicians will not experience the Divine Effulgence on that first night; but it has been my experience that those who continue their practices eventually have success.

Now What?

At the beginning of Aleister Crowley's *Book 4* (which also appears in the larger book, *Magick*), Crowley's secretary, Mary d'Este Sturges, using the name Soror Virakam (and probably acting as a voice for Crowley's own ideas) makes an important comment. She says that other religious leaders tell you to believe what they say while Crowley says, *"Don't* believe me!" Instead, use his book as a guide with "tips" and try it out for yourself.

I agree with this latter idea completely. Don't take my word that achieving the Divine Effulgence will occur. Rather, let the instructions I have given above merely be your guide. With this information, you now know what to do in order to experience the Divine Effulgence. However, in order to experience it you have no choice but to *do the work yourself!*

Unfortunately, about what happens during the experience of Divine Effulgence I can say little other than what I have already said. It is subjective and not quantifiable or qualifiable. It may be identical to another's experience, similar to it, or dramatically different. What I can say is that everyone who has experienced it—by accident or through work in the technique given above—is changed. Life is different. He or she has experienced something divinely unique.

At the same time, the life of such a person stays very much the same. There is a story I once heard about a man who came up to a Taoist priest and asked, "Is it true you are enlightened?"

The master replied, "Yes, it is true."

The seeker asked further, "What did you do before you were enlightened?"

The priest said, "Chopped wood. Boiled water. Cooked rice."

The seeker then asked, "And now that you're enlightened, what do you do?"

The priest shrugged his shoulders and said, "Chop wood. Boil water. Cook rice."

And that's true. After the experience of Divine Effulgence, you will do the same things as you did before. Chances are you will do them the same way you did them before. But you will be doing them with a new understanding of yourself, the universe, and the divine. Some of the attitudinal changes that occur may not even be conscious.

The experience of Divine Effulgence and its results are something that could not be conceived of or experienced if the source of that experience, the Godhead, did not exist. Just as the experience of either objectifying or being an object proves that the self and others exist, so, too, does the experience of Divine Effulgence prove the existence of the divine. To sum up, as a result of my experience of Divine Effulgence, as well as the descriptions of others who have had the same experience, I do believe, without a shadow of a doubt, that the gods do exist and that the Source of All, in its own way, is as real as you or me.

Perhaps more importantly, having the experience of Divine Effulgence will yield something far more important than "merely" proving that the divine exists. It will prove to you on an inner level so deep that it defies description, that you are part of the whole of the universe. This new reality and understanding will change you, make you part of the *novus homo sapiens,* the new evolution of humanity, that will face the future with joy, wisdom, elán, and hope.

About the Author

Donald Michael Kraig is the author of *Modern Magick,* one of the most popular books on the subject ever written. He is also the former editor of *The Llewellyn New Times* and is a regular contributor to several metaphysical publications. He has been been a student and teacher on a variety of metaphysical topics for over twenty years. After intense study, Don became a Certified Tarot Master (CTM), an honor bestowed upon him by The Associated Readers of Tarot, an international, not-for-profit educational organization. He has been a student of the Golden Dawn system for over fifteen years.

LOOK FOR THE CRESCENT MOON

Llewellyn publishes hundreds of books on your favorite subjects! To get these exciting books, including the ones on the following pages, check your local bookstore or order them directly from Llewellyn.

ORDER BY PHONE

- Call toll-free within the U.S. and Canada, 1-800-THE MOON
- In Minnesota, call (612) 291-1970
- We accept VISA, MasterCard, and American Express

ORDER BY MAIL

- Send the full price of your order (MN residents add 7% sales tax) in U.S. funds, plus postage & handling to:

  Llewellyn Worldwide
  P.O. Box 64383, Dept. K861-3
  St. Paul, MN 55164–0383, U.S.A.

POSTAGE & HANDLING

(For the U.S., Canada, and Mexico)

- $4 for orders $15 and under
- $5 for orders over $15
- No charge for orders over $100

We ship UPS in the continental United States. We ship standard mail to P.O. boxes. Orders shipped to Alaska, Hawaii, The Virgin Islands, and Puerto Rico are sent first-class mail. Orders shipped to Canada and Mexico are sent surface mail.

International orders: Airmail—add freight equal to price of each book to the total price of order, plus $5.00 for each non-book item (audio tapes, etc.).

Surface mail—Add $1.00 per item.

Allow 4–6 weeks for delivery on all orders.
Postage and handling rates subject to change.

DISCOUNTS

We offer a 20% discount to group leaders or agents. You must order a minimum of 5 copies of the same book to get our special quantity price.

FREE CATALOG

Get a free copy of our color catalog, *New Worlds of Mind and Spirit*. Subscribe for just $10.00 in the United States and Canada ($30.00 overseas, airmail). Many bookstores carry New Worlds—ask for it!

Visit our website at www.llewellyn.com for more information.

The *Golden Dawn Journal* series reflects the magical teachings and philosophy of the Hermetic Tradition. The books will seriously explore the techniques used in ceremonial magick and include practical ritual advice for the working magician. Each volume focuses on one theme, with contributions by various authors experienced in Western ceremonial magic.

**The Golden Dawn Journal
Book I: Divination**

**edited by Chic Cicero
and Sandra Tabatha Cicero**

Book I: Divination explores how and why the process of divination works, traditional techniques of tarot and geomancy (along with new information on both), new tarot spreads, historical information derived from the actual Tarot readings of an original member of th Golden Dawn, explorations of both Roman and Graeco-Egyptian divinatory techniques, gypsy runes, and new systems of divination developed by accomplished magicians in the field. All authors then respond to the question, "Can a Divination Always Be Trusted?"

As both an order and a Magickal Tradition, the Golden Dawn is responsible for planting many of the seeds of magick that have sprouted today in the form of numerous magickal organizations throughout the world.

1-56718-850-8, 304 pp., 6 x 9, softcover   **$12.00**

THE GOLDEN DAWN JOURNAL
Book II: Qabalah—Theory & Magic

edited by Chic Cicero and Sandra Tabatha Cicero

Book II: Qabalah—Theory & Magic explores the various aspects of this mystical system, both ancient and modern. These include the history and evolution of the Qabalah, inquiries into how the Qabalah is used for spiritual growth, traditional techniques of Gematria, Merkabah mysticism and Angel magic, comparisons between Qabalistic philosophy and the sciences of astrology, Alchemy, and psychology, investigations into the Goddess and feminine energies on the Tree of Life, sphere-workings, telesmatic magic, explorations into the Qabalistic aspects of Golden Dawn magic, and new Qabalistic rituals for today's practicing magicians.

- **The ABC's of Qabalah**—Harvey Newstrom
- **The Tree of Life: Jacob's Extending Ladder**—Gareth Knight
- **Sacred Images: A Qabalistic Analysis of the Neophyte Formula**—William Stoltz
- **The Restoration and Alchemy**—Steven Marshall
- **The Qabalistic World-view Behind the Golden Dawn System of Magic**—George Wilson
- **The Tree of the Sephiroth**—Donald Tyson
- **This Holy Invisible Companionship: Angels in the Hermetic Qabalah**—Adam P. Forrest
- **The Sacred Feminine on the Tree**—Madonna Compton
- **She Dances on the Tree**—Oz
- **The Equilibration of Jehovah: A Ritual of Healing**—M. Isidora Forrest
- **Shebilim Bahirim (The Bright Paths)**—Mitch and Gail Henson
- **Structural Implications in the Sepherot**—Sam Webster
- **Qabalistic Ritual**—Dolores Ashcroft-Nowicki
- **The Astrological Kaballah**—Lisa Roggow

1–56718–851–6, 456 pp., 6 x 9, softcover   **$16.00**

To order call 1-800 THE MOON.

Prices subject to change without notice.

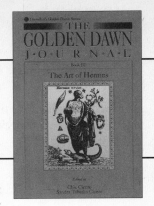

THE GOLDEN DAWN JOURNAL
BOOK III: The Art of Hermes

edited by Chic Cicero and Sandra Tabatha Cicero

Book III: The Art of Hermes focuses on Hermetic magic, upon which all Western occultism for the past five centuries is based. Hermes Trismegistus is the god of wisdom of the Graeco-Egyptian philosophers who lived in Egypt in the early centuries of the Christian era. He is linked with alchemy, medicine, magic and the mysteries. All secret schools and orders in the West that claim an occult tradition (such as Freemasonry) may be loosely linked with Hermes. The editors trace the course of the Hermetic tradition from ancient Egypt, through Greek philosophy and the Greek Mystery religions, Gnosticism, Neoplatonism and the Kabbalah, down to the modern occult revival and the Golden Dawn.

- **Hermes: Chief Patron of Magick** – William Stoltz
- **The Emerald Tablet of Hermes and the Invocation of the Holy Guardian Angel** – Lon Milo DuQuette
- **The Hermetic Isis** – M. Isidora Forrest
- **Logos Revealed: Hermetic and Kabbalistic Influences on the Renaissance Humanists** – Madonna Compton
- **God-Making** – Donald Tyson
- **The Hall of Thmaa: Sources of the Golden Dawn Lodge System** – John Michael Greer
- **The Pillar of Osiris** – Adam P. Forrest
- **Invocation of Hermes Trismegistus and the Vision of the Poimandres: Two Ritual Pathworkings** – Oz
- **Of Hermes Mercurius** – Sam Webster
- **Images of Growth in the Hermetic Arts** – Gareth Knight
- **Magical Notebooks: A Survey of the Grimoires in the Golden Dawn** – Mitch and Gail Henson
- **Women, Qabala, and Masonry** – Fran Holt-Underwood

1-56178-852-4, 360 pp., 6 x 9, softcover   **$20.00**

To order call 1-800 THE MOON.

Prices subject to change without notice.